Russ L. Howard Library for House of Howard Publishing

## The King of Three Bloods:

**TheKingofThreeBloods.com**

Visit the author on Facebook:

**TheKingofThreeBloods.com/fb**

BOOK EIGHT:

# BREKKA

## THE KING OF THREE BLOODS

# RUSS L. HOWARD

Copyright © 2019 by Russ L. Howard
Cover Art: Deranged Doctor Design
Formatting: Deranged Doctor Design
Publishing: House of Howard Publishing

ISBN: 978-1-945130-12-0

**TheKingofThreeBloods.com**

# ACKNOWLEDGMENTS

I EXTEND MY GRATITUDE TO PAULA Riggs whose tireless editing spanned seven years, much of which required her to endure my corny jokes, and to her husband Carl who had to endure the many blood drenched battle scenes in the book. Much appreciated help came from Jeff Day in preserving my sanity through dealing with my hated computer and for computer and technical assistance above and beyond waking hours. Particular thanks to Susie Stokes for her exquisite artistic talents and formatting despite her own busy schedule, and she, too, gave endless hours of technical direction. I give praise to my beloved wife whose constant feed-back and aide has always inspired me, and to my son, Adam, who gave continuous encouragement and deeply thought out opinions when asked. I thank my many children and my devoted friends who repeatedly asked, "Is it done yet?" Unto them I say, "Here it is."

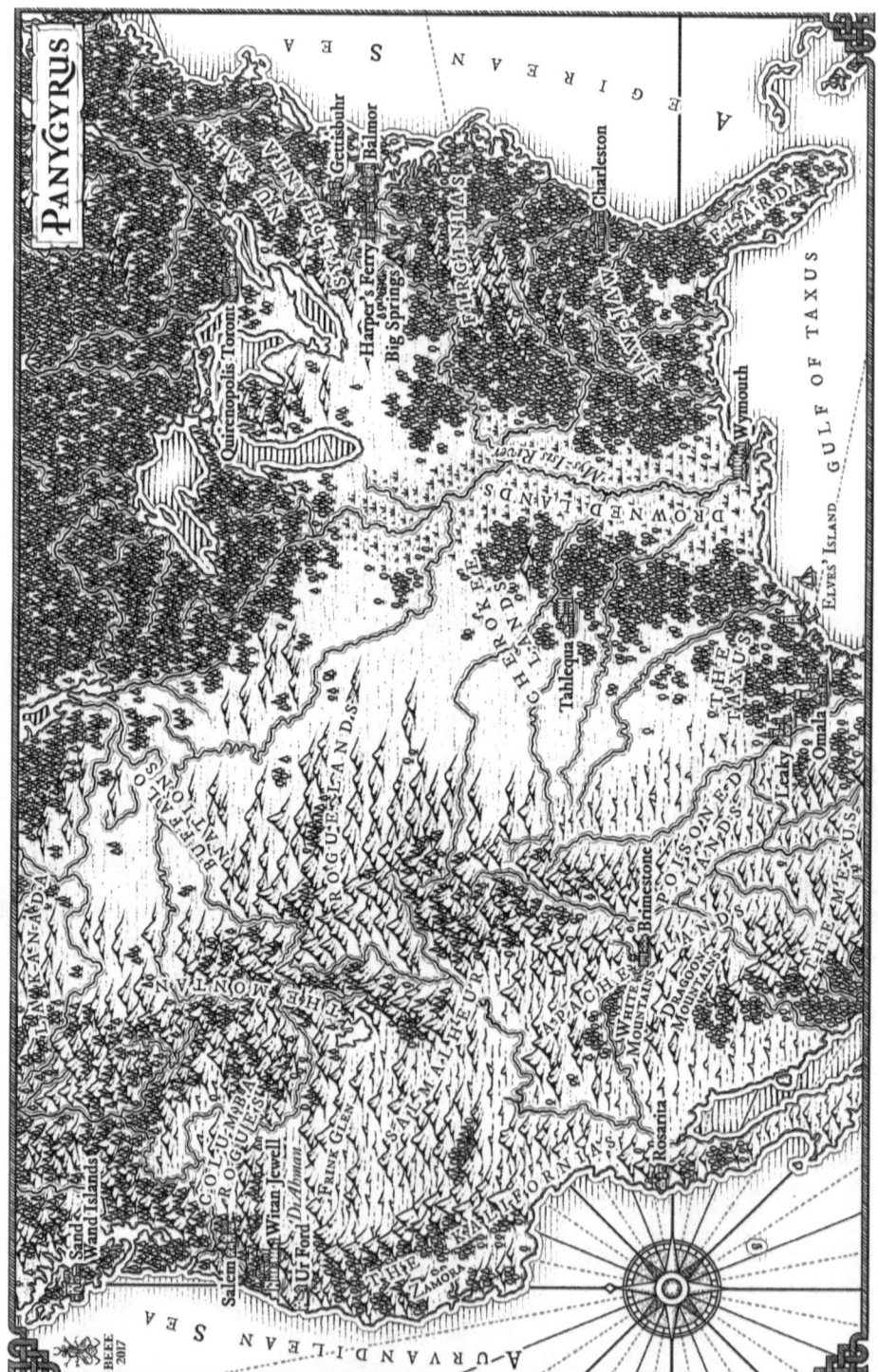

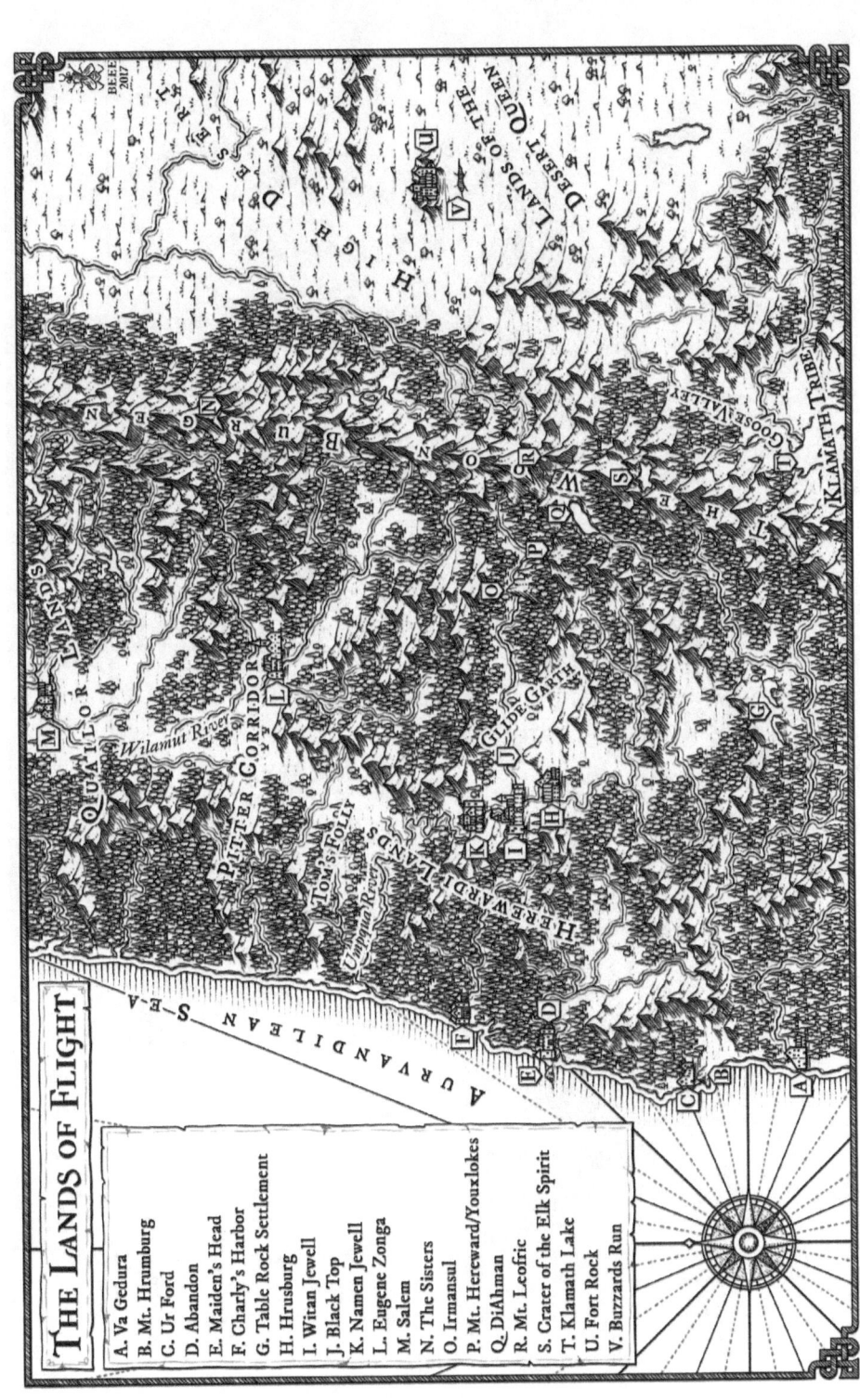

# THE LANDS OF FLIGHT

A. Va Gedura
B. Mt. Hrumburg
C. Ur Ford
D. Abandon
E. Maiden's Head
F. Charly's Harbor
G. Table Rock Settlement
H. Hrusburg
I. Witan Jewell
J. Black Top
K. Namen Jewell
L. Eugene Zonga
M. Salem
N. The Sisters
O. Irmansul
P. Mt. Hereward/Yourlokes
Q. DiAhman
R. Mt. Leofric
S. Crater of the Elk Spirit
T. Klamath Lake
U. Fort Rock
V. Buzzards Run

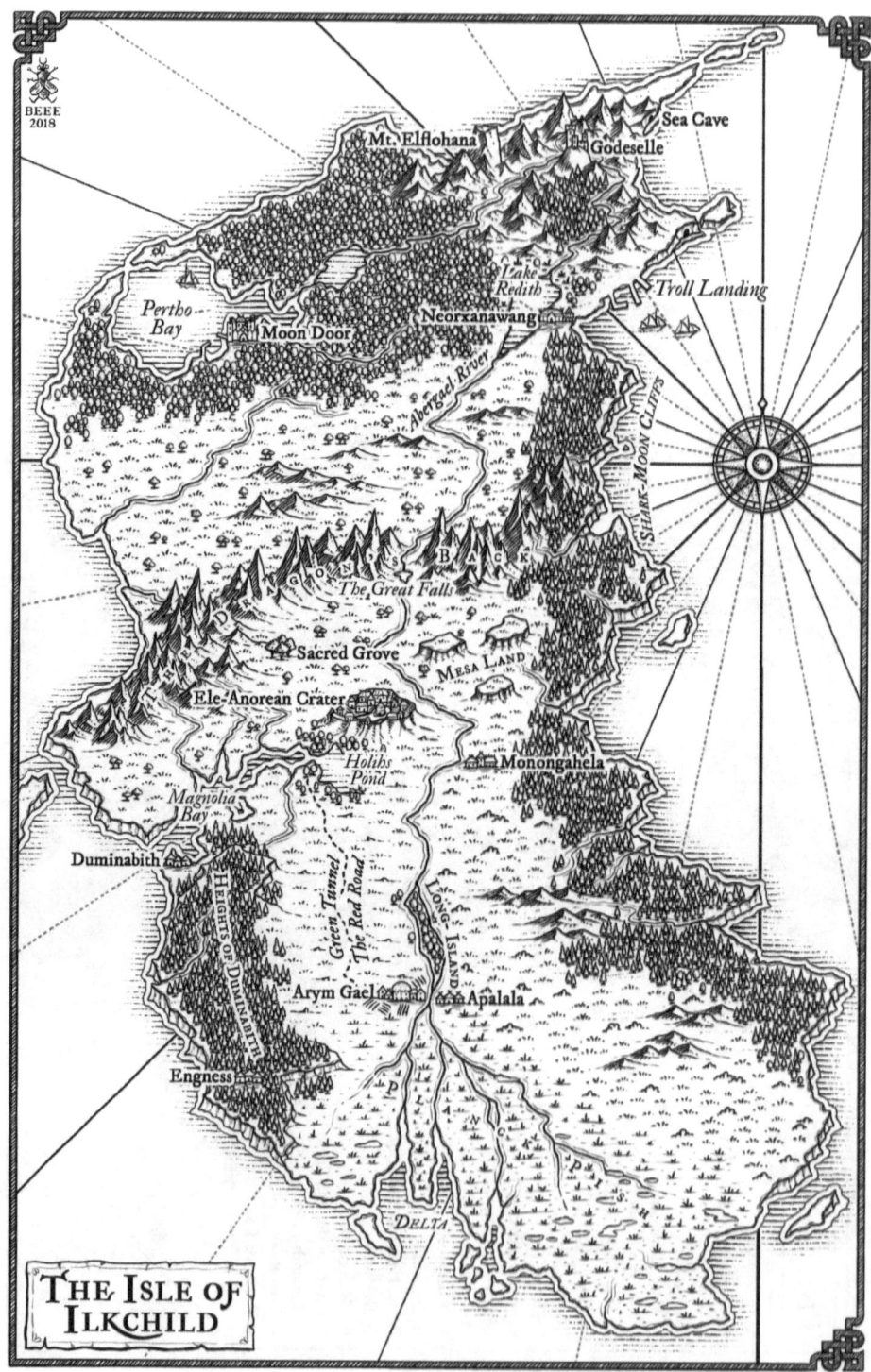

THE ISLE OF ILKCHILD

# TABLE OF CONTENTS

# CHAPTER 1 :
## THE CLASH OF CULTURE CONTINUES

*The official record of Syrdom as transcribed by Lord Long Swan,
prothonotary scribe of the kingdom of Syr Folk:*

IT IS THE MOONTH OF SKIPPING *Lambs in the year 603 HSO as
reckoned from the slaying of the Herewardi King and Longfather,
Hrus-Syr-Os. It is the twentieth year after the great eclipse when
the Lord Prince Sur Sceaf, The King of Three Bloods, Heir to the
Swan Throne of the Herewardi Kingdom, was given his commission to
unite the Herewardi, Sharaka, and Quailor Tribes. Since that time of
beginning when the confederation was in its infancy, many other tribes
kindred, tongues, and peoples on the Isle of Ilkchild and the Main Land
of Panygyrus have joined the confederation of sovereign states.*

*As I scribe this log in the Moonth of the Skipping Lambs, it has
been fifteen years from the defeat of the legions of the Pitter commander
Balaban at the Battle of Moon Door on the Isle of Ilkchild--what we Syr
Folk have come to call the time of the cleansing. Since then, the isle has
been free of Pitters, their allies, and their ilk, thus making this place an
island of sanity and sanctuary in a world that had otherwise become
insanely mad, as judged by any normal man or woman of the mould.*

*It was also the time when the Lord Prince Sur Sceaf had been elevated to be
the High King of the Syr Folk. A time celebrated annually to mark his kingship as
well as the elevation of the lord mayors of the city-states throughout the isle.*

*After numerous severe attacks on the Pitter zongas, the Herewardi reestablished their sovereign strongholds at Witan Jewel and have regained their lands in the Umpqua, the Table Tops, and upon Shasta.*

*However, the Pitter legions, due to their vast superiority in numbers, have re-conquered most of the peoples of the Kalifornias and the Mexus Lands. They are now pushing further south into the unknown regions of the Nether Lands which lay south of Guatemala, in an effort to garner slaves and resources to feed the increasing appetite of their gluttonous empire.*

*Since the formation of the confederation and its ruling body, led by King Sur Sceaf and the Council of Sovereign Nations, the Pitters have not encountered our full forces. The Roufytrof, who are the ruling body of the Herewardi Nation, convinced the Council of Sovereign Nations that the armies must be sufficiently built up in numbers before the Great War can be launched and any true military muscle flexed.*

*It had taken nearly two generations before sufficient armies and navies were built. When attacked, our fyrds have responded to drive the Pitters back, killing more enemy forces than we lose. Also, forays into Pitter zongas have been made from time to time to free captives, and to test the enemy's points of strength. Thus, the status quo and the balance of power have been maintained in check for the past fifteen years. Now, the Syr Folk have appointed this year as the time of an offensive thrust that will be executed with lightning strikes at all the major Pitter zongas at once. This war must be won swiftly before the next bamboo bloom, as the bamboo fruit triggers population explosions among the Pitters, resulting in litters of offspring rather than their usual one or two gets. Were this to happen, it could turn the tide of war indefinitely in the Pitter's favor within a mere eight or nine years time.*

*The past fifteen years have seen many changes on the blessed isle of Ilkchild. Additional fortresses have been built at the strategic landing places of Arym Gael, Magnolia Bay, the Isle of Isles, and Moon Door. The ever-increasing armies of the Syr Folk have fully manned and maintained the fortresses and repelled any attacks against their isle. Joining troops have been rigorously trained for the coming war. Bush masters, rangers, Cherokee Dragooners, Jywdic Lions, and Pyringean Pirates in their sea stallions have sorely afflicted the Pitters along the Great Aurvandilean Sea Board of the west, and destroyed roaming bands of Pitter rat packs throughout the mountains and deserts.*

*The massive campaign is soon to begin, with the High King Sur Sceaf in over-all command, and the Sharaka Chief, Mendaka, second in command. A war council composed of representatives from all nations and headed by Jon Dee Lee deals with all matters concerning war, including supplies, ground support, hospitalers, transportation, and refugee placement. Just as in the government of the Confederation of Sovereign Nations, the armies are formed in much the same way. Some armies are combined, while others maintain their own command.*

*Sur Sceaf's eldest son, the Lord Arundel, an acclaimed strategist and warrior, and a king in his own right, has tactical command, while younger son, Il-Alim, is in command of the irregular forces. Sur Sceaf's daughter, the Lady Brekka, Commander of the Order of Lady Knights, has been given the commission by both the Roufytrof of the Herewardi, and the Council of Sovereign Nations to launch the offensive campaign against the Pitter Empire and their Vardropi and Growling allies on the Main Land of Panygyrus in an all-out assault on the combined forces of the Pitter Emperor, Hryre Seath. It is the beginning of the Great War.*

Dawn was breaking over the wooded hill where Brekka and Custus Ruhm Lee had, due to heavy fog, involuntarily elected to spend the night together. Brekka awoke in the hushed old oaken forest, her senses already alert and her focus sharp. Overhead, the hanging mosses swayed in a westerly breeze, and the heavy morning mist had taken on the surreal golden glow of the rising sun.

To her relief, the gorgeous man beside her was still asleep, his rhythmic breathing causing his grey and red cape to rise and fall over his broad chest. His handsome face with its strong Hickoryan features and tan skin was relaxed, his lips slightly parted. A familiar frisson of pleasure coursed through her.

Not only had she spent the night with a warrior, but also the most handsome of the lot.

She lay awake in the twitter light wondering how she was ever going to lead her lady knights in the most terrible battles the world would probably ever see, and how she was ever going to find the Holy Mound of Heredom that housed the secrets and treasures of her race, so long resting in the Ea-Urth, in a place where the folk mouth said heathen kings still slept in their dolmans.

She alone was commissioned by the Roufytrof to discover the Holy Mound. As prophesied, it was required to be uncovered by a virgin of Hereward's descent. Should she fail, her life's sacrifice would be in vain, and the prophecies of five hundred years would have to await another seed, for the gods always have a backup plan when they prophecy to the sons and daughters of Man.

She lifted her head, looked around, and saw off in the distance her brother, Il-Alim, riding through the grove on his white steed, with Merriman the Hunt Master on his bay Hanoverian mount. She breathed a sigh of relief. As they approached, she noticed how Il-Alim had grown into such an impressively tall man, with his muscular warrior's frame, raven black hair, white porcelain skin, so unlike the rest of Taneshewa's children with their golden skin color. His eyes flashed with the color of indigo. Fa Mo Mo Redith said he was likely a throwback to his elven ancestry, and those eyes attested to the blooming of elven seed in his bloodline.

It seemed only yesterday she was changing Ily's diapers, and wiping the drool of porridge from his face with a spoon. But now, he cut a dashing figure from his strenuous training in the martial arts under the apt tutelage of the Master of Crypsis himself, Starkwulf, King of Fort Rock. She was honored to have taken Il-Alim under her arm, even as Arundel had taken her under his. There was a strong link among the three of them that went deeper than the blood they shared, something from more ancient times and places, some bond from the Fore Earthly World.

She had groomed Alim into an elite warrior for the war to come. And he was a warrior through and through. She was doubly sure Alim was proud of his mixed heritage. After all, he was the son of both the High King Sur Sceaf, and his beauteous red-skinned mother, Ahyyyokah Taneshewa, daughter of the great Chief Onamingo, of noblest descent, and now Chief Judge of the Syr Folk.

Brekka was only thirteen when her father had taken Taneshewa as his seventh wife. Over the years she had come to value Ahy as a trusted friend as well as a nigh-mother. Perhaps it was because Taneshewa was much more attuned to Brekka's warlike nature than her own sweet Quailor mother, Lana, her father's second wife.

As Alim saluted her from afar, she marveled that his face shone fairer than an elf's in the morning light. Seeing him approach eased her heart. She was suspect of this meeting ever taking place after the events of last night, for Ruhm had arranged it. His plans landing them alone in the deep forest made her doubly suspicious. Such suspicions come with being a warrioress.

What was now evident, was that Ruhm had not tricked her into some scheme to seduce her in the foggy wood of yestereve. He had claimed Alim was going to ask Merriman for his daughter's hand, and had requested Brekka and Ruhm to assist him in that endeavor. It meant a lot to her that she could now trust Ruhm's integrity. It showed that her vested trust in him had never been misplaced, and now this trial alone with him in the forest had proven so. She would need such a trustworthy man in her quest to find Heredom, the Sacred Mound of Herewardi origins.

At some future date she hoped to marry Ruhm, stubborn son of a bitch that he was, harder than hickory in his opinions, and as immovable as a rock in his will.

She knew from his steady breathing that Ruhm was still fast asleep. Looking at the line of rocks she had erected as a barrier between them in the foggy night caused her to laugh. She had been taught all her life that a maiden can never be too careful. Particularly in such places as here in Freya's garden, filled with woodland faeries and water nymphs, who can fill the mind with mists of forgetfulness, and one's veins with the liqueur of love and the sap of sensuality. Such faeries and nymphs feed on the delicious behaviors of young lovers, as surely as bees suck up nectar from tender blooms.

She had told Ruhm if he crossed that line, she'd cut off his yard and gut him like a white bellied fish. He had laughed heartily and assured her, she was safe as a dove under his wing. Am I? She had thought.

Yestereve, she and Ruhm had stopped to rest at the woodland grotto at the place called Elfbeard's Moss Falls. The musical splash of the crystal clear water on the moss-covered rocks, and the perfume of the lush flowers and Daphne in the grotto had somehow cast a magic spell over them. They had hugged and kissed until she was breathless with yearning, so much so that she had felt the husband's bulge through his clothing whenever he pressed into her.

She had immediately backed off, and realized things were getting dangerously intimate. That's when a swirling mist had beset them like a faery wind. Within minutes, it had become so thick that the landmarks in the hushed old wood had been rendered invisible. That's when Ruhm decided they would have to make camp for the night, and she had reluctantly agreed; there being no other choice, with the blanket of darkness and the curtain of thick fog moving in.

It was known to the Herewardi that mischievous and tricky sprites took a special liking to the fog, so as to work their conniving trickery and bedevilment, often weaving hearts and bodies together that were never meant to be one. There could be evil, there could be good, but what was certain was that magic had shrouded the forest for a purpose, to test the strength of her faith over the will of her flesh.

*My power lies in my chastity. Take that away, and I am like every other woman. Protect it, and I become Woon's champion and Freya's charge.*

From her first meeting with Ruhm at age thirteen, she had felt a magical attraction to him. By the gods she loved just about every part of him. Here it was once again, moving into the season of marrying and manmaking, and once again she would have to refuse all proposals of marriage, despite the attraction they held for each other. Nevertheless, her commission gave her an excuse, a way to justifiably refuse a marriage proposal.

Her love of Ruhm was an ancient and pre-earthly power with the force to pull her away from her holy calling. She feared it.

She reached over the line of rocks that divided them and prodded Ruhm on his broad shoulders until he stirred awake. His eyes heavy, but pleasantly inviting, greeted her with their smile. "Good morning! What a lovely sight to awaken to."

"They're here, coming down off that hill over there in the oaks." She gestured toward the two riders closing in on them.

"Who?" he asked drowsily, trying to see what she was pointing at through his half closed lids. This time she bracketed his face with her hands and turned his head toward the horsemen making their way through the witch-hazel thicket, which was in full blow with yellow tasseled blossoms, and intermittent splashes of red coming from the flowering currants abloom beneath them.

"Alim and Merri are coming through the wood, even now."

Ruhm smiled. "Then I better get up. Wouldn't want Old Man Merriman to get the wrong idea."

"Wait." She rested a hand on the arm he'd used to throw off his cape. "Ruhm, you have no idea how much I value the restraint you showed last night. It speaks to your integrity and character."

He offered her a crooked grin. "Brekka, I adore you, and I want you so bad that I'm bursting. God knows, I was tempted and ached half the night for you. I'm pretty sure I've ground my teeth down to nubs trying to restrain my urges."

She couldn't keep from laughing at the frustration he expressed just in the tone of his voice.

"You think that's funny, do you?" He reached out to tug gently on one of her long curly locks. His laughing eyes met hers.

*I have known this man before. I have loved this man before. He is mine and I am his.*

Time seemed to stand still. And then Ruhm's eyes darkened. He gripped both her hands in his. Still holding her gaze, he said slowly and with clear emotion, "I know that you have had your doubts about me, but I swear, I will never deceive you or try to take advantage of you. But you also need to know that I don't know how long I can wait like this."

She searched his face. Beneath the handsome façade was a decent and honorable man. A man she could trust.

"Do you believe me?" he asked, breaking the intense silence.

"Yes, I believe you, and I understand your frustration. I care deeply for you, but, Ruhm, I'm not free to act on my feelings at this time. As I have told you before, I must be virgin to fulfill Woon's calling. And particularly, as the commander of the Lady Knights, it is imperative that no one cast any aspersions over my maidenhood, so I hope you will not speak to your compatriots about this night in the woods together. That weasel Hoth already questions my virginity because of our familiarity with one another in public."

Ruhm frowned. "Why on earth—"

"Because, he claims you're quite the gadabout, and have a string of Hickoryan ladies who favor your bed, from one end of the isle to the other."

Ruhm turned red. "That bastard!" He sighed. "Brekka, you have my word, I'll never speak of this night. As for Hoth's claims, well, I won't pretend to be as chaste as you. But, if he prints one more word of untruth about you, I will nail his scrawny ass to the ground with my dueling sword, and cram my other fist down his slanderous throat. Then I'll tear that lying bastard's tongue out by its roots and plant it in the sands of the sea where the tide comes in twice in twenty four hours. That's the only justice that slanderer will ever understand."

"Wouldn't we all love that! You'd be lauded by most everyone in the land."

Smiling at his passion, she waved to Alim and Merri who were now entering their camp.

As Il-Alim came upon them he noted the line of jagged rocks between the two of them, and grinned.

"Hail and was Sael, Brekka, Ruhm. We were expecting you two last night at the Jack Daw Megalith. Saw you strike up a fire last night, but didn't want to fight the slippery and unforgiving terrain of this forest with its ferny slopes to get to you. As soon as dawn broke we could see the trails and came down."

Merriman gave out a loud roar of laughter. His big hand grabbed the saddle horn as he dismounted. "I see the lady knight built a wall. Kept you in your place, didn't she, Ruhm?" Another rumbling laugh followed that nearly shook the leaves from the trees. "It'll be a damned lucky man who lands this little copper-head."

Alim tied his horse to a faery bush. "I know the purity of your heart, Sis. Still, take heed; there is much Maywood here under these old oaks, though they are not yet ablow. The elves and faeries can work cunning magic over the hearts of lovers in such an enchanted wood. See there, you slept in the greenwood spray of an eildon tree, enough to drown out the strongest resolve of any maid or gent. You can thank the elves the Hawthorn yet sleeps."

Merriman shot a disapproving glance at Alim and said, "Is this the kind of heathen hogwash you share with my daughter?"

Alim was taken aback. "I can only tell you, I learned such things in the loving arms of my dear mother. Your belief in angels is not all that different."

"We believe angels are real, but we are not in the habit of seeing them flit about through the forests and glens like you are with your faeries and elves. They spoke to us long ago and gave us everything we need. All we need now is the word."

Tension mounted, and Brekka was about to say something when Ruhm grinned and responded, "No need to worry about elves or angels having their way last night. Brekka's resolve is stronger than either. She laid down a virgin, and she rises this morning ever much the maiden she was, but not through any design or resolve of mine, I assure you."

While hunting together over the years, Alim and Merri had built powerful bonds of friendship and trust, but they still had difficulty understanding one another's thinking. After spending so much time at the Hickoryan's homestead, Alim had developed a fine liking for Merri's daughter, Lorna Wallanwood, a brilliant, chestnut-brunette beauty of the Hickoryan people. From the first moment he spied her shepherding her sheep in the Savannah Lands while he chased hounds across the meadows, his heart was captured, and it remained imprinted with her love.

He took unmeasured pride in his Herewardi bloodline and heritage, and thus, had deliberated long and hard on the sacrifices that would have to be made if they were to marry. Finally, he decided that like his grandfather, Onamingo, had told him, he must follow the rope of love wherever it led. Though it would limit his choices in life, the ur fyr had prompted him to choose this woman or regret it the rest of his life. Therefore, he was willing to do whatever it took to win her hand in marriage.

Today was Walpurga, the day that marked the change from the Skipping Moonth to the Radiant Moonth of Albespiene. When Merri had invited him to the First Kudu Hunt of the season, he decided to seize the opportunity to ask for Lorna's hand. For the past two moonths, Alim had choreographed this moment, but now that the time had arrived, the tension of the approaching conversation was killing him. Merriman was such an exceptionally intolerant man. He lit like whale oil whenever you questioned a tenet of his faith. He was so self-deceived that any contrary reason one proffered him only fortified his 'faith' all the more.

Because Merriman had taught his Christ catechism to Ruhm, Alim had asked him to come along. If anyone could understand his dilemma, he was sure it had to be Ruhm. Ruhm could act as mediator, even though he did not fully embrace Merri's teachings. Ruhm lived by the axiom that churches were prisons in disguise, but Merri considered him a devout pupil who was only temporally straying from the fold. And, indeed Ruhm had come under the sway of the old man's teachings, as attested to by his numerous disagreements with Herewardi on cultural matters.

Brekka had suggested elopement, but that did not sit well with Lorna. She loved and respected her parents, and was reluctant to depart from her father's teachings, and still more fearful of the concept of a bride-covey, having been disallowed much exposure to it. Alim tried to persuade her to accept the Herewardi practice but to no avail.

While Alim saddled their horses, Brekka and Ruhm quickly packed their gear, and then made them all a delicious breakfast of eggs, side meat, and hardtack. Ruhm was teasing Brekka with a particularly succulent piece of side meat which she swiftly snatched from him and quickly ate while Ruhm feigned outrage.

After a brief clean up by everyone, they mounted. The burly huntsman took the lead, and rode off to the Kudu Lek. Soon Merriman turned in the saddle to shout, "Not far from here is a locust grove overlooking the savannah, and I've oft seen a herd of kudu cows browsing amongst the ceanothus that grows there. I reckon there ought to be a bull or two there as well."

Brekka pulled her hair back and pinned it up with her hawthorn swan claw. "If there is no objection, I claim the horns."

"What for?" Ruhm inquired.

"I promised El Yid as many Kudu horns as possible to use for shofars aboard his sea stallions. He said blowing the shofar signals spiritual warfare against their enemies."

Merriman's smile revealed his large teeth. He tipped his hat to her in a surprisingly courtly gesture and said, "They're all yours, my lady." Merri held the Lady Brekka in great esteem, but Alim was sure that that respect could as easily change to contempt if she told him how narrow she found his beliefs. Brekka was feisty enough that she wasn't afraid to take anyone on. She had sorely berated Alim for yielding to Merri's bigotry.

'Marriage decisions are only between the parties involved in living it. This man is spiritually harnessing you to the yoke of his pitiful faith.'

Had Alim not put her on stand down, Merriman would have been spiritually gutted by now.

As they rode through lingering patches of fog toward a wooded savannah famous for large kudu, Alim squeezed the saddle horn tighter and tighter, and his hands sweat more and more as he tried to pick the opportune moment to ask for the hand of Merri's daughter. Lorna had told him the best way to ask her father would be when he was focusing on the hunt. Now that that moment had arrived, Alim had no idea what the outcome would be, simply because Merri had never allowed even a discussion of marriage.

Merri had, however, shot more than one barb at Sur Sceaf in Alim's presence. On Alim's last visit to Lorna, Merri had remarked that Sur Sceaf had built the homes of his wives so far apart just to keep them from throwing stones at each other.

The fog was just beginning to lift as the cool eye of the winter sun grew brighter against high noon, sending out a saffron hue over the grasslands. The air filled with the hum of bees working the yellow Acacia bloom for the spring bust. Upon passing through a sparse grove of Locust trees they heard the clashing of horns in a nearby tight Acacia thicket.

"Damn bucks got their horns in a tangle," Merri exclaimed with a scowl. Beneath their sharp hooves, the ground had been gouged and furrowed, as though plowed. Their horns were hopelessly interlocked, so that the bucks could only seesaw back and forth in an attempt to best the other. They would in all likelihood never be capable of disengaging from this death lock they were in. Only the sheer masculine dictates of nature kept them driving back and forth at one another.

Merriman lifted his hands up to sign, and then said, "What the hell, let's take them down before they both die of exhaustion. Problem is, there are too many bucks in this herd anyway. Only need one or two to service a herd this big; makes for too much fighting for dominance. We'll take these two and then look for some others for the larder. Then you shall have your horns, Little Miss Brekka Copper Locks." He winked.

It amazed Alim that Merriman understood the principles of nature in the beasts, but couldn't relate them to man.

Alim thought briefly, *Is that what's going to happen to us out here? Are our differences going to force us into a deadlock that spiritually kills us both? And after our mutual enemy, the Pitter, is destroyed, what then? Will Herewardi and Hickoryans lock horns like this? Fa has always taught, 'Only a common enemy keeps us united with the other tribes.'*

Ily nocked an arrow and drew back his bowstring. The others did the same. Simultaneously, they released and the kudus twisted into an entangled heap. The four of them got down from their mounts, tied the reins to the thicket of golden wattles, and took a good ten minutes disengaging the kudu horns. The bucks were as tall as the horses, and their bodies still hot from their struggles.

Brekka and Ruhm retrieved their ropes, threw them over the branches of a nearby elm, and with the help of Merri and Alim hefted the bucks into the air until their hooves were a few inches above the ground. After securely tying off the ropes, they took out their knives. It dawned on Alim that Elms hate man. He wondered if the field was giving him a bad omen of what was to come.

While Brekka and Ruhm field dressed one buck, Alim helped Merri gut the other, using an ulu knife he had haggled from one of the Snow Men traders, Red Men who had come out of the Great North. The unique crescent shape of the knife blade made the skinning a lot easier.

As Alim peeled the hide from the kudu's body like one takes off one's pants, he considered Merri probably thought of him as some hunter only wanting to strip his daughter out of her pants. *After all, isn't that what these pastors all claimed; that Herewardi men are so lustful, and delight in filling their harems with big breasted women.*

He shook his head. The pleasurable imagery of large breasts made him jerk his own reins of thinking. He aligned his thoughts to the task at hand, to persuade Merri of his genuine and honorable intent. His oath would be the key. After all, Merri knew that no Herewardi would break an oath. Ruhm and Brekka had come along as Alim's oath-helpers.

*In my heart, I will always be Os-true to my word, for one does not lie to the gods. Only to one's self.*

He couldn't stop thinking of Lorna, her beautiful smile, the pleasure he took in her hug, the comfort of her presence, her gentle kindness, her warm embraces. *If Merri says no, what will I do?*

In another year she would be eighteen, and under Syr Folk law she could make her own decisions. But he could not wait, for by then he would be fully engaged in the End War, and far away from the isle. As he had explained to Lorna, he had specific orders as Commander of the Irregulars to fight the Pitters in as little as three moonths, and there was no way to know how long he would be away, nor how long the war would go on. Now was the time to marry. He had never been so transfixed by any other woman before and when he gave his heart it would be in totality.

Alim sucked in a deep breath. "You know Merri, Lorna and I have taken a real liking to one another."

In his usual gruff manner Merriman turned his hard dark eyes on Alim as if to measure him. "Man would have to be blind to not see that, boy; all your kissing and hugging, and endless hours dallying in the garden and woods about the house. Only reason I've allowed it is 'cause I know you can be trusted. Damned pity you got yourself all worked up for nothing, though, cause I really like you. You already know that. We've been hunting buddies a long time, and you know well that we don't see eye to eye on this marriage issue. There just ain't no place for my daughter in an ungodly Herewardi harem. So there is no use in your thinking of marriage or the likes of such."

Alim sucked in air and squared his shoulders for a horn clashing. "Merri, the Herewardi practice is a moral science; we always strive for excellence and proper deportment with the goal of improving our race."

Merri shook his bull-like head. "It's not a question of morality or improvement. I know you Herewardi are all upright men. God help the man who thinks they could out think a lore master. But your traditions have blinded you to the way the one god intended us to live. One man and one woman established by holy writ."

"But Onamingo said there is no one universal law for marriage," Alim argued as calmly as he could.

Merriman lifted his head and thrust out his jaw. "And now I would expect that of a heathen red man who gave his own daughter to be your father's seventh wife."

Alim considered himself an expert in flyting, the Herewardi sport of word wrestling, but he was already on the slippery slope and couldn't push this issue much further. Hickoryans usually took great offense at flyting. "Onamingo has only one wife. Yet he saw that love is rare enough that it should be grown whereever it's planted."

Merriman shook his head even more emphatically. "No use in going there, my boy. You know where I stand. If you truly want my daughter, then you need to step into my tent; for I'll not have my daughter living in the tent of a harem."

Alim had carefully rehearsed this conversation in a hundred different forms, so he was ready for this. He put his ulu in its sheath and said with firm resolve, "I thought you'd be of that mind, Merri. I had hoped knowing me so well might change your mind. I don't want us to end up like these two kudus, locked in a battle that would kill us both. So I'm retracting my horns and asking you, if I marry Lorna as an only wife, and bind it with an oath, my two oath-helpers here standing as my witnesses, will you give us your blessing?"

Merri stopped sawing at a horn and turned to look at him with both surprise and suspicion. "You mean to tell me you'd live one man and one woman with her, until death do you part?"

"Yes, until death do us part!"

Merri studied him intently for several long moments with that fierce bull-like gaze of his. Slowly, his hard look turned to one of satisfaction and even delight. "Why boy, I gotta tell you, that'd be damned pleasing to me." He chuckled. "One thing's for sure, I don't care a hog's piss about any of the other boys that have been courtin' her." He paused as if considering them. "They're poor white trash; bunch of damned worthless peckerwoods. But you, you got some good breeding, and you were always respectful, and would be like a son to me. By God, I already think of you as one of us."

Ruhm smiled big. "Congratulations, Alim. She'll make a fine wife."

Brekka looked down, tugged at a kudu horn and began sawing at it more vigorously with her folding saw. Her tight lips bit back vehement protest. Her silence masked a brewing storm.

Merri glanced at Brekka before giving Alim another big toothed grin. "I can tell the little ginger lady wants to eat me from the inside out. I appreciate your silence, Miss Brekka."

Brekka gave him a fiery look. "Don't count on that happening again. My voice is only reined in by an oath I gave my brother to not tell you what I really think of your ruining his life."

Merri gave her a good-natured smile. "I wouldn't have expected anything less from a fire-haired wild cat." He gently chided her. "Fact of the matter is, this is your brother's decision and not yours to make."

He turned to Alim. "And I'm sure your many parents aren't going to want any part of this business either, but it's the only way it can be, Son. There is no other way."

"You are right, my parents will not like it, but they allow me the freedom to make my own decisions." He glanced at Brekka, who frowned her disapproval.

"As much as I love you, Alim, if you ever betray this oath, I'll cut your heart out and feed it to my hogs."

# CHAPTER 2 :
## TILL DEATH US DO PART

THE DELIVERY OF ALIM'S WEDDING oath and the ceremony of handfasting was held at the harrow stone on the shore of Lake Redith at a place called Larkspur Rise. It was the middle of the moonth of Albespiene, when weather was usually unpredictable, but the gods graced them with a warm, sunny day.

This particular harrow stone had been erected in a grove of dark yews, as designated by the swan queen, Paloma, who was directed by the Ur Fyr as to its placement. The ancient stone rose out of the earth to equal the height of a very tall man. Covered in moss, it had been carried by many generations of Herewardi migrants and had witnessed the pledges of countless couples.

Behind the stone, the broad expanse of the lake shimmered with irridescent fire. Reflected in the azure surface, the snow-capped monolith of Mount Elflohana rose majestically into the sky, a benevolent witness to this most solemn of ceremonies.

On one side of the stone stood Sur Sceaf, the children still residing on the isle, and the invited guests. On the other side stood the Hickoryans, Merriman and Lorna Wallanwood, along with various family members and guests. The Seven Women of the Swannery, attired in their priestly aubergine robes, stood directly behind the harrow stone to perform their office of witnessing the marriage and handfasting.

The bride was dressed in a long white dress with ruffles, frills, and a train. To her side were the three Hickoryan pastors who would officiate in the Hickoryan marriage rite to follow. On Alim's side stood three Herewardi priestesses from the swannery, as it was customary that women sanctioned marriage among the Herewardi, and men among the Hickoryans. Ruhm and Brekka also stood as civil witnesses. They would also sign the civil certificate of marriage attesting to the legality that both parties were legitimately married under the cannons of both cultures' laws, as well as Syr Folk law.

Herewardi musicians played the lute, the rebec, and the recorder as wedding guests assembled.

Sur Sceaf and his seven wives stood regaled in their most costly attire; green and blue silks, perfect white buckskins, and costly adornments of precious metals and gems. Paloma and Taneshewa held yew branches to lay before the bride and groom, likening their marriage to the yew tree, ever-living and enduring in strength forever.

After kissing his mother, Il-Alim walked over to the harrow stone to kiss his bride and take her hand in his. It was the last time he would wear the red sash.

In Sur Sceaf's memory there were six such other marriages he had witnessed where the man was required to renounce the Herewardi practice of multiple wives. Each one of them had aroused the same mix of emotion--one part happiness, and nine parts pain. To a Herewardi, such a marriage represented a form of spiritual death to be grieved in silent prayer. It was a capitulation to the intolerance of dominant cultures, rather than to the will of those betrothed.

Sur Sceaf loved all his wives and never doubted that they loved him, each in her own way. He hoped his son would find as much love with his one wife as he had with his seven queens. It was not what he would have chosen for Alim, but took some small comfort in the young blood's happiness. As soon as Alim had announced his betrothal, Redith had wisely implored the family to trust in Alim's good judgment, honor his decision, rejoice with him, and leave his fate in the hand of the Norns.

The music stopped and the Lady Redith stepped forward. The ancient sage announced, "We are here to witness and honor the vows and oaths spoken through the harrow stone. Let us all honor the choices of these two who will this day be wed according to the laws of the Syr Folk regarding the marriage between two disparate cultures." Under her direction Il-Alim stood on the west side of the stone, and Lorna stood on the east.

Il-Alim stepped up to the well-worn altar stone to pronounce his oath. Lorna's father assisted her to the altar, and she spoke her vows. Both said 'Until death do us part.'

Sur Sceaf whispered to Paloma, "I am pleased, Merriman is taking this in good grace."

Paloma whispered back, "Why shouldn't he, he's getting his way. He's done his best to prune this tree of a man into a mere bush."

The nuptials moved to the harrow stone. Alim stretched forth his right hand through the hole in the top of the harrow stone and took Lorna by hers in the handshake of a solemn pledge. "I, Il-Alim, descendant of Herewardi kings and Sharaka chiefs, do solemnly declare before the gods, elves, and these witnesses here gathered, that I do promise and swear to take Lorna Wallanwood, daughter of Merriman and Selma, as my lawfully wedded wife throughout eternity, and swear to take none other throughout all the years of her life until death do us part, so help me Odhin, and keep me steadfast in this resolve."

Lorna then spoke her troth, "I, Lorna Wallanwood, do solemnly swear and promise that no man shall cover me, save only Il-Alim, and that I shall worship him and none other with my body, heart, and mind all the days of my life, and throughout eternity."

Redith stepped forward, "In the eyes of all present, I declare this couple to be of one flesh, heart, and mind."

The Hickoryans said, "Amen" and the Herewardi said, "So mote it be." The bride and groom kissed, and everyone cheered as the little Herewardi girls in their wispy aubergine dresses with feathery yew garlands wreathing their heads, danced around the bride and groom. Willowy, green clad Herewardi boys played their flutes and fifes and followed the bride and groom in the dance of joy.

Selma and her daughters had decorated a bower in a nearby willow grove where those Hickoryans who had refused to attend the heathen Herewardi ceremony had awaited. Following Redith's counsel, none of the Herewardi refused to attend.

It was a simple ceremony, and after the couple exchanged vows, the three pastors gave lengthy speeches on the necessity of one man and one woman as the only acceptable form of marriage in the eyes of their god. They belabored the point so much that even the Hickoryans threatened to fall asleep.

After the final ceremony, Sur Sceaf whispered to both Paloma and Taneshewa, "Oddly, according to their scriptures, their god was a god of polygynous prophets."

Taneshewa said, "As Thunder Horse taught me, there is no point in talking to those who sit under the noon day sun and say it does not exist."

Once the ceremony concluded with the nuptial kiss, the wedding party made their way slowly up the hill and into the gates of Godeselle. The trumpets blasted to announce their passing. Finally, the happy procession made its way into the Great Stone Hall of the palace.

Sur Sceaf sent his wives ahead, declaring that he wished to stay behind to offer his own prayers for the young couple. As he stared at the stone, memories of his own seven weddings played through his mind. Only Ahy had initially balked at sharing him with his other wives. Had he not been able to help her resolve her fears, he would have lost her, for it would not have been possible for him to violate the Forty-Four Laws. He wept for Alim.

Placing his hand against the soft moss, he contemplated the solemn promises Alim had made this day. It was true that his son had been raised as a Herewardi royal, but he was also a member of the Syr Folk, and a citizen of the Confederation of Sovereign Nations.

As they had stood there at that harrow stone, and his son reached through its hole to take the hand of his bride, a golden cock crowed from the large oak, and in the sycamores peacocks cried out throughout the betrothal. Weren't these all good omens?

So many changes had occurred since he had first set out on his commission to unite the three tribes. He had fought hard to preserve the Herewardi heritage and culture, but instead of assimilating the other tribes, the Herewardi traditions were in grave danger of being compromised.

His son had taken an oath of wedlock, promising to only have one wife during her mortality. It saddened him, for he knew the young man was of the finest cut, yet one wife would deprive him of the many offspring his brothers, sisters, and friends would have, and seriously limit his domains. The bride, Lorna, was smart, charming, and nurturing, and no one could ask for a finer nature than her pleasant and engaging spirit. Certainly, no one could doubt her love for Alim. Most importantly, to Sur Sceaf anyway, she was the woman Alim wanted, so that is the way it had to be. He took comfort in the idea that they would at least likely have lovely children, who, in the next generation, might be grafted back into the Herewardi ways. The Forty-Four Laws were written to preserve the Herewardi in the Ea-Urth. Any compromise would, ultimately, result in their dissolution, rendering the Herewardi without an identity or the expression of their uniqueness, floating in a sea of mediocrity, a bland monoculture that melted into the masses of lost souls that teamed the seas of confusion covering the Ea-Urth.

Closing his eyes, he prayed, "All Father Woon and Holy Freya, what is becoming of my kingdom? How is it my beloved son, the firstborn of Taneshewa, has been made so limited in his growth? Bless them that they may find a full measure of happiness in the world they have chosen, and help me that this choice of his does not diminish him in my eyes. Be with Alim, that he may find joy and rejoicing in his life even with the newly imposed limitations. And be no less a god to him, for he has chosen correctly, in that he has chosen the path of love."

By the time Sur Sceaf made it back to the great stone hall, the sky was darkening, and a tiny fallen crescent moon was shining clearly overhead. The celebration was still in full sway, and laughter mingled with the mouth-watering smells of the still heavily laden festive board.

The Hickoryans had decorated the hall with ivy and wildflowers. The crackling fire in the massive fireplace burned gold bright, sending sprays of sparks into the chimney. The many ram's head sconces lit up the peaked arches, and illuminated the tapestries portraying the history of the Isle of Ilkchild as well as the heroic deeds of yore.

Once again, his eyes were drawn to the tapestry of Ilkchild the Fair being swallowed by a shark-wyrm in the thrashing sea. He remembered the day it happened like it was yesterday, how Ilkchild had miraculously cut his way out of the wyrm to later appear before them hale and whole. The tapestry was a portrayal of the day they found this isle.

His gaze shifted to the tapestry portraying the Battle at Moon Door, with the woven intestines of their enemies mounted beside it. That was the high water mark of the Pitter Empire when the united Syr Folk races destroyed the last of the enemy's hosts upon this sacred isle, and the Norn Sisters wove their enemies ill fates into such a gristly tapestry.

From that day, the Pitters had been confined to the Main Land of Panygyrus, and the isle continued to be a sanctuary for all freedom loving peoples and races. Much had been achieved, but the tree of tolerance had not yet taken full root in all the peoples' hearts. Still, people had grown far more tolerant of each other's cultures than when they first came to the isle. Perhaps another great moon would pass before the tree of tolerance would bear its true fruit. On the other hand, perhaps it never would.

He soon spotted Ahy among the colorful throng and walked over to give her a kiss. "How's my beloved holding up?"

Though she smiled, her eyes were troubled. "As fine as can be expected. I am well pleased with the bride, and believe she will make Ily a very fine wife. I understand the way her parents think, for I once thought that way myself, but a lifetime of experience has shown me there are other roads to happiness. So I'm just going to make this as special for Ily and Lorna as possible, and let the Norn Sisters spin what fate they will." She glanced at the newlyweds who stood, arms linked, chatting with her parents by the fireplace. "'One to spin the thread, one to measure, and one to cut it.' Ain't that what Redith always says?"

Sur Sceaf smiled, "You're doing a great job of giving it your best. And yes, Redith says it." Sur Sceaf folded Taneshewa's arm over his left arm and walked over to welcome his new daughter-in-law.

"Lorna," he said, looking into her deep grey eyes, "You are a most welcome addition to our family, and I hope you will spend many days with us at our estate. We have prepared the swan bark for you honeymooners, and loaded it with mead and provisions. When you return we shall feast together."

Her warm eyes shone as she replied, "We shall make it so, my lord."

Taneshewa said, "I don't think I've ever seen a more beautiful couple. Hopefully, by thrice three moonths we'll have a little lamb crawling around our hearth."

"I hope so, too—if it is god's will," the peachy complexioned girl said, "If it's a boy we'll name him Hereward-Il. And if it's a girl we'll name her Taneshe-Lana."

Taneshewa nodded her approval. "That would be most pleasing. He always loved Lana as much as me, and she gave him great comfort in his day."

A slight frown cover Merriman's face. Sur Sceaf reached out his hand and said, "Thank you for this beautiful daughter, Master Huntsman."

Merriman smiled, "And thank you for my new son. Always did like that boy."

"Well, the truth be told, he already had quite the bond with you."

"Yes, he is a fine boy and we have a long hunting history together. It's gonna be hard letting him go off to war. I was talkin' with his mother. Maybe, someday, he will wrench my homeland of Jimson, in the Virginias from the Pitters."

Some Hickoryan relatives came up and began greeting the bride and groom. Sur Sceaf said to Taneshewa, "I have a sudden craving for some of Govannon's ale. Can I bring you something to eat or drink?"

Ahy shook her head. "I'm already stuffed."

"Then I'll leave you to be with your son." He bent down to kiss her before excusing himself.

He found Lana filling a plate with some schnitz and knepp, as she called her dried apples and dumplings. Instead of the usual Herewardi banquet with beautifully decorated tables, colorful table cloths, place cards and attentive serving staff, Selma had planned a more casual affair, with the guests helping themselves to the food and drink before finding places at the bare tables.

As he filled a krug with ale, Milkchild and Shining Moon joined them. "A lot of the little ones were getting tired, so Swan Hilde and Paloma took them home," Milkchild told him.

"I fear many of the older ones are becoming bored," Shining Moon added. "I hope the dancing begins soon. Otherwise, some of them may get into mischief."

Lana sighed. "It seems we're to just piffle here until the bride's mother sayeth what we do next." She rolled her eyes. "Honestly, I feel like we've been put in the back seats at our own son's wedding. They chust want to run the whole show with no thought to us or our ways at all. And then there's that schnickelintz, Hoth Ev'Rhettson. No doubt, he hath come to gloat over our son becoming a monogamist. It wondereth me. Why else would he even bother to come?"

Lana was blushing nearly as red as Sur Sceaf's sash, a sure sign she was upset. He planted a kiss on her hot cheek and said, "It's twitter-light, already, my little flitter-mouse. It won't be long before this is all over."

"I'm not stupid," Lana retorted. "It chust feeleth all so inconsiderate and selfish. They expect us to accommodate them, and take no thought to our ways or customs at all. After all, we are chust heathen wood lords. It wondereth me that we ever thought the intolerance would have an end."

"I hope it is not meant to be that way, my sweet honey sop. We may not have tolerance yet, but we have set the bounds of intolerance, and that is enough of an accomplishment for one generation. Let's not let conflict sour our mood. They just don't celebrate like we do. Let it be our son's moment and we'll rejoice with him. It's the life he has chosen, and he's no less our son for it. By the time his children grow, methinks a more tolerant spirit for us will prevail in the land."

Milkchild nudged Shining Moon. "Looks like young love is a-bloom between Brekka and Ruhm, does it not?"

Lana sighed. "I fear Ruhm will be disappointed if he is hoping to marry soon."

"You have to admire the boy's persistence," Sur Sceaf said before taking a hefty swig of ale. "He so hangs on to her."

"And Brekka's willpower," Milkchild replied with a chuckle. "I remember how I wanted to melt every time you came calling, my love." Her eyes flirted with him. "But you were a true gentleman. Ruhm is more like a wild and randy buck."

Shining Moon laughed. "I'm not worried about Brekka doing any melting. Even as a child, it was clear she had the heart of a true warrior. It's in her blood. Though, this Hickoryan is a tamer of horses, he does not yet know the way to tame Brekka. I can sense the frustration in him."

"Hi Fa! I've been looking all over for you."

Sur Sceaf's four year old daughter, Fae-Earendil, of Faechild's hearth, stuck her little hand into his. Behind her came his seven year old son, Woon-Ulf, of Shining Moon's hearth, and fifteen-year-old Ethel-Flicka, daughter of Swan Hilde's hearth.

"Will I be able to have a beautiful dress like Lorna's some day?" Fae-Earendil looked up at him with wistful blue eyes.

He deposited his krug on the table before scooping her into his arms for a kiss on the cheek. "Even prettier."

"I sure hope their kids look like me and have black hair," Woon-Ulf declared fiercely."

Ethel-Flicka tugged on one of Fae's beribboned pigtails. "They are a beautiful couple, sure enough, Fa, but I hope brother's seed takes before he goes to battle, or that line may be doomed to die out, forever."

Sur Sceaf turned to his teen daughter, lifted his brows, and said, "Ethel, we all hope that, but let us not speak evil things. We do not wish to tempt the fates or call down the black faery upon his bride."

Fae-Earendil looked puzzled. "Is Alim planting a garden?"

Sur Sceaf hid a smile. "In a way." He kissed Fae on the cheek and winked at Ethel. "Someday soon, Ethel's going to be a bride, and you will be her brides-maid."

"When?" The little girl demanded.

"Ethel will let you know, won't you, dearling?"

Ethel frowned. "Fa, you know I'm going to be a lady knight as soon as I'm sixteen."

"If you pass the tests," Sur Sceaf reminded her with a gentle smile.

"I'm not worried. Alim and Brekka have been training me."

"Finally, the dancing's about to start," Milkchild declared.

"C'mon, Fae," Woon-Ulf urged. "Let's go dance!"

"Put me down, Fa," Fae ordered.

Sur Sceaf hid a smile. "Your wish is my command, my lady," he said solemnly as he lowered her to the floor.

She took Woon-Ulf's hand and they headed for the dance floor. As he watched them with amused pleasure, he caught sight of Paloma coming toward him. His pulse accelerated. He was to spend tonight with her.

After explaining to her sisters that Swan Hilde would be returning shortly, Paloma leaned closer to whisper, "Honestly, my lord, Selma is running this wedding like a cross-eyed friscan marketeer. I swear they don't know whether to buy, sell, or trade."

He laughed, "The newlyweds can forget all that in bed tonight; besides the Hickoryans might surprise us, so I recommend you suspend judgment for now."

"Well, I know somebody that won't forget that comment in bed tonight." She winked.

The musicians began to play. The sound of the fiddle, banjo, and dulcimer rang out in the hall. Alim led his bride onto the floor for their first dance as husband and wife. Soon other couples took to the floor including Fae and Woon-Ulf.

Alim was as graceful on the dance floor as he was in the fencing ring. He was an unusually powerful man, filled with strength and cunning like few warriors. This was the reason he was to command the elite force of the bush masters in the coming Great War, despite his extreme youthfulness. When Redith blessed him as an infant, she said he was of purest elven blood, and would likely enter the bloom early as had Sur Sceaf. The bloom was the Herewardi process of opening a person's seed code to its full potential, and happened only rarely in the sons and daughters of man, but once activated, one continued to progress in spiritual and mental faculties.

The next thing Sur Sceaf knew, Milkchild and Shining Moon were tugging him toward the dance floor where Faechild and Ahy waited impatiently to join in a Hickoryan reel. In the swirling mass of merrymakers, he caught sight of Brekka dancing with Ruhm. Ruhm's cocky grin taunted his fellow cavalrymen as he went quagswagging in the jargogle of the dance.

One of the fiddlers, with a mouth as wide as a frog's, was fiddling at a feverish pace, while another ancient, Old Duff, who resembled an old white rooster, plucked away at the banjo the same way a fighting cock dances in an arena.

On the fringes, Hickoryan farmers drew out the corks of their glass bottles of brandy and whiskey, and passed shots of it around, along with beer by the tankard. Others spat their thick tobacco juice in the fireplace, warranting a look of utter disgust from Milkchild.

Swan Hilde scowled. "Do you see Brekka corrade with all those Hickoryan cavalry officers? She is right there gathered about the scuttlebutt with them. And if you ask me, she's showing a might bit too much interest in that purdy dillydowne, Ruhm."

Sur Sceaf offered a reassuring smile. "You don't need to worry about Brekka, my darling Hildy. She's Herewardi to her core, and she'll never abandon her commission. Ease your soul. Either Ruhm will be Herewardi by the time the end war is over, or she will not take him to the marriage bed. Before you comment on Il-Alim let me just say he consulted with the gods, and this is the answer he received, 'follow the path of love'."

As the Hickoryans began to shout and take their pleasure on the dance floor, Sur Sceaf noticed the slander monger, Hoth, took his leave. He was sure Hoth would not be missed by either Hickoryan or Herewardi, and could only wonder what smut he would connive to print next. Such bitterness as he printed could only pour out of the mouth of a man that was fatherless. Sur Sceaf had seen it before, boys reared without the presence of a father or uncle tended to be wanting in the nobler aspects of manliness.

Shortly after Hoth exited the hall, the Lady Redith entered with Muryh and his wife. Soon they were followed by Surrey's good friends, the Quailor Hartmut Hegele and his Sharaka wife, Mendaho, bearing gifts. Mendaho immediately found her way over to hug her friend Taneshewa, while Hartmut escorted them toward their party. Though his grandmother Redith was nearing one hundred and five winters, she was still spry and her grey eyes radiated both kindness and humor. Her wit was as sharp as ever.

Sur Sceaf put his arms around her and said, "So good to have you here Mo Mo."

"I wouldn't miss my great grandson's wedding for anything. Look at his bride there. Isn't she a beauty?"

"That she is," Sur Sceaf said. "I hate that in three moonths he'll be off to war with his green rascals. I can only pray the gods preserve him and he returns alive."

"And I pray you all return alive," Redith said. "Sadly, it was only yesterday, when you were his age and I was sending you off to war. This time, I shall not live to see any of your returns, and I grieve the day of your departures worse than my coming death."

# CHAPTER 3 :
## THE JOURNEY BEGINS

THE CALL TO WAR HAD gone forth throughout Syrdom. The Bell of War had been rung at Godeselle. The distinctive full-throated peal was heard as far away as Neorxnawang where its announcement was repeated from the stone towers from one end of the land to the other. It was a bell which could not be un-rung. The forces it would unleash could never be recalled. Nor could the resolve of five centuries be abated in the hearts of the warriors going forth.

Lord Arundel, King of Ele-Anor-Ness, had spent the two weeks since his younger brother Il-Alim's wedding at Ele-Anor-Ness. Leaving Zschamillah, his bride-covey, and his beloved children was one of the hardest things he had ever done. There was no telling when they would ever be reunited again. His ship had ported in Troll Landing the night before and he had stayed at the home of his mother, who held a farewell party for him before he headed for Godeselle in the morning. His fyrd had camped out on the beach at Troll Landing, on Shark-Wyrm Bay.

King Sur Sceaf had sent a formal dispatch commanding King Arundel to appear before him at Godeselle in a meeting in the upper chamber of the Stone Hall. In addition, he was to bring his fyrd in preparation for full deployment. The Lord Arundel dismounted from his white steed and handed the reins to a green-clad stable boy, no more than thirteen winters of age and beaming with excitement. The tow-headed youth took the reins and bowed at the neck, "My Lord Arundel. The honor is all mine. Your name is on all the lips of the fyrd commanders and the Roufytrof."

Ary smiled. "What are you rattling there, lad?"

The freckle-faced boy took a deep breath, held the reins, and said, "Everyone that rides in has your name on their lips. Some say you are the greatest strategist in Herewardom, and others say the gods have marked you as their champion and even marked the command runes on your cradle. Others say you were born to be the heiland, having come from the core of the previous world and the circle of noblest godlings."

Ary was taken aback. "What is your name, son?"

"Sygna, son of Cwichelm," the lad said, as he stroked Sky Strider's neck.

"Sygna," Ary said, "Although I was born in a royal household, I once worked as a stable boy, as a shepherd, and as a beekeeper. Each of those jobs did much to prepare me to be a warrior. The gods always start us low before they exalt us through day-to-day tasks. Unless we reach mastery degree by degree, no calling bestowed upon us can be properly fulfilled."

Sygna smiled wide revealing a noticeable gap between his front teeth. "In two more years I'll be ready to join you on the battlefield as a beetle."

"Of that, I have little doubt. You are a bright boy. If we should ever cross paths on the battlefield, you make it a point to come and see me. You hear?"

"I hear, my lord, and I shall train like the devil to be worthy to fight with you."

Ary said, "I shall look forward to it." He ruffled Sygna's hair as the boy led Ary's stallion safely into the livery with pride. He caught the other stable boys looking on in wonder.

It was early morning, and the streets were a bustle with workers and craftsmen making their way to fields of labor, toting carpet-bag tool sacks in hand. A wolf pack of fyrd warriors was arriving at the Stone Hall, and the merchants of Godeselle were unpacking their goods and setting up their stalls along the streets. Chickens were clucking from all the jostling in their cages.

Ary pinned up his two hair braids at his temples on either side of his head over his freshly washed long hair. Long hair had long been the pride of Herewardi royalty and nobility since distant times, and Ary took particular pride in his thick suit of braids.

Several members of the Roufytrof were gathered before the peaked archway, dressed in their customary Saxon green, hooded robes. Only Heimdal wore the white, the mark of a lore master. They smiled and saluted Ary. He knew many of them from his days at the Academy, and he had numerous times sat in deep council with them rehearsing law and battle strategies.

Master Heimdal approached him with a broad smile and mischievous twinkle in his eye. "Big news tonight, Ary." The powerfully built blond pointed to the upper chamber. "We've been at it for three days."

"At what?" Ary asked.

Heimdal lifted his eye brows and in a low breath declared, "Selecting the grand commander and laying out the war road, the master plan. Whoops! Just remembered, I must go. Your father asked me to tell him the moment you arrived. I'll see you up in the chamber." Heimdal rushed back up the stairs and into the hall.

Ary bowed at the neck to the members of the Roufytrof before walking through the royal arch into the great stone hall thinking, *This is it! I have been officially chosen as the grand commander. Why else that twinkle in Heimdal's eye? He nearly let the cat out of the bag.*

It was a good thing Arundel had dressed in his fyrd uniform of rich red wool with golden Herewardi wake knots embroidered around the collar and sleeves. His knee-high black boots sounded out his approach as he trod across the terra cotta tiled floor. Alabaster ram's head wall sconces lit his way. Licking his dry lips, he swallowed hard as the full impact of such a calling finally struck him. Now, a powerful sense of humility filled his chest and, though he wanted this command, he knew he must not in any wise fail.

This hall was the see of the High King Sur Sceaf's government, and was well built out of thick granite stone sent in from the stockpiles of Panygyrus by Ary's grand father, Sur Spear. As he opened the large black walnut door to the antechamber with their sculpted swirling green-eyed dragons on them, the two elderly doormen, one heavy and one thin as a rail, ritualistically brought him to a halt with their spear tips. The thin one said, "Heimdal went to announce your arrival. You are to wait here for an answer from the high lord."

Ary said, "I notice you wear the badge of Witan Jewell. Are you from there?"

"Sure am, served there for sixteen years as a doorman for your Fa Fa, Sur Spear, after the seat of government was moved here to Godeselle. Name is Od. I hail from the Viceroyalty of Stonyford."

The skinny doorman peaked through the door and up the stairs where Heimdal could be seen nodding. He then returned and announced, "Permission to allow him to enter the upper chamber has been granted." He bowed to Ary before adding, "If you will follow me, Lord Arundel. They're almost through with business and will see you as soon as they finish up their last point."

He was led up a winding stairwell into an upper chamber of polished oak floors where the smell of copal incense permeated the air as if the walls and woodwork were breathing its sweet essence. Ram's head sconces fueled by whale oil glowed brightly. Above the door to the upper chamber was mounted the proud head of a mighty bull wisent, shot by Mendaka on a hunt with Sur Sceaf, Brekka, and himself.

Ary was brimming with excitement. He took one more deep breath and squeezed his fist to relieve some of the tension. For as long as he could remember, his parents and friends had told him he would someday lead the forces of liberty against the might of the Pitter Empire. And by every indication the gods had ratified this approval.

He had trained most of the fyrds of this generation and had proven each one of them in skirmishes and campaigns of one sort or another on the Main Land of Panygyrus, tried them on treks of endurance into the Arid Zone, and ran them through endless tournaments, maneuvers, and mock combats, until every unit was a proven, crack fighting force. At his request, Degataga had put them through the rigorous training on the Auvandilean Sea, and recently, he had Il-Alim train them in crypsis. This generation of fyrds was as ready as he and his lieutenants could make them.

The tiler grabbed the door and gestured for Ary to enter.

Ramrod straight, he crossed the threshold, paused and bowed at the neck. Looking up, his father, the High King Sur Sceaf sat at the head of the polished, oval-shaped, kauri-wood table. Dressed in his official robes, golden crown shimmering in the candlelight, his father was as regal and dangerous as a tiger. Were it not for the great love they bore for one another there would be cause to tremble.

This was an August assembly and a historic moment. White robed Godhi sat six to each side of the table. One of them was Ary's dear uncle and friend, the Lore Master, Long Swan, who resembled a gentler version of Sur Sceaf with the same regal demeanor and long brown hair, powerful physique, and that god-like handsomeness which was the legacy of the Herewardi royalty.

Once they settled a formality, King Sur Sceaf turned his attention back to Arundel, and motioned him forth, to receive his instructions from the twelve ruling members of the Forty-Four membered Roufytrof. Many plans had been gone over in the Sovereign Council of Syr Folk, but this meeting was attended by the ruling members only.

At a nod from his father, Arundel knelt on his right knee and gave the swan salute. This was executed by raising his left arm to the square, making a fist, and striking his chest with it. Then he repeated the salute, alternating with right arm and kneeling on his left knee.

In a thunderous voice that shook the hall, Sur Sceaf said, "Lord Arundel, you have been commissioned as the Heretoga of all the fyrds and as grand commander of all the forces of the confederation on the march to the Taxus Lands. Your mission shall be a campaign of total war, with the express goal of the destruction of the Pitter Empire in its entirety by severing it root by root.

"I will join you on 'the war road' at the Omala. In military matters no one but me supersedes you in authority. But we know, for we have proven you in days that are past, that as a tactician, you are most excellent and will deliver us the victories we have planned and meet the set target dates for the same. Even so, the All Father has shown his approval over you your entire life. I, therefore, charge you, in the name of Odhin to bring us victory over the vile offspring of Ish and Vardrop, the occupiers and usurpers of the inheritances of all the races of Man. A victory which may only come through the hardest and swiftest blows you are capable of delivering according to the timelines set forth by the War Council of All Tribes. May Tyranus be with you! May he strike death's threatening waves before you?"

"It shall be done, Father!" Arundel said. Pride and honor swelled his chest as he scanned the wise faces of the Godhi. He had come to greatly respect these priests in his younger days at the Skaldic Academy. There sat Heimdal the Wise who taught him the strategies of history. Across from him, Ethelthor, who had taught him field medicine, Goldcyg, who taught him the proper employment and use of phalanxes and finally,

Vanstem, who, along with Starkwulf, taught him and Il-Alim advanced crypsis. The other eight were various teachers of politics, language, culture, and law, whom he had learned so much from.

His breast was full to bursting at the confidence these elders of the folk had invested in him, and it was easy to read his father's pride in his smiling eyes alone. Even the air in the chamber exuded with spirit like some great reservoir of luck from which he could draw on so as to be stronger than his mortal frame would otherwise permit. For unto the Herewardi, **luck** was the accumulated spiritual power one acquired through good and courageous deeds, which he would most assuredly need. For this was to be a long war, fraught with great costs of resources, blood, and losses.

Sur Sceaf rose up from his chair and faced Arundel squarely on. "Son, on the morrow you will depart this isle and travel against the direction of the sun until not one Pitter occupier is left to stand against a wall, from sea to sea. I charge you to cut out their evil root at their heart in Hormah, while my armies strike before the next bamboo bloom in Flar-Dah and the south lands, thereby staying their abominations in the Ea-Urth before it is everlastingly too late; for if they have the benefit of even one more bamboo fruiting, it will tip the scale in their favour, and they will multiply exponentially and overrun us.

"We face extinction if you fail. Take with you the dogs of war and the doves of peace. Break the yokes off the necks of the oppressed races in bondage, and set free the captives of the foul and sinister Emperor Hryre Seath. Bring the captives and oppressed nations into our covenant. Strive with all due speed to meet the target dates we have set for, the War Road." He paused then belted out in his deep guttural voice, "Now go and shape it so!"

"So mote it be!" echoed the white-robed Godhi of the Roufytrof. Ary caught a nod of approval from Long Swan, saluted his father, and knelt on the wool sack and honeycomb the Tiler placed on the floor in front of him.

The High King walked slowly over to the kauri table and picked up a horn of oil, and returned. Ary bowed his head, and the king poured the magnolia scented oil over his crown while saying, "Arundel, son of Sur Sceaf, son of Sur Spear, descendant of Arundel the Great, I anoint your head with this holiest of oil and consecrate you as the Grand Commander of all Syr Folk forces."

The Twelve stood and drew their swords as the oil trickled down over Ary's brow and ran into his beard. They raised their blades to the ceiling. Then, with a shouted accolade, they chorused, "Os wills it!" and brought the points of their swords down to rest upon his head.

Long Swan intoned in his resonant voice, "We consecrate, dedicate, and sanctify you to bear the sword of righteous judgment to the nations and races of man, in Panygyrus, and throughout the whole of the Ea-Urth."

All intoned, "So mote it be!"

After closing the meeting in due and ancient form, Sur Sceaf removed his crown and saxon robe, once again becoming Arundel's father. He walked over to a closet and hauled out a barrel of high desert ale, which he poured into leather flagons for Long Swan to pass around. The men drank to one another's health, shouted curses to the Pitters, and then they sat for several hours going over the critical war plans known as the War Road.

At the end of the discussion, Sur Sceaf announced Long Swan would accompany Ary in all his campaigns unless otherwise deployed. Finally, with one last round of ale and song they left the upper chamber.

As Ary walked between his father and Long Swan down the winding stone staircase, his steps were light. He was utterly thrilled to have Long Swan assigned to him, for there were few men in the land gifted with more wisdom or intelligence. His counsel rarely failed. Not only was he an uncle, a fa bro, but he had virtually grown up with Ary, and their relationship was that of dearest of friends.

Long Swan was known as one who never showed fear or favor, but always spoke truth. He, like Ary, had learned to lean unto the Ur Fyr for his understanding. He always judged and chose aright, for which he had earned all the Herewardi's respect, insomuch, that his word was usually the final word. He was Os-true.

Ary leaped down the last three stairs and would have danced, except the guards gave him a queer look. But inside he was bursting for joy. As he exited the pointed stone archway, he shouted into the trees. "Thor, Almighty Thunder God, into your hands I commend my spirit. Let us strike down the image of Pitterdom."

It was a beautiful starlit night as Ruhm inspected his cavalry along with his two lieutenants, Seamisch and Loosestrife. In the flickering torchlight they made it a point to check the tackle, and gear, and the shoes of each horse before inspecting each cavalryman.

As they inspected the last trooper, Ruhm intimated to his two lieutenants, "I want us to be the handsomest and most disciplined and skilled cavalry the world has ever known. By God these horses and men are the finest I've ever seen. Wait until Brekka sees us ride into Godeselle tomorrow."

Seamisch shook his head. "Jesus, if you can't get the woman off your mind for one minute, why don't you just wed and bed her before we go to war? Won't be much time for loving once the battles start."

"I'd wed her in a flash if she'd have me. She's stuck on being Odhin's battle maiden."

After inspecting all four feet, Loosestrife slapped the final horse on the rump and said, "Then why don't you just bed her."

"Can't do it. It wouldn't be right."

"Wouldn't be right?" the skinny goateed officer mocked. "Hell, Ruhm, you didn't seem to mind parting Ellie Lou's thighs last week at that hoedown in Hockney-In-the-Hole."

"I've made it a policy to never violate a virgin. It's a place no man should ever go unless fully invited, and then only with the sublime intent of full commitment afterwards. Making love to someone who is not a virgin is altogether different. It's not a breaking and entering. It's not a long term commitment. It's only an invitation to a party that's already in progress."

Seamisch grinned. "Then why do you only ever go to the party one time?"

Ruhm paused to think. "If you feed stray dogs they'll hang around, and then you can't send them home."

"Can't say I ever had the opportunity to know a virgin. My own wife didn't even afford me that comfort."

Loosestrife probed, "How about it, Ruhm, I mean, I've read Hoth's Kat Sheet, about the two of you. You ever seen the mcgillicutty on that redhead you've been courting." He laughed loud and long. "Can you be sure she's a virgin?"

"Brekka is one, regardless of that crap you read in Hoth's Kat Sheet and I intend to honor that."

"Oh, wee! It's going to be a tight fit when he finally gets in there," Loosestrife said as he slapped Seamisch on the back.

Ruhm felt his temper flare. "I warn you both, close friends or not, do not jest about the woman I love. I hold her as sacred as my mother, and I'll damned well lay you both out cold on the spot if you ever sully her name with your loud laughter and evil speaking again."

# CHAPTER 4 :
## BREKKA'S TRIUMPHAL DEPARTURE

**J**ESSE BEN DAVID'S LOG: I *am Jesse ben David, of the Jywdic Tribe. I write this as personal scribe to the Lady Brekka, Daughter of the High King Sur Sceaf as well as Heretoga of her Fyrd of Lady Knights, and Commander of the Young Blood Spanix Warriors. My new calling required of me to be trained in scribing in the Herewardi flame alphabet that only Herewardi lore masters and royal lords can decipher, so that, should they fall into the wrong hands, none of our communications can be understood or interpreted by the enemy. The writing is difficult to learn, but is the purest of delights when mastered.*

*The Moonth of May or Albispiene of this year, 603 HSO marks the beginning of the New Age, and the Lady Brekka has a major role to play in the coming war against the Pitters. From this time forward, the campaign will switch from one of defensive, marauding, and consolidating tactics, to a total war of aggression and offensive tactics.*

*As a symbolic gesture, the official start of the war will begin with the lighting of the spring equinox fanisk, or as we Jywdic people call it, 'the mazzaroth.' These bonfires will burn throughout the land, heralding an all out invasion of the Pitter Empire, which has for so long yoked the nations, peoples, and races of the main land of Panygyrus.*

*The Pitter occupiers have been oppressing and enslaving all free peoples for over five-hundred years, systematically eliminating whole races, religions, and nations of people. Were it not for the stiff Herewardi resistance, they would have long ago conquered and subdued all the nations of the world.*

*Their elitist politics are based on total acquisition, oppressive social hierarchies, and compulsive programs of racial homogenization and genocide. Compounding this, their scientific priesthood has endarkened the nations that fell under their persuasion or the misfortune of their legion's crushing foot, so that the humanity that was in their seed code has now been obliterated, or so weakly burns that it resembles the last flicker of a candle's wick.*

The Moonth of Albespiene broke with the explosion of white blossoming Hawthorn on the Isle of Ilkchild. Added to the Hawthorn's thick honey scent were the erupting fragrance of the yellow flowering gorse and the brine of fresh sea air. Brekka breathed deeply the smells of her island home for one last time, stirring nostalgic memories of former more playful days. The blow of Hawthorn was the season that marked the call for mating, and man-making, as well as battle. It was also a delightful time of merry-making. Even in her meditations she had already drank the cup of war and prepared her heart for the bruising.

The storm clouds had been gathering for moonths. For twenty years the Roufytrof had been planning for this war. The melding of the tribes by her father when she was but thirteen had been the first step. Now that the fateful time was at hand, the very air seemed filled with the sharp scent of aggression, and the moving of armies stirred in the blood of every warrior. The horsey odors added their pungent whiffs to the thunderous sounds of hooves, steel-rimmed wagon wheels, and cheering crowds. The air was filled with May Knots hurled by the maidens. In the distance she caught sight of the handsome Firginia cavalry Commander parading his horses and men before the throngs of a cheering Godeselle.

War! Unlike her Quailor Mother, Lana, it was not something terrible to her. It was something exciting, thrilling, and glorious. She was animated at the prospect of full-scale combat leading to the freeing of endless captives and nations. Indeed, it was her fate to be the midwife unto those oppressed races. More importantly, the commission had endued her to find the Lost Mound of Heredom; for she knew that unto this purpose she was born.

That morning, during false dawn, she had bathed in the lake next to Neorxnawang under the gaze of a phalanx of swans until the bloom of the star marks faded into pink dawn. Among the Herewardi, this was the custom of baptism into warfare or any great undertaking. She now pressed to Godeselle on her white mount along with her White Buffalo, and the shaman, Talks-As-He-Walks who cared for the buffalo. She wished to say her final farewell to a city that had nurtured her through her most formative years. Once she reached Troll Landing, she would board the sea swan and sail across the Auvandilean Ocean to the Main Land of Panygyrus where conflict would soon ignite in the dramaturges of a holy war long since prophesied.

She looked up at the sky with a prayer of gratitude to Woon. The sun was growing warmer as it climbed the sky, having passed through the equinox into the warm-eyed moonths of spring, and the spirit of life and death filled the air. For this was the time when kings went to war.

The highly trained armies were assembling for loading on the docks below the city of Godeselle. As she rode slowly through the stone city to join her warriors and greet her admirers at the end of the parade of troops, a renewed hail of excitement, like a tree full of birds suddenly taking flight, came from those who had gathered to cheer her off.

Although the fyrds were under the supreme command of her brother, the excellent Lord Arundel, Brekka as the archetype of a New Day, had come to symbolize the glory of the Syr Folk. Arundel told her the people loved her, and they held great expectations of her and her band of Lady Knights.

As she stretched down to touch the hands of admiring girls, the leather of her saddle creaked and groaned. Older women pressed in close, to touch her legs and speak their blessings. Hands grazed her legs and their shouted blessings poured over her. "Bless you, War-Woman. Bless you Shield Maiden of Woon. Bless you Spear-Shaker. The Norns weave you good fate." As she looked into their smiling faces, she was determined to see their charges to full fruition.

This fortress at Godeselle was the strongest bastion of the Syr Folk. Here, the city-state of Godeselle boasted its mighty Rams Head Fortress upon the stone hilltop above the sea, and it was poised for battle and protection as needed. Few enemies had ever dared to besiege this colossal tower of strength. Those that had were utterly broken upon its ramparts. This walled and templed city of the gods had been the seed bed for freedom, equality, liberty, and tolerance. It shone like a beacon to all the oppressed nations who fled from under the dark cloud of Pitter dominion on the main land called Panygyrus, meaning many races. She could still hear the words of Muryh at the temple's dedication: *In strength will I establish this mine house to stand firm forever through the force of truth, light, and reality.*

She remembered her father likening this city unto a large clam out of which the raven god, Woon, opened to let out his mighty armies so as to free the minds and bodies of all races of men. She drank in the limestone and marble structures, and knew how bright they shone in the liquid ocean over which they hovered. It was her city, and today the clam was opening to release her, the city's virgin arrow.

South of the fortress, rose the magnificent rounded, H-shaped temple as a tower of spiritual strength, with its center dome ensconced in two architectural swan wings, the masterpiece of the builder, Muryh. The swan-winged temple sat on a mound above the mirror lake. Beyond the lake laid a large valley of savannahs running south for hundreds of miles until it hit the rugged Dragon's Back, which rose through the middle of the land. The river Mahallah ran from north to south, and in conjuction with the Dragon's Back quartered the sacred island into the Nor Folk and the Suff Folk, the Es Folk and the Wes Folk.

With great emotional impact, she realized she would probably never lay eyes on this marvelous sight again, and choked on the tight lump in her throat. So many good times were held here. So many laughs, so many toasts, and feasts at the festive boards. Only last night she had sat in her canoe on the lake and watched the image of this white temple on its mirrored surface while she prayed to Odhin and the Idisi to bless her arms in battle, her mind with cunning, and her heart with wisdom.

The departing fyrds, newly initiated Young Bloods, Green Beetles, and Silver Harriers, too, were all praised and sung to as they passed along the road. Crowds of families, many with tear-filled eyes, hailed kith and kin off.

Recognizing her beloved grandmother standing with her dear mother, Lana, she motioned for the guards to permit her family to gather in. She had bade goodbye to her brothers and sisters the night before, but her mother and grandmother insisted on this one last farewell by positioning themselves strategically along her path to the Gorse Gate.

Dismounting from her white horse, Cycnus, she tied it to a madrone sapling and gave the lead of her white buffalo to her personal groom, Talks-As-He-Walks.

"Fa Mo Mo Redith!" With outstretched arms, she embraced the ancient matriarch of one-hundred and four winters goodbye.

In syncopated verse, Redith proclaimed in the crackling and aged tones of a prideful grandmother,

"Proud, bushy-haired, Brekka Copper Locks,
Here you stand in warrior's garb of silver ringlets
As glowing and glorious as the moon through cloudy mist.
Your red hair burns like a fire, a beacon atop the mountains,
Announcing to all the Ea-Urth, all the races, and all the nations,
A lady knight is finally come to right the wicked world
And turn the rivers, sands, and sea red with evil blood.
You shall redeem our people, branch, root, and stem!
And humanity will evermore be free, when this oppression ends!"

Redith gave her a warm embrace and kissed her goodbye on each of her cheeks.

Brekka loved this woman with all her soul. She had long realized Redith had been the driving force of her grandfather, Sur Spear, Father Sur Sceaf, her brother, Arundel, and of course, herself. Her wit, wisdom, steely resolve, and above all, her gift of seership had molded all of them into what they were; for it was her prophecies that guided them, her teachings that inflamed them. Her wisdom would forever be the light unto their feet long after she entered her sepulcher.

Brekka lingered long with watery eyes in the embrace of her grandmother. It was this old woman who sent her forth as an arrow of light into the enemy's heart, as surely as if she had pulled back the bowstring herself.

Struggling not to choke on the tears, she hugged Redith tightly and whispered, "Oh, Fa Mo Mo, I will probably never lay eyes on you again, but I shall never, ever, forget you. You are written on my soul, forever."

"Hush now! The gods are calling me home and I know I shall not likely pass through another winter. Muryh has already cast my sepulcher out of white marble in the shape of an owl. But I am content that my Dau Son Dau shall be the light of the new world of Panygyrus." Redith swished her hands as if she could chase away the tears. "Now go forth, sweet child of my soul, conquering and to conquer on your white horse. The gods have appointed this day. So, until we meet again on some distant shore, may the gods shine on you. On Ea-Urth, as it is in Heofonum," she said in the old tongue.

She gave Redith one final hug, then hugged each of her nigh-mothers. Taneshewa presented her with a wreath woven out of all of their hair as a talisman of protection for her to wear into battle and to remind her of their love and prayers for her.

Her Mother, Lana, a peace-loving Quailor, looked on in dismay at her bride-sisters and Redith. "Please don't encourage her. She ought to be marrying, not going off to war. Oh God, my baby is really going off to war!"

There had never been a time when Lana hadn't clucked and fussed about her like an over protective hen. She felt compassion for her, but fully comprehended her mother was of another nature, a peaceful nature, alien to the seed code Brekka had inherited from her father's side. For she knew every cell of her own body embraced the warlike, rageful, blood-drenched nature of her sire, with all its warlike ferocity and passion. She was nothing like Lana, her peace-loving Quailor mother. She was a tigress.

Through heart wrenching sobs, Lana declared, "I love thee with every fiber in my soul, child. May the gods grant we meet again?"

As their cheeks met, their mingled tears were a holy anointing, blessing each other with the purest of love. Reluctantly, Brekka released her mother and walked through the host of relatives and friends. Walks-As-He-Talks silently handed her the reins to Cycnus, who nickered impatiently as she mounted, and the family cheered her off.

Somehow, Brekka managed to resume the appearance of her royal composure. She must always remember that hers was a calling from the gods. Many were the strangers whom she encountered in forest, field, and woodland who had imparted her with great wisdom and then disappeared in an instant. She had to believe it was elven-kind who came to endow her with such knowledge.

Now the day had come when she was to ride forth as the shield maiden of woon. Her strict training for years as a swordsman by Ilkchild, her training in archery from her father and her brother, Arundel, was now to be put to the use for which it was meant. Finally, her excellent training in horsemanship by her brother Alfheah, helped to make her a highly skilled warrior.

She looked at the red man, Ma-Za-Ma's keeper, smiled, and said, "We go now."

Talks-As-He-Walks jerked his head in the direction of the tall Firginian dressed in grey, riding Brekka's way with two of her lieutenants close by. The red man said, "Methinks the handsome hick, still want to see you. He comes this way."

"He'll have to catch up to us then. Won't he?" She wiped a tear away with the back of her hand. Not wishing Ruhm to see her teary eyed.

Another cheer went up from the crowd as she gave one last look back at her family, she felt the knot in her throat tighten. While nearby gleemen delivered their melancholy songs of departure, and Herewardi banners with the eye of Howrus whipped in the sea breeze. The people tossed magnolia leaves before her path, and red-clad godhi priestesses shouted repeatedly, "May the Idisi go with you! May the Valkyrie light your way. And may All Father Woon ever have your back. For the love of Osir endures forever!"

Even though she was likely never to return here again, she smiled and shouted back, "The gods be with you till we meet again!"

Not long up the road to the gorse gate, she heard someone coming swiftly up behind her. The thwacking of horse's hooves on the cobblestone road let her know of their anxiousness to catch her. Soon she was joined on her right side by the grey clad commander of the Hickoryan cavalry. The red interior of his cape caught the sea breeze and whipped the sky like tongues of red flame.

It was Ruhm Lee; his usual tall, handsome, and eager self. He smiled at her, and his white teeth shone like pearls against his vermillion lips and tanned face. He was mounted on his blue-grey steed, and her two lady lieutenants, Freyxus and Verushka were accompanying him, and grinning like two schoolgirls on a first date.

Her heart rate quickened and she noted instantly how his nearness immediately stirred all her womanly senses. She put on a friendly smile as a mask, as Ruhm's sharp grey eyes searched hers. Without speaking, he removed the red scarf from around his neck and leaned forward to fasten it around hers. "To remind you that I love and want you." With one last roguish grin, he wheeled his horse and galloped off through the gorse gate.

Freyxus and Verushka now remained at her side while they went at Ma-Za-Ma's pace. The shouts, the singing, and the wind deafened her.

She had chosen the long blond, Freyxus, daughter of noble Aethelstan, for her excellent skill as a blade master and the best sword-maiden known, and Verushka, daughter of Rudolf the Quailor, because of her ability to weigh matters and deliver the wisest of options. She knew they were as attracted to Ruhm as much as she was, and this pleased her, for if Ruhm was ever to be Herewardi, she preferred to be surrounded with friends in her bride-covey. But, so far, he showed them no inkling of liking. He only ever treated them with gentlemanly kindness, and did not reciprocate their hints of affection. Together Brekka, Freyxus, and Verushka formed a formidable team. Brekka knew they were the head, heart, and liver of the Lady Knights fyrd.

The sentinels saluted as they passed down the dock, and pointed to her ship docked at the troll landing. Diving and swirling ravens flew above her. She could see the long beard boys, Forkbeard and Fairbeard, the sons of Elfbeard loading her faery-hounds on board the Sea Swan. These hounds were white with red heads, trained as war hounds, obedient and loyal to the core, and the pride of her personal breeding program.

Once Ma-Za-Ma and Walks-As-He-Talks were safely on board, along with Cycnus, she went in search of her father.

The dock was over a mile long, but even in the crowds of fyrd warriors dressed in their red surcoats, the hordes of Hickoryan in their grey uniforms, and Sharaka warriors dressed in buckskins, Brekka managed to spot her father in his saxon green robe. He stood apart, watching as sailors rolled barrels up planks, and wranglers led horses on board.

Calling out his name, she ran toward him, springing into his powerful arms like the little girl she no longer was. "Father, the day is come!"

"My beloved Brekka," he said in his deep voice. "May Os shine on you, as you shine in my heart, my dear, and may Woon gather his War Maidens to assist you in all your labors. I cannot bear to part with you, dear child, but know that I now must. Perhaps I shall not live to hear of your victories, but know that my heart is always with you. I hope after I secure the government of the Kalifornias and the Mexus under our umbrella that I may come join you in the final assault on the empire of Hryre Seath. If we do nothing else but secure all the lands from the Mys-Isys to the western sea, and destroy the bamboo bloom of the southern lands, it will be accomplishment enough for this generation."

"I could never have had a better father than you. All your works shine as a bright candle to light my path and show me the way into the future. I go as the vessel of your seed to deliver our enemy, Hryre Seath, into his grave, which has so long hungered for him. My sword shall not rest till the grave of our enemy has been thoroughly gorged, and his head placed on a pike in full sun. I vow that not another generation shall pass until the banner of Howrus on Heredom doth wave."

"I can only hope that your vow is fulfilled, and I live to see you have seed in the Ea-Urth, like your other sisters have been blessed with."

Brekka faced her father square on. "I dare not dream of such marvelous things. Today I am a warrioress. Perhaps in tomorrow's world I can take a husband and bear children, but today is a day of sacrifice and the field of family must lay fallow in me." She shot a glance in the direction of the Hickoryans--and Ruhm.

A silence fell. Her father's expression was that of a loving father concerned for the safety of his little girl, but he did not speak it. He wouldn't.

"Tell Tamfae, I am sorry I am not able to attend her wedding. Thank Mother Ahy for her wise counsel she gave me in regards to Ruhm. And take special care of Mama. She is not cut from the same breeding as we are."

"I shall do as you ask, my dearest," he promised. He reached into a lamb skin bag at his side. Reverently, he retrieved two stones. "Take these seer stones, for they will be a light unto your feet by which you may divine the outcomes of battles, and by which you can locate the weak points in enemy armies. These stones will help you ascertain the enemy's strengths and weaknesses, and aid you in following the Ur Fyr. They are the eyes by which your grandmother Redith scryed, they are the stones by which I scryed, and they are the peep stones by which your brother, Arundel, has scryed." He returned the stones to the pouch before removing it from his belt and handing it to her.

"Thank you, Fa. I will carry you in my heart until we meet again."

Sur Sceaf took her in his arms once again and hugged her tightly. He could not speak without weeping. His throat was closed. So they hugged one another long, in silence.

The surf was rhythmically pounding the sand. The crowded shore at Troll Landing was a buzz, and gulls mewed overhead. Ruhm stood on the dock watching the reflected light of sun cats running over the hulls of the rocking belly ships, as his men were loading into them. He directed the loading of his own horses and mules, ordering his men to secure them below deck.

Harriers, young men dressed in silver smocks, were releasing messenger pigeons with the help of Beetles, boys acting as pages and dressed in beetle-green uniforms. The pigeons were alerting the peoples of Urford and Witan Jewel that the fyrds were being launched to join with the fyrds of the main land, where they would meet fyrds from the islands and viceroyalties of the north, and the mountains, and viceroyalties of the south to form one grand host hell-bent on laying Pitters to the edge of their blades.

Finally, Ruhm finished directing the loading of his Hanoverian and Hackney horses and his men. His horse was the only grey stallion, so that his men might always know his whereabouts on the battlefield. The Hanoverian had been trained by the horse master Alfeah who gave it a Quailor name, Spitzer, which meant the "foremost" or "spearhead".

Rhum waited for the final supplies of food, weaponry, and medicines. Then, to one side of the dock he spied the tall Sharaka Shaman, the Thunder Horse, chanting his blessings over the campaign, sending up holy herbs on the winds, and motioning with his shamanic crook.

The red man's long grey hair was tied in braids hung over his shoulders. His face of tanned antiquity gave him the majesty of an eagle. He surveyed the preparations for the launch, taking sacred tobacco smoke into his mouth and blowing it over his people and goods.

Strangely, Rhum was drawn to Thunder Horse, like a boat without paddles is drawn over a waterfall. He couldn't explain it, but he felt somehow he must speak with the shaman. Long had he heard the tales of this Thunder Horse's wise counsel, particularly his deep insight into the matters of the heart, and his powerful abilities of seership.

Thunder Horse was the Chief Judge of the Suff Land, as the Great Seer of the Sharaka, whose predictions almost always came to pass. But Ruhm had never availed himself of such gifts as this Shaman was said to possess. It was a spiritual wisdom he could not comprehend and indeed his culture held it suspect. Instead, Ruhm relied only on his own logic and will to steer his course through life. He prided himself that he was led by his intellect, unlike both the Sharaka and Herewardi who were forever talking about encounters with strange beings such as elves, faeries, and gods.

But he had tried every logical avenue he could think of to win the heart of Brekka, and all of this to no avail. Now his desperation drove him for an answer. Willing to sacrifice his vain pride, he wondered why he had not thought to consult the wisest man in the world on such matters before.

He took a deep breath and mustered his courage, feeling strangely like he was walking into another world. "A good day to sail, is it not, Thunder Horse?"

"That it is, Young Lee." Thunder Horse paused, grabbed Ruhm by his upper arm and led him behind some large crates waiting to be loaded. "We shall be alone here. You have something you wish to ask of me?" he said, as if he knew everything in Ruhm's deep and aching heart.

"Why, yes as a matter of fact I do," he admitted, "but I know not how to ask it, as it is so personal."

"All things are personal at some level." The shaman stared up into the sky. "Ask only if you want truth, for I see your heart as a proud one."

"Thunder Horse, what is my future with Brekka? I feel such unending love for her, but she remains wholly committed to remaining virgin. I am willing to be patient, but I must know if she will be mine once her mission is complete. I've placed my whole life on hold for her and I have to know the wait will be worth it."

The Thunder Horse slowly turned his head from looking into the sky at the circling pigeons and diving ravens to Ruhm. It put him in mind of an eagle searching the spiritual horizon. The Shaman's eyes fastened on Ruhm's eyes like talons. They felt like they were drawing out the thoughts at the very bottom of his soul.

Suddenly, Thunder Horse clutched Ruhm by the shoulders with his strong hands. And in his gritty voice said: "Look at the golden shield the maiden carries." Ruhm shot a glance over at Brekka with her shield on her back. She was hugging her father.

"The golden shield is her virginity. See how she clings to her father. That tells you she embraces fully the Herewardi way and none other. She is her father's girl. The shield is the shield of her glory. If you would attempt to defeat that virginity, then look to her butterfly axe hanging there at her waist. Behold, like the shield it contains the Eye of Howrus at its core, at its heart. Mark that well!"

Ruhm frowned. The old man was speaking in riddles.

The shaman asked, "What does all that tell you?"

His tongue was tied and his brain stalled. He could not think of an answer. Instead his mind went confoundedly blank, and the Shaman's eyes penetrated even deeper, as if boring into his soul to the point that Ruhm felt naked and actually began to squirm.

All Ruhm could think to do was say, "The ways of revelation are not made known to me. I don't know what it means?"

"To wed her, you must become as Howrus. You must do the works of Howrus and embrace the Herewardi ways. Not that she is invincible or immortal, but the gods of the Herewardi keep close watch over their daughter, and they will slay any who bear her evil intent or try to draw her away from her fate.

"She is bound by blood, oath, and covenant to the core. For she entertains none, save only the pure of her kind inside there. She has permitted you into the outer courts, but you will have no key to the inner court without becoming like Howrus and doing the works of Howrus."

"What does all that mean?" He darted a glance over at the dock, at Brekka still engaged in a conversation with the king. "Become like Howrus? I can't understand that, Thunder Horse. You speak in a hidden language I am not acquainted with."

But the Thunder Horse only stared at the pigeons flying out to sea. "Then you will have to wait to know what that means. For the heart does not reveal what the mind is not prepared to receive."

"But why tell me such then?"

"Because your pride blinds you, man, and the gods are purposed to sift you like wheat. They know your fate and wait for you to make the appropriate choice."

"Do you not think I am willing to give up my pride? I thought that's what I was doing by consulting you?"

"That was mere surface pride. Your pride runs deep to the core of your culture, young Lee. It blinds your eyes like the scales of a fish. The gods require a broken heart and a contrite spirit. You are far from there. Sadly, this prophecy will not be made known to you or have any meaning until the black cock crows through the hickory smoke. For in that day you will be brought through a refining crucible, and the day of deliverance will surely be at hand.

"I am telling you, this bird is yours, if you do not frighten it off by attempting to pen it in a lonely cage. She is a communal bird."

The conversation was interrupted by the grokking of a raven perched on one of the crates. As Ruhm turned from the shaman, Sunchild, Fairchild, and Bnimin rode up on their mules, clad in their black satin Jywdic uniforms. Behind them followed the dashing Jywdic fyrds.

"Which ship may we load our mules on?" Bnimin inquired.

Ruhm saluted and pointed to the loaders. The loaders flagged them to the next belly ship down the line where the Jywdic Pirate Captain, Zeru-Herewardi, called El Yid, was already waving his black flag to draw their attention.

Aboard each ship the Herewardi fyrds wore red, but the Jywdic Fyrds were dressed in all black, and Ruhm's own troops in their greys. The Jywdic ensign adorned with twelve rearing golden lions in a swirling fanisk on a black background fluttered in the sea breeze.

# CHAPTER 5 :
## WITAN JEWEL: STRONGHOLD OF THE UMPQUA

**J**ESSE BEN DAVID'S LOG: WE *arrived early in the Stronghold of Witan Jewel on the Half-Moonth of Albespiene 603 H.S.O. Located at the confluence of the North and South Umpqua River, and surrounded by fertile lands, the stronghold consists of a center fortress from which radiates tall, round, stone towers.*

*In the generation before the Syr Folk Confederation, it was the See of Herewardi rule under the High King Sur Spear, before he took up his role as Weardean in the Roufytrof, leaving his son Sur Sceaf the High Kingship. The Herewardi settlements sit amidst a mighty and impenetrable forest, like an island surrounded by a girdle of protective woods and reinforced by formidable mountains. All roads into the land are sealed and heavily guarded, making entry by any armies, without detection, all but impossible.*

*A war council has been convened in the Shepherd Hall, the large timbered lodge that in earlier times had been the navel of government before the rams head was built at Godeselle. Witan Jewel is now ruled over by Aonghus, one of the forty-four sons of Sur Spear. Aonghus is presiding in this war council as he is the sovereign in his own land.*

*Recently, Sur Sceaf gave over supreme command of all the fyrds, save his own, to his firstborn, King Arundel of Ele-Anor-Ness, a brilliant strategist and tested warrior and commander. Now, Arundel has been given the charge to march east to reclaim lands from the Pitter Empire, to take the Poisoned Lands, and the Taxus Zongas (Enemy Fortresses) as well.*

*The High King is sweeping through the Kalifornias and the Mexus Lands before his scheduled meeting with Arundel's forces at the Omala. From the Omala they plan a many pronged attack against the heart of the Pitter Empire at Hormah, so as to disorient the Pitter response and draw it thin. Brekka will march through the north and then into Toront, Arundel through the Appalachian Mountains, Kanarus through the Shenandoah, and Sur Sceaf will begin the destruction of the Zongas and bamboo plantations of the south, followed up by Il-Alim's forces. While this is all going on, the Jywdic fyrds in their sea stallions will do a pincer movement on the lands of Nu-Yalk. Lord Pyrsyrus will sting the eastern seaboard from his sea palace, offering reinforcements where they are needed.*

*Lord Arundel, as Supreme Heretoga of all the fyrds, has just been called upon by Aonghus to address the assembly of fyrd officers assembled here at Witan Jewell. The Herewardi write as the ox turns, so I shall have to re-write this.*

At the age of thirty-six, Arundel was in his prime. He had won numerous campaigns and major battles. Tall, broad-shouldered and agile, he had long brown hair worn in the traditional style of the Herewardi warrior, and intelligent green eyes that pierced one to the core. His voice was mellow of timbre, but forceful and confident.

The great wooden-hall came to a hush so still that the candles could be heard to flicker. Ary grabbed the walnut podium with his hands, feeling its smooth texture, and looked over the vast assemblage of warriors spread throughout the pews. Though the shepherd hall was filled to overflowing, he recognized many of the faces turned his way. In the council of women sat his wives Macbah and Ilklilith shooting him encouraging glances. Behind him sat the assembly of the Roufytrof, and on his right by the podium sat his Fa Fa, Sur Spear, looking regal as always in his white robes. Though he was nearly seventy-five winters with long white hair and neatly trimmed beard, his fierce green eyes reflected the fires that had set many of the forces of the syr folk into motion the generation before. Now it was Sur Sceaf's commission to take this baton of oneness and tolerance to the next generation in hopes that he could complete his kingship in like manner. The baton, Arundel understood, would ultimately come to rest in his hand as Chief Tactician.

The candlelit hall was warm and inviting with its highly polished and gleaming walls and colorful tapestries. Each of the forty-four columns sported a white banner with a red ewe's foot, and one of each of the Forty-Four Laws written in black runic letters on it.

Aware of the gravity of the subject he was to address, Arundel took a deep breath and plunged in. "Men and brethren, lords and ladies, this is the great year we have awaited a score of years for, and this is the appointed generation of the reclaiming of all of our ancestral lands. It is the great and terrible day of our peoples. We shall see whether we shall champion the race of humanity, or whether the Pitters shall champion their kind. For endless moonths we have had our peoples raped, enslaved, oppressed, tortured, and killed by the chronic and persistent evils of the Pitter Empire."

A mumble arose out of the audience. Arundel paused at the podium to wait for them to quiet. "We have won some notable battles at Shasta and in the High Desert. We cut off the Pitter supply lines running through Frink Glen. Brekka and the Spanix Fyrds destroyed the Pitter Legions in Zamora, showing the great battle cunning our Lady Knights are in possession of."

Many in the hall broke into a Syr-Haka stomp and a salute to Brekka. After it was finished Arundel stroked his goatee before continuing.

"Now, just before this year's Summer's Solstice we have assembled every Fyrd of Herewardom, all the braves of the Sharaka, every available soldier of the Free Folk, Spanix, and Jywdic Fyrds, and the eternal peace loving friends of us all, the Quailor, so as to begin the final battles of this Great War. We express our gratitude to the Quailor who have agreed to provision all our supply trains and to meet all of our nursing and medical needs in the long days ahead with their order of hospitalers."

A round of applause echoed around the hall.

As Arundel scanned the audience he spotted Melyngoch's son, Forsetti, who upon Melyngoch's death, was taken as the adopted son of Ilkchild. He was soon to be summoned to war in what would be called the second wave. In his heart, Ary thought, *The House of Melyngoch may yet one day be redeemed.*

He smiled at Forsetti and then continued. "Today our spirits are high, and we would break upon our enemies in a rage if we could. But this war has been a long one, and it will yet test the stamina and mettle of all of us before it can end. Every move must be with absolute calculated accuracy. The Skull Worm still maintains his massive legions in Frisco and Copperopolis where he daily seeks for another way in which to root us out of the Ea-Urth for good. Soon, my father will march against him. Skull Worm expects us to attack him first, so he drains his other zongas of their strength and draws them unto himself in Copperopolis. I tell you today, we shall be the first to strike. Spies inform us The Skull Worm's mighty nervous."

Ary's grandfather, Sur Spear, struck his staff to the floor and said. "Hear, hear!"

The audience all stamped their feet, the token that they marched with Arundel. The Council of Women cheered. Ary saw Brekka's eager and supporting look. Then the assembly broke into applause.

After the audience stilled once again, he commenced. "From time to time we will be required to re-purpose our goals so as to keep the enemy off balance and always guessing. All commands must be followed to the letter, trusting that your leaders know more than you when an unusual change or request comes, even when they don't know better than you. It is a hard thing I require. We must endure and persist with this mission throughout the dark and long days ahead. Unto this purpose was this generation born and raised. Let us not fail in this, for our hour upon the stage has arrived. The curtain call is at hand."

Great silence and awe filled the hall.

Aonghus called a recess for refreshment. As the stewards opened the doors for air, a mighty wind swept through the hall causing the whale oil lamps and candles to all flicker, and the sheep foot banners to flap as if some Great Spirit had just entered. Arundel took this as the sign of approval from the gods.

Brekka returned to the hall eager to learn what immediate role she was to play in the early days of the war. She and Ruhm along with her lieutenants, Freyxus and Verushka, had sampled several krugs of ale along with cheese and bread, and she was feeling slightly light-headed from it.

After making certain that only members of the military forces were in attendance, and guards were stationed at every entrance, Aonghus once again turned the floor over to Ary. As usual, he got right to the point.

"I shall now assign the fyrds to their various fields of battle."

He described the overall plan of sweeping from west to east, then executing a many pronged attack over the entire east. He gave out the various theaters of battle over which each Heretoga would have their own sovereign command. Finally, he assigned Brekka's fyrds to smite the Eugene zonga of the Pitters. This was the Zonga that had so sorely afflicted her mother's people in Salem, the peace-loving religious sect called the Quailor; a people who worshipped the one god. This zonga had long ago killed her great grandfather, Ludwig von Hollar, in the battle of Salem; a very costly battle that lasted for six agonizing moonths of privation.

When she heard she was to take on the most powerful zonga in the west, her heart skipped for joy. It was a token of her brother's absolute confidence and favor. Her fyrds, except for her twelver, were composed entirely of Spanix. Like every fyrd, she built hers of twelve wolf packs. The lead wolf pack or twelver was composed of her lady knights, with Freyxus as her first lieutenant and Verushka as her second. She shot a glance at Freyxus, and got a wink from Verushka.

This was her first command since Zamora, and all knew she was given the assignment based on her merits as well as her brother's favor. She was to attack the Zonga that had been used to subdue subjected peoples outside the Syr Folk realm of influence. Long had this Zonga been a thorn in the Syr Folk's flesh. Now her sword was given the honor of hewing down the first domino in the chain of Pitter strongholds. She wanted to shout for joy, but, instead, let a ghost of a smile of satisfaction trail over her face as all the other Heretogas looked on and applauded.

She was proud of her Spanix, too. Especially Xarela, Son of Arundel and of Maya Ixil's hearth, who was wise beyond his years and experience. He stood tall, dark-haired, and sported a thin mustache which he often combed with one finger. He was getting pats on his back from his lieutenants. Pata and Cisne, two of Brekka's lady knights and also Xarela's wives, stood by him. He was indeed young, a mere fifteen winters, and had just taken to himself these two wives under Maya Ixil's advisement. He was a highly skilled warrior as proven by his fighting skills in Zamora, and was as dedicated to the cause as she was. Not to mention he was filled with a double measure of the elven seed code.

In the Battle of Moon Door, almost sixteen years before, Guatemalan women had been freed from Pitter slavery. As very few men from their villages had been spared, the Herewardi men wed many of these deserted women--those who chose to be wives rather than remain spinsters. Thus they reared up an additional army of warriors in an effort to achieve some balance of numbers against the Pitter hordes. It was an experiment in social engineering conducted by the Council of Women, and now the tree was yielding good fruits. The Spanix had become in all their ways Herewardi, in their thinking and culture, but because their mothers spoke another tongue, which they were also given to speak, they were called 'Spanix.'

Each Heretoga was issued their commands in turn, showing that Arundel had highly favored and honored Brekka by issuing her the first and most important commission. As the meeting was closed in due and ancient form, Ary stepped down from the dais and moved toward Brekka. Xarela came over and congratulated her, while Ruhm stood silently nearby.

Ary nodded a greeting at Ruhm and Xarela. "This sister grew up on my arm and she is like a daughter unto me. As a matter of fact, as a child she could not be separated from me. I believe the Idisi willed it so for just such a day."

Ruhm frowned. "And yet you placed her against the most dangerous zonga in the west."

"No matter which way I have turned with this, by the gods of the ur fyr, by revelation, and by deep wrought inspiration, she has been called, chosen, and anointed by the Roufytrof, to go up against the Pitter Empire as a full-fledged warrior. It's time she try the wings the gods gave her, and bring the dark Commissar Tintregon to his knees."

Brekka felt her face flush at the praise, "I shall make it so, my lord."

Ruhm entered his tent along with his two lieutenants, Loosestrife and Seamisch. He lifted a candle lamp and lit it. Sitting at his writing table he began to enter the events of the day in his journal when Seamisch said, "Captain, do you think it wise the Herewardi lord appointed a woman to command us?"

Ruhm was shocked, "Why ever would you say that, Seamisch? You make it sound like we are not one with them."

"Oh, it's just that I see you two arguing a lot lately, and I'm not so sure these women are up to what a real battle is going to take."

Suddenly, he was aware of Brekka's accusation that the Hickoryans did not have high opinions of the strengths of a woman, so he tempered his answer with reason. "Seamisch, I have fought often with you and trained hard with you and know you to be a fine warrior, but it behooves us to give women more credit than our culture has been wont to do. I have also come to understand that these lady warriors are more than a match for any Pitter. The Herewardi have no trouble in placing their women on the battlefield, in government, in council, and I can tell you, my eyes have been opening to this. One of the wisest people I know is my mother, and I saw how courageous she was when we were attacked by a band of outlaws while passing through the flooded lands. I was but a boy, and she wielded her skinning knife as adeptly as any warrior. You heard how successful Brekka was in the Zamoran Campaign. I am not the least troubled about Brekka being in command over me."

Brekka awoke in the dark cool early summer morning to the bustle outside her tent. She lifted a side of the tent and was witness to large bands of Sharaka dog soldiers pouring into her camp. *But why? It was before sunrise. Then it dawned on her that now that she was on the Main Land of Panygyrus, the red tribes had come to see her and the White Buffalo, Ma-Za-Ma, just as Talk Walk had predicted.* Upon exiting her tent she heard whispers of 'Buffalo Woman.' 'She has our blood.' and 'Fire Head.' Many braves pointed at her.

Xarela came to her side and explained, "The Dog Soldiers from many outlying tribes wish to see you, my lady. They have heard from their fathers the tales of the Buffalo Woman who would break the bows of their enemies, and restore power to the red man, and put a final halt to their afflictions."

She nodded to Xarela. "I'm sure I'm not what they expected. I chust hope I can deliver what they hope for."

"Ju will," the tall commander confidently answered. "Ju will."

Ruhm came out of his tent near Brekka's camp, apparently attracted by all the commotion. He tucked his shirt tail in and combed his thick, tussled, brown hair with his fingers. "Brekka, why are there hordes of red men gathering into your camp?"

"I should have expected this, Ruhm. I have Ma-Za-Ma with me. It's a thing of holiness to them. They've come to behold him."

Xarela said, "To them, she is the Buffalo Woman of prophecy. It is a holy moment for them, just as it would be if your god showed up in camp."

As Brekka looked at the teaming masses of ponies and dog soldiers strung out through the mist laden woods in the early rays of the morning, she saw a particularly tall, muscular, lean brave approaching her.

He locked his eyes on her, and made a beeline to her, as if making eye contact were an invitation. When he arrived he declared, "My lady, I am Fox-On-Fire of the Sioux, from the Black Hills. I am come to see you. The Keeper of the White Buffalo said I would find the Flaming Hair through these woods."

"Os-Frith, Fox-On-Fire," Brekka said. She shook his hand, only to look up and see her brother walking towards her.

"Sister," Arundel said, "I am sorry I didn't tell you. Fox-on-Fire is chief of one of the many bands of red men I have sent word to. They have heard of your victory over the Zamoran Zonga, and that you rode the White Buffalo into battle. Such a thing is a great omen for them. They requested of me that they join 'the Flame Head' in battle. You will find fox a very accomplished war chief and a man of great honor throughout the buffalo nations."

Brekka looked at the tall, lean warrior with a red quill roach running down the middle of his head. "Such praise, I am sure, has been well-earned. I have heard of your great deeds, Fox-On-Fire, and how you have slain the Ice Bears and Dire-Wolves that plague the North Land. And tales have even been told of your encounters with the She-Wolf Banners of the Vardropi. Anything you can share about tactics against the Vardropi would be most useful to us. I take it to be a great honor to have you fight alongside us and lend your counsel to ours."

The towering Red Man smiled. "The honor is mine, Buffalo Woman."

"Fox-On-Fire, you may set up your corrals south of ours and your camp can be just there to the west of my tents along with Going Snake. His is the tipi with the four serpents. He will fill you in on our protocol." Brekka smiled. "And we hope you will join us in the council fire this evening."

He bowed his head, backed away, and then joined his braves in admiring Ma-Za-Ma.

"Also sis, I am going to place Custus Ruhm Lee and his calvary under your command. So you shall control the Spanix fyrds, the dog soldiers, and the calvary of Hickoryans. All I ask of you is that you give me the impossible Zonga of Eugene. If you can do that it will demonstrate to all that you are a major arm in this conflict."

"You know I will, my lord."

"Shape it so!"

As she darted a glance at the sleekly handsome Ruhm Lee, she noticed he was not taken by surprise in the least, and must have somehow already been apprised of Ary's decision.

"Your mission is to destroy the Pitter Zonga of Eugene within three moonths, and then join me at Fort Rock in the High Desert by the moonth of the equinox. I'm also assigning the Thunder Twins,

Russell and Ev'Rhett, as Heretogas of their fyrds to serve you. Eugene is, after all, a very powerful zonga. The Thunder Twins will do anything you ask. All I ask is that you allow them to do it their way. May long life attend you, and may you see your seed until the fourth and fifth generation. And sister, may god's light shine on you as you shine in my heart always. My prayers will be with you. Farewell, and travel under the cloud of the elves!"

"Thank you for this trust, brother. I shall not fail you."

"Of that I have never doubted, Bear Wrestler, Beast Stabber, and Buffalo Woman." The two laughed. Ary kissed her on the cheek and they parted.

The sun had barely risen, but the sky was bright with pink hues when another band of Red Men came through the madrone wood approaching Brekka's camp. A squat brave with a broad head led them in. The dark warrior dismounted before her and said, "Lady Brekka, I presume."

Brekka nodded.

"I am Jerome the Ndee, sent to ensure the safety of the Lady Wilona Saga-Jah-El-Ea, who travels just behind my Dog Soldiers. She bids me tell you of her approach."

At last, Brekka was to meet the famous Elf Maiden! Her heart pounded with excitement as Jerome continued, "By order of my Blood Brother, Kanarus, I am to shadow her until she meets the Buffalo Woman. If you show us where we may settle in, she'll be along presently."

Brekka's heart skipped several more beats. To think the Great Prophetess--some say the very daughter of Woon, sprung out of the loins of the All Father--is come to join my band of lady warriors. She swelled with excitement. Waiting was a great burden. The Grand Lady she had heard so many praiseworthy tales of was to join her.

When she had been to Govannon's forge as a young girl, she remembered meeting an ancient white haired man in a deep saxon green hood, who helped Govannon forge her shield. The Ancient One had told her, 'In the twilight dawn of your War Path, an Elf Maiden of Osgardean descent will teach you the truths from on high, and give you the keys of the heavens, that your seed code may bloom fully.'

Breaking her reverie, she turned her attention back to the fierce looking brave before her. Jerome presented as a stout, broad faced, bulldog like Ndee, with fierce black eyes looking out from under a red bandana. His appearance was at once both bold and shy. Brekka pointed out to him a place where he and his dog soldiers could pitch camp to the east of her Pfalz Command Tent, then anxiously waited for Wilona to arrive on her snow-white mount.

As Wilona approached through the wood, clad in shining silver cloth, a gown with slits all the way up the sides and silver pants, she appeared whiter than marble. Even from five horse lengths away her golden eyes struck one like opening a bush to discover the face of a tigress starring back at you. Like an exalted being, she was completely other worldly in her deportment, and at once felt more lady-like and more dangerous than any women Brekka had ever met. Such was the force that emanated from her presence, and it was veiled in the most lovely face and figure any lady ever cut.

The Elfsmith, Govannon, had told Brekka that Wilona was a master at the plying of fibers, and she had made her own silver cloth that repelled the heat of the sun and breathed coolness to her white skin. About the Great Lady's neck hung a shimmering silver cord which had a celestial brilliance to it more akin to moonlight, much like her garments but discernibly more metallic. Brekka had heard the special conditions attending the discovery of Wilona as an infant on a Golden Pond, and how she was delivered to Govannon by the All Father in an air and water ship. As the tales went, it was said that she came with this same silver cord she now wore, to remind everyone that this was not some common adoptee, but as the Seeress Redith said, 'Arriving on the waters as Woon's Maid.'

Wilona gave some indiscernible orders to her assistants and then turned with a smile. "I am the Lady Wilona."

"And I am the Lady Brekka, Daughter of Sur Sceaf." She gave the proper hailing, "Waes hael to Woon's White Woman, Faery Queen of Kanarus' Lair. Please, you and your attendees, join me in my shelter."

"Hail and well met, Brekka of the Copper Locks, Syr Sceaf's Daughter of Lana' Hearth. I am come to help, aid, and assist you in your holy calling. I have been fully informed by the Roufytrof of the sacredness of our cause."

"Then, please, join me in my tent, Great Lady," Brekka said, feeling her heart race at the honor of being joined by a woman whom many considered not of this world. After all, it was plain to see, Wilona was not a woman of the mould, but was much more. She was of celestial hue.

Brekka's Pfalz Tent was a large red tent which could hold up to twenty six people comfortably at capacity. At one end was Brekka's three tables, one with maps and books, and the other two that served for eating purposes. Here also was stored clothing in trunks, and chests which bore armaments as well. In the center was a fire hole above the fire pit, and all about the tent hung whale oil lanterns, just extinguished at dawn.

As they entered the tent, Brekka introduced Wilona to her personal handmaids, "This is Ynys and Wyth, my handmaids and friends. And this is Verushka and Freyxus, my chief lieutenants of the lady knights, the ten other shield maidens, the five Spanix and five Herewardi Lady Knights who compose my twelver."

Wilona bowed at the neck. "It is a marvelous sight to behold a fully constituted League of Lady Knights. I am honored."

Freyxus returned the bow, her long golden hair, dark in comparison to Wilona's white hair. "The honor is all ours, Daughter of Woon."

Verushka bowed and said, "The White Woman of Woon! What a great honor!"

Brekka smiled, "Wilona, your reputation as a seeress and prophetess have long preceded you. I understand you are capable of direct communion with the elven realms, that the directions of history are made known to you, and that you are a master of spirits and can even command the demons at will."

Freyxus declared, "It is even said, that you have the power to heal or slay from a distance, like the Faery-Queen's of olden times."

Brekka nodded. "Be assured you will have my full and honored approval to join me as an equal in battle. Together, you and I shall occupy the magical role of the Thirteenth Warrior in this league of Lady Knights."

"The honor is all mine," Wilona said. "My Father, whom you would have known as Govannon the Alchemist, wrote me many years ago telling me the tales of a young red-head of whom he saw great promise."

Brekka blushed. "When I was no more than a lass, I drew close to both Govannon and the Giant, Herman the Kettle Maker, for I lived in the Suff Lands where they dwelt among the Chartreuseans. They fashioned my shield befitting for a lady knight with great artifice and craftsmanship such as is known only among the gods. In the innocence of my youth I did not know that the two travelers the wizard entertained at the forge were Woon and Weyland. I only knew I felt magical in their presence and that they showed me the tenderest of regard."

"It is because you had found their favor in the council of the gods before your birth to Lana's hearth. Even the special golden arrow with the power to track down any enemy in the dark had virgin's milk alloy and was made 'with star power' which is beyond anything of this Ea-Urth."

Brekka walked over to a cloth draped table, lifted the cloth and presented the golden shield and Dwarven-Arrow for Wilona's examination while all the Lady Knights drew in close to watch. For most this was the first time they had heard of how favored Brekka was of the gods.

Wilona took each item to hand and caressed its golden sculptured surface with the whitest of fingers. Brekka marveled that such hands that were delicate and beautiful to look upon were also known to be deadly with blade and arrow alike.

Taking the shield in hand, Wilona said in a deeply reverent tone, "Fa was a great prophet; he would never have done this for anyone less than his favored godlings. When I heard he had presented you with the shield, I realized it was time to set my eye on the day you would be knighted. My children knew I would soon be required to leave their presence once my son Anghrus came of age. Likewise, my dear husband was pained to lose my companionship, for great has been his love to me and mine to him. The two of us have drank deeply the nectar of mortal love. Still, I told him I was born to make straight the way for my holy sister, the lady seed, and unto this end I must live, that I might fill the measure of my creation as appointed to me by the wyrd sisters." She delicately touched the shield. "The norns have willed it. We shall come to know each other deeply in the times ahead, Brekka; for we have had elsewhere the roots of our friendship, which the veil of this mould now strains to keep from our memories."

"Of that, I am sure;" Brekka said, placing a hand to her chest, "for the ur fyr burns like a furnace in your presence."

"As token of our bond, I wish to gift you with this sacred silver cord." Wilona lifted the shimmering silver cord from around her swanlike neck and handed it to Brekka. "It is the cord I was left with at birth; the necklace of Immortality. I was instructed to wear it until I had fulfilled the measure of my creation and then to give it to the one whom the gods want protected." Turning to the lady knights, Wilona emphasized, "This is for the ears of you lady knights only."

A gasp of amazement went up from the lady knights.

Brekka's eyes widened. "It's beautiful. I've never seen anything quite like it. It appears seamless and yet it is so flexible and smooth. The glow of it appears independent of reflected light. Most curious!"

"Wear it well. For it will not shield you from the harm of this world, but it will stop death's hand from taking you in an untimely death, for the only death that may take you is the one imposed by the entwined essence of your seed code. Surely it will shield you so that no dark elf may harm you."

Brekka had been so overwhelmed; she had neglected to introduce everyone in the tent to Wilona. When introduced she responded with genuine warmth to each one individually. Finally she came to the last two. "This is Pata and Cisne, the only married ladies in our band. They are both Xarela's wives and have taken an oath to refuse his seed until the War Road has ended."

"Such beautiful young maidens, and yet I believe it will be too difficult to refrain from receiving their husband's seed in bed. Is that really necessary?"

"We can't have lady knights birthing babies in the war road. They must always be battle ready."

"My Apache medicine woman can give you such herbs as prevent conception."

Brekka saw the brows of Pata and Cisne lift with renewed interest. "Well, Sisters, it would appear you may soon be able to afford yourselves a pleasure denied the rest of us." Their faces brightened into a blush.

After a long talk with Wilona, Brekka took her on a tour of her troops. Ruhm and his men were helping the Red Men position their camps, find feed, and set up temporary corrals so that they could accompany the Buffalo Woman. So she introduced him first.

"Ruhm, I wish to introduce you to a Herewardi Seeress of Great Name. She will be traveling with me as the Thirteenth Lady Knight. Which means she and I shall act as one in power, authority, and command. Permit me to introduce the Lady Wilona."

Ruhm took the hand of Wilona, knelt and kissed it. "I am pleased to meet you, Ma'am," Ruhm said, "Are you from a nearby Herewardi settlement?"

"No, actually, I have come from the White Mountains. Perhaps you will have heard of my husband, the Half-King, Lord Kanarus?"

"Indeed so, but I heard we shall not be joining him for months."

"That is correct. He has other wives to tend him now, and my children are in good hands." Wilona declared, "For I am come to fight at the side of my sister knight. Hopefully, the path of my husband and I shall cross before this dread war is over."

Ruhm looked up, stood, and said, "I shall never understand you Herewardi. I would have never let a wife as beautiful as you out of my clutches."

"Your words flatter me, but like Brekka, I have been appointed a special calling in this End War. Our lot does not allow us to fatten ourselves around a hearth and loom, but rather we have been called as lean she-wolves to take down a frothy rabid bear who has ravished the lands of Panygyrus for far too long. Our calling and election have been made sure by the weavings of the Norn Sisters, to do the will of our heavenly parents and none other."

Ruhm shook his head in disbelief.

Wilona turned a fastening eye on the Hickoryan commander. "I prophecy, Ruhm, that you shall become as a brother to my husband, and the two of you shall grow closer than friends before this war is over."

Ruhm's mouth dropped and he appeared stunned. "But I don't even know your husband. I wish someone would explain this prophecy stuff to me. How can you know things not yet transpired?"

Wilona smiled. "You will come to know him. The teacher is there when the pupil is willing. You would not have been called to this work nor brought under the influence of such great spirits as Brekka and Kanarus, if the gods had not already woven you into the fabric of our cloth in 'The World Before This World.' Here you will meet my husband under another sun and another moon. By-and-by, the gods will teach those who still nurse how to eat meat. For they will instruct you line upon line, precept upon precept until you are ready to see. Then your inner eye shall be opened for you to see aright; first through promptings of the ur fyr, then through pure intelligence flowing into you until you arrive fully at the stature and influence of a Godhi, which we call the elven bloom."

"I believe there is a god, but I cannot put a name on him. And even though I have always depended upon my own natural strength and wisdom to guide me, I must confess, I pray for help always. I just don't know to who or why."

Wilona placed a hand on Ruhm's shoulder. "It is because you are one of the sons of light, Ruhm, but you have been born into a very dark room. Your spirit can never be content in the darkness that blankets this age. That does not mean you will find your way into the light, for enlightenment is found through seeking and choice, and the darkness has its own allures for you, as well as the power to pull you off course into forbidden ways that can slow your progress. You may yet choose the wrong way."

As they left Ruhm to organizing the camps, Brekka perceived he was stuck in reflection over Wilona's words. She took Wilona by the hand and walked through an oaken grove to the East side of her camp. A camp of one red tent and twelve large white tents with one that had a red cyclone on a white field. Xarela's nick name among the Spanix was 'Cyclones'.

Brekka stepped near the tent entrance and yelled within, "Yo, Xarela, are you in there?"

"Si, my lady." The youthful, tall, dark-haired gentleman dressed in white pants and shirt with a flat, wide-brimmed black hat, and thin mustache lunged out of the tent, "Ju called me?"

Brekka smiled and said, "I want to introduce you to the wife of Kanarus. This is Wilona, daughter of Govannon, also known as Saga-Jah-El-Ea. She and I together will now constitute the Thirteenth Lady Knight. This means we are to be treated as equals in all matters."

Wilona presented her hand in customary fashion as Xarela bowed and knelt on one knee, and kissed her hand.

"Permit me to introduce Commander Xarela, Commander of the Spanix Fyrds."

"A great honor to meet ju," Xarela said. "If you are only half the jaguar the Lady Brekka is, then we shall wipe the land clean of Pitters in no time. We look forward to fighting with ju, my lady." He tipped his hat and bowed at the neck.

Brekka walked over to the hosts of Red Men gathered around the corral where Arundel was meeting with them. They watched and marveled in awe at the perambulations of the White Buffalo. Upon seeing Brekka they all reverently stood back and allowed her to pass. Some seemed to wonder whether Brekka or Wilona was the Buffalo Woman. Brekka saw Fox-On-Fire point to her.

"Lord Arundel," Brekka said, "see who has come to do battle at my side. It is the Faery Queen of Kanarus! Permit me to present you to the Lady Wilona."

Arundel looked Wilona wide eyed, knelt on one knee, and placed her hand to his forehead. "Lady Wilona, by the gods, it is a great honor to have you in our midst. It's been sixteen years since last we met."

"And how fares that great Bee Queen you married?" Wilona asked with uplifted brow.

"She fares very well. She shall join us once the Taxus has been taken," Arundel said with a smile. "My heart goes out to you in this great sacrifice of service you tender us. I hope it will not be long before we join forces with Kanarus, and you may rejoin your husband again."

One of the Apaches left the buffalo corral and came towards them with a determined look on his face.

Wilona's face brightened as she let out, "Chiggibbah! Are you here with your Dog Soldiers?"

"I am. It pleases me to see you here as well, Saga-Jah-El-Ea. We have come to join the Buffalo Woman in battle."

"As have I! As have I!"

Ruhm had spent the day seeing to it every cavalry rider had proper armoring, weapons, and essential supplies. Now he was happy the day had ended and he could bed down. Content that he had done everything possible to ensure his men's battle readiness. He had sent a third of his horses back to the smithy to be re-shod, as the rugged mountain pass through Coke Hill at Myrtle Pass had worn many of the shoes loose. He issued new armoring where needed, and had his men mend their tack and gear.

All through the day he met with the various dignitaries, commanders, and skilled cryptic warriors to get a feel for how to best prepare for the coming battles. Busy as he was, he couldn't get the sylph-like image of Wilona out of his mind. Her image burned in his heart. She had presented him with a true dilemma. He contemplated what Brekka once said to him, 'The Ur Fyr is in every man. Some simply choose to never listen or follow it, but if yielded to, the inner man is greater than the outer man.'

Ruhm said, "I cannot comprehend their gods, but I shall seek this light they talk of by praying to my own. Whoever or whatever he may be?"

Ruhm climbed into bed, lay on his back, and imagined he could see the Big Dipper through the white canvas ceiling of the tent. He prayed: "God, oh my God, show me the path I am to walk. Let me know thee as well as Brekka and Wilona know their gods and take away the scales from my eyes so that I can see the holy things they purport to see. Bless me that I will never require anything of my soldiers that I wouldn't do myself. Watch over my father and mother in their latter-years. Keep my sisters, Ruth and Rose safe. Bless me that I can know whether I am to marry Brekka or not. And if I am, please help me to remove the barriers between us. Amen"

Outside the tent Uhu the Eagle-Owl made her plaintive calls throughout the night.

He rolled over in his bed and remembered what his mother once said about Brekka. 'That girl is the most beautiful and pure thing I've ever laid eyes on, but Ruhm, in all honesty, she is wilder than a feral Mustang.' *What were her words*: Beautiful, wild, and fearless. I don't think you could ever break her for riding, and you are not the type of man that can be ridden.'

In the background he heard his men outside the tent talking about their families they had left behind. One even said he'd miss plowing the fields this year, and seeing his girlfriend help him sow the wheat crop. By-and-by he closed his eyes and drifted into a deep and dreamy sleep.

A large mirror stood before him and inside it stood Brekka, or was it her fetch as the Herewardi say? She was clothed in a pure white gown that glowed brilliantly. She beckoned him to follow. They were communicating clearly, but not with their mouths. They spoke with one another through their minds and hearts. He was overcome by the intense joining and love he felt for her. Had he met god himself, he was sure nothing else could feel this exalting or uplifting.

He followed her into the mirror, whether afoot or floating, he could not tell, and then before him he saw a long row of oval upright mirrors, one after another. Each one he looked into portrayed some scene from Brekka's life from her prophesying as a child of four, to her shaking a spear as a maiden at a ferocious bear ready to devour her, he even saw their first encounter while traveling on a ship to Godeselle, then there was a hunting scene involving the two of them at the time they discovered the White Buffalo calf together. He saw many wonderful scenes with her and her great grand mother, and other very endearing scenes of her with her nigh mothers, scenes with Ary and her other siblings. Scene after scene they viewed the unfolding of Brekka's life. All the while his heart bathed in the warmest love he had ever been enwrapped in.

Then they came upon the mirrors of Brekka's future. He viewed battle scenes, some too horrible for him to bear looking into, and he averted his eyes.

All the while Brekka's gentle voice led him on saying, "Do not fear to look. It is for your eyes to see and understand."

He peeked through closed fingers until he saw her hanging upside down from an old dead tree, the skies filled with crows or vultures, and she wrapped tight as a mummy in bloody strips of linen. His mind went black with terror and anguish, then dark clouds gathered around him. His heart broke, and a powerful clean light stilled his soul. All the darkness left. Next he was overcome with the warmest love he had ever experienced, and Brekka's loving face and form faded through the white ceiling of the tent.

He awoke and sat up, his heart still filled with indescribable emotion and love towards Brekka. Tears were streaming down his face and he gasped for breath from such indescribable elevated feelings. He had never connected at a spiritual level with anyone else before. He knew this is what the Herewardi called, a 'Night Vision.' The union his spirit felt was greater than anything of the flesh. He was left with the single thought and awareness, *Brekka is already a goddess.*

# CHAPTER 6 :
## THE FIREBRAND OF THE LADY KNIGHT

COMMISSAR MORTH TINTREGON, COMMANDANT OF the Eugene Zonga, was asleep in his quarters when he was awakened by an urgent knocking at the door. "Commandant, one of the scouts report an enemy army approaching, led by a witch with flaming hair" The voice belonged to his aide, Brokin.

Although he had heard reports of this warrior witch from Zamora, he feared neither her nor the fyrds, nor the Hickoryan calvary, and not even the hordes of Red Men that clustered about her like a swarm of bees.

Although Eugene had never been the target of a direct attack before, Morth was fully confident that no enemy force could breach his walls, withstand the might of his legions, or face his new secret weapons freshly arrived from the poisoned lands, the toulucans. Nevertheless, he immediately began preparing for the anticipated attack.

Getting up was always difficult, so he ordered, "Sound the alarm. Order the legions to mount and wait my arrival."

He sat up slowly. His cherry wood bedstead had been custom made with a soft mattress to accommodate his hunched back, and an extra railing to help him pull himself up. He chuckled inside, anticipating the coming clash with a certain sadistic delight, feeling confident of his ability to defeat the Witch within the first engagement.

Outside his austere room, which contained only a swivel mirror and a rough-hewn table and chair, he heard the horn blowing the alert, followed by the clamor of his troops assembling.

As he was dressing, Brokin, knocked again. "Commandant, the witch is bearing down hard. Scouts say she is now within ten miles from the southern wall."

"Enough! Do not trouble me again. I need no more reports."

His men knew to fear his moodiness and he relished their submissive looks and anxiety any time they approached him. So harsh was his rule that he had even once killed a servant boy by running him through with his walking cane for breaking one of his mother's dishes, which was a particularly cherished object because his twin brother had fought him so hard for it.

When he'd been assigned as commandant of the Eugene zonga, he had vowed to rule with an iron fist. It was the same iron fist that had won him the recognition of the Skull Worm and the title of commissar, infuriating his twin who was fast climbing in the emperor's court. No mutton-eating witch was going to make him move any faster than he intended to.

Leisurely, he took up his gnawing stick beside the bed and chewed on its hard wood to keep his yellow teeth worn down to manageable size. *I'll gnaw my way through this Herewardi army like this stick, and spit them out in so many splinters underfoot before this day's end.*

Impatiently, he shouted for his valet who had a small room adjoining his.

His valet handed him a towel and held a pan of warm water for him to wash his face in. "I shan't be shaving today so don't bother with making up any soap," he said with a discernible snarl that sent the valet exiting at a hurried pace. After wolfing down his breakfast the valet had placed by his bed, he walked over to the mirror again. As he turned the mirror he was disturbed by his bushy black protruding eyebrows joined in the middle over his pinched rat like nose. "What the hell, I'll trim them some other time."

Turning away from the mirror, he motioned with the claw like hand for his clothing. He had come to hate that defective hand, but was determined that he would conquer in spite of it. After dressing in his black uniform, he slowly pulled the black leather cape over his hunched back with the help of his valet, so as to disguise his horrible disfigurement.

Once again, he viewed himself in the mirror. The bump made it look like he wore a backpack under his cape. Despite his deformity from birth he had made it to the office of a commissar, and he was damned proud of that, for it made his deformed brother all the more jealous. His valet handed him his cane, bowed at the door, and the commandant went out to address his Pitter legions.

He awkwardly made his way to the platform at a place called Elfton Baker, adjacent to the main gate where the legions awaited him, a place where the Herewardi had once settled and where the early Eugeners worshipped ducks. He motioned for the scout to come and asked, "How long before the witch arrives?"

The khaki clad scout ran a worried hand over his bald head before reporting, "By all calculations she should arrive within an hour or less. Her army is no more than six miles south of here."

Mort swung his long leather cape around, surveyed the troops from the platform, and whispered a command to one of his lieutenants to prepare the toulucans for battle. Then he turned and addressed the legions.

"Followers of Angrar, the heathen are stirring. They come against us as one, hell bent on conquering us, but they shall leave split into many pieces. Their uprising has long been predicted by the blind seer, Katus. So this is how it starts! They think to humiliate us by sending a mere witchy woman to beat us, and thereby dishearten the other zongas. Perhaps, in their heathen arrogance, they even think to take us unawares.

"Look at yourselves. You are the mightiest legions ever assembled. Behind you is the safety of our fort. They claim this witch-woman took the Zamoran Zonga. First off, I don't believe it's a real woman, but one of those long-haired sorcerer-kings of the Herewardi, and probably as queer as the Vardropi." Loud laughter came from the legions.

"Well, I know their cunning, and they will not slide this one past me. We will beat them to hell and pursue them back to Witan Jewel with their tails between their legs like the bunch of frightened sheep they are." With a broad sweep of his good hand he yelled out, "Now, bring forth the toulucan!"

He beckoned with his skinny claw-like hand, the product of his mother having taken some sort of drug or too much bamboo fruit, but now his infirmity made no difference, for all bowed to him all the same.

The legions cheered, and soldiers ran into the fort to wheel out the toulucan. Mort could smell the horses on the morning air, heard the crows in the nearby trees, and the creaking metal wheels of the toulucan.

His First Lieutenant Mausmorg, a Dominiker from Hormah, wore the new blue uniforms of the emperor's newly risen caste of warriors. Mausmorg was a human convert to the religion of Angrar, and had been given a special dispensation from Hryre Seath along with orders that he be treated with special favor.

"Commissar Morth, pray enlighten me. What is this toulucan that it should inspire you to such confidence that we do not go out to meet the enemy?"

Why do you ask about the toulucan?"

"I would think it was something your first lieutenant should know."

He looked at Maus with disgust. He didn't really trust humans. They smelt funny. To think he had to grant special deference to a pure human soured in his crop. "The fewer that know about it, the better. It's part of the new magic that Queen Gloomullah is giving us in exchange for the young female slaves we are providing her."

Maus studied the large hollow metal container with its massive metal wheels and thick axle. Finally, he asked, "How does it work?"

"It is activated by placing an explosive powder down its mouth and then sliding a large metal ball on top of the powder. When you apply a torch to the toulucan's wick, it roars and spews the ball from its mouth for a great distance, wreaking as much havoc as boulders hurled from a catapult, but with far greater accuracy. I have full confidence that once the red-haired witch swallows one of these toulucan balls she'll beat a speedy retreat back to Witan Jewel. No army is a match for this weapon. With it, we shall break the teeth out of the entire world should anyone ever dare to oppose us. Now is the great day of our power." He laughed in sinister glee.

The main gate of the Eugene Zonga was no more than a hundred yards directly ahead. Brekka called a halt and surveyed the lay of the land.

As the sun moved into the west just above the skyline of the trees, she released a messenger dove. The dove announced to Ruhm that it was time to bring up the rear as far as Mount Goshen. There, half of her fyrds would meet him with the enemy in hot pursuit of Commander Xarela. Then Ruhm's army of tramps and cavalry would be joined by Russell's fyrd on the right and Ev'Rhett's fyrd on the left. At Mount Goshen she intended to mount a fiercely pitched battle where the Syr Folk would be able to command the high ground and rain down destruction on the Pitters from the protection of the Deep Forest of Goshen. All success depended on her being able to draw Morth out of his Zonga to the kill zone.

She clutched the two seer stones in the pouch at her side for a reminder of her faith in the gods. For it was through the stones that she had scryed this maneuver. However, the stones refused to reveal if her strategy would be successful. Once the plan had been set, she had to trust her commanders to properly execute every minute detail.

According to plan, she ordered the signaler to send forth a second messenger dove from a grove of trees behind her ranks, so as not to be seen by the Pitters. The dove originated from one of her spies in the Eugene Zonga and would return with the message that soon the resistance would be called upon to play their part.

Lieutenant Xarela of Brekka's Spanix fyrd settled his youthful stripling warriors into cavalry formation, and looked to Brekka, "It puzzles me, the guards in the towers must have seen us, so why have they not come out to engage us, my lady?"

"That is a riddle for which I have no answer." She turned to Wilona. "What do your senses tell you?"

Wilona stared fixedly at the timbered walls that stood two man lengths above the ground. In a nearby field, a killdeer gave its plaintive cry before taking flight. After flying only a short distance, the bird landed and feigned a broken wing. "Methinks they have a toulucan. Our spies report it is a new weapon from the Poison Lands."

"Father told me of it. I fear to go to close."

They waited for some time before the gates to the zonga opened. Pitter legionairres poured out upon the battle field and into their battle formations. Pikemen to the fore. Brekka commanded her fyrds forward. They marched, shields high, and spears forward.

The Pitters hurriedly wheeled the toulucan through the gates in her direction. She signalled her host and drove her horse with her heels. The fyrds surged forward, gaining momentum. Gaining speed on horseback, she released the war arrow into the Pitter host. It was followed by a shower of arrows from her fyrd that flew into the Pitter hoard, decimating their ranks. All the while the mouth of death was approaching in the form of that toulucan on its creaking metal wheels. Herewardi spies had informed Sur Sceaf of its function, they having tracked its usage and transport all the way from the Poison Lands. Lord Arundel had given Brekka several lessons on its usage, and as such its power was no secret to her. She knew timing was everything when dealing with the toulucan.

Ashe, Brekka's Lady Knight in charge over the bowmen, signaled for a second flight of arrows that went forth in a solid spray. The olive-khaki clad Pitters dropped on the field before them, appearing like bestrewn piles of cow manure. To Brekka it felt like that first thrust of a sickle through green barley. She shouted, "Yeoh Wah!"

She knew Morth would only allow for this much slaughter in hopes of leading her into the mouth of that toulucan where he could mow her down like a scythe, but she would not so easily be fooled and would not suffer such a reversal of strategies.

She signed to her lady knights, and with their swinging battle axes they clashed with the Pitter pike men. Hacking off their pikes with one side of the axe and swiftly slicing through enemy helms with the other side. Their sharp, blood drenched axes went into the synchronized motion of a cutting machine. Brekka kicked and hacked her way forward, using her stirrups for extra thrust. She joined with Xarela's men, chewing up the enemy ranks with their wedge assaults like the teeth of a panther. Even in the heat of the battle she could sense the enemy's lack of aggression stemmed from some sort of strategy they were employing; for few of her men fell. The enemy was obviously poised for another maneuver by which they hoped to destroy her.

She heard the blast of a quacking Pitter bugle. As soon as the Pitters parted, Brekka glimpsed a khaki-clad soldier lighting the torch for the toulucan. She swiftly reined in Cycnus, and signaled to Xarela to split as rehearsed. Xarela's troops quickly split to the south, and her troops split for the north, leaving the toulucan to fire its explosive breath into the empty foreground. The impact of the missile sent earth, turf, and stones flying through the two divisions of troops to either side of its hit, but leaving them virtually unaffected. This enraged Mort Tintregon. He was immediately helped to his horse to pursue Xarela with a fury.

Just as Brekka had calculated, at the explosion from the toulucan, she feigned a swift retreat, and raced off far ahead of Xarela who feigned a much slower, crippled retreat like the killdeer dragging his wing, drawing the advancing, angry Pitters' attention toward himself. He would only take flight when he had full pursuit and knew Brekka had safely swung around undetected through the woods to the north.

Morth shouted for victory at the routing of the Syr Folk. He could not contain himself for the sinister delight at this ease of victory. Jumping up into his saddle, he yelled aloud, "I told you we would route these damned fools. The thunder of my toulucan drives them before us like lambs before a bear. Now we'll drive the witch's sheep-eating mouth into the floor of a pit soon enough. Fools to send a mere woman against a commissar! Fools! I did not gain this rank by dealing in the slave trade. No, I got it marching on the bloody skulls of men, women, and children who opposed the great god, Angrar. Where I go, famine, fire, and ruin are in my wake."

"What now, exalted commissar?" Commander Mausmorg asked.

"Prepare for a forced march, we're going to mop these infidels up. It's just as I told you, now we pursue them back to Witan Jewell with their tails between their legs. Grant them no quarter, but preserve this witch alive for me. I will have her pitted, and her scalped muff hanging from my spear by sundown."

His men were over anxious to pursue, but he held them back till he could get his mount at the head of them. Then he bellowed out, "Now, cut the mutton-eating bastards to the ground."

He, his dark clothed lieutenants, and his minions rode off after Xarela at full speed like a charging pack of ravenous dogs.

Mausmorg rode close beside Morth. "Commissar, this has the makings of a trap to me."

"A trap, a trap you call this band of half-wits! It's led by a damned lily-livered woman. These sheep-eaters don't have the power to trap four legions even if they wanted to. If anything, it's their delusion that they will spring a trap on us, but we shall prevail. You'll see. We'll crush them the same as I crushed the Comanche Tricksters who attempted to defy me in the Taxus."

Xarela found a convenient hill to anchor his men down on against evening, and prepared for the onslaught of Tintregon's legion. He sent three wolf packs back to begin the fighting and to slow down the impact of the legion's charge. The wolf packs exchanged arrows with the enemy horde until the approaching legion broke its pace and proceeded much more cautiously by bringing a wall of armored horses and shields up before their cavalry, thus greatly slowing down their driving march to a slow crawl forward.

The Wolf Pack waited till they were near, and slowly eased its way back to Xarela's troops anchored on the wooded hill. Tintregon was incapable in the twilight of ascertaining the number of men he was fighting against. Xarela was but fifteen winters old, but he had learned his fighting skills from his father, Arundel, the Lord of War. He assumed Morth must conclude the entire fyrd was nestled in the wood on this hill. He knew at least that his Spanix were capable of firing volleys of arrows from the forest edge sufficient that the forest maze of dark woods would give Morth much cause for halting. As Xarela kept watch with his lieutenants, the Pitter legions withdrew a small ways off and hurriedly pitched camp with hopes of rousting the Syr Folk out of this wood in the light of the following dawn. For now, Xarela had the benefit of a wooded cover and high ground, with night moving in swiftly, giving him the cover for the surprise attacks he was planning. Tactics he had learned from his father.

Xarela had his men rested until two points of the medicine wheel before dawn. Then they began their penetration of the enemy camp. Cautiously he began to cut down the guards one by one. He silently snuck upon them, killing them with an awl then posing them by tying them against a tree and placing their spear in hand, so as to appear they were about their duty.

By dawn's twitter light Xarela was ready for the attack. He wore a smile on his face and felt elated that Brekka had trusted him whole-heartedly, as a Young-Blood, in executing this battle as he saw fit. He signaled for his Spanix Rangers to execute the plan by closing his fist above his head and bringing it swiftly into his chest.

Pitter campfires were mere coals and ash. Mist hung in the air obscuring visibility, and most legionnaires slept confident in their khaki tents. Thus, he caught them completely off guard. It was barely light enough to discern forms when his men sent flaming arrows into the Pitter's khaki tents, cut horses loose from corrals, and shot arrows at rallying legionnaires like rats in a barrel. Then Xarela signed with the palm of his hand up in the air, followed by swiftly dropping it to his chin and then drawing it across his throat. He launched this plunge into the Pitter encampment as an initial diversionary thrust, leaving a very great slaughter, but not bothering to stay for the marshaling of the legions, against which they could be no match with his small numbers. Dead guards lay slumped over their spears, horses stampeded and whinnied, screams arose from the tents, tomahawked faces gave their ghoulish and bloody stares, while commanders shouted into the chaos of alarmed troops trying to bring order and make sense of what had just happened. Conflicting bugle calls echoed against the forest. By the time Morth Tintregon had gathered his legionnaires to form a defensive machine, Xarela and his troops were off and up the road to the Forest of Mount Goshen and the dense fir cover it would offer.

After a hard ride, Silver Harrier scouts reported the progress back to Ruhm Lee in Goshen that Morth was enraged at the surprise attack and was taking the bait by pursuing, and he would be up on them within the hour.

By two hours before high-noon Xarela saw the wooded mount near Goshen. Ruhm was astride his Grey, awaiting him on the breast of the hill with signal flags directing his men to safety. As Xarela rode up, Ruhm approached on Spitzer, his banner flapping with a Red Bird on a white background.

The Hickoryan Commander smiled, "I see you were successful in teasing the Commissar and his Pitters out of their pit. Have your men follow the flags to safety, and I will assume command from here out."

Xarela widened his eyes for emphasis. "I hope to the gods you're ready for a swarm of yellow jackets. I stuck a stick down their hole and stirred it. They are madder than hell and won't be long in coming, Hick."

Ruhm gave a puzzled smile. "You can bet, we're ready! The ground is high, the cover is good. Even with their vast numbers, they can only get a cohort at a time in here. The thick wood funnels them into our blades, shields us from their arrows, and lets us stay their forward progress. Besides, we have Brekka's Faery-Hounds and their handlers. War-Hounds will wreak chaos and horror on the enemy such as they have never known."

As they awaited the approaching storm of battle, Ruhm readied his cavalry. He had them form a solid wall that charged head on. Then the cavalry split in two to join Russell and Ev'Rhett who were flanking the Pitter legion just as they were arriving. The Pitters plunged directly into Mount Goshen, unaware that they were being flanked. Soon they were met by a shower of Spanix arrows that filled Pitter skulls like a war bonnet and sent a good tenth of the Pitter cavalry to their deaths. Ev-Rhett and Russell's forces came smashing in from the sides, tearing the legions' sides open and disassembling their ranks. The young Spanix Warriors swept in from the front like packs of coyotes, accompanied by Brekka's Dogs of War, and tore the legions front ranks open, sending the legionnaires in the middle in a mad dash back out of the woods. Morth's losses became too great to sustain head on battle in this terrain for long. Their quacking bugles sounded a speedy retreat.

The Commissar had to concede an imminent defeat, if he didn't drop back in a retreat to re-group once again. A Pitter bugler sounded a retreat once again. Many of the Pitters had not heard the first, and stragglers were being hacked down by the Spanix Stripling Warriors and chewed up by the War Hounds. The Pitter buglers repeated the retreat signal over and over again. The legions clustered tightly and began drawing back down the mount like a snail recoils into its shell from an unexpected encounter with salt.

Ruhm posted double guard, redoubled his scouts, and called for a war council in the impenetrable wood on top of Mount Goshen. As Xarela entered Ruhm's tent, the Thunder Twins, Russell and Ev'Rhett, soon followed, tomahawks still adrip with Pitter blood.

Once they were all seated on the hides, Ruhm said, "It's obvious to me Commissar Tintregon is re-grouping in order to set up camp. I conjecture he hopes to draw our Syr Folk armies off the mount and out into the plains of Goshen, away from this high ground and protective cover of wood."

"For the Mother of Gods' sake, thousands of Pitters lay slain before us," Xarela said. "Do these fools not realize we have the high ground and have no need to fight them on their terms?"

Ruhm was amazed at the pluck and military genius of this Young Blood. To think the boy already had two wives and a command. He nodded, "I'm thinking, Morth's pride will not let him return to the Zonga and concede a defeat at the hands of a woman. I'll wager he stays and ventures to take us, even if he has to march over the corpses of his own men. High ground or not! He has to be seething in shame at this moment. We will hold him here and do him as much evil as we can invent until his armies are forced to limp back to Eugene where Brekka hopefully shall deal him his final blows."

Ev-Rhett shook his head. "I thought we were to be the distraction. I thought the plan was to drive them back to Eugene and, together with Brekka's troops, finish this cannibal off."

"Yet," Russell said, "he is incapable of taking us in this high wooded ground. We've got him trapped between our high ground and his pride. I don't think Brekka saw this in her scrying. He can't budge. The cannibal has come for supper. I'll wager you, he's taking a badger's stance and won't budge an inch. Why not accommodate him and make Brekka's job all the easier?"

"You're absolutely right, Lord Russell, which means I shall swoop down on them like an owl tonight with my Grey Ghosts. If we are all one, then Brekka will support our actions. How about it Xarela, are we all one?"

Xarela knew what his instructions were, but he also knew his Aunt Brekka honored on-site decisions, and she had given him the latitude to control his end of the battlefield. Xarela bit his lip before saying, "Jour counsel is good, Commander Ruhm. We are one."

They answered in unison, "We are all one. So mote it be!"

Ruhm smiled, "If you will approve, my lords, here's my plan."

For seven days cohort after cohort advanced against Ruhm. The battles were all in the funnel of wood. Neither side could fully engage the other. But in the woods the Syr Folk reined superior, sending battalion after battalion of Pitters to an early grave. The square cohorts of the Pitter legions could not operate as they were accustomed to in the rocky wood, and the Syr Folk were given to be masters of crypsis and unconventional warfare, whereby they dropped out of trees, sprang out of the ground, and appeared behind every tree and bush like striking rattle snakes.

Again and again Morth hurled his cohorts against the Syr Folk army to the point that even the grassland leading into the funnel became too clogged with fallen bodies for Morth to advance. When he attempted to clear the bodies, Ruhm's archers sorely afflicted them with their deadly accuracy, adding to an ever growing pile. Vultures filled the skies in ever increasing numbers.

Many of Ruhm's and Xarela's men bore wounds, and hundreds had died. Ruhm could not retrieve their bodies for the heavy fire the Pitters gave when they tried. Morth had latched onto them like a bull dog and was not about to let go no matter how much they boxed his ears. Ruhm knew that Brekka's plan was to draw them to Goshen, deal them a large blow and force them into a retreat back to the Eugene Zonga where she would be waiting for them to deal the final death blow. But Morth was not budging, and it was becoming too costly for the Syr Folk to continue this ploy much longer. He had to wound this serpent bad enough to force it back down its hole in the Zonga.

Ruhm had to develop a strategy to break the deadlock. He sent several Silver Harriers back to Brekka, keeping her abreast of his plans, and discussed with the commanders his strategy. Brekka sent a return Silver Harrier back that bore the message that if it was the voice of the commanders to keep the Pitters engaged, then she would support their counsel.

The Spanix kept vigilant watch over their camps, their horses, and their supplies. Beaucerons and Brekka's long-eared Faery-Hounds kept the camp safe from surprise attack. As night fell on the seventh day, Ruhm took his elite Hickoryan Night Warriors, the Grey Ghosts, who were all trained by Il Alim in crypsis. They were called 'the Grey Ghosts' by reason of the grey hooded capes they wore lined in deep red. By day they wore the cape grey side out, but at night they reversed it to red side out so that one only caught wisps of grey in the night, giving them a ghostly appearance moving through the wood. Each ghost took a substance that the Ele-Anoreans made, called 'Night Juice,' which they dripped into their eyes for greatly enhanced night vision.

Rhum felt the talons of his owl, Uhu, as she clung to his arm. Uhu was brought to induce terror in the Pitters, who had the disposition that owls were both demons and the harbingers of death, for it stirred up something deep and primal in their Rat Blood Seed Code, inducing some sort of primordial fear and terror in them that superseded reason.

Ruhm's Grey Ghosts, Xarela, and Going Snake penetrated the camp of the Pitters, stealthily bringing silent death to around forty legionnaires under the cover of night. They snuck from guard tent to guard tent. The Pitters could always be counted on to set up their camps in a predictable systematic way, whereby the guard tents were all marked with the Pitter word, 'Caveat.'

All through the night death dealt its silent blows with the poisoned awls, with never one alarm being sounded. As time ran out with morning approaching, Ruhm swiftly lifted the door flap on a Pitter tent, silently crept to the first legionnaire, pinched his nose so that his mouth opened, then stuffed a wad of cloth in his mouth, and slit his throat. Once the life drained out of the Pitter and he heard the blood gurgling up in the throat, he moved on to the next and the next, until every relief guard was summarily killed.

Upon exiting the tent he gave a whip-poor-will call signaling for everyone to return to their rendezvous point. He then headed for the grove of rowan trees on the breast of the hill. Soon he was joined there by Xarela and Going Snake who had accompanied him. Now Ruhm knew no one exceeded Going Snake in crypsis or effectiveness, save maybe only the Master of Crypsis, Il-Alim, and he had come to greatly value Going Snake's companionship.

Going Snake said, "We tucked them all in for the night, Ruhm."

"Well," Xarela said, "They will not wake up in the same place they laid down now, will they?"

"Of that much I'm sure." Ruhm said. "Any complications or injuries?"

Each commander said, "None."

Ruhm gave a sigh of relief. "Then it is done. Let us return to Mount Goshen and wait for the enemy camp to awaken."

Going Snake mounted and said, "It's a good thing the Syr Folk always keep well trained watch dogs in our camps to prevent the same such attack from ever overtaking us."

"Yes it is." Ruhm said as he waited for Xarela to join them on his horse. "Even so, no man is a match against our beauceron dogs and the Pitters scorn to befriend the dog. Going Snake, were you able to locate Morth Tintregon's tent?"

"Sure did. He'll be ready to lead his men into hell as soon as they discover him."

"Well, done. Let us return to camp and muster up the troops for the rising dawn." He hoped thereby to win favor with Brekka, but an agonizing gnawing in his gut at the memory of the night vision he had of Brekka hanging from that tree like a mummy haunted his mind. He prayed for her safety and well-being. *Oh Invisible God, that I do not know, please watch over my love, and suffer her to come to no harm.* He briefly considered, it was just a night vision, a dream, nothing more. *But no, that dream was more real than anything I've ever known. By god, that was a spiritual revelation. I've got to stop her before they kill her.*

According to Morth Tintregon's instructions to Mausmorg before bed, his lieutenants were to awaken camp two hours before dawn. His lieutenants attempted to do as they were instructed, but found numerous dead amongst their ranks setting them all at great unease. Mausmorg feared to sound a general alarm; he was, after all, a new commander, and merely a Dominiker. He decided to delay the alarm until the commissar awakened, knowing he would be enraged that they had once again been taken unawares in the night. The enemy was gone now, but what would he tell Morth. It could mean he would be decommissioned and possibly sent back to a labor camp.

If he went back to a labor camp, there would be those who remembered him there, and how he had betrayed them to become a Dominiker. They would remember that he was of Yengish blood, and had been converted a Dominiker; the name of abomination on the lips of commoners who didn't understand that no one could withstand the empire. The Dominikers had come to realize that the struggle against the Pitter Empire was utterly purposeless. *Better to have a good life of plenty than suffer as a peon scratching out a mere subsistence in some beet field,* he thought. Even his own family scorned knowing him after he had made the switch. He had hoped when he showed up with turkeys and hams on holiday that they would be grateful, but they threw him out of their house with his gifts, and told him the next time they saw him they would kill him, and said he served the devil. He could have had them all sent to labor camps for their treatment of a Dominiker, but he could not wish that on them. He was not capable of ignoring the love they had given him earlier in life when both his mother and father sacrificed their food so he and his siblings might have their bellies full.

He could however, never go back. He had stepped over the cliff, and there was no way to atone. He was as good as a Pitter now, even gave up his Yengish name of Rodney Mason and took a Pitter name the better to show his devotion to Angrar. He was one of the few but growing Dominikers risen to the rank of a commander. Only his wife appreciated his wisdom in this. His whole existence would now depend on Morth Tintregon's response to this night's attack, and it did not set easy on Mausmorg's nerves.

Commander Mausmorg grew steadily ill at ease, for he did not wish to be the one to break the bad news of all the dead in camp, so he just waited for the commissar to emerge from his tent until dawn. Then finally, Commander Mausmorg decided it couldn't wait any longer. It was time to tell Morth of all the casualties they had sustained in the night. He sent a soldier to Morth's tent, and braced for the explosive reaction he expected to follow. The soldier carefully opened Morth's tent door, then turned and said, "Commander, no one is inside!"

Mausmorg ordered a search about the camp for the commissar. After a nervous wait, a khaki clad soldier whose yellow incisors needed some grinding down ran up to Mausmorg and said, "I think he is standing about a hundred yards out of camp, sir. I dared not approach him; you know how angry he gets when thinking. He's killed soldiers for less. You know how he beckons you when he wants you to come, and chastises you if you enter his presence without invite. I wasn't about to disturb the commissar."

"T--yes, I know, but this is preposterous! Why didn't someone tell me he was up and about? I've wasted all my time waiting here for his command. I'll have to approach him myself. I don't need to remind you that shit rolls downhill."

He trudged out to greet the commissar in the mist of the morning. His dark form just standing there transfixed in thought, hunched over in his usual deformed body. Maus gave a hard look. Sure enough in the morning mist it appeared to be Morth, but as he approached, a large owl took flight right over his head. He ducked and his heart shuttered at what the Pitters had taught him was an evil omen. Surely that flaming-haired evil Lilith was near at hand, and mayhap the witch had shape-shifted into that huge owl. Horrible fear gripped his whole being, knowing there could be no worse evil omen than this before a battle.

Approaching very cautiously with shame, he cleared his throat, but said nothing. Again he was shaken by the owl hooting and swooping nearby, but the commissar was not in the least perplexed by such devilry. Commissar Tintregon with his black cape draped over him, was still likely focused on hearing the enemies every movement before the fog lifted. Mausmorg cleared his throat once again and whispered loudly, "Commissar Morth, the troops are ready to deploy."

No response came. He was sure Morth was deliberately ignoring him; shaming him for not having been ready for this guerilla encounter. The commissar was showing his total disapproval and would likely slay him at any moment.

"I am very sorry we had so many deaths in the night. I assure you we had taken every pre..."

His voice petered out as he came around to the front of the dark commissar only to see that his throat had been slit, and his bushy eyebrows were framing bulging, terror-stricken eyes. Examining how he could be standing he found that Morth had been tied to a post. Fear strangled his heart. *First the owl, and now the death of the commissar.*

*Maybe this was witchcraft. Maybe the owl had slit his throat?* He could no longer see his men in the fog, and slowly backed up till he heard them talking. All the while searching for the owl, the witch, or those ghosts whom his men reported slew so many of his soldiers.

Commander Mausmorg cried out for his lieutenants. When they ran to his beck, he said, "Get us the hell out of here. Order and sound a retreat and leave everything. This wood is the haunt of demons and wraiths. That Fire-Head is a Witch and Shape-Shifter. We're getting behind the walls of the Zonga, for this enemy is not of this world, and we'll defeat these mutton-eaters in the safety of the Zonga with the toulucan."

As soon as Mausmorg was brought his mount he had a retreat sounded by the bugler. They left their entire camp and all of its supplies and fled by horseback. Then suddenly, out of the fog, they were flanked by Hickoryan Cavalry in their grey uniforms and flapping red cloaks. Numerous Dog Soldiers poured out of the woods, which must have waited parked on their painted horses until this very moment. The chase was on. The dogs were nipping at his heels. He would not be enticed to turn his massive calvary around on them. No, he wouldn't let them whittle away at his armies like Tintregon had done. Mausmorg knew he only had to make it inside the Zonga walls to obtain the high ground, and from there he would slay these Syr Folk dogs like squealing puppies in a pen.

While Ruhm, Xarela, Russell, Ev'Rhett, and Going Snake wreaked havoc on the retreating Pitter legions at Goshen, longer than planned, Brekka and her company were busy shaping her designs on the Eugene Zonga.

At the Eugene Zonga there lived a lady among the Eugeners called Belle Filer, long time Resistance fighter. She had for many years formed a hidden alliance with the Syr Folk, meeting in mountain glades with spies and representatives of the Herewardi to share information and plans. For twenty years she had waited for this day to awaken the resistance in an uprising against the Pitters. This uprising had been fomenting and welling up behind the Zonga walls for some time. Hardly a day passed that she hadn't groomed several new recruits for the Resistance.

Belle Filer had painstakingly kept track of all the Pitter's comings and goings, their numbers, supplies, positions and maps of their compounds, and even got the names of the young slave girls that were weekly hauled off to the Growlings. She and the Resistance had built tunnels and planted shrubbery to disguise circulatory paths for spies to come and go without detection.

When she received Brekka's messenger dove telling her the day had arrived, she sent a rider out to the secret rendezvous point. At pre-dawn of the following day the message had been received, and the rider lead Brekka's seventy-two elite fyrd troops, her Lady Knights, Chiggibbah's Apaches, and Fox-On-Fire's Warriors into the heart of the Zonga by way of those dark covert pathways.

Once they were all safely and covertly inside the fort walls of the Eugene Zonga, Belle signaled the resistance by lighting a lamp in the bell tower of the Christ Church steeple. The Resistance all wore the agreed upon white, so as not to be mistaken for Dominikers. Word was spread through messenger trees to stay indoors unless engaged in the fighting. At the given signal, they rose up and attacked their pre-assigned targets with a vengeance for the wrongs they had endured, and charged with a thirst for true liberty.

Meanwhile, Brekka's Syr Folk troops prepared to slay the Pitter guards manning the Zonga. They rode leisurely and quietly up to the first dormitory on their horses. No one even suspected an attack could come from inside the gates. She quietly dismounted, and signed for her Lady Knights to wait while she walked up the stairs to the sleeping guards before the dorm. The legionnaires laid in a horrible state of laxness with her waveblade. She stuck the first sleeping guard through the back of his neck with such force it severed his brain stem. She brought the sword around over her head, and swiftly severed the second awaking guard's head from his body. The head hit with a thud as it thumped down the stairs like a watermelon. She returned to her horse and mounted. Brekka rode up the stairs, and broke through the dormitory doors with her horse. The Lady Knights followed. They rode down through the center of the building, stabbing and hacking the awakening soldiers in their beds where they broke too late for their weapons.

As she rode back out into the dawning sunlit streets she was signaled with a red lantern in the square that the Resistance had slain most of the Pitter administrators and Dominiker sympathizers in their homes. The children of the Pitter sympathizers under age twelve were spared and escorted to a building for safety. Even with the surprise uprising, some Dominikers fled the Zonga on swift horses and wagons.

As the two guards of the second dorm ran to engage them, Brekka and Freyxus shot them down with arrows. The awakening Pitters had had time enough to grab their weapons, and flew through the door. The Lady Knights went forth slaying and to slay wave of Pitters after wave of Pitters. One grabbed a spear and ran at Brekka with a demonic look on his rat-like face. She grabbed her spear and hurled it at the charging soldier so quickly that it drove hard into the demon's chest and came out his back. The rest of the Pitters abandoned their fighting spirit and attempted to leave through the windows and doors. Many spears were released on the fleeing mass of soldiers. The commander in charge yelled for order, and persuaded some of the Pitters to return to the fight. Brekka whistled to Freyxus and signed, 'spear that one,' she pointed. Freyxus hurled her spear through the air at the commander, and struck at the place where the neck joins the head, at the top most vertebrae, severing both tendons so that the head fell to his chest. After a long pause, his body crumpled to the floor. Cisne and Pata slew the remainder with their battle axes, and followed Brekka out the back of the dorm.

Chiggibbah and his Dog Soldiers, were doing likewise, for as Brekka exited the second dorm, Chigibbah's men poured out the back door of another dorm pursuing fleeing Pitters.

Brekka thought, *Times like these seduce the good judgment of even the most sensible leaders. I must focus and be vigilant to the end.*

By the time she made it to the third dorm a Pitter guard had rung the alarm bell, and the five remaining dorms came pouring into the square only to be met by a storm of arrows from Fox-On-Fire's warriors dropping the fleeing Pitters and piling them up like dominos.

A squadron of Pitters formed a turtle cohort to shield themselves from the arrows. Brekka sent Cisne, as her runner to bid Fox-On-Fire to hold his arrows. Cisne returned, and the Lady Knights formed into their silver-armored phalanx like a tight knit kit. Their prancing warhorses trampled the Pitter cohort underfoot, breaking the enemy's formation.

The Lady Knights leaned from their horses with swinging battle-axes to cleave off sword arms, split shields, and sever heads.

Brekka deflected a sword aimed at her belly, as a mace hammered her shield. She gave a knee command and her horse trampled the assailant under foot until he ceased moving. She sat mounted, assessing the scene when one of the Pitter's she'd shot and thought she'd killed, came running up behind her with sword drawn, only to receive an arrow through the eye from Pata's swift reflexes.

Suddenly, Brekka turned her mount and looked over the brazen wings of her horse's helmet at another cohort of Pitters. They struck her Lady Knights like the impact of a swollen squall strikes a skiff at sea. The knights twisted the reins of their horses and commanded them to stamp the enemy under hoof before them. The Pitters were so fierce that Brekka had to swing her axe on one side and slash with her sword at the same time on the other. Only the superior height and strength of the horses allowed them to prevail against this unexpected cohort, but soon Fox-On-Fire and Chiggibbah brought their death dealing blows with their tomahawks to relieve the pressure.

She scanned the city. Every street in view had a red lantern burning on its street sign. This was the signal that the Resistance had put to death any Pitter, Dominiker males, or sympathizers on that street. No matter which direction Brekka looked, the enemy was dead. She signaled with a green lantern and the Resistance let ring the bells of the Christ Church for victory.

An exquisite saffron and pink dawn broke over the horizon as the church bells pealed out the message of freedom. The Eugener Resistance gathered in the streets en masse, flying a green and yellow duck flag of victory. Most of the city was in total confusion at why the alarm had been sounded. They were greeted by the Resistance fighters dancing in the streets and hailing Brekka as their deliverer. Enormous crowds formed, unsure whether to believe what they heard and saw.

As the Resistance brought forth the final Pitter escapees, Brekka dismounted and drew her elf blade. She slit each Pitter's throat and said, "Gather their filthy corpses. Soon we will have them burned. Never again shall a Pitter cross the threshold of Eugene. Never again."

Soon the non-resistance citizens started realizing their good fortune as news spread that their city had indeed been freed. They belted out their cheers, and joined in heaping the bodies and the corpses on a pile prepared for the bonfire in the middle of the town. But they were bidden by the Lady Knights to await the final battle with the returning legions before setting it to flames, so as not to alert the legions to anything unusual within the Zonga walls. After four days had passed, the stacked Pitter bodies began to stink so bad that Brekka ordered they be burned anyway.

By the following day the bodies had been thoroughly consumed to ash due to the use of whale oil. Brekka stared out the fortress doors awaiting a Silver Harrier to announce the return of Morth's legions. *Now is the time to perform 'the Estoque,' plunging the killing sword into the Pitter Legions, as Xarela had so aptly named this move.*

The wind raced through Commander Mausmorg's hair, and the horse's mane swished in his face from the hard ride. He was shocked that Morth Tintregon was dead, but yes, oh yes! He secretly delighted in it and had visions of he and his wife Janet Holly Ender ascending to the high places in the Pitter government. After all, the commissars would have to concede, he saved the day by pulling away from the impossible battle Morth had so recklessly plunged them into by leaving the safety of the Zonga. A Zonga they had been charged to never desert. The commissars would want to hold this Zonga above all others. The most powerful beachhead the Pitters had ever enjoyed into the Herewardi territories, and it never lacked for legions.

He had visions of taking over all the slave plantations in the Salem Valley, abusing the captive women for his own pleasure, and could even imagine the untold wealth, power, and influence when he took the Eugene Zonga. Maybe he would even be elevated to be a commissar like Balaban had been.

He pressed his men with yells as he happily fled the Syr Folk, straining to keep from smiling about his new found power. His ass hurt from the hard ride, but he was grateful to see a band of Pitters coming out to greet him. He couldn't help but laugh at his great fortune. He would now be rid of the pursuing Syr Folk armies and promoted to be the new commissar. He could hardly contain his sinister joy. But soon things began to take on a queer appearance. What was that army waiting before the Zonga. As his eyes focused he could see it was a wall of lady knights, the witch, and a host of Sharaka lined up just outside the Zonga fortress.

It was worse than the sight of Morth strung to a post with a shape-shifting owl overhead, for now, just before him was mounted that horrible blazon-headed Witch with the Golden Shield ready to swoop in on him like a blood thirsty eagle-owl. She had flown back to the Zonga. He couldn't turn back, and there was nothing but terror that beckoned him. He couldn't turn right or left, as he was sore pressed on the rear by calvary and Dog Soldiers on either side.

In his terror he screamed to dismount and form a turtle cohort. Bringing his mount to an abrupt halt, the troops clashed behind him and to his sides. Soon all his troops were dismounting and gathering around him with shields up. Horses ran off, panic stricken, and the outer fringes of the army began crumbling. Mausmorg tripped over a bow someone had clumsily dropped, and quickly scrambled back up to his feet as his legions closed rank around him. He felt the security of the shield wall go up, and ordered a march straight for the Zonga just ahead. *Why aren't the legionnaires of the Zonga coming to my aid? Where are their lazy asses?*

They advanced twenty yards when his legions came to a grinding halt. All Mausmorg could see were the pounding tomahawks and the Golden Shielded Witch in her silver armor mounted on her white horse with a band of silver-clad women warriors tramping down his legionnaires like marsh grass. *This couldn't be happening.* He thought. But she kept moving ever closer on a direct course for him. He ordered his men to fire a volley of arrows at her, but they had all left or dropped their bows when they dismounted.

Panic and terror set into his ranks. No order he shouted was having any effect. The field had degenerated into every man for himself. Even the three guards he had assigned to shield him went their own way. He saw one get a tomahawk to the head, and the other had a boulder smash into his chest and fell beyond his view.

Spear clashed against shield, and the armor rang with tomahawk blows on every side. The fury of the ensuing battle left little doubt of the outcome. A great din arose with moans and shouts of killers and the killed. Soon there was hardly a piece of ground that was not drenched in slippery blood. He was penned in like a rat in a cage, and these Herewardi Harpies were breaking through his defenses in a direct bee line for him. He grabbed the reins of a wandering horse, but as he started to mount it an arrow pierced the top of its head where the hairs of the mane begin, and the horse collapsed dead under him so that he had to pull his leg free from its crushing weight. With a deafening roar, the angry Red Men rained hundreds of arrows on them. His armor rattled from all the arrows deflecting off it, but his men fell in piles all around him. Some of his soldiers fell with arrows through the eye and others through the neck or in the cracks of their armor. He could only be glad no arrow had found his exposed body parts.

After the shower of arrows came the fierce attack of the Red Men like the blast of a sudden squall on a stormy sea. Their wild cries stirred the free running horses to trampling the legionnaires, adding to the chaotic melee. A fellow legionnaire was coughing up blood beside him, and spears were hurled beyond the wall of shields. The long-haired harpies were in determined pursuit of him, and they drove panic through his ranks. Evil was coming swiftly upon him. *If only I could get a horse and ride out of here to Salem?*

The flaming-haired witch moved in towards him. Pitter horses were working havoc from their terror, and occasionally a herd would pass through the ranks screaming and kicking wildly. When the witch got close, she dismounted. Mausmorg charged, only to have that golden shield deflect his sword. She hurled him back into his own men which were the only thing that kept him afoot. He stabbed with his blade, trying to work it between her and her shield only to have her swing his arm up into the air with such force that he nearly lost the blade. He had never felt such force in any combatant before. To the witch's right and to her left stood two fierce shield maidens and one who was as white as driven snow. He now understood he was the prey, and she was coming straight on for him. This was to be his end.

A herd of horses passed between him and the shield maidens, giving him some reprieve, whereupon he seized reins and brought a horse under his control; hoping in the terror of the moment to get away. He swung his leg over the saddle and kicked the horse onward. He glanced back at the witch who pushed her shield to her back and drew an arrow from her breast. It was like a witch arrow. It shimmered, glowed, and appeared to be a shaft of golden sunlight, magically singling him out. Though he ducked, it struck his head. He fell into the dust and was trampled beneath the feet of his own legions, darkness closed his eyes and poured over him.

*Jesse ben David's Log: It took the better part of the day to finish off the scattered legions. Brekka had her arrow retrieved and the body of Mausmorg was brought to her. He who had once plagued Herewardi settlements was burnt, and his ashes scattered to the four winds so that he might not have a grave in the Earth, and that he might never be known amongst men or the Syr Folk again. Morth Tintregon was eaten by crows and left to hang in what is now called Hunchback Hollow above Goshen. Janet Holly Ender was given over to the Eugeners who burned her alive at the stake for all of her years of cruelty. This war is gruesome, and I still shudder to hear her screams coming out of those devouring flames. The Herewardi and Sharaka don't even flinch, but as for me, I have never witnessed such blood and destruction before, and it troubles me in my heart as to what horrors I shall witness in the future, for this war is only in its infancy.*

*After the seizure of the Zonga, Belle Filer had the puppet Mayor of Eugene, Bo Lawrence brought out before the citizenry of Eugene and asked, "Brekka, what shall we do with him, he has bled our people for over twenty years and made our lives a bitter living hell? He turned deaf ears to the oppression heaped upon us, ground the face of the widow and orphan, and took the young women all against their will."*

*Without hesitation, Brekka rode over to him, drew her wave blade, reached down and grabbed him by his sparse hair. In one slice of her sword, she severed his head and trampled his body with her horse. All the hosts of Eugene witnessed. As she held up the blood dripping head she said, "People of Eugene, I slew this tyrant under King Law, you shall never have to endure this type of tyranny again. Neither Pitters nor their lackeys, nor traitorous Dominikers shall trouble your lands anymore."*

*The crowds hailed her with joy as she commanded, "Hang this head in the sun for all to see the fate of tyranny." She heaved the blood soaked head into the air, which thing I can never forget, for it struck the ground like the thud of a pumpkin. She and her Lady Knights rode into the Zonga like she had merely tossed a rotten fruit into the compost. The rest of the day was spent setting up a provisional government under Belle Filer, with Eugene as a sovereign city-state under the terms of confederation.*

*Eugene was originally settled by its earliest inhabitants from the Rogue Nations and others who had fled to the mountains for refuge from the floods. The floods came by reason of the burning stars devouring the forest and leaving the soils naked of vegetation when the rains came. Since the Herewardi, Quailor, and Sharaka were all new settlers and took up much of the remaining niches, the Eugeners were suspicious of them and their motives. Then upon learning that the Herewardi had the strange practice of having many wives, the Eugeners chose rather to do business with the Pitters. The Pitters paid them handsomely to cultivate a foothold so as to obtain the sea ports of New Port and Florence. But too late did the good citizens of Eugene discover that a cuckoo had laid her eggs in their nest. It was not long before they were ground fine in the Pitter mill of oppression and made to render lives of bitter servitude as second class citizens in their own land. By the Great Year most of the citizenry of Eugene were ripe for resistance.*

***Jesse ben David's Log:*** *Syr Folk ambassadors from Godeselle were sent to finish the negotiations with the charter city-state of Eugene and to make them full members in the Syr Folk confederacy. Brekka and Ruhm then took their armies to the north, freed the plantation slaves, and set up once again the charter city state of Salem under the rule of Elijah*

*von Hollar's Son, Marion "Buddy" Hollar. Syr Folk, and particularly Quailor settlers, returned to claim their original inheritances from which they had been forced to forsake a generation before under Pitter pressure. With all the Pitter might now broken in the northwest, Brekka and her armies reported to Fort Rock where she met Arundel under the Jaquarundi Banners of Syr Elf, her cousin, the Lord of the High Desert and City-State of Syr-Rus-Salem.*

*Syr Elf has completed the cleansing sweep throughout Salem, the Whilumut Valley, and the High Desert to eliminate any and all Pitter bands or outposts. He will now accompany Brekka with his Fyrds thence to the White Mountains. There they will operate under the command of the cunning Half-King, Kanarus, whom the Ndee refer to as the White Apache.*

*After the meeting in Fort Rock of the Grand Council, in Fort Rock, Arundel split and took his fyrds into the Rockies where the Presteric, Jywdic, Hutteric, and Buffalo Tribes will join their armies under Lord Arundel's command.*

*The High King, Sur Sceaf is keeping the Isle of Ilkchild safe while the enemy, Skull Worm trembles in Frisco fearing his eminent attack any day, for much word has been sent to the Skull Worm by his Rat Packs and spies that Sur Sceaf has a master plan for taking the Kalifornias and the Mexus Lands. Only the Roufytrof has been apprised of Sur Sceaf's actual plan of attack against the Pitter Zongas of the Kalifornias and Mexus and so far, we have no word of their progress.*

# CHAPTER 7 :
## THE TRIBULATIONS OF ANGHRUS

**F**AR AWAY FROM THE WESTERN coast of the Aurvandilean Sea in the deserts of the Apache Lands, the son of Kanarus, Anghrus, was undergoing his proofing as an initiate in the rite of Long Hair as all boys of eight winters are wont to do. The anthill was dangerously close. As Anghrus opened his eyes to the blazing sun burning down on him, he saw the red denizens of the desert sands moving about on the hot earthen floor. He tried to recall the past few days. He remembered watching two previous suns pass overhead. Yes, and two shivering cold nights of darkness. While he lay in the shadow of the large Saguaro Cactus, too sick and too weak to move from the rattle snake venom still coursing through his veins, he remembered, he had been bitten when five winters old and may have died were it not for Red Knife's doctoring. Red Knife had told him then that he would be much stronger for having survived it. That was the only reason he could think as to why he was still alive.

Three days earlier he had been released into the desert by the Young Blood Warriors to begin his proofing in the rite of the Long Hair, so as to join their ranks. He would have to return to Kanarus' lair by the third day in order to pass the test, and ensure his qualification to become a Kaninchen Young Blood. He had been stripped down to just his loin cloth on that day, given a pouch of chia seed, and a scramasax, then told to find his way home through the deserts within the allotted time of the three suns.

On his trek he had run out into the desert, located a water hole, covered his fair skin with red ochre, drank deep, and placed his thumbnail up against the evening sky to chart where he needed to pass through the mountains on the eastern skyline. Then in the darkening hour after sunset he heard the rattler, felt its fire pierce his ankle, and jumped on one leg to a nearby rock shelf to cut the bite open for bleeding out when a second rattler struck him in the back. Pain of the worst order beset his body and wracked his being with horrible swellings, incomprehensible aches, pains, and excruciating head pain. Extreme vomiting overtook him. Unconsciousness, nausea, delirium, and confusion alternately took possession of him. The following day, he couldn't even remember what point the sun was in the sky as he stumbled back to the water hole in a delirium for more water. Several times he passed back and forth over the border of this world and that of the spirit world where he imagined he saw his mother, Wilona, beckoning unto him out in the desert. Only with the visitation of his mother's spirit did he feel any hold on this world coming back to him.

It was already the third day. He could never make it back to Kanarus' lair in time. He only vaguely remembered climbing into the shadow of that Saguaro. Now and again some logic started forming in his mind. The fiery desert storm in his mind began lifting to more lucid thinking. Suddenly, he was aware of the fire and stings on his skin. He shook the ants off himself with a shiver from thinking what more damage they might have done to him had he not regained consciousness soon enough; their bites and stings already compounding his overwhelming misery.

It was painfully clear he had failed this first test to join the Young Blood fyrd and would not be allowed to grow his magically long hair to show he was an initiate until the next trial coming up in six moonths. His fellow initiates would have already received their spears, the first step of becoming a warrior. He imagined them holding their spears in the fire circle while pronking to the beat of drums and deer whistles about now. His father, Kanarus, would be there wondering what had happened to his son, what had delayed him. He had expressed such confidence in him that he had personally forged the scramasax and carved the two serpents into its handle for him. This he knew, that above the pain of rattlers and ants, nausea and unconsciousness, it would be even harder to face his father's disappointment.

Anghrus saw a cloud of dust rising in the distance and felt immediate shame cover him as shivers passed over him. He was sure it was the Young Bloods coming to rescue him. Or maybe it was even worse, his father and the fyrd. *I'm not going to allow them to shame me. I'm going to show at least that I can make it back to the lair on my own without their help.* But then they would be able to track him. It dawned on him; they would not be sending a rescue party out this soon. They would wait until the fourth day. The cloud of dust grew even larger as it approached.

This was the only water hole within a day's journey in any direction. What else could this mean? Perhaps it was a dust storm to add to his already miserable condition? It would delay him yet another day, and he was already powerfully hungry. He raised a hand full of red earth and let it fall to determine there was no wind. Whoever was stirring the dust up like a hoard of buffalo was definitely in great need of water; for they were making a direct course for it.

Anghrus saw a cleft rock near the water hole, picked up a stick and struck it on the rocks in the floor of the cleft to scare off any rattlers that might be denning there. He had to get to cover. Rogue tribes were known to sell loners for the slave trade. He wedged himself back into the crevice so that he could comfortably hide himself and blend into the rocks. After a long wait, with sweat dripping from being confined inside the hot rocks, he heard the thunderous roar of thousands of hooves shaking the ground like an avalanche and echoing against the tight walls of his vantage point.

He peeked out of the dark cleft to see it was an immense army approaching; stretching all the way from the farthest horizon. Banners with a large skull in the center and the Mark of Ish on the forehead with a winding black worm weaving out of the mouth and through the eye awoke every sense in his body to danger. He gasped in horror. These were Pitters. Worse yet, this was the personal Banner of the Skull Worm, a commissar who had earned the name of the Anti-Life, by reason of his horrific tortures and dark deeds.

The horses pressed for the water hole as the men held them back so that they themselves might drink first, bullying, and shoving one another to jostle for position. The horses shied and snorted for the liquid life just out of reach. An ugly large man rode up. His nose appeared to have been smashed against his face. He stood out from the rest. He took off his turban, revealing a shaven head with the Mark of the Ish tattooed like a chicken's foot print right between his eyes. He shouted atop the skinny nag he rode, "Drink slow, you fools or you'll never lay eyes on the Kaninchens. You, you there!" Pointing to a rat-faced, buck toothed, young soldier in khaki attire, "Bring me a drink."

The skinny man with rotting buck teeth caught the flask that was tossed to him, smiled, spit out tobacco, and said, "Yes, Master Skull Worm." He ran into the muddy hole to fill the leather flask. He returned with the skin dripping with water. The soldier averted his eyes to the ground as he handed the dripping flask up to the Skull Worm.

Anghrus was so afraid he could hardly bring himself to breathe. The blood pounded in his ears in a steady beat. He thought, *there should not be a Pitter horde coming from the West. Pitters usually come from the east, and are easily spotted by the Ndee who patrol the routes into the land from the east. This means father is probably not aware of this coming attack. Here I am completely trapped in a snake pit, and somehow, I gotta be the one to get a warning off to my people.*

Crunched and hurting in the cramped quarters of the cave he waited as the sun's hot complexion marched further across the sky. His stomach growled and twisted tight from hunger. He opened his small pouch of chia seed hanging at his waist and put some to his mouth. He began to feel the saliva welling up under his tongue as the nutty tiny seeds drew moisture there. He twisted to see what the enemy was doing when a rattle snake slithered out of a crevice just under foot. He smote it hard with his stick, pushed and ground till its head was utterly crushed. Then, without hesitation, reached down and grabbed the recoiling writhing serpent. He ripped the scaled skin open with his teeth and took bite after bite of the fishy flesh until he had consumed it in its entirety. He wiped his mouth, only to feel a retch coming on. He struggled to subdue the sound, re-swallowed and endured the rumbles in his belly which the cramped quarters seemed to compound as if the hot rocks were equally ready to spew him out.

The sun began to set. It became all too apparent that the Pitters were going to make camp here for the night. The Skull Worm had his black command tent set up first, and then a chuck wagon pulled up alongside it. Anghrus's mouth watered at the sight of hot food being passed out. He yearned for real food, even though his stomach still threatened to heave its contents. In no time, the Skull Worm was being served piping hot food by slave girls, dark of hair and brown of skin; Anghrus assumed Mexus, but they did not dress like Mexus. The other Pitters began their drinking and gambling outside their tents, waiting their turn to eat. Anghrus suppressed another retch, fearing they would surely hear him if he did.

During all the activities of the camp, Anghrus studied where all the guards were posted and plotted a safe course around and through them. He knew there was no way to blend in. He had inherited the glorious golden hair of his father, as had all the children of the Baldurean Race, but even whiter because of his mother Wilona's extreme fairness. No, he must place mud in his fuzz of hair to tone its shimmering brilliance down. He had to give up precious spit on the red earth that he rubbed over his face and hair to cut down on his fairness after the sweat had washed away much of the ochre. His mouth grew dry and he was reluctant to give up any more of his body's already depleted moisture.

As he left his crevice, he could hear his own heart pounding loud in his ears, stepping softly under the darkness of night he hid in moon shadows. Ever so cautiously he wove in and around tents, under a line of horses and past a camp of slaves. He swallowed some more chia seed from the bag tied to his loin cloth while waiting for some drunken Pitters to pass. He sucked long on the tiny seeds to relieve that nagging thirst, and remembered the fine rabbit feasts his mother oft made him. As he passed the tents of the Mexus slave girls they were screaming as if someone was hurting them.

For what seemed like hours, he safely wove his way through the Pitter encampment with all its loud laughter and course talk. He had to duck some water bearing slaves as they passed, and he sucked his lips at the thought of a mere drink from one of those dripping leather pails right now. Finally he came upon a patch of rough rock over which no one camped. Taking the cover of its shadow, he ran along this rocky ridge into the dark desert, only stopping long enough to catch his breath. Then stealthily stole away with the Pitter campfires burning behind him. In the moonlit night he held his thumb up to the mountains to make sure he was still on course. After several hours of travel, the land started inclining upward once again towards the mountainous high desert. He came upon a large grouping of Cacti, pulled out his scramasax and cut open a barrel cactus. He knew it would do little more than give him the pleasure of a wet mouth, but that was all he needed. He let the cactus prick him and smeared the blood on its base. His mother had taught him, 'The blood is your sacrifice to the plant for its gift to you.'

Sucking its bitter juices and mouthing its bitter pulp, it gave little relief at all to his cottony mouth and at this moment he thought how marvelously quenching the crystal spring brook by his father's tent ran. He pressed on, crossing up and over the mountain and into the pass as the darkness was interrupted by the brilliant morning star, then dawn broke with first, promise, and then increasing warmth. It didn't take long for the return of the burning rays of the sun to drink up the shadows and the coolness of morning. Sensing the need for hydration, he realized it was now getting to the critical point.

Red Knife had told him of men who survived the desert by eating lizards, bats, and bugs and even subsisting off their own urine. He remembered his father telling him the means for survival are all about us if we just use our heads. He would not be able to make it back to the Lair without water. He didn't even have an urge to urinate. But that would not stop him from trying. *How in Woon's name can I use my head?* Then just ahead in a small swale out in the desert he saw a beautiful sheet of water. He began walking with a perky pace only to realize he had been in these parts before. There was no water out there. None for miles.

Betrayed by the mirage, he summoned new energy from his exhausted body and aching legs. He trudged on, remembering Red Knife's description of a poor wayfarer he had once found whose tongue was so swollen from thirst that he could not speak, and whose lips looked like they had been chewed off, and how the man could only cry tears of blood, but he couldn't remember whether Red Knife said the man lived or died. Even so, Red Knife said, 'the biggest killer is always panic.'

Ahead of him, his eyes slid beyond the occasional Mesquite and Cactus to a herd of wild-asses moving up a gradual slope through the pass. This must mean there is water in the pass, but where. He'd have to track the asses. He went to where he had last seen them and followed their trail as long as the daylight permitted before darkness moved in like a stealthy cat and covered the land with a refreshing coolness his skin welcomed once again. As refreshing as the night was, he was angry that the asses had not led him to water before he lost track of them.

While trudging through the long pass, he noted the moon had marched half way over the sky. A piercing panther cry split the night air. Once again he fetched his scramasax from his leg. Scanning the rocks above for any sign of the large cat in the moon lit landscape, he continued to pick up his pace and run ever eastward through the long, cool hours of the night. Now and then he caught the sight of the large cat leaping from one rock to another paralleling him. His father's words came once again to his mind, 'Odhin will try the reins of your soul like you lounge a horse, but if you endure well, he will bring you to life and victory.'

The morning star appeared in the eastern sky once again and soon dawn spread its multicolored wings over the sage and cacti. There was not much strength left in Anghrus' legs, and his lungs felt like dry sacks of dust. His tongue cleaved in thick sticky saliva to the roof of his mouth and his breath grew labored under the rising heat of the sun insomuch that it even hurt to breathe. His dry, cracked lips wanted only to be moistened.

He continued moving ever eastward toward the stronghold in the Chiricahua Mountains remembering how his father had told him how he once made it across a desert just by repeatedly counting forty-four steps over and over until he finally looked up to see home. He counted forty-four steps, twenty seven times until by mid-morning he grew powerfully thirsty beyond anything he could possibly endure. His lips cracked so wide it felt like lizards were eating them and they grew too sore to touch. He tried touching them with his sticky tongue only to taste salt and blood.

He thought he saw a flicker of movement and waited for the cat to emerge. To his delight two ravens rose up and settled on a creosote bush near him. Straightening he said a prayer his Father had taught him, "Odhin, All Father, preserve me to fulfill the measure of my creation that I may join the long line of my ancestors in honor in the upper world at the finish of my life."

The hot world candle of noon pressed fiercely down upon him. He staggered ever towards the lair. His lungs ached and the sun's golden eye still beat down on him with unrelenting merciless heat. He stumbled, and his legs and arms barely lifted him enough to rise again. Upon rising, he reached to his arm to pull out the cactus spicules he had fallen upon. Now, almost numb to pain, he could no longer remember how many times he had counted to forty-four. He counted one more step, "Thirty-three." Then all went dark.

When he awoke, the coolness of wet water was running over his brow and chest and he tasted its sweet coolness on his parched tongue and lips. The deep voice he heard leapt in his memory. "You be alright boy."

It felt as if his very skin was absorbing and sucking up the water as moist fingers touched his lips. Struggling to make his eyelids open, the bright sunlight forced them to quickly shut. In that quick flash, above him was the face of an old Ndee warrior of many winters. Anghrus struggled to speak; his tongue swollen with thirst, insomuch that his voice came out hoarse and crackling, "Red---Knife!"

Struggling to force his eyelids open he saw the ancient face smiling. The old brave's earth baked face looked like the surrounding dry cliffs. "The spirits have really put the hurt to you Young Rabbit. Relax now. Drink slowly. Your raven brothers have shown me where you fell."

The old brave ran his wet hand over Anghrus's face and poured the water in his fuzzy hair catching on the sprigs of Sage as he did. "It will take a while and you will revive. Don't try to speak just yet?"

Out the corner of his eye he saw Red Knife fashioning an umbrella of sorts from a branch. Over which he threw a blanket to further shade him.

Anghrus relaxed as long as he could; which was less than the time it took Red Knife to finish tying the umbrella. "Red Knife," he croaked hoarsely, "you must get me to father. It's urgent."

"No call for urgent, boy. You come in late. No problem, you run again in six moons. Then you grow magic hair like others."

"No ...you don't understand," he said as he sat up feeling the effects of the sunburn, ant bites, and exhaustion overtaking him once again. "It's the..." he could barely say the words before he was compelled to lay back down from the dizziness. Why was he so woozy and faint? Why wouldn't his body and lips obey? Breathlessly he squeezed out the words, "It's the Pitters."

"What about the Pitters?"

He tried shaking his head to gain clarity. "They come. Many come from the west." He barely had the energy to motion westward.

"Are you sure? Maybe desert take your mind? Heat stroke, searing sands, sun-poisoning. All soul-crushing things that can play devilish tricks on the mind."

He could feel the effects of the water reviving him even as he answered, "It's the Skull Worm." He grabbed Red Knife's arm.

"Skull Worm no come here, Young Rabbit."

"But I saw his banner. It was a worm weaving out the eye socket of a skull." He made a twisting motion with his finger.

A look of consternation covered Red Knife's usually stoic face. He quickly took the blanket he used for the umbrella, wetted it, and wrapped Anghrus with it. Then he tossed him over his horse like a sack of potatoes, and rode off. Anghrus just let himself mould to the horses back as Red Knife rode for Kanarus' Lair.

Upon arriving in camp, Anghrus turned his head to see a large group of Young Bloods were gathering around. Red Knife unloaded him to the ground. Before him was his father's tent with the painted rabbits over it. A flush of relief came over him. He was home. He could hear the cool brook in the background. The tent flap opened and the burnished yellow braids of his father popped out the door. Anghrus smiled down at him. Suddenly he became aware of all his young peers standing with their spears in hand, gathering around. He felt shame at not having completed his return on time and averted his eyes from theirs which only forced him to imagine what they must surely be thinking. Only one word stood out in his mind: FAILURE.

From a large oak near the stream that ran through their camp he saw a heavily stuffed white cow hanging from the tree. If he had successfully completed the Rite of Hair he would have been permitted to cut down the cow, but if it was determined he failed, then the cow would hang near his tent for six more moonths, reminding him that he was still not a young blood, but a Mama's Boy.

Before he could speak, Red Knife said, "I found him in the desert about five miles from here. He looks bad. Ant bites, sunburn, rattlesnake bites. He says Pitters are come; said it was the Skull Worm."

Kanarus reached down and placed his hand tenderly on Anghrus' head, "I should have known it would have taken something very big to have stopped you. What happened, son?"

Anghrus sat up and said, "I was bitten by a rattler and set about fixin' the bite when another one bit me on the back. I returned back for the water hole and I saw the night pass twice, and the sun was on its third journey when I awakened under attack of fire ants. As my mind grew clearer, I realized an army was approaching the water hole. So I hid myself in a crevice of the large rock outcroppings near Saguaro Pond.

While hidden, I saw the Skull Worm himself and the black banners with the skull and worm flying on them. They're even now there at Saguaro Pond, west of here."

Kanarus said, "Well, done son. This feat you have performed and this trial you underwent has earned you the right to grow your hair long and take up your position with your brothers in a Wolf-Pack with the Young Blood fyrd." He saw his father motion to Ilkleif, a Young Blood Pack Leader who soon returned with an Elm Leaf Spear. His father took the spear and handed it to Anghrus. "This is yours, son. There can be no doubt, you earned it. All that remains for you to do is to cut down Milky White."

Anghrus smiled and glanced over at the white cow with big pink udders hanging from the tree.

Though still utterly exhausted, Anghrus did not want to wait to cut down the cow. He could not endure looking at it for even another moment. He signed for his Wolf-Pack to join him, walked over gingerly on sore feet to the large oak tree, from which hung the stuffed felt white cow, and smote it down with his newly acquired spear. The cow's contents burst open and sweet cookies fell everywhere. Symbolizing he had left the world of women and had just entered the world of men.

He shot glances around at his peers and read approval on their faces. He choked on the words, "I am honored." His wolf-pack began trilling their approval and acceptance and chanted "Anghrus, Anghrus, Anghrus. One of us. One of us. One of us."

Then Anghrus nodded his approval, and he and his wolf-pack darted for the fallen cookies.

Kanarus reached down to pick up a cookie, stood back up, took a bite, and said, "I'm glad your mother is not here to hear what happened to her son. She'd be spearing me like Milky White for sure."

He motioned for the Quailor hospitalers to take care of his son, and then turned to his First Officer, "Mesculera, summon the fyrd and the ndee. It's obvious the Skull Worm is pulling his legions out of the Kalifornias and is heading for the Taxus Lands to bolster them in a last stand."

Mesculera frowned, "But why so soon?"

"I have to assume he is thinking he would be annihilated by Sur Sceaf's fyrds, and is fleeing for the safety of the Taxus lands before we can get there and cut the Pitter empire in half. We need to cripple him and wear them down by intercepting and delaying them with guerilla tactics as much as we can."

# CHAPTER 8 :

## FRISCO'S FREEDOM

THE JYWDIC DRAGOONS' BANNERS OF Golden Prancing Lions flapped in the cool sea breeze. On the rail of the poop deck a gull strutted up and down, squawking to be fed. Ignoring the bitching bird, El Yid frowned suspiciously at the lack of activity in the Frisco Bay. Ships tied to the piers bobbed on the incoming tides, their decks devoid of sailors.

"What in the hell is going on in there, Hamos?"

The squat helmsman shook his head. "Not much that I can see. Not even a canoe moving."

"That's what's got me worried, Hamos. This port is always teaming with warships and merchant vessels. Now look at it. Our ports at ur ford are even busier than that on a shabbat."

Shading his eyes, he shot a look up at the crow's nest, half-veiled by the melting fog. "Moshe, what are you seeing up there?" he yelled.

A lanky youth leaned over the crow's nest and shouted, "Nothing, Captain. Port looks empty. Not a Pitter banner in sight, and only a few looters scattering off the docks at our approach."

El Yid could not refrain from smiling. "Sur Sceaf, you Old Fox, I argued with him to send me to Newport and instead he sent me here for reconnaissance and I'll be damned if it weren't a good idea after all." He grinned at his childhood friend and helmsman. "Hamos, I think life is going to be getting a lot better. Set for port. The rats have fled."

As the dragoons pulled up along a deserted pier, some onlookers scurried away, while several others waved. The dragon neck of the ship ran under the water and rose up out of the bay some ten feet before the ship, giving the appearance of a swimming dragon.

A dark complexioned, bearded man dressed in the dirty white shirt and the knickers of a fisherman hailed him from the dock. "Hail, oh Herewardi! Hail! Welcome to Frisco."

"Hail!" Yid returned. After checking that the deck guards were watching from the rigging in order to forestall an ambush, he jumped from the dragoon to the pier, sending a flurry of mewing gulls into the air.

The fisherman stepped forward and reached forth his hand for a shake. His heavily calloused palm gave a firm grip. His broad smile was missing several teeth, and a purple scar slashed one cheek. "Name's Ridelli--Sonny to my friends--and that there's my fishing boat, the Maria Clara." He pointed to a nag of a ship.

Yid returned his smile. "I am Zeru-Herewardi called El Yid. I am the commodore of this fleet of dragoons, which is an arm of the Pyringean Pirates fighting for the Syr Folk Confederation."

"Oh yes. Heard the tales of your looting the Zongas and setting the captives free. You shall be a welcomed sight for most of the people here. Myself included."

"Have to admit I expected to fight my way in here, but the only Pitter ships I see appear abandoned."

"Damn Hell Rats started pullin' out the beginning of last month, just after we got word of one of their Zongas up north got captured by you folks. The last of the Skull Worm's legions left three weeks ago for the Mexus. Left only a few legions behind for cleanup, but they didn't stay long. Might be somethin' spooked 'em."

Yid glanced down the docks where two men were staggering under a load of boxes. "Looks like the looters don't expect them back anytime soon."

Sonny nodded. "Can't really blame 'em. Been going on for the past few weeks. Some damned good cargo still left aboard, too. Most of it just going to waste."

"And you haven't seen fit to do any looting yourself?"

"I had my boys haul some barrels of wine and dried meat away, but I've got a large family to feed and fishing's the only way I know to do it. Once all them supplies are gone, it'll be back to scraping for a living as usual."

El Yid studied the man carefully. Even though he was dark of hair and complexion, he was not Mexus. His face was the face of an honest man, a family man. He looked the man in the eye. Yid got a good feeling about this fellow.

"Sonny," Yid said, shaking back his side locks, "what say you be my guide in this city? I am claiming it for the Syr Folk and those Friscans who took refuge under our wing."

"Anything for the old race of Herewardi. We still tell stories of the Golden Freyxus in the Coliseum. A beautiful golden warrioress, a Herewardi Lioness and sword-maiden. You should have seen her humble the Pitters to the dust before my very eyes. You can believe me, you will be gladly received by anyone left alive in this town, though for now there are fifty some advocates for the leadership of the city and still some gangs that think muscle means government."

"I should tell you that, although my mother is Herewardi, I am of the Jywdic race." He gestured toward the banner proudly waving overhead.

"Don't see how that matters much, since, like you said, you're part of them Syr Folk. You bein' here will represent order, especially to those of us who remember the days before the Pitters. Fact of the matter is, most of the Friscans have fled to the countryside on account of all the burgling and raping and such goin' on. Been here all my life and saw it when it was the jewel of the whole Pacific Coast. Then Skull Worm came and stripped the whole city of everything of any value. Killed till there was nowhere to turn without seeing a dead body. And oh god, that awful colosseum, the circuses were a living hell. If you shunned the circus as a spectator, they'd soon see to it you were a participant. Then there was the years of giving up six tenths of everything I caught to their ungodly detailed accountants and tax collectors in their damned shiny blue uniforms. You and your kind will be like a fresh air blowing the filth and stench out of this rotten place."

Three days had passed since El Yid took over command of the city of Frisco. On the morning of the fourth, he sent a young boy out to the precipice over the harbour, and told the boy to alert him as soon as he saw any ships coming through the narrows into Frisco Bay. Peoples of all sorts were now moving back into the city upon hearing that the Syr Folk had come to bring order.

The main section of the city was composed of large mansions, the enormous colosseum, and endless small homes painted pink, white, or blue. Gone were all the large merchant stores of former days. And the beautiful trading vessels for which this city had originally been known stood in ruins around the docks and marshes like the bones of cuddle fish, bleached by sun and brine.

After securing the city, El Yid commenced organizing a government under the aegis of the Syr Folk. Several times his pirates slew robber bands or drove them from the city. Yid estimated that twenty thousand people had poured back into the city. By-and-by, the inhabitants of Frisco began in large measure to lend their allegiance to Yid as they realized that he represented order, reason, and their best chance at survival. Still, there were factions that believed the Pitters would return and were hesitant to participate.

Yid formed a police squad from the men Sonny said were honorable men. He authorized them to operate with his full authority. He set Sonny up as the mayor under the terms of confederation. Sonny was bright, he was honest, and he held some sort of informal sway with many of the citizens.

Additionally, Yid met in secret with members of the Sire Sheaf, the Herewardi secret spy web who resided at Frisco. They promised to support Sonny during the coming transition without revealing their identities.

Long ago, the Roufytrof had chosen members of the Sire Sheaf and placed them strategically in guise throughout many cities and peoples to act as leaven for just such a day. During that time, they functioned as an underground stream to supply the Syr Folk with information and assist in any way they could secretly. Now they were to assist the Friscans in rebuilding their city under the terms of confederation, allowing Yid to move back on to the war road where he would be of greater use.

From the command tent set up in a large eucalyptus forest Yid oversaw the settlement of refugees, and met with the trusted Friscans for ideas on how to rebuild their city. He saw to it that several members of the governing board were members of the Sire Sheaf as well as several merchants Sonny had recommended.

He had just adjourned a meeting with a group of returning Friscans and was making notes when Sonny's young son, Marco, darted past the guards at the tent's entrance. The breathless youth, who appeared to be around thirteen winters said excitedly, "There are Herewardi warriors coming, and their leader is black. Black as a crow, I tell you."

El Yid laughed. "Thank you, Marco, but I've already been informed by the outpost. That would be Khem Welsh." He gave the boy a ticket entitling him to an extra dole from the commandeered Pitter storehouses, and said, "Tell the escorts I have sent you, and lead Khem to me here. That way you get to see a real black man. I'll have another ticket for your family when you return."

"Yes sir! Thank you, El Yid!" The boy spun on his heel and darted back for the docks.

Within an hour Khem entered the command tent with his fyrds assembling on the edge of the forest.

The tall, broad-shouldered, black man came through the tent door and embraced El Yid firmly. "Good to see you again, my old friend. I see you still have your curly cues there. Don't they ever get in your eyes?"

"Not in the least. And likewise, commander, it's good to see you," El Yid said as he received the leather instructions Sur Sceaf had sent. He unrolled the vellum and read: *Well done, my good and faithful sea master. As always, I am pleased with your heroic works. Zeru-Herewardi, I need your services once again for yet another mission. Khem will take over your command of Frisco. I want you to run the coasts and see what the situation is in Citriodora, Rosarita, and as far south as Guatemala. Report back to me before a fort night. Spies are reporting the Mexus Lands are in a great upheaval. We must determine the cause and get a clearer picture of what's going on there.*

El Yid rolled up the vellum and said, "It would seem, Khem, the command of Frisco is yours. We've appointed Sonny Ridelli as mayor.

The High King wants me to scout the coasts and report back to him within a fortnight, so I'd better show you the ropes and introduce you as the new viceroy. I think you'll find most of the people here very cooperative. I'll show you the fortress you can occupy before I depart tonight with my dragoons. And then it's all yours."

Sur Sceaf was received on the docks of Frisco by Khem, as ship after ship arrived with his active fyrds. He and Mendaka walked shoulder to shoulder across the bridge to Khem.

Khem saluted and said, "Welcome to the city state of Frisco, my friends. It is good to see you again."

"And you, Khem," Sur Sceaf replied as they shook hands.

"Damn, Khem, when did your hair turn to cotton?" Mendaka teased as he, too, robustly shook Khem's hand.

"Bout the same time your mane took on those silver stripes."

Both he and Mendaka glanced at Sur Sceaf, still laughing. "Don't say it. My wives tease me enough about my white hair!"

After asking Khem about his wives and children, Sur Sceaf glanced around. The city streets were bustling with activity. Carts and wagons moved here and there. Women shopped at an outdoor fish market at one end of the dock, and there were so many fishing vessels in the bay that the belly ships carrying his army had to maneuver with caution.

"It seems Yid was right, Mendaka. This place has taken on new life."

Khem nodded. "Yid accomplished a great many important tasks in the short time he was here. Along with stopping the looting and convincing those who had fled to return, he selected new leaders and instructed them in our system of government. The surrounding villages are sending ambassadors to learn what we expect from them. They have been informed that they will fall under the overarching power of Lord Sigmund of Zamora, and I've explained the channels of authority and the respective order to them."

"Tis well, Khem. I will have you stay here and set up the provisional government until the Zamoran lord over the city-state arrives. Then I want you to join me when I send for you. On the morrow I will take half of our forces and sail for Citriodora. El Yid has sent pigeons saying the Pitters are abandoning all their Zongas along the coast. Word from our Citriodoran spies is that a powerful tribe is moving up from the south called the Moxo, and the Pitters are fleeing because they think we have an alliance with them. They're pouring into the Taxus Zongas because they fear being trapped in a pincer movement. Once I have securely placed the city-state of Citriodora under the Syr Folk wing, you will join me in the march south to Rosarita. It would seem the moment the Pitters left that a Mexus robber band took possession of it. After we secure Rosarita I hope we shall be able to ascertain who these Moxo are and what their motives truly are, then we can begin our drive for the Omala in the Taxus lands."

Khem frowned. "I hope to hell they are not another race like the Pitters. All we need is for the odds to tip even more in the emperor's favor."

"All I know at this point is that they have already crushed all the South Mexus Zonga's, and they've proven to be both swift and fierce in their overthrows. The few Mexus that have escaped say they are as oppressive and ruthless as the Pitters."

*Long Swan's Log: Once again I follow the High King to render a detailed account of his workings in the Ea-Urth. Sur Sceaf set up a Citriodoran named Moke as the Governor of Citriodora. He had developed a long term relationship with Moke, who fled the initial Pitter conquest of his city sixteen years before and sought sanctuary at Godeselle. Sur Sceaf knew Moke would be acceptable to the Citriodorans and was comfortable with his understanding of the expectations of the Syr Folk confederation, having seen it in operation.*

*The arrival of the Moxo in the Mexus Lands causes us much anxiety. Droves of Mexus refugees have come like flocks of birds fleeing north into the Kalifornias to escape the wrath of these fierce Moxo warriors.*

*Pyrsyrus' navy is due to follow Sur Sceaf to Rosarita and eventually move their supplies from there over land to the Omala. The Moxo could possibly force a change of plan.*

Moke hailed Sur Sceaf and the fyrds off. Khem's fyrds joined them shortly. The citriodorans had, prior to the Pitter invasion, been a prosperous city-state, though it was corrupt before its fall. Even though in decline from former times; Sur Sceaf hoped Moke would be able to restore it to its former glory.

He thought on what a beautiful city Citriodora once was before the pitters destroyed it and humbled the citizenry under the yoke of their harsh dominion. He remembered the thriving market place, the rich farmlands, and the philosophical nature of the citriodorans with their love of wisdom and the arts. Now the city looked like a dusty, dirty ghost town. Not even the shadow of its former glory.

Together, Khem's fyrds and Sur Sceaf's fyrds marched south for six days. They came upon some high ground outside Rosarita and embedded their armies in the defensible space the flat mound offered. Khem had been appointed as second lieutenant after the death of Crooked Jack. He was both a close friend and a good tactician, but Crooked Jack's rumbling feedback before every battle was sorely missed. Jack's feedback had always made Sur Sceaf weigh his tactics much more carefully.

After Sur Sceaf determined they would hold there for three days, Khem rode up and said, "My lord, they look ripe for the taking now. Why hold back?"

Sur Sceaf smiled. It was as if the spirit of Crooked Jack was speaking through Khem. Sur Sceaf sat mounted on Rekindler, and overlooked Rosarita from a nearby hill. He responded to Khem as if he was talking to his Old Lieutenant. "Nothing disarms an enemy more than suspense, Khem. The next three days will be sheer anxiety upon those Robbers. El Yid waits out at sea with his dragoons, and has lit the flames in their dragon's head to let us know he's here. Soon Juan Carlos will join him. Then we make a unified strike on Rosarita, so as to surgically remove the robbers and spare the populace."

"But why wait!" Khem raised an eyebrow. "These robbers are no match for our fyrds."

As Sur Sceaf looked into the black face of Khem he could have sworn Crooked Jack was looking back through those eyes. "Because, Khem, there is more to a battle than winning."

Khem shook his head. "I don't understand. We've got them in our jaws. Why not finish them?"

"These robbers are Mexus. They are not Pitters. With the Pitters it is vain to show mercy, for their seed code and blood memory makes them beyond redemption. But it mayhap some of these Mexus robbers are good men, and circumstances merely compelled them to choose survival over death. Juan Carlos is from this city. When he arrives, the citizens will hail him as one of theirs, and he will be able to sift and discern who should live and who warrants the administration of proper justice."

"Your wisdom never ceases to amaze me, my lord. My blood was up and my hand anxious to finish this fight, but I see you eventually want to make these Mexus part of the confederation. Don't you?"

Sur Sceaf smiled, "I salute you Khem for your keen observations. We are the creators of a Re-Made world. That awesome responsibility dictates we make it a world that is filled with light and life for as many nations as choose it. We must be protective of the rights of all men. We tread on hallowed ground here."

"Does that world contain a Black Nation?" Khem said with a hopeful smile.

"You bet it does Khem. So stick with me, and don't get yourself killed, because the laws upon which that nation shall be governed are all carefully written on your heart."

"My lord, there is one thing that puzzles me." Khem said as he twisted his seating on his mount.

"What is that?"

Khem pursed his lips. "Why would the Skull Worm and Sanangrar pick up without a fight and flee?"

Sur Sceaf thought for a moment then said, "I contemplated the same. I think there are many reasons. First off, his spies are reporting that we have an alliance with all the Red Men and Rogue Tribes. Secondly, the Pitter Zongas in Eugene, Salem, and the High Desert have all been destroyed. Now, apparently, the Moxo are busy destroying Sanangrar's legions to the south faster than he can evacuate. And it is my guess that Hryre Seath has ordered his legions back to protect his core. This much I know. We must never underestimate the evil designs of the enemy and must ever be ready for some sort of surprise."

Sur Sceaf continued to stare over Rosarita and meditate. El Yid had reported that these robber bands under Maximillius were even more barbaric and ruthless to the citizens of Rosarita than Sanangrar had been, as they were vying for control over the entirety of the Mexus Lands, and had before times served the will of Sanangrar as puppet governments, just like many of the North Easters became Dominikers.

On the third day, a messenger pigeon was sent to Commodore Yid's naval forces, and Sur Sceaf immediately marched against the Rosarita Band of Robbers. Khem swung around to the south of the city while Sur Sceaf marched from the north, and El Yid and Juan Carlos made an attack from ship on the port. The mere sight of the Toreador Banner of Juan Carlos struck fear into the hearts of the robber band and caused their resistance to melt in the Matador's presence. Rather than engage, the robbers fled behind the adobe walls of the city. Since they were surrounded, they prepared for a stiff resistance. By reason of their many evil deeds they feared horrible retribution and were, therefore, not likely to surrender easily, fearing to be tried as the war criminals they were.

El Yid and Juan Carlos made it into Sur Sceaf's camp to discuss the siege on the city when Maximillius appeared high up on the wall of the city and said, "Sur Sceaf, Juan Carlos, and El Yid, for every day you surround us we will kill every tenth person until ju leave us alone. Is that clear?"

Sur Sceaf rode up to the wall and shouted up. "If you even kill so much as one person, I will see to it you are disemboweled on a pole for all to watch. If you surrender now, we can promise you a trial and a punishment that will fit your crimes."

Maximillius flipped him a crude gesture and disappeared behind the wall. Sur Sceaf rode back to his men.

Juan observed, "He will never accept those terms my lord. He has too much to lose by letting justice take its course."

"But the people of Rosarita have too much to lose if justice does not have its way," Sur Sceaf said. "I just wish there were another way into that city."

Juan drew his face tight, his eyes widened, "There just may be. There used to be a well over on the south wall. When it went completely dry, I would use it to smuggle goods into the city and help captives to escape. The well wall was knocked down and a large capstone placed over the tunnel. I am sure with a little digging we could unearth it and have our way in."

"What are we waiting for? Khem I want you to make like you're planning a frontal assault on the north gate. Make it look good, cut some timber down like a battering ram. All you need do is posture an attack. Don't suffer anyone to get killed." Then turning to Juan he said, "Show us that tunnel. Yid, bring your men and follow me. They will not see us under the cover of dark night."

They assembled in the wooded area south of Rosarita in a large Old Cottonwood and Cypress Grove and waited for the sun to set. There was a sliver of a moon that could barely light ones feet as Juan led them to the mark on the south wall. The mark was a double rose made from baked clay and fastened firmly to the adobe. Others would have only thought it a decoration.

After they dug down about four inches they struck the capstone and began shoveling the dirt off it until they had a clear handle on all sides of the four inch thick granite. It took three men to heft it, and Sur Sceaf could feel the cool trapped air escape over his sweaty face. They let the air clear for a while before entering. A musty, fetid smell entered his nostrils from the depths as they descended undetected beneath the city.

Juan said, "Everyone be careful going down, this old ladder could easily give way."

One by one they climbed down, with Juan first and Sur Sceaf following. Once Sur Sceaf was in, he lit a candle and shielded the light from flashing brightly out the tunnel. There was a large cellar with some very old dusty barrels, hundreds of krugs of wine, and one dust covered table. No one had been there for a very long while.

After the last of Yid's pirates had entered, Juan said, "Once we top these stairs, I will unlock the door, for it is barred from down here, not from above. It will place us under the veranda that surrounds the town square. I reckon most of Maximillius' men are up atop watching for an attack. The rest are likely in the tavern that will be to our left."

Sur Sceaf directed, "Juan, you take your men to the tavern, I'll take my men to the right. We'll go under the veranda and up the stairs to the walls. El Yid, you take your men to the left, lift the gate and open it for Khem. Give him the signal and then join me on the walls."

Yid whispered, "So mote it be!"

All present whispered, "So mote it be," as each group of warriors filed out accordingly.

Soon, Sur Sceaf was running under the veranda. He bumped into two young lovers who at first looked terrified, but upon seeing the Herewardi uniform hunkered silently into a nearby alcove. A couple of drunks tried loading some sacks of 'cafe' on their donkeys, but were laughing so hard they were having little success. The donkey sensing the swift movement of warriors jerked its head and attempted to break free of them. Sur Sceaf was glad for the distraction the loud braying caused, because the patter of numerous feet was somewhat drowned out as they ran up the stairs. Looking out the side of his eye he saw the gate swing open. El Yid fired a dummy arrow with a white handkerchief attached to it. The robbers that stood atop the wall were distracted by looking out at Khem and trying to figure out what the white flash before them meant when Sur Sceaf and his Bush Masters struck them from behind with their swords.

Sur Sceaf thrusted his blade through the kidneys and up as he heaved the small man over the wall screaming. He quickly slashed the head off the next many and now the battle was on. One of them managed to sound a bugle, and the tavern doors burst open. Juan and his men cut their way in.

"Shield up, push with buckler, then stab from underneath." Sur Sceaf had thrown at least ten robbers over the wall, and his men were busy hacking and stabbing the robbers, not even taking time to remove them from the path. A group of six guards with swords drawn charged together at Sur Sceaf. He hit them right down the middle and shoved two over the railing to his left as he went, slicing the ones on the right with his stiffly held blade.

He turned quickly to assess three of the robbers were nursing wounds. One, though a good blades-man, was met by the speed, cunning, and ferocity that many years of training gave a warrior. Sur Sceaf parried his jab and brought his blade across the back of his neck, nearly severing the head off. The other three fled. All through the city streets the clamor of war and the clash of blades sounded out, as groans and yells reverberated from the walls. The smells of blood and split entrails filled the air.

Down in the town square, Khem poured through the gates with his fyrds like the surge of a mighty ocean wave. Shortly thereafter Mendaka rode through the square with his dog soldiers whose archers cleaned out the remainder of robbers from along the walls. As quick as a summer thunderstorm, it was over. There was no more resistance. The remaining robbers threw down their arms and pled for mercy.

A wailing woman attempted to leave by the gates with a band of saloon girls. They were halted by El Yid, and he quickly determined the woman was no woman at all, but was Maximillius, cowardly disguised as a woman and hiding in a group of their camp whores.

The camp whores evidently bore him no special love, nor respect, and they pointed the bully out.

Sur Sceaf laughed and said, "He is way too fat to pass for a whore."

"And far too ugly." Mendaka added.

Khem smiled. "I guess it was worth the try, my lord, but I don't even think he passes for much of a man." Khem belted out a laugh. "He looks to be a Mexus midget."

"That's the way it usually is. Little men often try to compensate for size by being ruthless. A poor substitute for manliness at best."

Word spread fast. Gaspar Maximillius was bound with the rest of the robbers to be held for trial by the citizens of Rosarita. Sur Sceaf waited in the upper room of the fort, as Juan Carlos was delayed in the square. The teeming citizens began rushing out of the countryside to greet him. All hailed Carlos as their deliverer. The one time favorite Matador had returned to his people. Although dark night, the oppressed citizenry waived scarfs and shouted out names. Many of Juan's men came from Rosarita and had maintained clandestine contact with their families and friends throughout the years. Indeed, many had been a vital source of information on the Pitter movements, but for now the streets of Rosarita rang with the joy of home coming.

His Toreador Banners had been recognized by all the Rosarita citizens, for not only had he swooped in from time to time to rescue a distressed Mexus brother, but he was their own Toreador that once graced their arenas in times long past. Tales of his piracy on the seas in his Clipper ships had long been told around their hearths. These tales were a constant warming hope in all the market places and in the privacy of the homes of Rosarita, and nurtured the belief that one day their deliverer could return.

Juan Carlos marched with his Mexus pirates up to Sur Sceaf in the town square. Together they walked down the stairs and out into a large sandy flat area where a well and water trough were centered, over which stretched a long lattice of roses lit bright by all the torches and lamps. The people of Rosarita attempted squeezing into the square.

Juan Carlos took off his black fedora and bowed before Sur Sceaf showing the people of Rosarita his allegiance. Juan embraced Sur Sceaf for effect, and Sur Sceaf said, "Juan, I want you to set Rosarita up as a city-state in the confederation of Syr Folk before joining Pyrsyrus in his march to the Omala."

He looked up surprised. "What would you have me do?"

"Appoint a governor, and educate them to our principles of constitutionalism and the rule of law. Set up judges in the land, and pass out allotments for them to ranch and farm, so that the wealth is not all concentrated into the hands of a few such as the robber band of Maximillius had done. The confederation is based on the idea that economic growth must spread horizontally as well as vertically."

"My lord, this could take several years to teach such concepts," his eye brows rose toward the silver hair at the base of his dark black hair.

"You will need to boil that down to about one or two moonths or less then." Sur Sceaf mirrored Juan's eyebrows to reflect Juan's response.

"My lord, you have always been very kind to me and just in all your ways, but unlike you, I have only one wife and I scorn to not be with her."

"I understand that all too well." Sur Sceaf said as he plucked a red rose from the lattice above and twirled it in his fingers. "As soon as we know what the true motives of the Moxo are, you may send for Tree Song and have her join Pyrsyrus' wives and travel here with them."

Juan gave a large smile and said, "Two moons. It shall be done."

A black breasted red rooster crowed from the top of the lattice, thinking all the torch light was dawn. It briefly interrupted their conversation with a shared laugh. A pleasant expression spread over Juan's face. Then Sur

Sceaf said, "Don't get too comfortable here. I want you to join me in the Taxus lands when I send for you. Pyrsyrus, you, and Yid will build a naval force for the confederation at Elves Island. Once we know the motives of these Moxo, we'll use Rosarita to port our naval supplies and haul them over land to the Taxus where we can reassemble them."

The crowd began chanting, "Juan Carlos, Juan Carlos, Juan Carlos." The nearby heavy laden Jack began to bray. Sur Sceaf watched as young men came up to touch Juan by the arm, believing it would impart some virtue of the famed bull fighter to them. A heavily wrinkled old lady with a colorful shawl over her head smiled at them. The square was now filled to capacity, with people still pouring in from the surrounding countryside. The Matador Banners had drawn them to observe the battle.

Sur Sceaf gave Juan a nudging nod, and Juan addressed the people of Rosarita in their tongue. Sur Sceaf could discern from the expressions of the people that they were more than pleased with Juan. Once Juan had delivered his speech to them, he began to entertain questions from them and to listen to their concerns. Several Mexus seamen gathered close to Juan asking questions with agitated fervor.

Juan squinted and frowned, turned to Sur Sceaf and said, "What do you know of the Moxo? Do we know yet if they are dangerous to us?"

Sur Sceaf spoke through Juan. "All we know is they are from the deep interior of the South Main Land, a place called Paz. Up until now they have not had many dealings with any of the people we usually deal with. They certainly know little if anything of us. We do know that they very much hate the Pitters, and yet, it is possible they could be just as evil as the Pitters and Vardropi. My hunch tells me they are just another people advancing northward and somehow the Pitters have managed to greatly offend them. Hopefully, they will act with reason, law, and civility."

Juan said, "These fishermen tell me they are marching through the Mexus Lands with a vengeance, flying a Banner of a Jaguar, and that they could not enter several ports south of here for fear of having their cargo seized. From the few ports they landed in, the people report the Moxo have massive armies, but few horsemen, and that they have already gutted several Pitter legions and seized the wealth and captives as their own, and even enslaved some villages of the Mexus."

"Sur Sceaf, if they prove to be civilized, perhaps we can persuade them to join our confederation." Juan held his fedora in both hands.

Then he slid a hand to his sword at his side. "But if not, I fear this may prove a major setback for your plans to seize the Taxus."

Sur Sceaf pondered for a moment. "There is so much we don't know about the world outside of our influence. The spies report that the Moxo have been in pursuit of the Pitters on a course heading towards the White Mountains of the Arid Zone. My intent is to head back north up the Baja and over to intercept them at Nogales, for neither I nor the Apache, I am sure, will suffer them to advance any further. It is my hope they are a people like unto us, whom we can bargain with, and we can head for the Taxus with them. Another ally in this war would be most welcome."

"If so, can I still bring my wife as agreed?" Juan asked.

"If the Moxo are willing to in no way thwart us in our designs, then yes, you can bring Tree Song with you to the Taxus. But first we have got to make sure it is safe."

A smile spread across his heretofore serious face. "And my men's families?"

"As you wish. A family man is the best security of any kingdom. Perhaps you shall take up a new home on Elves Island."

"So mote it be, my lord. I will make it so."

# CHAPTER 9 :

## SKALDIC FRIENDS AT THE LYCEUM

I**T WAS THE MOONTH OF BIRD** Song as the Ele-Anoreans called it or the moonth of Skipping Lambs as the Herewardi would say, yet some called it the Jester moonth, but in Moon Door one would likely hear all terms used interchangeably. Forsetti liked the blend of cultures he found so prevalent there. Against the back drop of the large blue Bay of Pertha, with all its sail boats, merchant and fishing vessels, stood the towering White Marble Lyceum of Moon Door. It was Forsetti's favorite place to spend time with his friends and fellow academicians.

Moon Door itself was also known as the Marble City of the Wizards due to the large number of philosophers, skalds, alchemists, mystics, and Lore Masters who resided in this city. The most prominent of these learned men and women was the Philosopher King, the Lord Ilkchild himself.

The Lyceum was framed on one side by an ancient windswept Monterey Cypress and on the other by a large cluster of silver-fronded Blue Bismarck Palms and one large swollen trunked Kauri Tree standing erect as a lone sentinel in the five acre lawn. Through the twelve large white columns arranged in a semi-circle, a gentle warm sea breeze blew in off the bay from the west.

At the end of the academic year in the Skaldic Academy, Forsetti's Nigh-Father, Ilkchild the Fire-Salamander, would summon the graduating class of Skalds to an academic contest at the Lyceum. The contest began in the mud moonth and ended on the full moon of Albispiene. The contest would be judged by the seven ladies of the council of women, and the victor would be announced at the masquerade ball, which was to follow. Each contestant was required to submit an expose to determine whose writing contributed the most to the lyceum as adjudged by the seven ladies. Their writings could be epic, poetry, philosophy, mathematics, song, history, botany, or any study that would benefit the academy.

By the moonth of bird song only five contestants remained. Two males, Forsetti himself, Son of Melyngoch and Yr Uehelwydd Son of Duv-Ba, and the Three Sisters, Ka-Luna, Da-Bocia, and Er-Yca, the brilliant and acclaimed triplet Daughters of Long Swan and Ysys.

Each of the five contestants had chosen a different theme. Forsetti had chosen to do a well-researched history of the Battle of Charly's Harbor in which his Father, the Lord Melyngoch, had fallen while defending against an overwhelming host of Pitter Legions from the Eugene Zonga. It was his greatest hope that his offering would dispel the cloud of shame that hung over his family. Yr wrote his on the War of the Trees, which was a beautiful poetic rendition of all the Oracle Trees on the Isle. Ka-Luna did hers on 'the Medicinal Qualities of Mushrooms'. Da-Bocia did hers on 'the Costs and Benefits of Sovereignty in a Confederation', and Er-Yca did a treatise on 'Family Constellations' and just how they repeat themselves generation after generation in certain seed codes.

Forsetti was feeling the pressure acutely. He had been personally schooled by Ilkchild and wished to make him proud. Ilkchild, knowing firsthand the pain of losing a father, took Forsetti's Mother, Swanyard, to wife. Thus, Forsetti became a near-son. In his three years at the academy he had grown very close to the other four contestants and, in fact, had developed a romantic interest in Ka-Luna that he could not extinguish. But his good friend, Yr, fancied himself to be Luna's love, and tension between himself and Yr was daily approaching the boiling point. Every encounter with Yr became more and more strained.

Approaching from the Flammeum jungle path that led through some towering Strangler Figs from the academy, Ka-Luna was the first of Forsetti's friends to arrive. Forsey took Ka-Luna's hand and whispered, "Listen, I want you to hear this." The two of them stood next to one of the twelve marble columns fronting the portico and listened to a drift of Oropendola birds trilling their mating songs.

The cool marble floor was a splendid relief from the humid heat of the day. This was the place where each day the five contestants met to go over their writings together, offering suggestions and critiques.

Forsey loved those times when he was in Luna's presence. She was the most beautiful girl he'd ever met, with her long reddish-blond hair, rosy lips, and a dignified sharp nose with its slight arch. He found it easy to get lost in those sapphire eyes and her hauntingly husky feminine voice.

Luna was laughing at the antics of the large green birds when Forsey turned to her and said earnestly, "It's time we stop pretending. I've never felt as warmly towards anyone as I do you, Luna."

She didn't draw back, but smiled, and tightened her grip on his fingers. "And I've grown to enjoy your company so much Forsey, but..." She pulled her hand back slightly and looked at the approaching troop of friends and frowned. "What about Yr?"

"What about Yr? He was just your practice for getting to me. You know it. I've seen it in your eyes for the past moonth."

Luna, threw back her reddish hair, "But, ... but, I wanted to let go of him softly." The bay breeze swept her hair up over her face.

"And what? Drag his pain and misery out all the more? Don't fool yourself. He knows what's going on. Anything else is a slow knife, at best."

"It's just that, before I met you, I had offered him so much promise. It feels like I'm cheating. I want to ease him out of it and let him down lightly."

"I suppose I must respect that, but do you think we could at least find some time alone away from our group? Maybe after Yca's reading, you and I could go for a walk together?"

Luna's eyes brightened. "I would like that, but it has to be some place private where we wouldn't be seen."

Forsey's heart leaped in him, "Then we will go to Onamingo's Dolman out by Turtle Duck's Point."

"That sounds..."

"Hey," Yr said, suddenly appearing from around the column, "are you horning in on my girl again, Forsey? By the gods, you'd think she was yours by the way you two are huddled together behind this column."

Forsey looked down at Luna's hand still holding his arm, "Hey, yourself. I don't remember seeing you speak your troth through a Harrow Stone yet."

"So what, idiot," Yr said gritting his teeth. "Everyone already knows Luna is mine. That's the way it's been for the past year."

Luna let go of Forsey's arm and slid back. Forsey countered, "Everyone knows you keep saying that, but I haven't heard her say it."

Yr turned scarlet. "That's as far as this will go, Forsey! Everyone knows your Fa Mo's the bitch responsible for the Invasion of Charly Harbor and now you are trying to re-write history to make it feel like the invasion was somehow unavoidable. Do you really think anybody is going to buy that cow shit?"

Forsey got directly in his face. "You bastard! You don't even know what happened there. My father gave his life to stop that invasion and my Fa Mo stood her ground when others deserted to defend her manor before she gave up the ghost." He felt his blood kindling as it had done many times before in similar circumstances.

"It was a miracle that my mother escaped with her children and that Ilkchild, in his mercy, took her to wife. You have no idea the costs my family paid in that battle, Yr. Besides, my Fa Mo may have been an extravagant lady, but she does not deserve having her name dragged through the mud for something that was totally unavoidable."

"I'm just warning you, stay away from my maiden or you and I shall come to blades."

"Name the place! Name the time."

Luna slid between the two of them, pushed them apart, and said, "Alright, alright, this has gone far enough. You're supposed to be intelligent academicians." She turned to Yr. "Yr we are good friends and there was a time when we were even closer, but I am not your maiden. We exchanged no promise."

The rest of Forsey's friends had arrived during the argument and were now exchanging shocked looks. Yr's jaw muscle tightened. "None of this would have happened, if Forsey hadn't horned in on us. He just acted like he was everyone's friend, and now that he's got what he wants he sticks the knife in my back. Friends don't take friend's women."

Forsey was close to losing his temper. "Yr, you just don't know when it's over and time for you to get lost, do you? It's open season on any woman who has not spoken her troth through a harrow stone."

"Alright Forsey, that's it, you've broken the branch. It's you and me in a duel. Bring your blade. This evening. The Stone Circle at Blood Water is the place. Fourth point on the Sundial."

Since Yr had issued the challenge, Forsey had the choice of weapons. A skilled fencer, he chose rapiers. Forsey tested his rapier, slicing the air like swift tongues of lightening cutting across the sky. His nine friends, and the Triplets, including Ka-Luna, had all gathered to observe. This was the chosen place for the Lek or Rink for the combatants. And Yr had brought only two Ele-Anorean friends.

Ruibe-Ur-Salla, Son of Long Swan and a friend of both Forsey and Yr, was the mutually agreed upon Umpire. The tall tawny haired youth examined both blades and handed them back. Ruibe took his staff and scratched a circle in the dirt to form the Lek which was about half the size of the Stone Circle they were in. The large stone monoliths had been placed in a circle as a memorial for the fallen in the Battle of Moon Door. Some said it was a place haunted by wraiths.

The blades were designed to slice but not stab. Forsey's intention was to win with a slice, for he bore no deep malice. He had always respected Yr Uehewydd, until he failed to yield and concede that Ka-Luna was now favoring him. After all, she stood amongst Forsey's friends at this duel and not Yr's.

Ruibe raised his hand for the duelers to attend him so that he could explain the rules of engagement. "Whoever draws first blood will be declared the victor. There can be no serious maiming or wounding. No injury may be rendered to the eyes or the man parts." He took Forsey by the shoulders and placed him at one end of the circle, then walked back to Yr and placed him at the opposite side of the circle. He saluted the friends of each, saluted the duelers, and then stepped out of the Rink.

Adrenaline pumped through Forsey's veins as Ruibe addressed those present. "If I may be so bold, the purpose of this duel, as I understand, is to gain satisfaction on Yr's behalf against Forsey for attempting to steal his girlfriend, Ka-Luna and for assuming that Herewardi are by nature alone, better fighters. And now on the other hand, Forsey seeks satisfaction for Yr's insult to his family and in particular the insult directed at his Fa Mo, Clotilde."

Ruibe held his staff in his right hand and pulled back his silver robe, "I bare my breast to declare openly before you that though I am a Skald after the Order of the Salamander King, I clearly state that this is a Clandestine Duel and has no formal sanction, except to satisfy this conflict, that it may go no further than the outcome of this rink and that we may forever put an end to it."

Ruibe then stretched out his staff and pointed at everyone present. "He who draws first blood shall be the victor and that is where all this nonsense stops and I shall end it. Agreed?"

All present said, "Agreed."

Forsey nodded his head that he was ready, gripped his rapier, and assumed battle stance. Yr got into position across the circle from him and shot a piercing look back. Ruibe held up a red handkerchief and dropped it. Forsey rushed into the frenzy of a parrying blade.

Yr's blade was swift, showing he was nothing less than an accomplished blade-master, but Forsey knew he was going to best him. Too many were the fights he had to endure growing up because of his Fa Mo's bad reputation and rumored folly.

"You bastard," Yr shouted. "You think you're privileged just like your weird grandmother. You don't care beans about anybody else's feelings and always think you hold the trump card in your seed code, don't you? Well, I come from some good breeding myself, of a royal sort, and this day will show it."

Forsey felt the taste of metal in his mouth and he no longer considered anything, but making this loud mouthed ass shut up and stop with his braying insults. He swung wildly, his blade whirring like an enraged bumble bee. Dark anger blinded him. But Yr was matching him blow for blow and parrying much better than anticipated. He quickly swung his blade for a thigh, was blocked and then smacked pommels in mid-air to foil a counter slash.

Forsey realized his anger was sapping his strategic moves and tried to turn the tables with an insult. "Yr, your people have been peace-mongers for too long. Forced everyone else to fight their battles for them."

It didn't work, Yr was equally angry, yet remained calm and calculating, frightfully confidant and cool.

Once again they locked blades and had to push each other off to re-position. Forsey studied Yr's feet and legs carefully and saw his thighs turn away from him. The moment of blood had arrived. As quick as Forsey could, he positioned himself to counter Yr's turn and moved to anticipate his move with delight. But Yr's blade was not there. Yr had tricked him with his legs.

He felt a burning cut along his left cheek and saw Ruibe's staff fall down between them. "Over! It's all over!"

Forsetti stood back, took a deep breath, and felt the hot blood trickling down his cheek. He watched as Ruibe took Yr by the arm and raised it in the air, "Here is our victor. The satisfaction goes to Yr."

Forsey chastised himself for having lost. It was obvious Yr had been trained to use deceptive body language and he had plied it well. It was not something he had expected. He had underestimated his opponent. He would have to chalk this one up to pride and over confidence.

Yr stuck his foil in the ground and walked over to Forsey offering his hand of peace. "Os-Frith, Forsetti. No hard feelings. As the saying goes, 'The duel settles all'."

Forsetti held his bleeding cheek with one hand and with the other took Yr's firmly. "No hard feelings. You have taken the duel, but Luna and I shall remain together so really it doesn't change much. Does it?"

"Perhaps not for you, but it satisfies the wound of having lost the love of Ka-Luna. It was not what you did that offended me as much as how you did it."

"Then I am glad you got your satisfaction. I only regret it cost us so much."

"Perhaps next time you will think better of us Ele-Anoreans." Yr furrowed his brow, and then stated with pride, "After all, we were originally the keepers of this land. It is our blood and soul that fashioned this Isle and breathed life into it. There's hardly a plant or animal on this Isle that wasn't shaped by us."

"I will think better of you. For I can only think better of a man who has honorably bettered me and holds no vindictiveness in his heart." The two smiled and squeezed each other's hands firmly once again.

# CHAPTER 10 :
## THE LORD KANARUS AND THE MIGHTY NDEE

**H**IGH IN THE WHITE MOUNTAINS of the Apaches, far away from
the blessed Isle of Ilkchild, Kanarus rode out of the lair astride
his White Horse, Sun Chaser. Before him rose impossible rock
formations, which formed a maze of twists and turns and dead-ends,
effectively entrapping any enemy crazy enough to try and enter the
labyrinths of its well defended folds. Kanarus could strike far greater
forces than his own and disappear into the safety of this natural maze to
the enemy's total frustration.

In the sixteenth winter of his youth, Kanarus had come here under the
name of Kane. He came as the Heretoga of an irregular Young Blood Fyrd
for training in hopes of reclaiming the Taxus. His father had already led
advanced attack parties into Taxus and resettled much of their Ancestral
Home Lands only to be presumed slain in a battle near the Omala. Kanarus
thereby became a Half-King operating out of the White Mountains to avenge
the death of his father, Ilker, who was believed to have found his grave
there, although his body was never found. Kane grieved with a vengeance
for four long years. Had it not been for the love he bore for his wives, he
would have taken the path of sworn vengeance and become a Wose.

On the edge of the fifth year of his grief, word came that his father
was not dead. But rather, Ilker had been compelled to live secretly
among the enemy until he rose out of the Book of the Dead and back
onto the pages of the living.

Though he greatly rejoiced at his father's return, he firmly believed the gods had placed him in the Apache Lands for a reason known only to them. He chose to continue with the life he had built in his mountain lair, and continued to harass the Pitters relentlessly.

It was from this impenetrable lair that he became the nemesis of Pitter Bands, and won the praise of the mighty Ndee. Though he was of the Royal Herewardi Blood Line, Chief Mangas invited him to take up permanent residence in the Sacred Mountain as a White Apache. From that time forth, the lair became the base of Kanarus' fyrd's operations. He also changed his name from Kane to Kanarus; meaning Kane the Son of Ar and Hrus, the Great Herewardi Patriarchs, Arundel and Howrus. Because he had no official sanction from the Roufytrof, he was designated the Half-King.

Upon the death of Chief Mangas Mesculera, one of his twin Sons, Chise, became the young Chief. Chise continued the strong alliance with Kanarus out of both respect and gratitude. Fifteen years earlier, in the time of what is now known as the Days of Preparation, days of slim hope, when immanent destruction loomed on every horizon, both he and his brother, Zoot, had been rescued from Pitter slavery and an almost certain death in Copperopolis. Starkwulf, the Herewardi Destroying Angel then called the Wose had rescued them.

Kanarus was partially responsible for the shift from a defensive to an offensive stance against the forces of the Skull Worm and his unholy alliance. Now the Skull Worm himself had been delivered by the Norns right to the threshold of Kanarus' Lair. Kanarus was sure it was fate and the weavings of the Norn. Kanarus was not about to let him escape without delivering several vicious bites to his heels and flanks.

As he and his fyrd traversed the cleverly hidden trail leading from the lair, the bugling of elks and the shriek of a golden eagle could be heard in the hills. Behind them rose the sacred mountain Dzil Nchaa Si Ann, where Chief Mangas' bones rested in an unmarked grave. It was where the God Ussen sent the Mountain Spirits to prepare a land for his people. It was also where Kanarus' father-in-law, Govannon the Elfsmith, was presented with Kanarus' wife, Wilona Saga-Jah-El-Ea, as an infant at the Golden Pond of Ussen.

As soon as Anghrus had delivered the startling news of the Pitter forces, Kanarus had sent two scouts ahead of his fyrd to ascertain the attack strategies and the most likely places to strike the Pitter legions, tight places that were too narrow for the maneuvering of the legions. Before the scouts even got half way to Saguaro Pond, they returned with their report. The Skull Worm was already on the move.

Now Scouts Elffle and Signy, two of Kanarus' sons, rode up and saluted Kanarus. Elffle reported excitedly, "My lord, the Skull Worm's troops are so numerous that they cannot be counted. But from their direction, they are heading due south, towards the Mexus, where they can enter the poisoned lands through the safety of the south gate. Moreover, we counted twenty of those toulucans the runners had told us about, moving with them."

Kanarus frowned. "Then we must re-direct them. If we can force them to go through the north gate of the Poisoned Lands they shall incur the most losses. But why are they on the move? Can Sur Sceaf and Arundel's forces truly be in command of the West Lands? Methinks not. At least no riders have arrived here as of yet. What do you deduce, Signy?"

Signy thought for a moment. "Well, we got word of Lady Brekka's victory over the Eugene Zonga, and Syr Elf reports several victories in the High Desert. He also reported Arundel cleared the Pitters out of Salem." He turned his horse to better address Kanarus. "Word came just two days ago that Sigmund had re-taken Zamora after Brekka had destroyed their Zonga a moonth before. I conclude it is possible Sur Sceaf has already taken Frisco. What is for sure is that this must constitute the bulk of the Skull Worm's legions. So my guess is, Sur Sceaf has already begun his march south to Rosarita, and these rats are merely fleeing before him."

Elffle nodded. "I agree. We'll probably get a Silver Harrier in with the news any day now." He pulled his horse in near to Kanarus and added, "At the tail of the Skull Worm's armies is an enormous slave train, heavily guarded. They must be valuable cargo to have so many guards on them; appeared to be mostly young women."

Signy said, "If we strike from the rear the costs to the captives could be devastating, as they would not hesitate to turn their toulucans on their own captives, if only to hit us."

"The best strategy," Elffle said, "if you will permit me to say so Father?"

Kanarus said, "Please, speak your strategy. I haven't been teaching you all these years for nothing. Show me you can be the generals I raised you up to be."

Effle shot a confirming glance at Signy, his Elder Brother of fifteen winters by one moonth. "The best strategy would be to hold back until they get far away from the water source. Then we can strike them in the front of their lines. Pin them down and over stress their horses with thirst to the point they can't make it to the south gate. We'll hit hard and keep them too busy to re-position. By the time they maneuver and set up their toulucans, we will be off to a safe distance. Then we can repeat the harassment every time they begin to inch forward. We've simply got to make it too costly to continue going south."

"That is as it shall be; Elffle, that is a good strategy. You are worthy of being called a tactician." Kanarus shot a proud glance at Elffle. "We'll have their legions crawling on bloody knees all the way into the poisoned lands and half their cavalry will collapse right under them from thirst. We must hamstring these rats before they can add to the might of the Taxus Zongas and Bastions. By forcing them to take the northern route into the poisoned lands, they'll be further crippled in the night by the creeps. At the slow rate such a large army is required to move, they'll spend two to three nights at least in the Creep Zone before they can even make it to the safety of the Growling Fortress."

Signy said, "Do you wish for me to assemble the fyrds, Fa, and send word of our plans for Chise and Zoot to join with us?"

"Yes, immediately. Summon the fyrds."

As soon as the fyrds joined him, Kanarus led them the ten miles to the Pitter encampment at Ghost Rock. "Make camp here. Make it light so we can pick up at a moment's notice. As soon as the scouts report the legions are moving, we'll ride in and attack at the head of their armies. Fire your arrows from your mounts coming and going."

Elffle saluted. "We will make it so, my lord."

Kanarus then sent a pigeon message to Chief Chise informing him of their location and requesting that he assist in cutting off all possibilities of the Skull Worm turning south into Mexus lands. He chuckled at the thought of forcing the Pitter Army into the Poisoned lands through the north gate. *No people are wont to go there. They fear the creeps, the muckle-mark steppers, skin-walkers, and monsters untold that are the denizens of those dark lands. But the Skull Worm will not be given another choice.*

After two days of camping under open sky, a scout rode into camp and reported the Pitter legions were still marching south towards the south gate. Kanarus and his men quickly packed up and mounted to rejoin the fyrds, who waited hidden in the canyons, armed and ready for conflict. "Men of the Herewardi, today we ride against one of the most formidable enemy hosts on earth. In all likelihood they will look upon us as little more than a pesky hornet to be avoided. But today we are going to render a very costly assault to their legions; one that will force their march through the dread north gate. In the name of the gods that love us, move out, and give it your all."

Coming upon the Pitter armies at Ghost Rock, Kanarus and his scouts hid behind the rocky crags and looked out over the Pitter black banners flapping in the wind. The massive legions crept over the desert scape like a black blanket. The whole desert floor seemed covered with a dark mass, like a black oil that spilled out of the ground to suffocate desert life. Kanarus split his fyrd and sent them out for an attack on the east and west of the southerly moving army to pinch them and halt their progress. He knew he had to create enough pressure to turn them back and to break the will of so great an army.

"Sons of sheep eating bitches!" the Skull Worm yelled as he ran his hand over his clean shaven head. "They're supposed to be Wood Lords. What in the hell are they attacking us in this god damned desert for? Do they think to possibly beat us with such a tiny force? This is all the work of that bastard Kanarus, whose father we ground into the earth down in Taxus, isn't it?"

"Yes, Master." Lupuspedia acceded. "We slew his father, but never recovered the body of the Wood Lord."

"Then that explains the bastard's persistence. Let's give him hell. I've got a strategy that will throw his ass for a loop."

Lupispedia grinned through his bared teeth, "You're going to blast him with the toulucans."

"Ain't that for sure, but I have something far more cunning to pull on this feral Swan Lord, the outcast of heathen spawn. A maneuver he will never suspect."

Lupispedia laughed hard, "You will fire all the toulucans at once."

"No, you fool. Those damned toulucans are good for little else but a siege weapon. Besides Gloomullah says they will have some built by the Growlings that will swivel and won't be difficult to turn. What I'm thinking is that we'll let this coyote pester us for a while yet, and then I'll take the back door right out of here. I will simply drop into the Poisoned Lands from the north. And you know what is best of all?"

"What?"

"They think to pin us down here, force us to fight and drain our horses and men of precious liquid. Scouts say the Ndee forces are moving up to reinforce the heathens. Well, the Poisoned lands are a strict taboo to the Ndee. They'll never cross into them and I'm willing to bet, neither will the Heathen Half-King."

"But Master Commissar," Lupispedia declared, "What about the skin walkers and creeps."

"What about them? Everything living shits and bleeds. Don't it?"

"Sure they bleed, but so do we. And what about water? We are too far from any water sources. I don't think the horses will hold up under battle conditions. Is there water through the North Gate? And didn't Hryre Seath send a Mandamus that we are to do no unnecessary fighting?"

"You whine too much for me, Lupi. For years this heathen spawn has wreaked havoc on my supply lines and Rat Packs. It's time we did some pay backs now that we have him out in the open desert. And stop worrying about water. Once we get through the North Gate, there is a stream about fifteen miles in. In any military campaign the victory belongs to the most daring, the most calculating, and the boldest. I'd like to see that wooly-headed bastard of Ilker follow us into the Dead

Zone." He laughed loud. "But first, we're going to show them a little of our wrath. Before I pull my maneuver I'm going to give this coyote the death blow he deserves. This is open desert and they have no good cover for at least ten miles."

The Arid Zone was Kanarus' playground. He knew every water hole, pine thicket, and cactus. Here in the Great Apache Desert, he was master. And with the hot noon day sun beating down hard, he was sure those khaki and black uniforms of the Pitters were like ovens inside; nor was Pitter horse flesh known for endurance.

Kanarus' swift attack and maneuver had caused the Pitters to stop and realign their toulucans east and west. Skull Worm waited with his toulucans for another attack to come from behind, but Kanarus instructed his troops to rejoin at a rendezvous point. Once they gathered, they came back in a full charge down the front of the Pitter line. They dropped Pitters by the hundreds with their strong horse-bows, whilst their war horses and the Apache's lightning ponies kept them out of the reach of Pitter arrows. All these sudden percussive attacks, he was sure, were too fast for the Skull Worm to re-configure battle formations.

He pulled reins in on Sun Chaser. His men followed suit and lined up on either side of him. The Pitters hurriedly sent out a legion to engage them and Kanarus sent forth his messengers of death, the arrows thick as rain which fell into their midst. Shower after shower of arrows from their bows dropped a third of the engaging Pitter legion while the other legions tried to move on their course forward.

As Kanarus fought the Pitter legion that tried distracting them, five hundred more Apache Warriors arrived under the Twin Chiefs, Zoot and Chise. They quickly joined in the fray, and together, made easy work of the legionnaires in their circling cavalry charges; shooting as they arrived, then turning backwards on their horses while shooting arrows upon leaving.

Zoot was so effective that when his horse sprung unexpectedly over a large barrel cactus, he still shot three Pitters with arrows before he hit the ground. Kanarus marveled that he dusted himself off and swiftly remounted. It wasn't long before Pitter ranks were so decimated that they huddled down into black shield phalanxes that made them look like massive black turtles crossing the desert scape. Then another wave of legions came to reinforce the first, and the process was repeated until the numbers of legions were too high to engage head on anymore, so Kanarus signaled for the trumpeter to sound for a re-grouping and a new strategy.

The Skull Worm attempted to press ever southward with Kanarus tightly nibbling at his flanks. At the same time, the Apaches made their flash attacks and retreats that drove the worm hastily onward. Kanarus' horses were watered at secret water holes, refreshed, and because they were accustomed to the heat, they did not faint. Not so with the Pitters. By midafternoon, the Pitter horses began frothing at the mouths and collapsing.

"Shit!" Skull Worm said. "Those damned mud farmers and sheep-rapists."

"What is it Master. What ails you so?" Lupispedia asked.

"I failed to account for this heat of the desert sun. Call a halt. Because of our great thirst the horses will need drink." He signaled for a halt.

"I hope it does not offend you that I mentioned that would be a problem earlier. And need I remind you of Hryre Seath's admonition to bring his legions back to him whole. He needs every one of them. What would you have us do, Commissar, to keep the Emperor's orders?"

"We've got to turn back for the Saguaro Pond. And I'll thank you to make no mention of this in your reports back east. Just say we ran into impossible odds and water shortages in the deserts. Tell them it's a drought year. You know. Fix the report in our favor."

"If it isn't written, it didn't happen. I know the routine."

But before he could force his way to the source of water, the Apache Chief, Chise, had sent forth a thousand Dog Soldiers he had held back for this moment. As they amassed on the flanks of the Pitter army, Skull Worm's anger rose into a rage. "Damned piss ants. Won't even let us get the water we need."

"I see you getting worked into a frenzy." Lupispedia said, "Need I remind you of the emperor's edict. And as you know a thousand Apaches is equal to any ten thousand of a Rogue Nation."

"Bring the toulucans! Place them on the legion's flanks again and direct them at those dog soldiers."

As soon as the legionnaires raised torches to light the firing fuses, the damned Dog Soldiers shifted. Furious, Skull Worm shouted, "Swing the toulucans in opposite directions! Don't let them scatter." His strategy worked, though the damage done to the enemy was less than expected. Still, the Dog Soldiers appeared far more cautious in their follow up attacks.

Over the next few hours and only inch by painful inch, the Skull Worm cut his way at a great price to the water hole at Saguaro Pond, which, because the Apache ponies had previously been watered there, was now little more than a muddy pool of water and no longer sufficient for all their horses.

"I'm not about to waste my legions on a bunch of desert dogs when they'll be needed back east!" He shot Lupispedia a warning look. If the bastard dared to gloat, it would be the last thing he ever did.

"A wise decision, Master. It'll please the emperor."

"Abandon the captives, the wagons of shoot powder and the toulucans. Bugle a retreat," Skull Worm commanded before whirling his horse and galloping toward the Northern Hell's Gate leading directly into the Creep Zone. He would lose some horses, but they had plenty. Perhaps the captives he was leaving would slow the Kaninchens down. It would certainly tap their resources. Kind of like leaving a lizard's tail behind for them. Finding water was crucial, and he knew there was water not too many miles from the gate. Best of all, everyone knew the Red Bastards were deathly afraid of the Haints in that section of the Arid Zone.

He glanced back, and sure enough, the Sheep-Eaters and their savage slaves had stopped short, raising a cloud of dust. He threw back his head, laughing loud and long as he passed through the North Gate.

Kanarus sat atop his horse before the Gates of Hell and considered his next move. No doubt, Skull Worm thought that he and the Ndee were entirely too superstitious and fearful to enter the Poisoned land. The Hell Rat was wrong. Kanarus respected the Poisoned lands, but did not fear them.

Like a foul-smelling khaki and black dragon, the tail end of the legions rode through the large X's that marked the northern limits of the Poisoned lands. If the creeps did attack, the Pitter armies were sufficiently large enough to ward them off, but it would still be very costly to the bastards. The more Pitters that were killed by the creeps the less they had to fight.

Once the legions had slithered behind some red stone canyons, Kanarus rode back to Chiefs Chise and Zoot where they were watching as their warriors rummaged through the wagons and collected weapons left behind. "Hail and Os-Frith!"

"Hail, Kanarus." Chise said, his braids of raven black hair and war-painted face framing a smile of soul-deep satisfaction. "We ran the rats right into the sack. Didn't we?"

"Sure did. Now, I recommend we lay up here for the night. Let the creeps soften them up and do a lot of the work for us before we enter."

"What about the captives?" Zoot inquired.

"Send a scout to the Quailor to let them know a train of refugees is in need of hospitalers, and have the refugees taken back to the stronghold."

Like a mirror image to Chise, Zoot, his twin, used the Ndee's name for Kanarus, meaning Yellow Rabbit, "It shall be done, Sikyatavo! This is a double victory for us, is it not? Our losses are few, but we slaughtered many, and now we have them funneled right into the Creep Zone where you wanted them. And look at the booty they've left us."

Zoot shot a glance at Chise, who nodded. "This morning some of my braves came across a wayfaring man traveling alone through the desert. Says he is a friend of the Syr Folk. Has the name of Trader Johnson, and he had the wax seal of Sur Sceaf in hand. He reports there is a mighty host of warriors heading this way called Moxo. Says the Moxo travel swiftly north through the Mexus Lands near Nogales."

Kanarus frowned. "I know this Trader Johnson. He's been a friend of Sur Sceaf and the Wose for many years. I'm sure he can be trusted, but who in Middle Earth would the Moxo be?"

"We have never heard of them either. We thought you might have," Zoot said. "I know of no other large armies to the south besides the Pitter legions."

Kanarus gazed into the distance where the disturbed dust still hung in the air. "Nor do I." He sighed. "We close one door on the enemy, and perhaps open the door to another threat. At any rate, we cannot be diverted, and must proceed according to the master plan Sur Sceaf issued in the decrees of the War Road. The War Road was agreed to by all the nations of the confederation and it alters not without Sur Sceaf's approval.

"This was a victory over the Pitters today, and according to plan, sent them into the jaws of the creeps, where they shall surely suffer great afflictions. Now, our forces can do a full scale attack when Brekka and Syr Elf arrive with their Fyrds and allies. In the meantime, bring Trader Johnson to me. With luck, I'll get a clearer picture of the Moxo from him. I suggest you send a band of your best warriors south to investigate the approach of these Moxo and get a report back as soon as possible."

# CHAPTER 11 :

## MASQUERADE

**T**HE MOON OVER THE ISLE of Ilkchild illuminated the misty lyceum, giving it the appearance of an enchanted faery realm. As the white-robed Godhi priest lit the black candles and placed them in the blue glass globes, wisps of brine-scented sea mist rolled in through the white marbled pillars, adding to the illusion of a place out of time and space. The silver palms and the Monterey Cypress created the perfect framing of this marvelous ritual space.

Musicians played lively dance tunes, while students in elaborate costumes swirled around the lantern-lit lawn. Laughter and shouts of recognition were carried on the breeze as the dancers attempted to guess the identity of their masked partners. Forsetti stood at the south end of the pavilion, wearing a long-nosed mask and curly ram horns to hide his thick red-gold hair.

He danced every dance, for he had determined he would find Ka-Luna first. He managed to guess Da-Bocia early in the merriment in her butterfly mask, though she could not guess who he was. And even though she made a valiant attempt at disguising her voice, he recognized the way she always turned her feet out. Then he danced with Er-Yca, dressed all in black with a scrolled black mask of the Black Faery over her face. Her voice and accent gave her instantly away with that Ele-Anorean lilt that so enriched their tongue. Surprisingly, no one had guessed his identity yet, although he had danced with as many as ten girls.

Forsey recognized Yr easily from the stance he had assumed in the rink. He had chosen a Wyrm Kat costume, complete with long tail, cat mask, and cat-like ears. He and Da-Bocia appeared to have formed a romantic attachment, for they seldom parted company and often held hands.

But no matter where he looked he could not discover Ka-Luna. Once he thought it might be a lady dressed like a hen, and then he considered she might be the Toreador, the perfect disguise, but upon closer inspection he saw the bulge in the crotch and realized it was Syr-Kraki, one of his male classmates. He looked at several other people clothed as Jesters, some as ghosts with long pointy hats, so eerie in the black lights with the dark hollows looking back at him. Then there were the two woodwoses, who passed dressed in flax and green, but no one who had the makings or hour glass shape of Ka-Luna was discernible.

A couple of ladies passed him in lovely ball gowns with elaborate feathered masks. Two boys passed him by, sporting booger masks while pursuing a girl dressed as a swan. He walked out on to the lawn, and there, standing still and silent in the black light by a globe, dressed in an Eagle-Owl costume and attire, was Luna. That was her. That had to be Ka-Luna. He could not see it, but he could feel it.

He covered the lawn with ease and declared, "I should have known Luna, that you would be an Eagle-Owl."

The voice came back, "You can't imagine the fun I've had watching you dance and hunt all over for me, and I just stood here loving it all. Best of all you danced with Lady Russella, she's an easy eighty winters old." They laughed.

"I thought she was awfully light, but why all the subterfuge?" Forsey asked. "We could have been dancing all this time."

"I'm sorry it just became an enticing game to trick the hunter for a change. Nobody has guessed me so far. What about you?"

"Not a soul, unless I count you. How did you recognize me?"

"Oh, that was easy enough. No other young man has your physique. Come on! Let's dance before they turn on the lights of revelation."

She grabbed his hand and together they ran to join the nearest dance circle, eased into the round, grabbing hands, and with crisscrossed feet leaped with the rest of the dancers; the costumed musicians doing their best to keep the gigs light and airy.

Precisely at midnight, Ilkchild stood up from his seat and stepped forward to the rostrum. Moonlight shimmered over the silver silk robe, denoting his status as Wizard or one of Elven-Lord status, granted him by the Roufytrof as a Lore Master of Excellence. For those who did not know him, he appeared whole. The long robes and the Kauri wood limbs crafted by Govannon to replace his amputated arm and leg were hidden beneath the robe. Behind him sat his thirty wives, along with faculty members and the Seven Learned Ladies of Moon Door.

Ilkchild held up his Fire-Salamander staff, and the music and dancing ceased. With the second wave of his staff the torches on the twelve columns were lit, creating a golden warm ambience. The students gathered closer. Forsey and Luna wished each other luck. His heart was thundering so loud he was certain those close to him had to hear it, even over the music.

Forty-four maidens sang paeans to the god Baldur, the patron god of Moon Door, as well as the redeemer and benefactor of mankind. Baldur was the healer and protector from evil, and some claimed that Ilkchild communed with him on a moonthly basis.

At the conclusion of the singing, Ilkchild waited for the applause to die down. "Before we announce our contest winner, let us take a moment of silence to reflect on all the sacrifices our people are making for us over on the Main Land of Panygyrus, where Kanarus and Brekka fight in the deserts, where Sur Sceaf and Mendaka sweep through the Mexus Lands, and where Lord Arundel marches for the Omala in the Taxus lands, so that they might bring an end to the Pitter Empire. We have all rejoiced in the news of their triumphs, and mourned those who have been lost. Most certainly more casualties will come. Loved ones will be lost. Not a soul amongst us will go unaffected. And so it is imperative for us to comfort those that grieve, and help those with burdens, encourage those with missing body parts, and all of us must pull together to bring down this horrible evil that has grown so formidable in these last days."

The audience went silent. "Everyone, please, let us be silent for twelve bells, and hold our loved ones in thought, and pray for those who now wield the sword of righteousness in our behalf."

The Godhi gently tapped on the bell as all bowed their heads in silent prayer and gratitude. After the twelve bells were sounded, Ilkchild said, "And now comes our announcement and the conclusion of our masquerade. I am delighted to tell you that this year it will be done very differently; for the seven ladies have chosen not one winner, but two. The works of which, though very different, we shall all be enriched by. May I call forth as our winners the Lady Ka-Luna and the young Prince of the House of Melyngoch, Forsetti."

Forsey grabbed Ka-Luna, and the two held each other by the hands, jumping up and down for joy. They walked up to the apex of the Lyceum, and approached Ilkchild who held a Golden Head Band of Magnolia leaves for each. Every imaginable emotion swelled in Forsetti's breast, but most prevalent was the shear relief of having rendered an accurate account of the battle of Charly's Harbor. He had finally redeemed his father's and his grandmother's names, though he in no way glossed over their flaws.

"Forsetti has rendered a historically accurate account of the Battle of Charly Harbor confirmed and approved by the Roufytrof, in which his father made a noble last stand against an overwhelming host of Pitter legions, and his grandmother fought to her death and stood her ground against the Pitters defending the Wood Palace she so loved."

Russella shouted from the audience in her cracking voice, "Remember Charly's Harbor."

Ilkchild smiled at the Grand Dame and continued. "And Ka-Luna," he paused, "Luna, one of my favorite students, has rendered in writing a most beneficial medical treatise on healing mushrooms for the benefit of all the Syr Folk, which contains the learning of Xelph and the secrets of Zschamillah for the first time ever in print."

Ilkchild took the Golden Magnolia Leaf Crowns and placed them upon each of their heads, and everyone applauded. Luna and Forsetti hugged. Forsetti was overwhelmed with the emotion of the moment, but tried hard to smile.

"Will Yr, Da-Bocia, and Er-Yca come forth." Ilkchild paused as the three made their way to the center point of the lyceum. Once they arrived, Ilkchild handed each one a silver leafed laurel for their heads which they knelt to receive.

"And I think," Ilkchild said, "I shall never live to see another five contestants so determined to bring us light in a very dark world. Please, everyone, give these contestants our deepest appreciation for their noble efforts with cheers and applause."

The crowd roared and applauded. Holding tightly to Luna's hand, Forsey smiled and thought how remarkable every one of the writings were and how difficult it must have been to choose a winner from among them.

Then Ilkchild said, "Whether we speak of god the noun, or god the verb, the Ur-Fyr is the creative urge of this world. These contestants we honor have tapped into this holy creative urge, and I have learned as the Master Govannon taught, 'I will become what I will become.' You, too, shall become what you become, through drinking from the ever-flowing creative force. You will feed the masses with the heavenly manna. All of you will be the sheath of the God-Force."

The audience all said in one voice, "As above, so below."

"Now, I have somewhat more to say and predict." He lifted his family banner out of its base and placed it in a holder on one of the marble columns, so that the rising sea breeze would catch and unfurl it to better view. The banner portrayed the family device of the yellow and black fire-salamander on a white background surrounded by a ring of red flames. The whole banner crackled with mysticism. "The tribes, which the armies of the free folk now go to free, have all been ideologically deflowered. I prophecy, that in not more than four years, you graduates of Moon Door Academy shall be called upon as Skalds to go to Taxus and go to the Firginias, and even to the far stretches of Panygyrus to be Bringers of Light to those who have had their souls and spirits drank out of them. Go! Give them your light to drink from. Make a world of light, liberty, and happiness. Deliver to them this Heavenly Manna. Smite fear and ignorance before you. Spread the wings of tolerance, and fill those lands with more light and joy than they have known in their endarkened state."

The audience roared.

Then Ilkchild held up his hand for quiet. "In fact, I am almost sure; these five shall soon follow the next Fyrd to Godeselle, and be in the next caravan to Panygyrus. For there will be a need of such teachers as these in the Omala, and in Wymouth, and from thence into the Firginias. For the battle with the sword on the War Road is but half the battle. After the defeat of the enemy by sword will come the battle with the powers of the spirit; winning the hearts and minds of those who have sat in darkness for so long. I may proudly proclaim, you five and the graduating class of this academy are ideally suited to teach them."

Ilkchild then signed for the Sisters Three to sing their powerful song as the evening of the Masquerade drew slowly to an end.

Smoke signals rose at mid-day throughout the Arid zone for hundreds of miles, as Jerome led Brekka, Wilona, Syr Elf, and Ruhm on a circuitous route through the rocky mazes of the canyons to the Lair of Kanarus. Colorful walls of rock canyons and dusty red earth under foot wove through the huge boulders with the resinous smell of chaparral giving off its heady fragrance.

Brekka uncorked her leather bottle for a most welcome drink of water. Between the heat and the dust, she was finding herself increasingly thirst driven. Behind her rode her Twelver with the Keeper of the White Buffalo, Talks-As-He-Walks, the Spanix Fyrds, Going Snake and his Dog Soldiers, Fox-On-Fire of the Sioux and his Warriors, White Crow of the Cheyenne and his Warriors. Pulling up the rear was Syr Elf with his fyrds and the Hickoryan Calvary on their Hanoverian and Hackney mounts. Ruhm alone among them rode his blue-grey mount, Spitzer. Chiggibbah tailed with his renegade warriors on their painted ponies. They made for a formidable host, and Brekka felt great comfort and joy with Ruhm there at her side.

As Xarela rode up near her to kiss his wives, she made it a point to later tell him to move his private tent further from her command tent. She was kept awake for the past week on the trail by the moaning from either Pata or Cisne as they made love. It had caused her to burn, and she was sure it tortured the other lady knights as well. How it made her wish she could make such sounds with Ruhm.

As they wound their way through the mysterious maze into Kanarus' lair, scouts watched from their high perches on the stone cliffs. They would not have been perceptible by the untrained eye. Nor would any enemy have made it this far. Coming into the stronghold, row upon row of colorful tipis with runic lettering and exotic animal paintings abounded. Brekka now understood why they called it the camp of the White Apache. For, in most respects, it looked more like an Apache Camp than a Herewardi Camp. The only exception was that the people were almost all Herewardi with red, blond, and brown haired children predominating.

Jerome said, "This is the home of the Kaninchen. We will likely find the Yellow Rabbit, Kanarus at his Long Lodge, just ahead."

As she looked at the Long Lodge with leaping yellow rabbits and eggs painted on one side, and men and women with rabbit heads on the other, children ran in from the brush to stare at them, and wives gathered about their fires. There sat Kanarus mounted on a white steed, with his officers and several chiefs awaiting their arrival.

She knew it had to be him, for he looked like an older version of Ilkchild with the same golden locks that shone like pure sunlight in this brilliant mid-day sun, the reason they called him Yellow Rabbit. Jerome led her up to Kanarus, who dismounted, and walked over to her to assist her off her horse, and smiled.

Kanarus' had fierce green eyes set in one of the most pleasant of faces she had ever seen, framed with his brilliant golden hair; she could see why so many women had told tales of his handsomeness. In fact, it was difficult to not believe it was Ilkchild, so much did his features bear the same imprint. He reached out with a sun-golden hand, and took her hand in the swan grip, "The Lady Brekka, I presume. Os-Frith and Waes Hael."

As she stepped down to the ground she said, "The Lord Kanarus, I presume. Os Frith unto the house of the Yellow Rabbit."

He took her hand and touched it to his forehead, as he bowed from the waist in customary manner.

"My lord, it is my understanding that my armies are to be placed at your disposal. Where would you have us set up camp?"

"You shall camp south of my lodge where there is plenty of water, but you have no need to worry about such things now. My stewards will accommodate your every need, and Jerome will guide you anywhere you wish to go."

A wave of pleasant emotion passed over Kanarus's face like sunshine on a cloudy winter's day. He suddenly turned his attention to Wilona, who was still sitting saddled on her horse. He took her hand with a big smile and helped her down. "My lady Wilona, what a blessed sight you are." Shaking his head back and forth, "What a beautiful sight you are." He repeated himself as if entranced. "An eye could never tire of looking at such beauties."

She jumped into his arms and he swung her around to plant a kiss on her lips.

Wilona was slightly dizzy as she uttered, "I shall have to leave more often to get this kind of treatment. I only hope my kids are all still alive."

They laughed and embraced with the deepest of affection. Brekka shot a brief glance at Ruhm who seemed to be in a trance. She wondered what he was thinking.

A young tow-headed man dressed in green-beetle attire, for such he was now by right of the hair, though only nine winters at most, ran up and grabbed Wilona by the arm. As she turned to see him, he clung tightly to her in a hug.

"Mother, I so missed you!"

"Well, I see you must have earned your spear; for your hair is starting to grow like a man's should." She tousled his fuzzy hair with her fingers. "That tells me something. You've passed into your young blood pack. Are you happy?"

"Yes! I'm a beetle now." The boy looked like a young Kanarus, only fairer of complexion. "Mother, you will never believe what I went through in the Rite of Magical Hair. I was bitten by two rattle snakes, practically eaten by fire ants, and almost roasted by the Skull Worm himself."

With raised eyebrows she said, "Well, it sounds like your father took very good care of you while I was gone, as per my request." She shot a fierce frown at Kanarus who shrugged his shoulders and smiled before she looked over at an old Apache Warrior who winked at her.

"Just a few complications, dear. We'll explain later," Kanarus said, and then turning to Brekka clarified, "This is my Young Prince, Anghrus."

"Pleased to meet you, Young Prince. I see you have passed through the Rite of Long Hair. Soon, you will be a warrior such as your father."

"But I want to be a pirate like Uncle Pyrsyrus someday, and explore the Sea of Aegir. My grandfather says he has heard tell there are undiscovered lands beyond the Sea of Aegir, with strange peoples and strange animals." He paused briefly and placed his index finger and thumb to his chin and stared Brekka square on. "So you are Brekka? I've heard a lot about you. They said you are a pretty red."

"That's right, I'm Brekka. Whatever did you hear?"

"Fa says Pitters are rats. The best way to catch a rat is with a cat. And that Mo Fa said you are the puss purposed to catch the rat."

"Your Mo Fa, Govannon, was a Great Wizard, indeed. I knew him well and spent many days at his forge learning. And if he says there are lands beyond the eastern sea, then you can bet they are there. But I can only hope I am the puss that catches the rat." Again they all laughed.

As Brekka looked around, she saw the chiefs and the officers were gathering to look at the White Buffalo, Ma-Za-Ma. Anghrus followed her gaze, exclaimed in surprise, and then darted off to examine it with some of the other boys already there admiring the beast.

Kanarus looked at her and said, "Shall we?" Brekka followed.

They walked together over to examine Ma-Za-Ma.

"What an extraordinary Beast!" Kanarus said, "Eyes as blue as sapphire."

"He is my jewel." Brekka said with pride, running a hand through the thick white fur atop Ma-Za-Ma's massive woolly head. She tilted her head at the shaman dressed in his white buckskins with weasel tails she said, "This is his Keeper, Talks-As-He-Walks, Talk Walk for short."

"I am glad to meet the keeper of such a fine animal. It must be a great comfort to be his guardian Talk Walk."

"It truly is." The Old Sioux Warrior said. "Sometimes I hear the spirits of my ancestors speaking to me. 'In yet a little while, the red man and the red gods will return so that none shall come to hurt or make afraid. It shall be a day when the great herds are re-born and their thunder heard roaring over the plains again.'"

Kanarus smiled at him, "So mote it be. And it can come none too soon for us all. For the prophecies of the Herewardi say the red man is the proper steward of the earth. The great mother has made them her guardians from the beginning of times."

Kanarus hooked Brekka's arm and led her around to the other side of Ma-Za-Ma to a young man with raven black hair and chiseled features, "Lady Brekka, permit me to introduce Chief Chise of the Chiricahua Apaches."

Brekka was surprised to see how young Chise was, probably on the edge of twenty and three winters, at the most. He dressed in leather breeches and loin cloth, and wore only a leather vest with no under shirt. He stood tall with a leather head band studded with gold solidus over his clean raven black hair. His eyes were a piercing hazel, his skin a golden brown. He had a countenance that radiated both intelligence and wisdom. "It is an honor to meet you, Chief Chise."

"The honor is all mine. Meeting the Buffalo Woman is the honor of a lifetime. Many have been the stories of the fire hair and her power as a warrior. The prophecy of all Red Nations is that the Buffalo Woman will give the red man great dominion over all the land. Already, since I was a child we awaited your coming. Though none of us thought it would be a White Woman. But I have found the race of elves is always full of many surprises. For many generations the Shamans have danced around the fire and prayed for your star to rise. And to think, I live to see this day. You are truly as beautiful as the mountain spirits."

"You do me honor with such recognition, and though white, you must know that I do bear some Sharaka blood as well. I am sure I shall look forward to sojourning here."

Kanarus put one hand over Chise's shoulder and the other over Brekka's, then said, "May we get you and your troops settled in? I wish to invite you to a moot in my long lodge at sunset. We have much to discuss before we attack the Poison lands, and I have a very important guest to introduce." He turned to a very old Apache warrior and said, "This is Red Knife, Anghrus' teacher. He will show you the corral for your buffalo, and then bring you to our Council Fire."

# CHAPTER 12 :
## MEETING THE MOXO

RIDING OVER THE HILLS INTO Nogales in the Mexus Land, Sur Sceaf yearned for some fresh water in the arid desert that surrounded him. His horses and men were weary from the fast ride and searing heat and had only a little water left in their flasks. Ahead of him was a community of small adobe homes scattered all over the rugged rocky hills, with distant dry mountains lining the back ground. As they approached the village cautiously, the scratchy sounds of insect song could be heard in the sun bleached grasses that grew sparsely about the ground. Approximately a mile ahead of them he could make out a group of villagers approaching them wearily.

Sur Sceaf signaled for Khem and rode over to him. "It looks like we meet the Moxo here."

Khem said, "All I can think of its getting out of this hot sun and getting a fresh drink of cool water."

Mendaka laughed and added, "Even the grasshoppers have to hop a mile between meals here. There's not enough grass to feed one horse, let alone our army."

"Well," Sur Sceaf said as he turned in his saddle and waved for Gorge to join him, "You're going to get your wish soon enough. That village ahead has trees, and as for the horses, you'll be surprised at how well they will thrive on this chaparral."

Khem smiled, "I think if we stay in the sun much longer, Sur Sceaf, you'll be as black as me."

"I can get quite dark, that's for sure." He studied the villa ahead. "Depending on what happens here at Nogales, we still have the two Mother Mountain Ranges to cross before entering the Taxus, and just maybe by then you'll have another black brother, Khem." Sur Sceaf laughed.

Gorge reined in his Grulla as he came to a halt, saluted with a hand above his brow and said, "My lord, you summoned."

"Yes." Sur Sceaf said, gazing at the villagers gathering on the road ahead. "I'm going to need you to translate the espagnol for me. Though I often understand, I also often misunderstand just as much."

As Sur Sceaf led out with his weary band of fyrd warriors following him, the villagers parted. One man stood alone, dressed in a white cotton smock and white pants, barefoot, and baked brown as mahogany by the hot climate. The soiled white hat atop his head shaded the suspicious look on his face. The man looked to be in his mid-thirties. He held up his hand, and Sur Sceaf signaled a halt.

The earth baked man said, "Hola."

Sur Sceaf said, "We come in peace." Gorge translated. "We are of the Syr Folk confederation." After Gorge translated, he saw a big smile light the man's face up.

Gorge said, "His name is Juan Pinedo. He said he is a shepherd and the leader of this village; that he has heard of the Syr Folk. And that we are most welcome as enemies to the Pitters; who have only ever robbed them and left them to subsist on less than one can live on. He said they were forced to live off the desert and to suffer many indignities to themselves and their women."

"Ask him," Sur Sceaf said as he studied Juan Pinedo, "has he ever heard of the Moxo."

Sur Sceaf waited for the translation as the man's face took on a deeply concerned visage. Gorge said, "He said the Pitters have pulled out their Rat-Packs and legions. That they talked of being overwhelmed by the great number of Moxo, and that they know the Moxo are coming like an army of ants. But more he does not know."

"Ask him if he has heard where they are located," Sur Sceaf said. He surveyed the adobe homes and corrals full of goats and sheep and none too few burros on the outskirts of the adobe village.

Soon Gorge translated, "They are probably three or four days south of here by now. The Pitters fled them over a week ago. He said he has heard their chief is called Ehira Sache and that there are two other armies traveling; one up the east coast and the other up the west coast of the Mexus corridor. The one on the east is commanded by a chief named Yuku, and the one to the west by Nubube. He says they treat Mexus and Pitters both as enemies."

Sur Sceaf was amazed at the detail of information Juan Pinedo was able to supply, so he inquired, "How is it you came by such detailed information, Juan?"

Gorge put forth the question then translated. "My sister, Rosie Pinedo, was forced to service the Pitter Commander Sanangrar. She escaped his camp during a march north, and overheard much. She said that Ehira speaks espagnol, but prefers his native tongue. They are tribes of red men from the deep lands and woods of the south. And she said Sanangrar operates under the belief that you, the Herewardi chief, have set them on to him."

"Well, that is certainly most valuable information and it explains a hell of a lot as to why Sanangrar is fleeing," Sur Sceaf said. He signaled for his quarter master, and waited as the stocky built, bewhiskered Columba Rogue rode forward. "Richmond, see to it these villagers get some tools, and shears, and a barrel of honey for their troubles."

The Quarter Master said, "I will make it so, my lord." Saluted and rode off to the supply wagons.

Sur Sceaf looked around at the other villagers who lurked back, cowering and wary of these strangers. He could see that many had serious injuries; presumably caused by the rough treatment from the Pitters when they passed through. He saw the seepage of wounds on several of their backs, and knew the pain of the whip himself from former days. "Khem, would you have the Quailor Hospitalers come forth and treat the wounds of these folk."

"I will make it so, my lord," he said, as he twisted the reins and rode off through the dusty desert.

Sur Sceaf then told Gorge to tell Juan Pinedo that they wished to offer him some gifts for his kindness, and that they had medicine to share. Juan looked delighted, bowed his head over and over, and the villagers lost their suspicious looks and raised a chorus of "Gracias! Gracias!"

Sur Sceaf knew his men and animals needed shade and could not make comfortable camp in the open where they now stood, so he asked through the translator, "May we camp in the trees of your village?"

Juan said through the translator, "Si, you may camp in the Cottonwood Grove, backed against the hills, where there is plenty of running water."

"Thank you," Sur Sceaf said, "And may we purchase some goats and sheep from you?"

Gorge translated, "He said that would be good and that he even has a large sow he could butcher for you, should you wish."

Sur Sceaf delighted in the company of Juan Pinedo. His men enjoyed the reprieve from the hot desert march. The Cottonwoods providing them the ample shade they so desparately needed to revive their mounts. Close to when Juan had told them, a fyrd scout reported on the fourth day that the Moxo were marching and now, only a half day off from Nogales.

Sur Sceaf turned to Mendaka, "I want you to take over command of the fyrds Mendaka. I'm going to meet with this Chief Ehira."

Mendaka protested, "My King, best of friends, I do not think it wise that you go to negotiate with these fierce Moxo. We know little of them. Rather I and Gorge should go."

Sur Sceaf frowned, "Not so Mendaka. People here have already testified he is after the Pitters. That places him on our side of the wall. He has an enormous army and a man of such power will want to speak with a King. Such a mighty chief will not take to bantering with underlings and consider my coming in person as a sign of great trust and honor. And should I die, I have faith that you will always be the advocate of my will; for no one knows my heart like you, my Blood Brother."

Mendaka nodded approval, "I see it must be so, my lord."

Sur Sceaf took Khem, Gorge, and the Quailor hospitaler named Doctor Walter Schanks with him. They rode south to offer peace to the Moxo and to ascertain their purposes in the Mexus Lands.

After crossing many miles of desert, they came upon the march of the Moxo. They were indeed an endless company of foot warriors. They stretched in an endless procession to the south, stirring great clouds of dust into the air for as far as the eye could see. The Moxo were dressed for the most part in red. They consisted of tramps and foot soldiers, with very few cavalry for such a large army. Large jaguar banners flapped in the desert wind. Sur Sceaf remained mounted by a large Joshua tree, and he prayed, "Almighty Odhin, God of Many Names, guard me well as I engage these strange people of the southern woods. The ur fyr guides me to do what I must do, but now my heart begins to have doubts whether it is wise at all. Please, strengthen my fortitude to trust in the ur fyr, and do not abandon thy son in his hour of need."

The dust alone from the Moxo army clouded the southern horizon and blotted out the view of how long the army actually stretched behind them. Sur Sceaf could only wonder what motive drove so great a force towards them. Were they to be a new menace to be reckoned with? Were they imperialist robbers, or evil-intentioned in ways only to be imagined?

Sur Sceaf took a deep breath and said, "You ready for this, Khem and Walter?"

Khem said, "It feels somewhat like facing a mountain lion with bare hands. You know they have the power to shred you, but you hope they won't. And by all the black gods, I fear they have the power to do us great harm."

Walter said, out from under his black brimmed hat, "You two are warriors, I am a man of peace. All I can do is hope that the good spark of the lord's spirit is somehow in the hearts of these men too. But I am with thee Khem, it's a very scary scene we are riding into. Maketh me wonder why thou broughtest me, Sur Sceaf?"

"If they have been fighting, they will have wounded amongst them. You, my friend shall show them the wondrous curative powers you possess."

Gorge said, "Here comes their scout right now. Jesus, Joseph, and Mary, I pray they are friendly."

The scout rode on a bay horse. He wore a red sock cap and was clothed in what looked like a heavy red cotton robe. He pulled up to about ten feet in front of them and spoke a tongue no one understood. When he got no response he tried another tongue.

Then Gorge clearly understood, answered him and said, "Si. He speaks espagnol, my lord."

The scout looked fierce, as if he would cut no quarter nor give any bargaining as he spoke. Then Gorge said, "He wants to know why we are here and what we want in the Mexus Lands. Seeing as we are obviously not Mexus, and he has asked if Khem paints himself black. Walter white, and how you came by your hair, the color of wood."

"Tell him," Sur Sceaf said, "we are the Syr Folk, and that we come in peace, and are of many races. Tell him we are also enemies of the Pitters whom they fight."

The scout looked surprised. Then told Gorge to wait while he rode back to speak to his chief.

Khem said, "Did you see the way he stared at us? It was as if he was ready to spit in our faces and cut our throats on the spot."

Walter remarked, "I'm sure they have not seen a white man, though the Pitters are ashen, and me thinketh certainly not a black man before."

Gorge said, "It seemed more than that. More like he did not trust our motives, but was confused at our answer."

Suddenly, the thwacking of horse hooves was heard. Sur Sceaf looked down the road to see ten horsemen approaching at a rapid gait.

"Gentlemen," he said, "this does not bode well at all. If they trusted us they would have invited us to join them, but they are sending ten warriors. If we do not return, Xelph and Mendaka have my instructions to regard the Moxo as enemies on a par with the Pitters."

The Moxo Warriors rode up and surrounded them with spears pointing at them and compelled them to ride back with them. Sur Sceaf began to calculate strengths and weaknesses. He knew he could easily break out of this band, as could Khem, but Gorge and Walter would be bait for crows if they tried. So instead, he went along with their captors, and determined he would seek another solution for his men's sake.

Soon they were taken down the road to a large cluster of warriors. The great chief took leave of the cluster of braves. He was a fierce looking, tall red man, dressed in red, with a head dress that spread out flat above his head like that of a peacocks tail. His face turned, and he eyed them with great suspicion and a fierce demeanor. He motioned and several of his men pulled Sur Sceaf and his men down from their horses, took their weapons, and held them by the arms to bring them before the chief. They were handled roughly and forced to the ground with a knock of the spears on the back of their knees as they knelt before the chief in forced submission.

The chief had a heavy red robe and carried an ornate spiraling staff. On his right breast was an embroidered Jaguar. The leader had an expression of cruel satisfaction such as a cat has when it has secured its prey firmly in its claws. Sur Sceaf was loath to think that those brooding eyes showed no signs of mercy or acceptance, and that he and his men might end up at best in bondage. The Chief spoke, and Gorge translated. "Who is your leader?"

Gorge pointed to Sur Sceaf with his head and said, "He is. This is the High Lord, Sur Sceaf, King of Kings."

"And I am Chief Ehira. What manner of man are you then?" Ehira asked, his sun baked face looking as tough as saddle leather, and his stern expression reflecting both a mix of contempt and irritation. Yet his eyes still betrayed a hint of curiosity. But his Moxo warriors all showed tightened senses and readiness to do harm, like dogs at bay waiting for their master's final signal to kill.

Sur Sceaf thought *this is a grim Pow Wow if ever I've seen.* Then he spoke while Gorge translated.

"I am Sur Sceaf, the High Lord of the Syr Folk, and High King of the Herewardi."

Ehira got a stern look on his face then went silent while several of his counselors discussed among themselves in their strange tongue. Ehira's face had a visually detectable change come over it when he heard Gorge say Herewardi. The stern face took on a warm glow and he broke into a broad, approving smile, revealing perfectly white teeth. The whole expression changed from the former scowl to a friendly demeanor in less than the twinkling of an eye. "The Syr Folk I have not heard of, but I have heard of these Herewardi. My father told me of the goodness of the White Lords years ago, and how he had met one that taught him much goodness of government. It has been told how you are the enemy of the Pitters, and that they hate no one as much as you. Obviously not for who you are, but for who you will become. Their death! And to think you are the High King, come to see me in person, please let me show you the hospitality we are capable of, and forgive us our roughness. We did not know who you were, nor that kings took such humble paths in these parts, but you must still be proven."

Immediately his lieutenants changed their countenances and showed friendly faces. With one twist of Ehira's hand upward, his guards released Sur Sceaf and his men, and they stood to their feet. The feeling of acceptance was now palpably clear.

Sur Sceaf could see the attitude shift throughout the Moxo ranks, and laughter spread through the ranks as their body language, the tenseness, and all the expressions of hostility ceased. Ehira led Sur Sceaf and his men back to his tent near a large water hole in the desert. The tent was a red canvas tent that allowed for approximately twenty men to sit and stand comfortably. At one end the earth had been freshly heaved up and pounded into a mound or platform big enough for five or six men to sit comfortably on. Ehira motioned for them to sit with him on the platform on some decorated mats, while many of his under chiefs sat below them. He clapped his hands and servants brought in some freshly cooked hot chicken with beans, and cooked cactus slabs dressed with pablano peppers like the ones Surrey's Guatemalan friends often proffered him at feasts.

Ehira said, "I have seen the white skin among the Mexus, but this black man with you," pointing to Khem, "is he truly black or does he paint himself so?"

Khem answered through Gorge, "I am truly black, and there are many more of us to the far southeast."

Ehira had an expression of amazement on his face as Gorge translated.

Sur Sceaf said, "And there are green and blue men on the island I came from."

Ehira responded through the interpreter. "There are strange things in this world. We should not have discovered so many had the Pitters not come upon us with their slave trains led by the filthy Mexus traders. They ravaged our outer settlements. I am sure the Pitters had no idea they grabbed the tail of the jaguar, for they took three of my daughters whom I hold dear to my heart." He turned his head to one side and spat. "We followed the slavers to the Mexus, then sent our armies to conquer the Mexus Lands, but have never come upon the stolen daughters of our land, and we have found no one that can tell us their whereabouts. They just point to the north and say they go that way."

"I am very sure," Sur Sceaf said, "I can take you to where your daughters have been taken. It is to an underground city called the Citadel, ruled over by an evil Queen named Gloomullah."

"And are our daughters there made to be whores?" Ehira asked.

"No, that is not likely, though it is possible," Sur Sceaf said, "Usually, they are used for their bodily secretions. The blood of menses is harvested from them to make the people of the Citadel younger."

Gorge translated, and Ehira's eyes grew as big as his face, and his men wrinkled their faces with disgust.

"This thing you tell me is beyond my hearing." Ehira said, as his counselors mumbled what appeared to be disbelief.

"It was at first hard for us to believe too, but nothing is too dark or evil for the Poisoned Lands. Nothing is beneath the blood swollen queen that reigns there in the Underworld like some monster black widow spider."

"And these Poisoned lands, how far are they from here?" Ehira leaned over his legs to hear Gorge give answer.

Gorge said, "Likely two to three weeks from Nogales, the village just to the north of here."

"You will lead us there?" Ehira said, placing an arm on Sur Sceaf.

Sur Sceaf said, "I command many armies, and we follow a master plan given to us by our priests, the Godhi of the Roufytrof. Our plan is to destroy the citadel, free its captives, and safely deliver them to the people of the mountains called the Presters. But we can sort your daughters out and have them brought to you in the Taxus where we are scheduled to rendezvous with our other armies."

Ehira squirmed uneasily on his haunches, "Why not we go get them right away?"

"Such an endeavor would ruin our coordinated attacks and plans. It will be better for your daughters if you allow us to extract them from the Under World of the Growlings and bring them to you."

"I do not know. This does not set well with me. I must prove you before I can trust you. Though I like you, you will understand, my daughters are everything to me."

"Prove me, then. Here I stand."

"If what you say is all true, then go intercept the fleeing legions who flee from Yuku's armies." He pointed to his lieutenant on the right. "Yuku will ride out with you. Slay the Pitter legions, and return to me at Nogales where Nubube's armies will meet us in two weeks' time." He pointed to the lieutenant on his left. "If you do this, it will show me you are as engaged in this fight as I am, and I shall join my forces to yours as soon as our daughters are returned safely to us. Yes, we shall lend our forces into battling these Pitters. They have erred greatly in taking my cubs. For as my father, Black Jaguar taught, 'The jaguar must ruthlessly crush any who harm her cubs, hunt them down, and eat their livers out'."

Sur Sceaf smiled, grateful that Ehira was going to lend his strength. Such an enormous army would be of untold value, even if it did slow him down some. He tore a piece of chicken off in his teeth and ate a pablano with it, savoring the warmth and flavor. At the same time he started reconfiguring his plans for marches through the south lands.

Picking up a cactus slab Ehira placed it on his mat and said, "For my friends, I have a gift." He clapped his hands and some beautiful Mexus girls were led in. "See they will dance for us and then you may pleasure yourself with them. Look upon them and feast. Have you ever seen such beauty? Are they not as pretty as the desert flowers that bloom here about?"

Sur Sceaf smiled as Gorge translated. "We would be very pleased to see the girls dance, but I have seven wives and may not be untrue to them."

Ehira said, "What, you have seven wives? Then why not pleasure yourself with these Mexus girls. Surely, such a stud must have endless needs."

Sur Sceaf cleared his throat, noted how curious the counselors were, as they all leaned in to hear Gorge explain. "I am bound by sacred and ancient law to not have sexual relations with any woman except those whom I am legally and lawfully wed to."

"A strange practice," Ehira said, "I have but one wife, and still take my pleasure where I will. These are just Mexus Mestizas," Gorge's eyes grew big as he translated, "mere mutts. They have no kingdom. They have no chief. No one will know or care what happens to them."

"Thank you, but no, my friend." Sur Sceaf said. "We have many Mexus who are our friends, and it would be a wrong to them as well if we despoiled their sisters."

Ehira threw his head back in shock. "What! You are friends with the Mexus. They were in league with the Pitters."

Sur Sceaf laid down the cactus slab he had just taken a bite out of, swallowed hard and said, "They were compelled and forced to fight for the Pitters. It was not their natural inclination or choice to do so. We treat the Mexus we capture as free people, and they have served us well against the Pitters. I think you will find they are nothing like the Pitters."

"A very queer matter," Ehira said. "Black Jaguar told me the Herewardi were filled with mercy. Then you must think I should free the cities of the Mexus Lands back to them, is that it?"

"We Syr Folk are a powerful alliance of many tribes and peoples." Sur Sceaf said, "We have found it is always better to give each tribe their own say and sovereignty over their own affairs, and not to hold any people in subjugation, but to govern all by fair laws, treaties, agreements, and an invitation to join our confederation of nations."

Ehira glanced over at his counselors who were busy digesting what Sur Sceaf had said. The one called Nubube seemed opposed, and the one called Yuku was making an argument for treating the Mexus better. Ehira's headdress swept the air, and he looked back again at Sur Sceaf. "But then how would we feed our vast armies and satisfy our men with ample women? Such a practice would turn my men queer on me." Ehira made a motion with his hand for the dancing maidens to leave the tent.

Nubube put his spear in front of them, then Ehira gave him a frown and he let them pass.

Sur Sceaf shot a smile at Gorge. Gorge was the kind who favored male sexual partners, and Sur Sceaf pondered the possible ramifications of what he was being asked. "I realize the way you have been doing business in Mexus is part of something that has worked very well for you. I am merely saying that it is the way of the Syr Folk to afford all men the same rights that we enjoy. If you join with us we can supply your armies. Otherwise this army you have will have to forage all the way back to your homelands. We have vast stockpiles and supply lines at our disposal which many nations have contributed to. For all armies must ultimately go on their stomachs."

"Would you even give the Pitters these rights?" Ehira said as he nudged Gorge with his hand for a swift answer while starring squarely on at Sur Sceaf.

"Were it possible." Sur Sceaf said, watching Ehira's eyes grow big. "But it is not possible. For the Pitters are not fully human."

"What do you mean?" Ehira said, his counselors discussing back and forth what they were hearing.

"The Pitters had their blood code altered hundreds of years ago. They are not fully human, but have the seed code of rats and wolves placed in them. This has supplanted their humanity. They cannot even have fertile offspring if they mate with us. Have you not noticed their prominent front teeth?"

"Impossible," Ehira said as he looked at his counselors and they seemed to think such was also not in the realm of possibility. "How can a rat mate with a human or a wolf? What sort of witchcraft could do such?"

Sur Sceaf said, "In the long dark past there lived a people called the Amerikans. They possessed very dark magic and had the power to alter the seed codes of man, animal, and plant. They could even poison the earth. Some works they did were good, but some were darkly sinister. They attempted to create a police force by making the Pitters, but when the gods caused the earth changes, the Pitters emerged as the dominant race on the lands northward. For over five hundred years my people have fought to set the balance right again by destroying the Pitters."

"Our elders have spoken of such dark times. Times in which they said the other nations were controlled with water. But not our people! We owned our water!" Ehira declared emphatically. "These Pitters are like those Water Controllers of long ago. They want control of all of our resources. You have my word, if you can defeat the legions of Grindlseath, and I get my daughters back we will assist you, Sur Sceaf of the Herewardi. What you see here is but a third part of my armies. I have two more armies besides this one and we do not want rat-people ever running into our land again. No matter how far away they dwell."

Sur Sceaf said a silent prayer of gratitude to Odhin the All Father, smiled, and resumed eating as Ehira and his counselors discussed everything they had heard. Though he did not understand much of what they were saying, he could see they were very animated in their expressions.

Within four days of Sur Sceaf's meeting with Ehira, Mendaka followed him into battle against the evil Pitter Commissar Che Grindlseath. He knew it was not in the plan of the War Road, but to win the alliance of Ehira, it would be a necessary side show. Mendaka had spent many campaigns with Sur Sceaf. In all his experience, Sur Sceaf had the prowess of a lion, the cunning of a fox, the dogged persistence of a mule, and above all the constant and abiding love of his people. He knew the Moxo would come to admire him for his position, his wealth and power, and his adeptness at warfare. But they could not know the goodness of Sur Sceaf's heart, the nobility of his spirit, nor his persistence in pursuing a righteous world that ensured the dignity and welfare of everyone under a government that guaranteed all tolerance and sovereignty. For inside this man, Mendaka believed was the spirit of a god. To him, Sur Sceaf was a Manitou trapped in a human body and dearer than any brother could be.

The insect voices of the night drowned out the stealth of Sur Sceaf's fyrds as they circled the encampment of Che Grindlseath in the early pre-dawn hours. Mendaka could hear Sur Sceaf breathing next to him, and felt the sage brush in front of him as the two waited for the proper moment to fall upon the enemy. As false dawn began, Mendaka looked over at Sur Sceaf, his thick brown hair with streaks of white, braided as the Herewardi do. His skin, though white, covered the facial features of a Red Man. His beard, always well-trimmed and neat, reflected his attention to cleanliness.

Most of all, Mendaka had always admired how he had a way with women, children, horses, and sheep. Indeed he even had the same effect on warriors. Now, Sur Sceaf stood behind the sage with him. He held his hands on his hips and elbows pointing back. Mendaka had come to know it was the sign Sur Sceaf was ready for action, and all hell was soon to break loose. He looked down and saw the signet ring of the Herewardi, which designated him as the anointed and chosen of the Roufytrof and watched as Sur Sceaf's hand tightened around his sword. He saw the fyrds and dog soldiers all poised for the attack on the enemy's camp, and he thanked the Manitou's he stood at the side of his dearest friend.

Sur Sceaf commanded his fyrd commanders, Asser, Geat, and Heremod to swing around from the rear of the Pitters. Sur Sceaf slowly drew his sword and raised his arm to the sky. "In the name of the gods that love us, Lay on, men! Lay on!"

The Herewardi and Sharaka raised their rebel cries and trilled their tongues. Mendaka felt his heart pound out a war beat. Together they fell upon the camp of Grindlseath. With a mighty charge, Mendaka felt his legs moving faster than his body, as together he laid down one guard and Sur Sceaf another. Then with his battle axe he split open the command tent of Grindlseath. He and Sur Sceaf entered together. The commissar rose from his bed and shouted in alarm, "Hell's devil's! Where in the hell..."

Mendaka split the skull of one of the lieutenants and swung around with a whirl to smash the jaw of the second lieutenant. Sur Sceaf had already grabbed the commissar savagely and slit his throat with his broad sword. Then, while hurling Grindlseath to the ground gasping through the bloody slit that ran the length of his throat, Sur Sceaf ducked and plunged his blade into a large assailant coming from the corner of the tent; The commissar's personal body guard. In the fray the lantern had been knocked from its stand, but everyone in the tent was dead or in death throes. Together Sur Sceaf and Mendaka darted out of the tent and re-joined the fyrds. Several tents were now burning from fiery arrows. Blood stained ground showed the work of the fyrds through the dancing red flames that engulfed the chaotic camp. The eyes of the Pitters gleamed with a reflection unseen in human eyes, making the enemy easy to spot in the eerie light. Both men had the stealth and easy movements of stalking panthers, and together cut awakening Pitters down, careful to cover each other in their advances.

They were forced to grope their way through the eerie twilight, looking for the reflection of those beady inhuman eyes and slashing at rustling sounds or the shadowy vignettes of Pitters. The spirit of war and berserker rage overtook them as they, bloody-handed, grabbed a group of cowled priests by their robes and hacked their heads open one by one. In the dim light the yellow teeth and beast-eyed Pitter rats let out their snarls and curses and sought to stab at them, only to be parried and dealt their death blows.

Mendaka strained his eyes to catch any telltale movement from the Pitters. All too soon the quiet ended with a fresh wave of legionnaires charging in. A huge form charged for Sur Sceaf like some dark ghost expelled from a grave. The great bulk of a Pitter rose up with little warning and was about to bring his sword down over the head of Sur Sceaf when Mendaka hurled his battle axe, splitting the sullen giant's spine and freezing any further motion. The creature fell as he fell like a great timber right behind Sur Sceaf.

As he wrenched the battle axe from the monster's back, Sur Sceaf turned and nodded his approval, and together the two advanced once again against the legionnaires. Mendaka came upon a group of priests whose eyes glimmered like the eyes of snakes ready to strike. Weird fetishes of scalps and ears decorated their necks in the twilight, and their yellow teeth were gnashing out curses. "Sheep-eating bastards," their leader said. His narrow hog-like eyes blinked repeatedly, "We'll have your ears for this."

Minutes flew by, and the priests were closing in on Surrey and Dak when both went into their cold, calculating, skillful thrusts; soon to be joined by their Wolf Packs in a cyclone of blades.

Sur Sceaf plunged his blade into the hog-eyed priest who grinned savagely and mockingly, not knowing the blade had entered him. His breath swiftly hissed out of him and his grinning turned to an ugly snarl. The priest reeled back, knocking the rest of his men off balance. Mendaka and the Wolf Pack finished the last of the resistance off, while the fyrd dispensed any Pitter that moved. In the calm that followed, they set to gathering up the camp whores and freeing the captive laborers.

Mendaka looked over at Sur Sceaf. The two of them were still catching their breath, covered in blood from head to toe, and utterly exhausted. Mendaka let out a loud laugh as he sucked in air. "Sur Sceaf, this gets harder and harder every year."

Sur Sceaf lifted up his head, "We're getting too old, Mendaka. It gets harder every moonth." He took a moment to catch his breath. "The truth be said, I would have retired long ago if I didn't have old Crooked Jack to remind me that he was at least five years older than you and I when he came to his end in battle."

Mendaka laughed, "Old Crooked Jack! What a hell of a warrior he was. God, I miss him." Mendaka couldn't refrain from laughing.

"Alright," Sur Sceaf said, still trying to catch his breath, "What's so damned funny."

"Yellow Horse!" Mendaka said through his laughs.

"What about him?"

"I just thought about the time those Mexus Merchants brought the red dye to the Lady Paloma under escort of Crooked Jack. Yellow Horse was there when Paloma asked what the red dye was."

"You mean Cochineal?" Sur Sceaf inquired.

"Yes, but Yellow Horse answered her with a riddle. He said, 'Lady Paloma, what's first white and then red. It's often found in a bed and there's not a lady in the land that wouldn't gladly take it in her hand.'" Mendaka could not refrain from laughing. "Then Crooked Jack grabbed Yellow Horse by the neck to throttle him while Lady Paloma said, 'Jack, stop, He's a Jester. You will incur the wrath of the law if you touch him.' Jack released the Joker and Yellow Horse said, 'The answer is Cochineal.'"

Sur Sceaf laughed. Then with a serious longing look said, "By the God's I miss Paloma's company."

"How about Yellow Horse's?"

"Yes, I miss that damned crazy fool, and I still grieve the loss of Crooked Jack like my right arm."

"Well, what could be better than a rest and a laugh?" Then in a more serious vein, he asked, "What now my lord?"

"We'll secure the supplies, take their horses for food, prepare the captives for our march into the Taxus, and field dress our wounded while we wait for Nubube and Ehira to join us at the rendezvous point. Yuku will report our victory to them."

Mendaka said, "I don't see how he cannot be impressed with your swift victory."

"He will be impressed, but I only hope he is a man of his word. Once Kanarus and Brekka have secured the Citadel, we should be able to fulfill the second half of our agreement and deliver his daughters safely into his charge. His men won't even have to fight. The mere sight of their numbers will strike such a terror in the Pitter heart, it will force them to call in their far flung Zongas."

"We could sure use the help of the Moxo in destroying the bamboo plantations though." Mendaka smiled wide, "Who would have ever thought we'd secure additional armies in this waste howling wilderness? I tell you, Sur Sceaf, the gods and thunder beings favor you."

# CHAPTER 13 :

## YISKA

**T**HE FIRE IN THE KITCHEN fireplace was crackling hot. Using hot pads, Paloma removed her raisin bread, baked in a cloche and carefully placed it on a trivet on the table around which all her bride-sisters sat. Some were darning, others placing bacon on the griddle while discussing the coming trek to the Apache lands, which had been long planned.

Paloma glanced toward the door, wondering as she sliced the hot bread why the Lady Redith had not yet appeared. She was usually the first down for the prayer circle and breakfast. As Paloma buttered the slices, Milkchild laid a sheet of paper on the table. "Eryfae got me one of Hoth's kat sheets last night. I've read it and wanted to comment on it with all the bride-sisters."

Paloma shot an irritated glance at the newspaper. "More slanderous back-biting, you mean; and so early in the morning, Milkchild, must we?"

Milkchild raised her eyebrows. "With Sur Sceaf and Ary gone, Hoth has no one else to rail upon besides you, Queen Zschamillah, and his all-time favorite whipping boy, Ilkchild. Or 'the Crippled Stallion,' as Hoth always calls him. But, this time, he's written something that has me greatly concerned." She leaned over, ran a finger halfway down the printed page before she began reading, "'The Queen Paloma, the Queen Zschamillah, and all the great ladies of the isle are due to depart any day now for the arid zone.' I ask you, how did he know that?"

Paloma was disgusted. "There are enough loose tongues in these parts to sink the whole damned isle, but the only hole in the boat I see is Hoth's big mouth. The Pitters don't need spies when they have Hoth revealing our nakedness to everyone. By the gods, I wish we had a newspaper that would promote and inspire the noblest in us all instead of bantering over Hoth's filth."

Faechild's eyes flashed. "Muck-raking makes for more exciting reading. Look how fast it sells out."

Paloma heaved a sigh, "The real problem is the Roufytrof has defined his paper as part of 'Flyting,' the contest of quarreling, and therefore legal. But no one is wounding Hoth back with words. It's a one edged sword. He just wants to yelp about wicked things and call us all a brood of serpents. I'm still fuming over what he said about Brekka being a Dark Witch and having incest with her brother. Hoth is just a witless drunk, who has never taken up a sword in behalf of his people, but instead enjoys throwing fiery darts and lies at all that do. Don't you think it's time we start showing him our fangs. I only wish we had Yellow Horse here. The Master Jester would give Hoth a tongue lashing that would drive him to the utmost bounds of the Ea-Urth." Paloma paused, and then with a devilish smile added, "Why don't we start a paper of our own?"

Taneshewa looked intrigued. "How would we get stories?"

"That wouldn't be hard to figure out," Paloma said, passing around the plates of bread. "Mendaho can write very well. She's brilliant, colorful, and ten times the wit of that shrunken larva of a man, Hoth."

Taneshewa frowned. "She'd be perfect. But Meny and Tree Song are planning on traveling with us to see their husbands."

Paloma shook her head. "I hate that Ilkchild has to endure the fire of this swine-dog's breath over and over, but like the Fire-King he is, he will have one more fire to pass through unscathed."

"I wouldn't worry about the Salamander King," Swan Hilde said, "he's got his Skaldic Academy on this one, and I've been hearing the students are now fiercely eating Hoth alive. Heard they have a paper of their own, called 'Revealed by Moonlight.' I've requested a copy of it. And in it, they have addressed and discredited every one of Hoth's low blows. Would you believe, its editor is Forsetti, the Son of Melyngoch?"

"A good lamb from a flawed ewe," Paloma said, and then froze in thought for a moment. "Swan Hilde, do you think we could get someone in Godeselle to print the 'Revealed by Moonlight' here?"

Lana, who had remained silent working out a lesson plan for the grandchildren, said, "The Quailor despise Hoth's kat sheet. He has so maligned their way of life. I could probably get someone in the downs or eweward to copy it for Godeselle before we leave for the Apache Lands."

"Make it so, Lana," Paloma charged. After another glance at the empty doorway, she asked in a voice filled with concern, "Should I be concerned that the Lady Redith has not come in for prayer or breakfast yet?"

"She is growing very old, and the stress of us all leaving has worried her much." Milkchild leaped up and ran to the hearth. "Oh, my goodness, I almost burned the pancakes."

Lana bolted from the table. "I'll check on Redith. It's not like her to ever be late, she was moving very slow yester eve."

Taneshewa looked up from the baby blanket she was sewing to say, "This Hoth is like the Herewardi version of Fromer Muckenschnabel. I only wish there was a far off land we could send all such people to."

Paloma smiled. "It's called 'Here,' Ahy. Because only here would anybody tolerate the noble and the ignoble and extend the same rights to both."

"I'm going to pull off the bacon; it's taking Lana way too long." Shining Moon said, "By the time Lana and Redith get here it'll be time to wake the children."

"Go right ahead," Paloma agreed before catching sight of Lana's sad face coming through the door.

"She's gone," Lana whispered, tears running down her cheeks. "Our dear Redith has passed through the veil."

The bride sisters took a silent dirge behind Lana and walked up to Redith's room where they wept. Paloma straightened out Redith's arms, smoothed her white hair and removed Redith's favorite silk gown from the armoire. The room filled with grief as the other Bride-Sisters helped ready the elderly lady for her funeral. Lana passed out handkerchiefs and they all made free use of them.

Paloma could only say her thought aloud, "What will Sur Sceaf do when he gets this news? He loved her so much and all of our souls were so inseparably knit to hers. It is a sad day in the land. Mayhap the gods knew her frail body would never survive the trek to the Taxus, and she so wanted to go with us. Now, the sweet old thing is going to go with us in spirit."

High in the Apache Mountains the coyotes sent out their cries. Brekka took a deep breath of desert air. As she entered Kanarus' lodge, all the leadership stood up and waited for her to take her seat on the blankets around a large central fire of fragrant burning pine wood. All along the lodge poles ran duel serpent engravings with the mark of Howrus carved and painted at the top of each one. Along the sides of the lodge ran rabbits painted on hides in various poses of running, jumping, and standing. Behind Kanarus were two banners featuring a man's body with a yellow rabbit's head springing over a crescent moon, the flag of the Kaninchens. Before him, candle lanterns illuminated several open maps.

"Please, Lady Brekka, sit here to my right with me," Kanarus motioned. "Permit me to introduce you to our special guest."

As Brekka settled crossed-legged on a cow hide, she smiled at the exquisitely beautiful, dark-haired maiden sitting on a woven blanket across from them. The lady wore a buckskin dress with beaded Thunder Beings sending forth their lightning bolts from their hands.

Kanarus smiled. "This is Yiska of the Navajo, or as they say, the Diney Tribe."

Brekka nodded her head. The maiden was no more than sixteen or seventeen winters and seemed of an unusually demure nature, both sober and quiet. But to be included as an honored guest in this august meeting meant she was of some greater importance than Brekka was capable of ascertaining.

As though reading her mind, Kanarus explained, "Yiska comes to us as a gift from the gods. Not only is she one of the very few survivors of the Poisoned lands, but she was also the one Gloomullah groomed to be the next Under Queen to replace Yggep. She has been to the very core of their realm, was Gloomullah's personal spokeswoman, and is here to help us tear down the Dark Queen from her throne in the Under World of the Citadel."

"This is indeed good news," Brekka said with widened eyes. "Does that mean she can lead us into the queen's chamber beneath the earth?"

"Precisely," Kanarus exclaimed, his eyes filled with excitement, "I have studied this problem for a long time. To begin with we will require a very large army to accomplish our ends." He smiled at Brekka. "Your armies shall serve that purpose. We shall have to pass through the Creep Zone of the Poisoned lands." Kanarus pointed to the map in front of them with a Juniper Wand. "And we have to do it as swiftly as possible so that we spend, at most, one night there before we breach the Citadel. I do not believe we could endure much more than that. The creeps and snucky punks come in the dark of the night. The creeps are the tiniest of the devils. They're the size of a squirrel, and the snucky punks about the size of a cat, but the nihtgangers are easily the size of a man. The nihtgangers take longer than the creeps to locate you, but they are far more dangerous. We don't want to have to deal with them if it can be helped. I hear they are absolutely impervious to pain." He glanced at Yiska, eyebrows raised in a question.

"This is what I have been told as well."

Brekka stared into the candle lantern, its honey scent filling the air and tried to imagine what these creatures must look like. *The nihtgangers can't be any worse than a grass beast and squirrels and cats can be kicked and clubbed easy enough.* "How would you propose we get past these trolls?"

"We must enter through Hell's Gate." Kanarus pointed to the X's at the north on the map. "That is so that the growlings will not suspect we are even coming. If we had chosen the south gate, their scouts would know of our arrival, and they would thwart any entry we attempted. We have just driven the Skull Worm through Hell's Gate and I know it took them more than two days to pass through at the speed they were moving. I am counting on them suffering much from the afflictions of the creep attacks. Perhaps enough we can overcome them in their weakened state."

Brekka nodded. "I can see where that will be advantageous to us." She noticed Yiska had not stopped staring at her since she entered the lodge; so uncustomary of the Navajos she had ever known.

Kanarus turned to an ancient looking Apache Shaman. "Red Knife, perhaps you should speak to this."

Red Knife's voice had a deep, raspy tone. "You bet! It be our advantage. Not only weaken legions, but they kill many thousands of creeps. Make way safer for us. That why we strike now, while legions weak with sickness and nihtgangers not find us."

The distinctive voice of Red Knife leapt in her memory, as did the broken English. It came to her that he had visited her Father with Kanarus when she lived on the isle. She remembered how much Govannon cherished his friendship. Brekka studied the map, looked back up at Red Knife and asked, "How do you mean weak?"

"I talk to Lone Dog. Him twice pass through Poison Land. Any bite. Any scratch from creep give festering wound. Much pain. Take two weeks to get well. Then still very sick. Sometimes death come."

Her head jolted back in surprise. "Did you say Lone Dog?" Brekka was hardly able to contain her shock. "From the Klamath Tribe?"

"That be him. Him come to aid Kanarus. Been great scout for twenty winters now."

Brekka searched her memory. *She was almost certain Lone Dog had been one of the three ruffians her father told her had tried to extort his commission out of him. And that he had fought along side the evil Standing Bull. But then hearts can change.*

Brekka shot out her next question. "However did Yiska make it out alive then?"

Red Knife looked out of his dark eyes that betrayed the cunning of a coyote, "She steal horse from Pitter. How do you say it in English?" He looked to Kanarus and spoke in the Ndee Tongue. Kanarus whispered back to him and he smiled then said, "She ride his heart out. Make it out in one day time. Then take long while to find us. Horse die. She eat it. Make way to Apache Land crossing desert, eating lizard, bugs, and bats."

Yiska smiled at Brekka and said, "I also stole some of the repellant the Grodor use to move about unmolested by the creeps--or should I say, at least, they won't eat you. No good for the scratches and bites though." She rolled a sleeve up to show several crisscrossing scars.

"Alright," Brekka said, "so it will take us a day and a night to get into the area where the growling compound and slave camps all are. Once there, what do we do? I've heard they are walled high."

Red Knife grunted. "That big problem, Lone Dog say. Growling wall have biting rope. Kill many men. Not able to cross over wall. Must go through or under."

Kanarus explained, "We will take the black explosive powder we confiscated from the Pitters, and with it blast down their walls. Our armies will then wage war on the Skull Worm, his Legions, and the

Growlings. That is where you, my cousin, shall come in and perform a miracle for us."

"A miracle!" Brekka said, her eyes widening for effect.

"Precisely!" Kanarus' penetrating green eyes searched her face. Wilona smiled at her. Kanarus continued, "It is a shot in the dark, but that is how I've operated all these years. And nine out of ten times the shot in the dark is the one that pays off."

"Alright, what is this miracle I am to perform?" She shot a glance at Yiska who continued to stare at her as if she was weighing possibilities.

"When we get to the growling citadel, we shall engage the Pitters and Growlings in total warfare. All of our troops must take an oath to stand until victory or death overtakes us. No one will be allowed to go with us through Hell's Gate who is not absolutely committed to total victory at any cost. Lone Dog will lead us in."

"Does this oath include me?"

"You know it does."

"Perhaps you could be a little clearer as to what miracle I am to perform?"

"Yiska tells us she knows how to get into the Queen Gloomullah Elli Termis' Den where you shall slay the Harridan, while we are distracting their forces above ground."

"Perhaps, Yiska could explain to me in detail how I am to do this?"

"Most certainly." Kanarus lifted his eyebrows, smiled pleasantly and said, "Yiska, would you explain."

The demure Diney woman brightened, "My lady, the growlings have no great fondness for the queen. They know they are no more than a slave race to her, but serve due to their dependence on her medications. Their only loyalty to her is a chemical one. For she also controls everyone with what she calls 'Noogs,' which are medicines that make you crave them incessantly after taking them for a while. When I was her Under-Queen, I would cheek them as the Grodor passed them out to me and then save them to trade for favors from the growlings. Now, in addition to the Noogs, the growlings require a special medicine to keep them from aging rapidly. They are the children of the people who were once exposed to the poison that fell upon the Poisoned Lands in ages long forgotten. Poisons the corporations of the Amerikan Empire concocted to kill nine tenths of the inhabitants of the Ea-Urth. Since that time, which they were not supposed to survive, they are all born dying and covered with blisters and carbuncles on their skin. That's where the virgins come in."

"Yes," Brekka said, "what is all this fuss over virgins?"

"You see, the growlings procure the virgins because the virgin secretions contain more of the essence of the medicine they make from it, and the virgins are free and clear of any diseases. They get the virgins from the Pitters, and then condition them to follow orders by use of the Noogs, after which the growlings deliver them over to the race of eunuchs who live under the earth. They are called the grodor; pudgy little bald men who serve only the queen and her needs. They live in the Under World with her, like termites."

"How are the Grodor eunuchs? Does she castrate them?" Brekka inquired.

"Not with blades," Yiska said, "but again with medicines. The eunuchs are made with her medicines."

Brekka asked, "And the virgins? What medicines are made with their secretions?"

"It is from virginal secretions the medicines for staying young are made. Keeps the Hags, the Growlings, and the Grodor long lived. Then, when she is through with using the secretions from the virgins, usually when they are around the age of twenty-two winters, she selects the most beautiful of them and magically puts the seed of man in their wombs so that they conceive. The choicest of the male children thus begotten are selected and raised to be her paramours, provided they have good looks and are above average intelligence."

Brekka inquired, "And the males who are found lacking in beauty, what becomes of them?"

"She has Grodor medicine doctors take the child and feed it medicine that makes them turn into eunuchs whom she and the other Grodor groom as the servant race. If there is an excess of them, she simply sells them to the Pitters for laborers."

"But surely they have female babies as well?"

Yiska's eyes darkened. "No, they don't. She can even control their sex."

"What dark, dark magic could do such?"

"There is a greater darkness. Some of the virgins have strange practices performed on them by her doctors. They alter the child while it is still nestled in the womb. You will remember in your history the horrors reported about the Bitch Yggep at Brimestone."

"Yes, how she created creeps, snucky punks, and other monsters, and tortured children in her labor camps with medical experiments. Luckily, she found a fitting end in our land as crow-bait. Had her bowels woven by the very Pitters she served. But tell me, what did the Harridan do with the women who bore the altered children?"

"She trades them to the Pitters to be used for slaves and camp whores."

"Despicable and heartless," Brekka said, "Justice will surely find her at the tip of Mother Freya's blade."

"Two of them were my sisters. My father was a Galani, what we Diney call a drunkard and a wanderer. He left us living far out in the wilds, too exposed to the Pitter legions that often passed through. We were soon captured in the spider's web. Gloomullah cared nothing for those with less power than herself. I found her to be as soulless as the Pitters, but my Goddess, Hastseoltoi, allowed me to come into her favor, as she also chose you, so that together you and I may be her war arrows."

Brekka bit her lip and then said, "But you mentioned paramours being reared from babies. Wouldn't they be too young for her?"

"She seems to live forever," Yiska declared, "and even though she continues to age she stretches the natural bounds of it and has medicines that keep her and her hags burning for young lovers. So she has them groomed for being in her harem of male paramours. The paramours live a well-cared for life where they are pampered, privileged, and educated, and then when they are old enough to no longer suit her fancy she has them sold to the Pitters as slaves. They usually don't last for long under the Pitter lash. But she uses the seed of her favorite paramours to make a new crop of paramours and eunuch Grodor. There are three lines of seed code that she highly favors for production of the handsomest males. Thus the next cycle starts all over again. Her biggest mistake was that she made a child from the seed of the Skull Worm and Yggep. It was the first ever cross between human and Pitter. I'm sure you knew the child as the Cha'Kal. Half human, and the gods only know what the other parts really were. For, as you know, the two races cannot have fertile offspring and even those few who are birthed soon die or are sterile."

"The Cha'Kal was born as fertile offspring." Brekka said turning up the corner of her mouth. "Fortunately, he is no more. His life was ended by the Wose who smote him through the ears on the breast of the Ele-Anorean crater. I was there on that day he slew the monster." Brekka looked down and to the left as she recalled the events of that day and then snapped back. "But tell, me, Yiska, how do you know you will be able to get into Gloomullah's den? Won't we have to fight the Grodor to get into her underground chamber?"

"Not at all! The dangerous part is getting past the Growlings. Once you are taken below the earth into the caverns, the Grodor can see that you are a virgin." She paused in shock for a moment and raised a questioning eyebrow, "You are a virgin, right?"

"Of that I am certain; though I hope to never die of such a dire fate."

"Good! Don't ask me how they can tell. They just know by how you walk, and they will never harm a virgin. Once I saw a Quant woman who was a camp whore, who thought she could steal some extra medicine. But she was quickly slain by the Grodor and dispensed with. We virgins, on the other hand were free to roam about in the caverns at our leisure as long as we did not enter the level of the paramours or the ground floor."

"Why would that be?"

"Because nobody believed any of us could escape and very few ever tried. Once you know the evil monsters of the Poison Lands, you will know why they never even tried. Several virgins once tried to escape through the tunnels beneath the bottom floor and were destroyed."

"Destroyed! How?"

"By chapinapes; creatures with hair like a man, teeth like a wolf, and strength enough to rip off your limbs."

Brekka reached for her medicine bag at her side, pulled out some dried leaves of elf wort and sprinkled it over her candle lantern for luck. "Where does the Harridan Queen live in the Under World?"

"She has her own chamber where she sits, fatter than three sows, attended by her Grodor, and her carefully selected paramours.

"How does she communicate with the Growlings then?"

"Above ground, she has this magic mirror which makes her look like a lovely lady and she tells them that she is working on magic to make them look whole and beautiful like her someday. In reality she could easily cure them, but keeps them always expectant of drugs and beauty as well as an extended life."

"How incredibly and endlessly selfish this bitch must be."

Yiska nodded, "If any of the Growling are disobedient, she has medicine administered to them and they die a horrible death; which convinces all the rest of the Growlings she has all power. She can also speak from a great distance through this mirror. From deep in her chamber, she gives all the commands to the Growlings, and likewise bargains with the Pitters through this same mirror. But I know how to find the passage that leads straight into her den. I can take you there, as well as to the magic mirror; for I was her Under-Queen."

"It seems to me that Yggep once bore that title, too, and she betrayed our cause most horribly." Tales of the betrayal of Frink Glen came to her mind.

Kanarus stood up and said, "Lady Brekka, I assure you, Yiska is our friend, and nothing like Yggep Green Teeth. Do you need to think a night on this before you accept or reject the mission?"

"With your assurance of Yiska's trustworthiness, I need give it no more thought. If Yiska is brave enough to do it, and you trust her to be true, then I shall do it. For like your brother, Ilkchild, I intend to cut my way out of this worm, one way or the other."

As Kanarus awoke early in the morning and looked down at the beautiful sylph-like face of Wilona lying on the pillow. It felt so good to have his favorite wife with him once again, his pleasured hands running over the fine curves of her warm body as they entwined like newly-weds throughout the night. She was favored most because the two of them had been forged by the spirit into some alembic alchemical vessel that held an elixir that was only possessed by divine lovers. Somehow, they had emerged together in absolute harmony. This, in no way made her better than any of his other wives. It only meant they had arrived at that exulted holy place all lovers seek and yearn for. The place the lore masters say one enters after emerging from the dragon's blood bath; the place where love is made immortal. Someday, the rest of his wives would arrive, and Wilona had lit the pathway to it for them. It would now be easier for him to take them there one step at a time. Anytime was with Wilona there was that long rapturous silence that attended and the fear of the inevitable darkness, emptiness, and privation that came from separating from one another again, be it a minute, an hour, or a day.

So it was always with Wilona, no matter how much Kanarus took, there was always plenty more to take and plenty more to take. He looked down at his wrist and there, entwined about it, was a love bracelet made of her soft faery hair. She had kept watch over him while he slept, and now she slept.

He leaned over and gently kissed her bare swan-like neck. Rose up with a smile and dressed, while his eyes continued to feast on the voluptuous form of the now sleeping beauty. He gently draped the cotton blanket over her nude form and eased out of the tent backwards so as to let his eyes feast as long as they could before departing for his duties.

The long absence had bred a burning appetite for her that he yearned to satiate before leaving the tent, but his leadership required he be up early to make all things ready. As he stepped out into the cool morning air, a road runner zipped by him after a small rabbit, which made a quick zigzag turn and disappeared into thick brush. In the clear spring pool by his tent he saw his son, Anghrus, busy carving and floating toy dragoons.

Kanarus couldn't resist teasing Anghrus as he whispered, "Hey, little pirate, there's a fair lady lies asleep in this tent. Don't let anyone disturb her slumber."

The blond hair stuck up on Anghrus head like duck down as he turned in surprise and said, "I won't Dad. But did you know I sunk three Pitter ships of toads, and now my salamanders are king of the pond."

Kanarus laughed and tussled the long golden fuzz atop his son's head. He looked up at the sentinel on the cliff and saw a mirror reflecting sunlight, indicating that a Silver Harrier was coming in through the hidden pass. He splashed some water over his face, still smiling at the small boats of toads swimming across the pool. He rubbed his face dry with a towel, and waited as the silver-clad rider approached him.

"Hail, Lord Kanarus. I am Edelswan, Sur Sceaf's thane, come from Nogales in the Mexus Land with an urgent message from the High King."

"Please, Edelswan, dismount, give me the brief, and join me for breakfast." He knew the name as one who was a much accomplished

Bush Master, which is why Sur Sceaf had chosen him for one of his personal Silver Harriers.

The young blond warrior said, "The pleasure would be all mine, my lord."

He dismounted and handed Kanarus the brief. Kanarus opened and read:

*To my good and faithful friend, Kanarus:*

*May the gods ever keep you safe, hale, and whole. I have encountered an enormous army in the Mexus Lands called Moxo. They hail from the Deep Nether Lands of the south woods, upon which none of us have recollection of ever having tread. They are enemies to the Pitters, and they have had many of their daughters taken captive by the Pitters. Should you discover in your siege of the citadel any Moxo people, I beseech you to separate them, and bring them south with you into Kerr by the river in the Taxus. Some speak espangnol, but most know only their tribal tongue. They are highly attracted to the color red, should this help in identifying them. If their daughters are brought with you, the Moxo will be most grateful and join us in the over throw of the Pitter Empire. I cannot tell you how much such an army would be of value to us, particularly in destroying the immense bamboo plantations, which, should they bloom and fruit, will propel a Pitter population explosion beyond anything we have ever witnessed. I have sent word for vast supplies to be caravanned to the Taxus from our Suff land plantations, and look forward to greeting you and my fellow confederates there along with our families, according to the time lines established in the plan of the War Road.*

*Your High King, Sur Sceaf*

Brekka was eager to begin the battle for the citadel, as were her lady knights and the rest of her forces. The night before, after she'd returned to her tent from the war council, both Verushka and Freyxus had expressed reservations about the mission Kanarus had assigned her, but after expressing their doubts, reluctantly agreed that it must be undertaken. Gloomulah had been the creator of all the ungodly abominations that crept across the land of Panygyrus, and the mother of the wicked Pitters who sought to destroy mankind. Were Gloomulah to be left in the Poison Lands, her evil would grow from its roots there, and again infect the world with evil. Brekka was destined by reason and spirit to be the warrior to end the wretched hag's reign of grotesque horrors.

Her army and the Kaninchens with the Apaches had assembled on an open plain adjacent to the village. The familiar sounds of preparing their mounts and loading their gear helped to fuel her impatience. It was Kanarus himself who was causing the delay with his prolonged leave-taking, hugging and kissing each one of his numerous children, before tenderly embracing each of his beloved wives, who returned his affection in full measure. It was obvious that he loved all of his children, but seemed to have a powerful bond between he and his son, Anghrus, in particular.

Kanarus was so much like her father, Sur Sceaf, that she even thought for a moment, *If Ruhm can't make the transition to my culture, I should very much enjoy being married to Kanarus, and I would tell him so myself.* She remembered how Wilona said, 'Kanarus is like a bola. He's pulled by his warrior blood on one end and his desire to nurture his family on the other end.'

Finally, Kanarus helped Wilona into the saddle of her mare, Moon Chaser, before mounting his magnificent steed, Sun Chaser. Eagerly, Brekka took to her mount, Cycnus, and rode with them, leading out ahead of their troops with Chiggibbah showing the way.

Across the brazen wing helmet that her mount bore on its head she spotted Ruhm mustering his troops to join them, then looked back over at Kanarus and marveled how he represented everything she had ever thought a husband should be. For a moment she thought, *I would be so happy with Kanarus, and pleased as a pollywog in a pond with Wilona as my Faery-Queen. She's already like the dearest of sisters to me. But, oh Ruhm! I love you. I do hope you get your act together. Would to the gods, you were more like Kanarus!*

They rode all day before they came upon Hell's Gate, which consisted of many large timbers shaped like letter Xs. The dire warning was clear: *Do not pass here.* Other than the large Xs, which looked to be placed every two plough lengths, not much else looked different from the desert they had crossed. From the angle of the sun, she judged it to be two hours before twilight.

It wasn't long before Kanarus called a halt. "We will make camp here for the night. Only a fool would enter into the Poisoned Lands in the dark of night. Such would be a shear demonic nightmare."

Brekka dismounted and led Cycnus over to the spot where her handmaids, Ynys and Wyth were efficiently setting up the command tent, which doubled as sleeping quarters for Brekka and the two girls and her troupe.

When she arrived, she directed her handmaid, "Ynys, fetch the barrels of repellent for me."

"Repellent" Ynys asked. "What is that?"

"Oh, you know, what's it called? The Thingamagig."

Ynys gave her a dumbfounded look.

"For the gods' sake, you know, the Gvorkel."

"Of course, my lady, you are fearful of an attack by ferocious beasts while we sleep?"

"Worse, I'm fearful of creeps." Brekka said.

The mules brayed while being unloaded.

Ynys' eyes widened and so did Wyth's. "What are creeps?" Ynys asked.

"They're vicious little creatures the size of a large house cat. They resemble a skinned cat with slimy skin, yellow teeth, and clutching claws that give you festering wounds which can take up to a fortnight to heal."

The two girls were clearly terrified. *Better that they should be prepared*, Brekka decided. "We ride in safety throughout the day, but when the night begins and the darkness falls, we'll find ourselves sitting in an anthill of creeps and other dark creatures unspeakable. The more fear you have, the less you will be able to face the gauntlet we must pass through."

Wyth ventured nervously, "You're saying they only come in the night?"

Brekka placed a comforting hand on Wyth's shoulder. "They spurn the sunlight. They are creatures of the night. What the Quailor here in the Ndee lands call 'Nachtzehrers'. Night Rippers." Brekka motioned with claw like hands, though she took a little enjoyment in rousing Ynys' fears. "They rip at you with their hook like claws and tear nasty little bites out of your flesh with their infectious teeth."

Wyth and Ynys exchanged worried looks. "Don't worry! We have ample troops, and besides the Pitter legions will have greatly thinned the ranks of the Nachtzehrers before we get there."

After the mules were all unloaded, Brekka went about undressing in the tent. She wished again that she could be as intimate with Ruhm as Kanarus and Wilona were with each other. She laid her head on her woolen bed roll, heard her handmaids whispering their fears to each other in the subdued candlelight of the tent, then got under her blanket and fell swiftly off to a peaceful sleep.

Ruhm awoke with his manhood prancing beneath the blankets. He had to sing himself to sleep to not hear the amorous sounds of Xarela in the neighboring tent with one of his wives. Breakfast was over before he could rise, and he wondered how many more nights he would have to endure before he could roll over and have Brekka lying on his arm. *Enough of those thoughts. This is the day of horror. Must be focused.* But it was all too clear to him he needed a woman in the worst of ways. He could have had a wife several times over; many lovely and talented Hickoryan girls had vied for his affections, but something kept him from accepting them. Something in his soul bound him tighter than instinct to Brekka. It felt as if it was a paradoxical torture god had designed to make his life thoroughly miserable and out of his control. Then he thought, *If she'd only let me touch those breasts. Oh God, if I could ever part those thighs and just rest my hand in her nest. That's all it would take. Stop it, damn it. Stop it! Gotta get control of my passions. Gotta refocus or I'll never be fit to leave this damned tent in my condition.*

Brekka stepped out of her tent door to a swift warming dawn. She took note that Ruhm was late in rising and chuckled to herself thinking he must have stayed up late playing chess or cards with his lieutenants. The clatter of loading mules, and horses, and the shuffle of moving feet showed everyone was busy preparing for the day except for Ruhm. In their section of camp, Brekka's Sister-Knights were making ready for the march, dismantling tents and loading the mules.

She rubbed the sleep from her eyes and watched as Kanarus and Wilona were making jolly over the breakfast. He was now teasing her with a pancake. "Just give it to me, Kane, I'll give you the next one. I'm starved."

Brekka missed the stimulating conversations she had with Wilona before they came to Kanarus' lair, but was happy for her friend's absolute delight in her husband's presence. Once, Wilona had told her with deep sincerity, "It was my man that shaped me, and your man shall shape you. You shall be his consolation for waiting." As she looked over at Wilona frolicking, how she hoped that was a prophetic utterance. At least Xarela had moved his tent far enough away to stop the torment caused by their love making sounds. The mere thought that her little brother was now a man only served to remind her how fast her life was passing away.

Pretending to eat the cake, Kanarus opened his mouth wide and Wilona screamed, "Don't you dare. That one's mine."

Brekka walked over to them with Freyxus in tow and said, "And we wonder why the kids fight over the food."

Soon Ruhm exited his tent, stretched, and joined Kanarus for breakfast. Before long, Kanarus and Ruhm were playfully tossing berries at one another.

They both laughed and Kanarus teased Wilona with another cake, who now insisted that he take it. Brekka said, "Well, I can see this could go on all day. Reminds me of old Hans."

Freyxus said, "Hans who?"

"Oh, just a story my Quailor mother would tell me about a man named Hans in Schnecken-Haus who lived in a snail shell and everything he had, he didn't want. While everything he wanted, he didn't have."

They all laughed.

Kanarus said, "We're sorry, Brekka and Freyxus, it's just so good to be back together again after we were separated for so long. I hope we aren't annoying you."

"Not at all. Reminds me of my days in the House of Arundel. He and the Queen carried on like you two giddy lovers. But I need to tell you something. I should have probably revealed something to you in the Moot we had the other night. It wonders me, how it chust slipped my mind."

"What would that be?" Kanarus asked, a look of puzzlement settling over his face.

"The Queen of Ele-Anor-Ness, Arundel's wife, gave me several barrels of Gvorkel for this occasion."

"Is it an ale?" Wilona asked in a hopeful tone.

"No, it's a repellant. It'll stop any beast from attacking, or at least from eating you. Kind of like that repellant Yiska mentioned."

Kanarus lifted an eyebrow. "I have heard those Tree People have their powerful herbal concoctions. Do you think it would work as good against the creeps as the repellent Yiska used?"

"We'll find out soon enough. Zschamillah said just a few drops on your head and arms and any predatory beast is repelled. It's made from herbs and wolverine urine. I think the herbs mask the smell to us, but not to the predators."

"Yuck!"

Kanarus poured some more batter into the skillet and said, "It's worth a try. There's not much that offends the creeps though."

After a hearty breakfast, Brekka passed around the barrel of repellent, and all who wished dabbed a few drops of Gvorkel on their arms and head, placed a few on their horses and mules and had to wait until the horses grew accustomed to the odor, then mounted and rode off through the giant Xs of Hell's Gate, double file into the Poisoned lands.

Besides being very quiet, the land was beautifully filled with cacti and sage as far as the eye could see. By noon, they had passed through the red colored canyon, which Yiska said was the start of the creep Zone. They continued to ride all the rest of the day without incident until they arrived at a large box canyon, which Kanarus thought would be good to back into for the night. He ordered everyone to set up tents very close together and to gather ample fire wood before nightfall. Presently, large brush piles and stacks of wood could be seen throughout the canyon and soon crackling fires burned like sentinels on the perimeters of all the camps.

# CHAPTER 14 :
## CREEPS

**Y**ISKA STARED UP AT THE darkening sky before announcing to the Lady Knights, "Soon the hour of their movement will come, and when it is dark enough, they will be upon us with their clutching claws and wicked teeth like a cloud of locusts on green corn."

Brekka carried a basket containing loaves of bread out of the tent and passed them around to her handmaids, the Lady Knights, Kanarus and Ruhm. Eyes narrowed, she scanned the darkening desert floor, but nothing appeared to be moving. Standing together outside the command tent, they nibbled bread and watched the darkness deepen into a wall of solid black. No one had to be reminded to be hyper-vigilant after Yiska's dire warning.

Ynys moved closer to whisper, "Not a bird, nor even so much as a cricket to be heard anywhere."

"I suppose that's because the creeps eat anything bigger than a gnat." Kanarus murmured. "But Lone Dog says we can best them if we keep alert. They are vicious, but small. A solid clubbing will kill them." He motioned with his fist. "They do not like frontal attacks, but prefer to catch you on the unawares. Beware of their distractions and ignore their sounds. It's not the ones you see that you need to fear."

Yiska shuddered. "Lone Dog is right. Let your guard down once and there'll be five deep on your back and legs. And by all means keep your necks covered. They always go for the necks."

"What about our horses?" Wyth asked.

"We put Gvorkel on them too." Ruhm assured her he'd be at her side should they suffer an attack.

"The truth be known," Kanarus said, "they much prefer our naked skin to hairy horse flesh."

Wyth sidled up to Ruhm and grabbed his brawny arm, "Oh Ruhm, I'm so glad you are here to protect us."

Ynys grabbed his other arm and asked fearfully, "Why are we standing here in front of everyone else? Wouldn't it be safer if we dropped back a few lines?"

Brekka said, "We need to be on the front lines to inspire confidence. You won't be any safer behind us. Remember what Yiska told us? These demons are Shadow-Shooters and dart about faster than rabbits. They'll dash behind you and between your legs. Just wield your clubs and watch that you don't hit any of us when you strike." Suddenly, Brekka cocked an ear to what sounded like a shuffle in the sage. She heard the braying of the mules and knew they saw what was not yet visible to human eyes. Scanning the faces of her compeers she saw they all had their eyes peeled and their ears cocked to hear. The creeps were there, and though they could not yet see them, the hair on the back of her neck rose, and there was an awful sense of something evil lurking near and drawing closer.

"Time to pick up your clubs and weapons," she called. "Prepare to play lacrosse with the damned little demons' heads."

Ynys said, her voice quavering, "I don't think I'm ready for this."

Wilona shot her a disapproving look. "You damned well better be. Without the will to fight they'll focus right on you."

Brekka retrieved her war club from her belt and searched the dark desert brush casting dancing shadows from the fires strategically placed around the camp as a first wall of defense.

"They're here!" Yiska exclaimed.

Kanarus ordered briskly, "Ready a club and your scramasax."

Brekka thought she could see changing waves of movement in the brush, but was unsure if her imagination wasn't coming into play.

As the rising moon cast a silver sheen over the desert flora, Ysys whispered, "Did you see that?"

"See what?" Wyth demanded, wide eyed and alert. Ruhm removed their hands from his arms and gave each of them a club from a nearby supply.

"That and that," Ynys replied, pointing with the head of the club. "It's like shadows oozing from sage bush to sage bush, hundreds of them."

"I see it now. Probably why they call them Shadow-Shooters," Brekka said with sword in hand.

Ynys said, "They are like liquid ghosts, dripping from one shadow to the next, but their shape and forms remain imperceptible."

Kanarus declared, "I'm going to light a lantern."

As he stooped down and lit the whale oil lantern then turned it up bright and held it high, countless red beady eyes gleamed like hot coals from the sage brush. Strange chirping and clicking sounds came from every bush, as if they were somehow communicating with each other in some sort of devilish insect sounding tongue. At the same time a foul odor drifted in on the night air worse than a dog fart.

Kanarus and Wilona said in unison, "Arggh!"

Brekka flared her nostrils in disgust, but readied for engagement as she held her sword ready for slaughter.

Kanarus said, "So that's why the Ndee call them Shit Devils. Smells like someone emptied the latrines on us."

Wyth held her hand over her face. "That is the foulest odor I've ever smelled. How can anything smell so bad?"

Yiska answered, "They sleep in underground dens in their own shit. That's how. They have no concept of disgust or cleanliness."

Without warning, the creatures attacked. The armies fought back, cutting, clubbing, and kicking the swarm of catlike creatures running under foot. Despite the Gvorkel, the vermin bit and clawed mercilessly. Kanarus, ever the beacon of calmness, shouted "Son of a bitch!"

Brekka looked over and saw Wilona club one of the demons that had its teeth sunk into his shoulder. As if catching himself, he managed to pretend it didn't hurt. Everywhere she looked the warriors were doing dances to shake the vermin off their backs and club them off their fellows, while horses, donkeys, and mules sent up an alarm of braying and whinnying that added to the fray. The very ground crawled with creeps choking on their own blood, shrieking from severed limbs, clawing the ground with blade torn bellies, or crushed skulls and yet the flood of them poured in steadily without break like a flash flood from a hellish storm in the desert.

Brekka caught Kanarus and Wilona peering directly at her. Suddenly, as if they were communing telepathically with her, an idea popped into her head. Turning swiftly, she fought her way to her tent, grabbed her shield and shouted, "Kanarus, hold up your lamp!"

But he was already raising the lamp. Even more eyes appeared along the cliff walls. The creeps had come down the canyon walls as if gravity meant very little to them. Ruhm bashed the brains of one of the creeps assailing Ynys, who hysterically ran in circles screaming and batting at her long hair. Brekka held her iridium shield up behind the lamp. A beam of brilliant light shone forth. Slowly she turned in a circle, and everywhere the beam touched, the creeps were electrified.

"Look," Wyth said, "They're begun falling from the cliff walls like singed ants on a burning log. Oh, Brekka, don't let any more of them in here. Keep doing that thing you're doing!"

"Steady your heart, Wyth. This isn't even the start of it."

Wyth covered her head and ran back into the tent only to come back out screaming, "They're in the tent!"

Ruhm stepped near to Brekka and said, "That did it, Brekka! That got them running. How did you know your shield would do that?"

His deep voice was the most welcome of sounds. She answered, "I guessed. Govannon had once told me the shield does far more than protect one from swords and arrows. It has a power to render evil powerless. I have yet to discover all the powers of the shield, but I just added one more." In her heart she knew that some sort of psychic bond now existed between her, Wilona, and Kanarus. A bond that was very different than the one she held with Ruhm. It was a bond of Brother and Sister, but the bond with Ruhm was both spiritual and rooted in the nature of her feminine flesh as well as her heart.

She had just evolved into a higher level of communion with Kanarus and Wilona. Finally, after holding the shield up till her arms began to give out from weariness, Kanarus said, "I think it best if we all take turns holding the lamp and the shield while we take shifts sleeping. Let us know when you tire of it, Lady Brekka."

"That would be now, Kane."

Brekka held her shield up a few more moments until her arms gave out and she passed it over to Ruhm. They alternated off and on in what the Herewardi called 'the wolf-rage,' where they slew the creeps with the sheild in some sort of altered state, until Kanarus said, "You two have done that long enough. Try to get some sleep. Wilona and I will take it from here."

Ruhm shot Brekka a warm caring look before they parted. She had Freyxus tell Xarela and Pata to take the next watch. She attempted to sleep, despite the chattering and clicking sounds in the background. Her anxiety was compounded by the yipping of men being bitten or clawed, but she oddly found that all less disturbing than she had found Xarela's love making sounds on previous nights. Finally, she fell into a deep slumber.

The next morning, when Brekka awoke, she saw Wyth asleep sitting up. On the other hand Ynys sat wide awake, shuddering with a club in her hand. There was no bird song, just the coolness of the desert air and the pungent smell of juniper overlaying the stench of the dead shit-devils.

By the time Brekka came out of her tent with Ynys trailing close behind, the first rays of dawn had driven the remaining creeps back into their wretched haunts. Hundreds of their slimy, mangled carcasses littered the camp, their vicious faces frozen with yellow-teethed snarling poses. She sucked in a deep breath of fresh air blowing from the East, then hesitated to take another deep breath as her nostrils picked up a strange odor.

"What was that?" She lifted her head and sniffed the air again.

"What was what?" Ynys asked.

"That smell. Can't you smell that smell?" Brekka said intensely.

"You mean the Juniper? Or those shit things?"

"No," she said, and then called over to Ruhm who was busy feeding his campfire some wood, "Do you smell that, Ruhm?"

He lifted his nose and breathed in, "Yes, it's the smell of war." He pointed his nose to the sky and sniffed again. "It's rotten carnage."

"Do you think the creeps we killed would smell that soon?"

"I couldn't say. Maybe when we get rolling we'll see what happened to the vile little beggars."

Soon, the camp was up and eating breakfast dutifully while discussing the horrors of the night amidst the corpse-strewn camp. Kanarus ordered two scouts to ride ahead to look for signs of Pitters.

Then they saddled, and with the army, hit the trail for the Growling Citadel. As they rode, they looked for dead creeps the Pitters might have encountered, but saw none until they came upon some heavily disturbed land about two miles from where they had been camped. Looking down they saw dead creeps everywhere amidst several Pitter and horse skeletons.

Kanarus said, "This is where the Pitters encountered them."

Ruhm added, "There must be thousands of them dead. No way to tell. They're everywhere. The sight of them alone makes me sick to my stomach. Look at those bulging beady little eyes. They look like skinned muskrats."

"It is said," Yiska revealed, "that they avoid water, fire, and light. That is why they always come in the night. And they were made by Yggep at the torture camp of Brim or Brime from aborted human fetuses mixed with rat or other rodents."

"There were so many of them. But where do these creatures go in the day?" Ruhm asked. "Where did they disappear to?"

"They go into caves," Brekka said.

"How do you know that?" Yiska asked.

"Just listen to how hollow the earth sounds under the horse's feet. This land is loaded with caves and burrows."

As they rode on through the morning hours they started coming upon dead Pitters horribly gnawed upon, in some cases all the way to the bones. The creeps that were killed had distended stomachs from gorging on Pitter and human flesh.

"Yuck, this is so disgusting." Ynys said, attempting to block the smell with her arm to her face.

"Well," Wyth said, "I warned you."

"The only reason I let you come," Brekka said, "is because you're my friend, but I warned you too. You have to have a strong stomach, because you will see worse than this before it's all over."

Brekka spotted the two scouts returning in haste down the road ahead of them. They rode up swiftly beside her and Kanarus, and said, "Just over the next rise is the Growling Compound. They have twenty foot battlements with buzzing strings on top of the wall, and after you pass that hill there, you will see the citadel rising like an eland's horn, as high as a mountain."

Yiska said, "The buzzing string can kill you. That's how they keep the creeps and monsters from entering the citadel. We are lucky we didn't meet any of the monster skin walkers last night. You must instruct everyone to not touch those strings, no matter what."

Kanarus signaled for his green-clad beetles to carry the message along the line of troops and all the armies as they marched. Brekka noticed several bites up and down one of the lady's arms, but he gave no complaint, and it was obvious from the sheen that someone had put healing salve on the wounds. After the rider reported the message was disseminated, Kanarus stopped on his horse and thought for a moment. He began by issuing a command to the scout, "Go fetch Going Snake. He's been taught how the black powder of the toulucan works. We're going to need to use that explosive powder we found in the barrels. By the gods, I knew it would have its uses."

Shortly thereafter the scout returned with Going Snake.

Kanarus said, "I am told you know how to use the toulucan and understand the uses of the shoot powder."

"That is right, my lord, I was shown how it works by Il-Alim and how to employ the fire powder to make it explode."

Kanarus stood up in his stirrups, the leather in his saddle creaking under his repositioning. Brekka noted his confidence in command. "Can you take down a wall with such powder?"

"Sure! It's really quite simple, though dangerous," Going Snake said motioning with one hand over the other. "All you need is compression by covering the powder in dirt, and then a wrapper with the powder in it. Actually we don't even need the wrapper. We can just pour the powder in a solid line long enough for you to get safely away from the explosion. Then light it, run like hell, and duck." He let his hands fly up, "And boom. No more wall."

"Very well," Kanarus said, "I'll have the powder brought up to you right away. Set to it."

After passing through the canyons of the Creep Zone, the barrels arrived, and Going Snake said, "We can place the barrels along the wall, pack them with dirt and rocks and then just leave a trail of the powder and kaboom, down goes the wall just like a sheep's kidney in the fire, but be warned, we'll need to steady our horses or they will all take off, and we lose the whole kit and caboodle."

"Thanks, Going Snake. I'll send a team of quailor and quants to assist you, and you tell us when it's safe to make our charge. We'll wait for your return and then charge."

Kanarus turned to Brekka, Wilona, and Yiska, "Are you three now ready for your part?"

Brekka nodded.

Yiska said, "It would be advised that only Brekka and I go. Wilona is not a virgin, and the Grodor can detect it."

"In that case, Wilona, you stay with me." Kanarus said with a questioning frown. "As soon as we breach the wall, go like a rabbit before a coyote, and make for the Grodor hole."

Brekka said, "I will shape it so, my lord."

A full hour passed in the early dawn before they saw Going Snake and Lone Dog riding like the wind with their team toward them. He came to a skidding halt right in front of Kanarus, "All is ready, my lord. Bring up the men and I will show you as close as you can get. Then I will go light the powder and return. Did you remember to tell everyone to steady their mounts before charging?"

"I did. Sent Beetles in all directions. And I suppose you want to be at the head of your dog soldiers?"

"That I do, my lord." Going Snake said with a proud look.

"Then go fetch them here, and you lead the charge."

"I will shape it so, my lord."

Going Snake rode off and returned a few minutes later with his Dog Soldiers. Together they rode out of the canyons towards the citadel, which stood against the horizon like jagged peaks in the middle of a great plain.

As they approached the great wall of the compound, Brekka could see no guards at all, and the wall stretched for miles like an endless canyon. Obviously the product of slave labor, for no one else could afford the costs in labor such a project entailed. *Probably no guards,* she noted, *because they are not needed with such a high wall. What were those buzzing strings on top of the wall that was reported? How could a string have power to kill?*

Going Snake took a lance and cast it in the ground. He turned around and said to Kanarus, "Nobody may pass this lance until I return. Then, as soon as the explosions go off, I'll count to eighty eight, and we'll charge. There will be a gaping hole in the wall, and the Pitters and Growlings will wonder what in the hell hit them as we pour through. In the name of our father's gods, shape it so."

All those that heard raised their lances and the rest raised their spears and said, "Shape it so," which echoed throughout the ranks.

# CHAPTER 15 :

## FROM GLOOMULLAH TO THE HALL OF HAGS

**I**T WAS TIME TO STRIKE.

At a safe distance, Brekka, Ruhm, and the armies of Kanarus awaited the order to attack. Going Snake ran out ahead of them and lit the end of the line of powder snaking its way to the numerous barrels placed against the wall before the citadel. At least three man lengths in height; the stone wall was designed to protect the denizens of the citadel from the creatures that plagued the surrounding Poisoned Lands.

Going Snake quickly returned, held his hand up as the signal for all to wait and yelled, "Steady your horses and get ready for the blast."

Brekka's heart pounded. "Yiska, dismount and ride double with me so I can hear your directions, and so we don't get split up. For now, you are my eyes."

It seemed an eternity to Brekka before the explosions went off like thunderclaps. Dust, rock, and debris flew skyward in great dark grey clouds with thunderous shaking running through the earth beneath their feet and reverberating in their chests. Though thoroughly desensitized to battle alarm and noise, Brekka's mare Cycnus shied, snorted, and churned the soil beneath its feet in a war prance. As it reared up, Yiska came nigh to falling off, but Brekka felt her strong grip squeezing at her torso. Others were not so fortunate. Some warriors had been thrown and were now attempting to remount unsteady steeds.

Going Snake counted to eighty-eight rhythmically bouncing his hand up and down for all to see. Her whole focus was on getting inside the wall, and she found the delay trying to her patience. Finally, he dropped his hand and the charge was on. Leading the way Going Snake and his youthful Dog Soldiers galloped toward the dust cloud, and the hooves of thousands of horses were almost as deafening as the explosions that knocked down the walls. Once they entered the cloud, things were barely visible beyond thirty feet. Sure enough, the wall that was there moments ago had a gaping hole through it.

Passing through the wall's remnants, they funneled in and did not encounter anyone alive. Instead their eyes were greeted by numerous Pitter and Growling bodies with missing parts strewn all about the rubble of the compound like dusty, torn, and mangled dolls in an old barn. As the larger particles of dust fell to the earth, her eyes discerned the hosts of the Pitters fleeing south in a wave of shock.

Brekka left Going Snake to the hewing down of the fleeing legionnaires while she and Yiska rode on to perform their targeted mission. Cycnus' hooves devoured the earth beneath its feet. The thought crossed her mind that it was strange how Yiska had said it would be better if only the two of them entered the citadel. Somehow it seemed too easy. As a warrioress she considered the possible scenario that Yiska might indeed be a traitor after all. Yet, Kanarus was a proven judge of the spirits of people, and he had expressed full confidence in Yiska. The plan was what it was. It was too late to change anything, but Brekka was determined to be vigilant all the same.

Yiska said, "Turn right." Brekka broke off and headed her horse for the right with the lean of her reins.

"Go up this path towards the Citadel," Yiska shouted. Brekka goaded her mount on, peering through the brazen helmet wings. Cycnus responded in kind by eating the ground up with her hooves as only a horse of noblest breeding could do, dodging fleeing growlings too fearful to notice or even care about Brekka's intent.

The closer she got to the citadel the more she could see that Going Snake had the Pitters on a full run heading for the cover of their compound. The Growlings were fleeing en masse for the west towards the citadel with its jutting spires. Now, she wondered if they would be able to make it to the citadel before the growlings would. Then, before her eyes, as the smoke and dust began to thin, she was suddenly aware of how high the citadel rose. It was a large beige fortress with no windows on the first two stories and numerous windows in row upon row above. Its six towers pointed skyward like mighty twisted arrows rising out of the ground. It was, she had to admit, a marvelous architectural feat to behold. Standing tall like giant termite towers in the shape of kudu horns, she marveled anything so magnificent could be built.

Yiska said, "It's no good. The growlings are going for cover in their citadel. We can never get through them all to get to the entrance to the underworld chambers. I did not anticipate they would block our way to the first floor control center."

Brekka had not come this far to be impeded. "We go Yiska, come hell or high water. We stick to the plan."

Yiska shouted, "In that case, once they all get inside, they will attempt to seal the citadel. I know how to get in. I just don't know how to get through them to get in. The problem is, they may attack us before we can get to the door of the control center, which we absolutely need access to. Wait a moment, I just remembered, two of my old friends serve in the control center, Bithia and Natasha. If we can get to them, they will put the growlings on stand down and stop them from doing us harm. We must get into the control center first, or I fear they will overwhelm us."

Brekka redoubled her speed to get out ahead of the fleeing growlings, kicking and knocking them out of her way as she passed. "One way, or the other, I'm going to get in there. Hold on, and direct me to where the entrance to the underworld chamber is."

Yiska directed. "Turn left here. Now go to that lamp post." Cycnus plowed through solid clusters of growlings, and trampled some underfoot. Hearing their screams of terror as they fell under hoof, Brekka pressed on.

As they passed the lamp post, Yiska said, "It's right there, through that door where all those growlings are going in."

"How far inside that door are the control center and the way down to Gloomullah?"

"It's about three man lengths inside that door and on the right. It'll be a pink door. If we can get to it and inside, they will not follow us down. Everything below the ground belongs to the Grodor."

"Hold on and don't let go, no matter what."

Brekka spurred her mount on and charged up the steps, sending growlings against either side. The metal shoes of the horse clang out on the hard stairs, and she made it to the stair top just ahead of the coming hoard of panic stricken growlings. When she got to the top of the stairs she shouted, "Dismount!" Yiska slid off the back, and Brekka jumped off and grabbed Yiska by the arm, pulling her toward the entrance. She gave her horse a whistle command, and it immediately began rearing and trampling growlings, who then turned and fled for another door. Brekka gave Cycnus a command that would send her daring off to their camp outside the walls.

Yiska pecked at some buttons with her fingers, and the door clicked, then opened. Once inside the citadel she could see endless hallways. It appeared the building was made out of some sort of mud, for she saw no seams, as if it were pure hard clay or stone. Sure enough, the pink door lay straight ahead. Down the hallway were several growling guards, and they rushed after them, shouting to other growling soldiers to help. Their horrible blistered faces, apparent even from so great a distance, made Brekka think of charging bull dogs, and they were hell bent on sinking their teeth into her. Their labored, heavy breathing could be heard wheezing from their strained lungs as she positioned herself for combat.

They attacked head on. Brekka ducked their swords and laid both of their bellies open in one swing of her sword, only to be met by a wall of sword drawn growlings. Using the bodies of the two slain growlings laying in front of her as a barrier, she was able to keep their fierce attack at bay. Anytime one of the soldiers attempted to step over the bodies of the fallen guards she added another dead man to the pile. Soon a couple growling pike men ran up. They pushed their way up the hallway through the other soldiers. If Yiska didn't get that damned door open soon, Brekka could not hold much longer. The pink door opened into an eerie light. Brekka briefly glanced back to see her pursuers. The light came from long glowing canisters that ran the length of the ceilings of the "control center" as Yiska had called it.

Yiska said, "This way."

Brekka quickly backed into the control center, and together they slammed the large door. Yiska sealed it again. Brekka breathed a sigh of relief, thinking it was just like the time her and Going Snake had escaped a pack of wild dogs on a hunt and had just barely climbed a tree before the dogs got to them. Even at that, she had to kick several of them down who were so intent on killing them that they climbed up the tree after her and Going Snake. They were trapped up in the tree all night when Ruhm came a riding by with a road gang and put the pack to flight. She was never so glad to see someone, and she remembered Ruhm's reaction of tender concern, whereby he turned the road work over to a foreman and escorted them safely back to Ele-Anor-Ness. She knew it forced him to work a day longer, and noted the sacrifice he had made for her. Now, as she leaned breathless with the growlings pounding on the other side of the door, she surveyed her surroundings, and the images of those leaping snarling dogs kept flashing across her mind.

Suddenly, she spotted about twenty curious little pear-shaped, bald men approaching disinterestedly on a predetermined course, and it was as if the wild dogs were once again climbing the tree after her.

"What should we do?" Brekka asked. "Fight?"

"That won't be necessary. They are grodor, and do not see us as enemies. They have no idea what's happening outside these doors, and only see us as hosts of the queen. See, they move right by us without so much as even noticing us. The only time they would pay any attention to any of us was when we traded our menses for noogs."

"What if I was not a virgin?"

"Then they would have sensed it, and we'd be dead or enslaved."

"Unbelievable!" Brekka said. She watched the chubby little men pass them, and then hobble along out another door. She took a deep breath of relief and said, "Now where is the queen?"

"Much, much, much deeper. But first, we must go to the main room of the control center. Remember, I told you, I have some connections here."

Brekka saw a white towel on a nearby counter and used it to clean the blood off her sword before re-sheathing it.

Yiska beckoned, "Follow me."

Brekka followed her down a corridor to a round room inside of which sat a young woman dressed in a purple robe. She was surrounded by numerous other young women dressed in white. Yiska explained, "That looks like Natasha, and those are her laboratory assistants. Let's go in and I'll introduce you."

Yiska opened the door and walked in. The woman in the purple robe looked like she had seen a ghost. She had mousey brown hair, high cheek bones, and chalky, almost sallow white skin. Upon standing up from her desk she exclaimed, "Yiska! Yiska, can that be you?"

The two hugged each other, and then the purple-robed woman declared, "So you were the cause of the alarm at the doors." Then as if routine, she grabbed a metal rod about a foot in length and spoke into it. "Sargonus, we are alright. I am processing the strangers. Have your soldiers stand down, and see to it no Pitters enter the citadel. This may be their ploy to get in here. Post a guard unit at my door and stand by for further directives"

It was all very puzzling to Brekka. It appeared as if she was addressing the growlings outside the door, and yet they were a good hundred feet from the door they had come through.

Yiska turned and said, "This is my friend, Brekka, Daughter of Sur Sceaf, King of the Herewardi and High Lord of the Syr Folk Alliance," Brekka nodded. "And Brekka, this is Natasha, my dear friend. We spent many days of our lives together here in the control center when I was the Under Queen. Natasha and Bithia aided me in my escape and I promised I would come back for them someday."

Natasha laughed, "And we never thought she would survive the Creep Zone. How did you ever...?" She trailed off.

Yiska asked, "What did Gloomullah say when you told her I stole away with a Hickoryan merchant?"

"She did not take well to it. Had the Hickoryan merchant hunted down, but found no trace of you. Forbade traders to come into the citadel after that. She truly valued you, Yiska, and felt greatly betrayed."

A strange metallic voice came through the black metal box. "Natasha, this is Sargonus. There is a major breach in the wall, and an enemy host is pouring in from the north."

Natasha picked the metal box up and said, "Just secure the citadel, and everyone will be alright."

Brekka was growing most uneasy. This had the smell of a trap. Too much secrecy and intrigue made her mistrust and suspect everyone. Natasha triggered a warning in Brekka's heart that somehow put her in mind of a spider inching down on its web. She let her fingers dance over her sword hilt to relieve the paranoia that was setting in.

Yiska looked all about and said, "Where is Bithia? Was she promoted to Under Queen in my stead?"

"Oh, I am so sorry, Yiska." Natasha said with an overly pronounced expression of grief. "She incurred the wrath of Gloomullah by her strong stance against experimentation on the captives."

"But she was always opposed to Yggep's experiments. What made the difference?"

"It's the new bot fly and mosquito experiments we've been conducting. Bithia tried to stop them. Tried to kill the flies and destroy the warbles. After that rebellious act, she was a camp whore the next day. Poor thing! I mean going from virgin to a whore in one day. But enough of the bad news. Good thing the scientists are all down in the parlor grooming themselves for paramour day. They'd alert Gloomullah if they saw you here. I suppose that is why you are here?"

"Yes, but is Gloomullah aware that the citadel is under attack at this very moment?" Yiska inquired as if in disbelief.

"Why would I alert her?" Natasha said, "Isn't this the day we hoped for? She's been alerted that there is a disturbance at the wall, but so far no news has come in to us."

"We need to get to her as soon as possible. That is really why I am here."

"Don't be in such a hurry, my dear. Let me show you what I have planned, and why the world is our oyster. I can't believe my good fortune at running into you. You will be most useful."

Brekka could not endure the banter. She had come to slay Gloomullah not to participate in a class reunion. "Natasha, it would very much facilitate what is going to happen here today if we could find our way to Gloomullah."

"Patience, patience. Things have changed since Yiska left. I am now the Under-Queen, and I've got vital plans of my own. Please join me." She motioned for them to follow into what looked like a large hospital room full of patients lying in two rows of beds. Their blistered faces and haggard looks showing they had undergone some form of traumatic suffering. Natasha continued to guide them out the other side and into a well-lit laboratory where two glass rooms were before them. Behind the glass in the first room were tornadoes of mosquitos swirling all about. Then behind the glass in the second chamber were bot flies, so thick that one could barely see through them.

Natasha got a sinister look on her face. "These are my work."

"Your work!" Yiska said.

"Yes," Natasha said with a ghoulish smile. "My way to the queenship." She pulled open a drawer and there in a round glass container squirmed slimy, wriggling, white warbles, large grubs the size of a man's finger. "Don't you see," she held up her thumb and a finger a knife's width apart and said, "I am this close to becoming queen, Yiska. The mosquitoes carry the fly bots eggs on their beaks, and the fly bots have all been infected with the disfiguring disease the growlings have. You saw the patients in their sick beds."

"The growlings." Yiska asked.

"That's my point, Yiska. You won't believe it. Last month they were Hickoryan captives with skin as fair as yours and mine, and now look at them. Come let me show you." Natasha took them back out into the hospital room and picked up a sharp small knife beside the bed then proceeded to cut into a swollen boil on an unconscious girl's arm. "Two weeks ago, this girl was normal." After making the cut, Natasha reached into the slit and pulled out a wiggling warble the size of the first two digits on her finger. "All of them were exposed to the mosquitoes and within two weeks they are clearly immobile."

Brekka said, "What are you trying to tell us?"

Natasha's eyes grew wide, "Once I have perfected a way to repel the mosquitoes, within two weeks' time I could release this plague on any army and render it immobile. I've already worked out a deal with Tibereon, Grumpus' lieutenant, that we will use it once I am Queen."

Brekka was sickened by what she was hearing and was just about to cry foul when Yiska of her own accord said, "You have become another Yggep. You don't even see the suffering you've already released on these poor patients. You just want power. You've become drunk with power. And now I see why Bithia raised such a fuss. What's happened to you, Natasha? You've become a devil and a murderess. You vile..."

Yiska had not finished speaking when a group of Growling soldiers came running into the hospital room. Natasha said, "And I thought we were friends. I could have used your help."

Brekka drew her blade and severed the head from the first soldier to approach her, elbowed the next in the eye, and plunged her blade into another Natasha pulled a small flat rock off her belt and pointed it at Brekka. The next thing Brekka knew was a shocking sensation and buzzing sound on her neck. Her sword dropped, and her body collapsed involuntarily to the floor. She, along with Yiska, was pulled into a nearby room with no windows.

As soon as Brekka recovered her movement she said, "Some friends you have."

Yiska looked sad, "Had. She is no friend to me. She's turned evil. She was too long with Yggep, and now she's just like her."

Brekka looked all around the confinement room they had been thrown into. It was solid walls with only one slit of a window in the door. "Well, now we've got to get out of here, and I have to get my sword back." She looked down the alley of beds at where she had dropped her sword. It was still lying on the floor. She then felt for her two headed axe. "She has taken my labyrus! I swear, I will end this woman's miserable ambitions with a swift fury."

"How do you propose we do that, seeing as we are locked in here? The fact is that in all likelihood, you and I shall be camp whores by the morrow." Yiska said shaking her head and restraining a cry.

"That ain't going to happen. Kanarus will level this place to the ground if I don't meet him this afternoon. And Ruhm would never desert me. Besides, I've gotten through more secure locks than this when I was a kid. Ary and I made it a habit of sneaking into my mother's locked press for the cookies." Brekka pulled the hidden scramasax from her ankle and began plying the lock open. "And this little lock won't stop me." She stood up and looked out the small door window.

She fiddled with her blade, scraping and pressing at the bolt through a crack. Soon the lock released and she looked out the small window on the door again to see where the growlings and Natasha had gone. They were not there. Her sword still lay where she had fallen. She opened the door barely a crack and listened. She could see the hospital room in front of her and hear the voices of the growlings in the other room. Now was the time to strike.

She scurried across the floor in swift quiet steps, took up her blade and prayed to Odhin. *Empower my sword arm, oh Mighty Lord of Righteous Battle. Father Woon, let me send my enemies to hell.* She looked into the other room and saw only three growling soldiers and Natasha were left. Natasha was writing a note, and then gave it to one of the growlings who took off in haste. Brekka felt confident she could overpower them. She looked back and motioned for Yiska to follow. Once Yiska was near her she whispered. "When I slay them, can you secure this area?"

"If you can slay them, I can seal us in tighter than a turtle in its shell."

"Here, take my scramasax, but stand clear. I'll be swinging wildly. This time, I'm going to get that bitch before she uses her magic on me again. Now, let's lay on."

Brekka charged through the door and plunged her blade into the base of the neck of the nearest growling, sending his eyes bulging in shock. She quickly withdrew the blade and ran it through the teeth of Natasha who was just turning in her chair to see what the commotion was all about. Brekka plunged and twisted her blade to core Natasha's brains. She drove the blade with such force that she lifted Natasha off the ground, like a fisherman gaffs a large fish from the water, writhing and wet with blood. Like a fisherman lands his catch, Brekka hurled her up onto the nearby desk with a crashing thud.

The final growling tried to circle Brekka. She drew her blade out of Natasha's teeth, and waited for the soldier's next move. His eyes widened, peering out of his blistered face. Yiska had knifed him through the back. As he struck the floor, there stood Yiska holding the bloody scramasax, as if she had surprised even herself.

"Now! Secure the doors." Brekka commanded.

Yiska ran to a panel and pressed several buttons, after which a loud clank let Brekka know, the doors were secure. Yiska said, "There's no way they can get in now. Neither can they communicate the state of affairs to the Dark Queen."

Brekka searched the room and found her labyrus lying upon the ground. It had fallen when Brekka smashed Natasha down upon the desk. "And we," Brekka asked, "Can we still get to Gloomullah?"

"Yes, I can get you to her, but first we must destroy those mosquitoes, bots, and warbles or we'll all be looking as pitiful as those patients she's been conducting medical experiments on. Can you just imagine the pain those warbles give, tunneling through your flesh; not to mention the disease they'd leave strapped to you. All for power! All for power! Damn it, are there no humans left in this world anymore?"

"There are humans, Yiska, but you are one of the few better ones." Brekka said. Now, in full confidence of her loyalty, Brekka could proceed with her mission in comfort of mind.

Yiska busied herself looking through drawers until she found certain liquids that she mixed together and poured through a screened vent leading into the bots and mosquitoes. Then she carefully searched all the drawers for containers of warbles and poured the mixture over them. The mosquitoes, bots, and warbles ceased to move and littered the floors of the two glassed in rooms. Then she soaked a rag and proceeded washing the nine patients in the hospital room with the mix. Brekka took another cloth, soaked it in the substance, and assisted in cleaning up the suffering patients. Most were too weak to even move, but at least two of them were coherent enough to have realized what just happened and spoke their gratitude. As Brekka looked around at all the interesting buttons and lights she turned to see Yiska approaching. "There, we just averted a plague." Yiska washed her hands and said, "We can get Gloomullah now." She motioned for Brekka to follow her into a closed room. "This will take us down to her." Yiska said with a sweating furrowed brow. She was still breathing hard from the rapid pace she had been obliged to operate at. "This room will take us down." She pointed to two doors in front of them.

Brekka put her sword between the doors and pried it open only to see bottomless darkness and metal ropes that were moving like lines on a pulley. She felt Yiska take her by the arm and say, "Just wait. It will come and take us down." Suddenly a well-lit room or a box appeared before them. Yiska explained, "It took me a year to figure out how the Grodor went up and down the levels so fast. Look here. We press this bottom button to go down and the other button to go up."

The floor looked to be solid rock, and the room had no other doors. "Deep, how can a room go deep?"

"You will see," Yiska said wiping her sweating brow with a kerchief.

They stepped inside the small room and the doors closed behind them with a thud. Brekka felt her stomach lurch just like when one is on a boat, and she had the sensation that she was falling. Above the little room, she saw descending numbers from forty to one. They passed door after door and Brekka could not help but wonder what was behind each one. When the number one finally lit up, she heard a ding sound. The doors opened on their own into another long hallway, lit like the first one they had entered.

"We have gone down forty levels of caverns. This floor is the Hall of the Hags."

"You mean we have gone forty floors below ground."

"Forty! That's right. And it goes forty floors above the one we were on, the ground floor."

"How does this magic box go through the earth so fast?"

"It travels through a shaft on the metal ropes you saw. No different than dropping a bucket in a well."

"Why do you call this, the Hall of the Hags?" Brekka said as she eyed the strange furnishings through the windows.

"This is the Hall of Gloomullah's associates, what they call fellow scientists. They are practically as old as her; former lab assistants from a nursing school. Over there," She pointed to sinks and curious jars, "those are their laboratories where they usually work. We are in luck! It's their day off, and they get as giddy as teen girls." Yiska peeked through a window into a large room from which filtrated the sickening sweet odors of perfumes and powders. "I want you to look in here."

Brekka gazed through the crack in the curtain of the window. She saw hundreds of Grodor plucking, tweezing, and grooming the oldest women she had ever seen. Probably as many as twenty. "So that is why they call it the Hall of Hags?"

"Not exactly. That's what I named it. They call it the Scientists' Quarters, and this particular room is what they call the Beauty Parlor."

As Brekka looked through the cracks in the curtains, the Scientists were frail and wrinkled like dried out tomatoes. Some were very much enjoying the pedicures and manicures, as they laid limp in large white chairs that leaned back. Others enjoyed mud baths and massages from the chubby, baby-like, little Grodor who bounced around as happily as dwarves in a workshop. "More like the shop of horrors." She laughed, then said, "Well, I suppose, even an old barn looks better when it's painted."

"Yes," Yiska laughed, "It's Grooming Day; the day when they meet with the handsome paramours. That means most of the Grodor will be pre-occupied with the hags and the paramours. You'd think these hags were in their teens with the way they act and behave on grooming day. The Queen All-Giver dwells at this, the bottom level with them, just a little farther down the hall. She will be pleasuring herself with her personal grooms."

"How will we locate the Harridan?"

"It will be easy. Gloomullah goes nowhere. Her chamber is round with a large round bed in the center of the room. From there she watches magic mirrors of people in other worlds doing strange things. She will be surrounded by her paramours who only leave her chamber to be schooled or when she grows tired of them. After the shows on the mirrors she invites them to her bed. These paramours will be judged as three of the best. It's always been her preference to have three lovers at a time. And they will probably be slightly younger than the other hags prefer. Usually though, once they are twenty-four winters, she gives them to the other hags, or they are sold into slavery to the Pitters, who I have heard sell them in turn to the Vardropi who have a particular liking for pretty boys."

"I'm surprised that she has paramours at so great an age as she must surely be," Brekka said. "The thoughts alone sicken me to the gut."

"Things in here are nothing like things where we came from, Brekka. They are all twisted. This place has no seasons of life. And certainly no code of behavior you're familiar with."

"I suppose so. The Amerikan Empire became perverted and morally bankrupt by the time of its collapse."

"That is my belief." Yiska motioned to turn right to go down another hallway; at the end of which could be seen a large circular room, but glassed off and curtained off inside. They walked towards it.

Yiska said, "It took me years to figure out most of what I know and am showing you now." As they came up to the glass room she said, "See here, there are cracks in the curtains, and if you lean real close you can see Gloomullah."

Brekka put her head to the thick glass in front of her and peeked through the slit in the curtain. Sure enough, inside, propped up on cushions and pillows on a large round bed sat an enormously obese woman, and although fat, she was hideously wrinkled with crepe-like skin. On the bed with her were three Grodor who were massaging her back, her arms, and her legs, while she ate something that looked like large white flakes. Meanwhile, the other Grodor were busy cleaning and taking away her dishes.

Brekka shifted positions to see more of the room. Just as Yiska said, there were magic mirrors the size of small tables. It looked like some sort of play was going on inside them. Brekka pulled back and whispered, "I've never seen anything like this. The mirrors must be scrying stones or mirrors, but I actually think I heard them speaking and music coming out of them."

"It's what they watch all the time. It's called a screen," Then with a questioning look said, "Did you see her paramours?"

"No, they were not there. I only saw the Grodor massaging her and rubbing oil onto her horribly wrinkled skin. It was like a brood sow being cared for by little fat, hairless rats. Gives me the creeps." Brekka shook as if trying to shake off flies, those horrible warbles she had seen, or something else even more revolting. "It was morbidly grotesque in the highest. The Queen's just a bloated old sow. I expected something more sinister, more powerful looking."

"In her world she's powerful enough. Look again, I'm sure the paramours are nearby. She rotates them regularly. She hates to be alone, and she dotes upon her pretty boys daily."

She peeked back through the crack in the curtain. "No, I don't see them."

"Then come over here, there's another slit in the curtain."

Brekka, placed her eye against the glass and peeped through the crack in the curtain. This time she saw three young men who appeared twenty winters of age, maybe younger, and they wore make up. All were pleasing to the eye, tall, and yet, somewhat effeminate looking, with little muscle tone or hardness. As she studied them, they appeared to be scrying too. Just as Gloomullah, they were watching one of the mirrors with huge buildings inside, and chariots with people in them, but no horses pulling the chariots. All the while, they pressed black sticks in their hands and yelled like they were at a tournament.

Brekka said, "I see them now. They're so young and handsome. Eyes are painted, and it looks like they wear make-up. How on earth could they ever think to love that disgusting brood-sow? And how could they possibly arouse themselves enough to mount her?"

Yiska laughed, "They think she is a goddess. Besides, she gives them noogs. Did you see that jar full of white beads on the shelf by the blankets? Those are the noogs. Once you take noogs for a while, it becomes all you want. When I was captive here, I would cheek my noogs. I realized that they are how she controls everything that goes on here. She once told me in the days of the Amerikans, that whole countries of people were chemically controlled. It's how their politicians kept the peace. She has these noogs given to her paramours to make them service her and adore her. She gives them to the grodor to make them do her bidding, and she controls the Growlings outside with them as well. Now that the Pitters are dealing with her, you can be sure she will soon be controlling them with her noogs, and extending her control into the outer world as far as she can. Anyone who falls under the power of her noogs can never turn against her will."

"That would explain why our spies reported the Pitters are using the noogs."

"Yes, Yggep, introduced the pitters to them. She thought to gain power over them herself, but she obviously miscalculated the strength of the Syr Folk."

"But her paramours, don't they ever try to escape?"

"Why would they want to? She's had the Grodor rear them, and then they are taught she is the All-Giver and that life itself comes only at her bidding. She is the master of her world. To them she is the Great Mother."

"More like a fat spider feeding on juicy little honeybees." Brekka unconsciously placed her hand to her sword. "How do we get in to her?"

"There's a door to the back of this room, but the Grodor will be all over us in there."

"I only counted six. Are the paramours a problem?"

"No, it's not the paramours. Look back through the first crack."

Brekka walked swiftly back to the first crack in the curtain and looked through the slit.

Yiska said, "Do you see a stick that's attached to a black cord?"

"Just a moment," She cocked her head for a better view, "Yes, I'm seeing it."

"You must somehow cut that off first."

"Why?"

"Because she can press it when she wants something, or she can talk through it, and she can press it a certain way to make all the Grodor come to her aid in an instant. The only reason we've made it this far is because I turned off the warning systems, but that one is an emergency warning system which functions anytime the other one goes down. After you sever that cord, we must kill the remaining Grodor to get to the queen. If one escapes, they'll activate a lock down on all doors and release the nihtgangers or chapinapes."

"Chust show me the way," Brekka said.

On the backside of the glass chamber was a purple door. Brekka drew her labyrus axe out, charged in, and immediately hurled the labyrus, severing the black cord, sending it like a writhing snake spitting flames across the floor. Twirling, Brekka lopped the head off of one Grodor with her lady sword, and followed through with a blade thrust to drop another. She saw Yiska stuck one in the neck, and another one grabbed Brekka. Strong for its size it tried to topple her. Brekka brought the butt of her sword down on his head, and Yiska turned to stab him. The last one fled for the door. Brekka hurled her blade to stop it. He hit the door with a thud, and fell to the floor motionless as a pile of dough.

The paramours clustered like drones, as they expected to be the next to die, but Brekka immediately placed her blade, Snake Fang, to Gloomullah's throat and said, "Yiska, make sure those boys don't try anything, and tell them I'll cut them from nave to chaps if they move from where they now crouch."

"Yiska!" Gloomullah said in a husky voice, which Brekka could only ever remember hearing on an old Idoan woman who smoked tobacco incessantly, "Please, tell your friend I'll give you whatever it is you want. There is no need for bloodshed. I mean no harm. You, me, we can bargain."

"I am Brekka of the Herewardi, and I have been sent here to kill you. Not to bargain. There is a wrongness about this place which I shall right. Of this you may be sure, there will be no bargaining. The only bargain I will make with you is that you shall live only as long as you answer my questions. When I get the answers I want, I will put you to the sword and end this infestation of monstrosities you have begotten."

"Ask away, child," Gloomullah said in a gleefully evil and sinister tone. Then she shifted her weight to a more relaxed pose like a bloated catfish on a muddy river bank, and prepared to bargain like a Mexus Merchant. "Whatever do you wish to know, my child?"

"How old are you, and how did you get to be so old?"

"Perhaps, you'd be so kind as to tell me who you are first? You said Brekka, but where are you from?"

"I am Brekka, Sur Sceaf's daughter, of the Herewardi. That is all you need know."

"Very well. Now it is clear to me why there is this misunderstanding. Do you realize I am six hundred and sixty nine years old. To understand this, you must know that I come from the generation where society began to fray at the edges. Laws stacked on laws, and soon life was too rigid to move. Corporations were strip mining the Earth, and all governments were up for sale. The masses were dissatisfied, so they had to be controlled by police, imprisonment, and drugs. Race wars, religious wars, resource wars, all plagued us from one end of the planet to the other. We became like jungle animals at a dried up water hole. The government issued mandatory chemical prescriptions for any infraction. I being a scientist of drugs and pharmaceuticals, was put in this facility underground to determine the best way to control populations, and given full reign to experiment on population reduction techniques."

"I am not following. You are using words I do not fully understand."

"I am saying, the government controlled the mass of people through drugs, chemicals, and allocation of resources. You know, medicine, food, water." She motioned with a flabby arm and cupped her hand to the mouth. "We were a society that celebrated youth. Old age became despised. It was seen as a curse, and all sorts of chemicals were found to prolong life. There were drugs to increase your libido, drugs to allow one to be obese without any consequences. Most of the joys formerly only the benefit of youth were now available in medicinal drinks for people of any age, and were just a swallow away. It was believed artificial looks were better than any ugly natural reality. Breasts could be made bigger, sexes could be changed. One decade the style was to be fat, the next decade it was to be thin. People changed body shapes the way they changed clothing styles. Anyone with money could look anyway they wanted. I was sent here to the wilderness of New Mexico to head a team of scientists in what was called the Citadel Science and Research Lab. A corporation with government fingers, with the sole goals of learning how to extend the life span beyond its normal range and how to control behaviors chemically."

"What happened to make these lands poisonous?"

"There was a group of scientists in this building that worked on weaponized diseases. While transporting some of the vials, they were struck by an earthquake that released the poisons. The citadel was charged with the task of doing the cleanup, and the resulting disease that was released struck the exposed people and animals, causing them to age rapidly for the most part, and their few offspring began having the effects of aging right away."

"I had developed ways of treating them with hormones when the meteors... I'm sorry, you would say burning stars, struck the earth. And suddenly, society, as we formerly knew it, was no more. It happened over night. The citadel became a fortress against marauding bands above that were ravishing and sweeping the land like schools of sharks in those days. It was all chaos and bedlam above." She waved her flabby arms, "Out there. But I just stayed down below doing my research. I figured a way of collecting the hormones they needed from young women's menses to treat the growlings, and thereby learned that if I took it, it prolonged my life as well. Also, if we only used virgins the chance of disease was greatly diminished. We all used the menses in the beginning, then some were weary of life without youth. Two of my underlings, Doctor Afeerah Ish and Doctor James Vardrop stole my research and headed to New York and Toronto where they said they had a plan to heal the society by using their genetic research to end all strife and war forever. They gave me credit. Even called me the great She-Wolf because I begat them spiritually by teaching them all the genetic splicing or mixing of seed codes they knew. But I deliberately gave them a flawed formula, that if followed would lead to severe aggression in their offspring and an ashen skin color. It's what I call a Melanin Graft, a seed code from rats that increases the melanin in the body to dangerous levels, making you excessively aggressive, combined with the seed code of wolves to ensure absolute obedience. To my surprise, my dear servant, Kurtzig found an egg labeled Afeerah Ish, and I had a vial of Doctor Vardrop's seed. With it I created Yggep, and had her raised by the Grodor as my Under-Queen. Once Yggep grew up and started her medical experiments, two of my team members committed suicide. She was told that several male scientists were plotting to kill her, so she forced all the male scientists to leave. It wasn't long before we female scientists grew lonely and we had to conspire to check Yggep's power."

"You mean Yggep the Bitch?"

"That is strong language and certainly would have been called politically incorrect in my day. Is that what you call her?" Gloomullah said as she ate one of those white chips out of a nearby bowl. "She was like a daughter to me. I taught her science and medicine. Then when she asked for a man, she chose one of the Balmoran slaves. Barely bigger than a Grodor. That fitful, pitiful specimen of a real man, Jacob Walker. But then she lacked beauty herself, was rather manly looking as well. All my labor and hopes were gone. And the nerve of her to betray me like that! Together, her and Walker sought to extend my experiments with the sole aim of acquiring power of their own. I could not control her. Unlike her parents, who sought to use the seed code to raise up a police force from the prison population, Yggep's appetite for the bizarre knew no limit, and soon all sorts of monsters were running loose in the Poison lands. I had to tell her to leave or I would be forced to expel her. And she left in great disfavor. Then when this sweet little Navajo girl came in a slave gang I chose her, thinking she would be much more pliable to my will, but you see, even Yiska has betrayed me."

Yiska pressed against the large round bed. "But I never betrayed the Diney way. We, Navajo, put people before power."

"What about all the tortures I heard of?" Brekka said, glancing over at the still cowering paramours.

"Oh, the monstrosities and tortures that girl, Yggep, was involved in. None of those were my doing." She coughed. "Maybe a little of the mixing of naked mole seed codes with human seed codes, but none of the work done on the aborted fetuses. When I realized she had garnered so much power, she left with a vast supply of my noogs, and had even brought the Pitters into the compound. She even had a baby by the Skull Worm, if you can imagine crossing with those creatures. I then chose Yiska; someone with a soul, as another Under-Queen to replace her. Haven't I always done good by you, Yiska?"

"You may have thought so, but I was robbed from a loving family, which I would have much preferred over this sinister place. To me this place was always a place of darkness. The epitome of the darkness of domestication your evil generation was wont to spawn."

Yiska' expressions were pained when she talked about being separated from her family, but Gloomullah acted as coy, if all this was some sort of rehearsed play.

Brekka pressed her blade against the folds of Gloomullah's fat neck, and ordered, "Tell me more, for your life grows shorter as we wait, Dark Mother."

"Before I could ever discover the fates of Dr.s James Vardrop and Afeerah Ish and call them back, it was too late, for I wanted to stop them from making the race of tyrants they were working on, thinking they were creating a policing force. Their 'Super Humans' as they named them were no humans at all. It was too late."

"Why?"

"Because the burning stars and the earthquakes destroyed the last of social order, and I was left here for hundreds of years alone, surrounded by the Poisoned Lands with a perfectly operative citadel. The few survivors on the surface easily became pliable to my will, and I had all the knowledge in the world to rebuild my world from the ground up. The team of female scientists that worked with me were accustomed to my superior credentials and continued to follow my directives. It did not take me many generations to figure out that the pitters were the dark work of the Doctors Vardropi and Ish."

"Brekka said, but you supplied them with the seed code of the Pitters."

"Yes, because they wouldn't follow my directives. They teamed up against me. Made me an appendage to the very works I created. Then, when they implanted the flawed seed code I gave them in their 'Super Servants' which they had created from the prison populations of New York, I knew they were putting into place the plan to bring about world peace. Oh, that boy was so stuck on 'world peace'. But I knew it would not take long before their creations would spread and come under my control through my Noogs. Vardrop was hell-bent on world conquest and filled with his guilt-ridden religiosity, which he indoctrinated his pliable Pitters with. You see, he was once a priest of some sort and couldn't help infusing them with his own religiosity and personality flaws. Like father, like son. It seems they were particularly bent on conquering you Herewardi with their boiling hatred of your love of tolerance, your heathen gods, multiple brides, and self-rule. But Vardrop did not count on my chemical controls. I had him on a long leash and was just beginning to reel him in. He did not count on my commandeering his war machine through my Noogs. Even now, many Pitters are coming under my sway and bring me what I want. I've been able more than once to slow down their conquest or speed up their growth when I sold them the secret of the bamboo fruit causing rapid population increases." She smiled with a hollow, devilish grin that lifted her wrinkled cheeks like the smile of an old crocodile ready to swallow a cygnet. "You see, we can have the whole world eating out of our hand, if you let me show you how, Brekka, royal daughter of Sur Sceaf." She popped another chip in her mouth and offered Brekka some.

Brekka held her hand up. "Your ways do not tempt me, Troll-Wife. The spirit of life has departed from you long ago."

"Troll-Wife! Ha Ha. That is cute. Yes, you are Herewardi and I know your origins too. You are the offspring of that Doctor Howrus and his colleagues; professors of ancient cultures, history, and other anachronisms at Shepherd University on the Potomac. The things other globalist universities deemed irrelevant. Some said the old Virginia gentleman actually believed what he taught; sort of a revived heathen spiritualism. I heard he even believed he was in contact with Heavenly Elves. Some say he taught that the Elven Lords of olden times continued to visit men throughout the long ages of mankind right up until the collapse, and that the elves would continue forever in their ministrations to mankind. Doctor Howrus must have had one vivid imagination."

"See to it you take his name carefully upon your lips, Troll-Wife, for it is holy spoken by me. The Lore Masters have taught us that you Amerikans kept your people content and stupid with consumption, while you ate up the earth with your machines. We have heard how you sold your democracy to corporations, your republic for union, and your freedoms for security. It seems to me, you mean to sustain your selfish needs at the expense of everyone else, that is not my way, but I shall end your life and your evil now."

"Come on, Brekka, what is the difference between you and I. I will not pretend to the morality of my world, nor should you to yours. I know how your men have many wives. I can give you power over the Pitter's, and look at all my pretty boys. Isn't that what a woman of war really wants? Endless power and all the virile men you could ever hope to ride. See how they are so pleasing to look on and surround one's self with. Imagine troops of young men to do your every bidding. I could make you Queen of the World."

"Everything I do is for others, and as for our men, you will never find any men more willing to sacrifice for the common good. Everything you do is for yourself only. Had these paramours the wisdom and choice, they would spit you out like the rotten egg you are."

"But I can give you wisdom, power, riches, youth, even more paramours such as these. Whatever you desire, my dear. Just tell me what you want, and I can make it happen. But don't kill me. Don't shut these eyes which have wakened for six hundred and sixty nine years."

"I desire all those things you speak of, but only as they serve those I love in the order and moral science they were meant to be given. You, on the other hand, have become a lawless, immoral monster with no controls. You have ignored the laws of the Great Mother and violated and defiled all we hold sacred. You and that hell-spawned bitch, Yggep, have created the muckle-mark-steppers, creeps, skin-walkers, snucky punks, and other unnamable monstrosities. Look at you; you are a brood-sow that feeds like a vampyr on these innocent virgins and paramours for your own lusts sake." Brekka looked at the huddled boys who stared back wide-eyed and still bewildered. "These innocent boys are made to service you, rather than have their own lives. Need I remind you of all the souls you have already destroyed, and not one word of sorrow did I hear from your foul, gluttonous lips. The thick make up you wear can never hide your black heart, for you are a daughter of Hell, if ever I knew one. When I think of all the lives that went unlived chust for your wanton lusts, the abomination grieves me. And then you thought so little of them as to market them back to the Pitters as slaves for a life of certain Hell. This cries out for justice in my ears. And what of those beautiful young ladies you gave to the Pitters for camp whores. By the Holy Ur Mother, I slay you in the name of holiness and extinguish your darkness out of the Ea-Urth forever."

Gloomullah shrunk back in horror like a frightened pig into its burrow. Her eyes were yellow-brown like tobacco stained onion skin glaring out of swinish hollows of madness.

"Please, Yiska, stop her."

Yiska stood over the cowering paramours and said, "I have long yearned to see the world set right. Brekka bears the sword of righteousness. Her will is my will."

With that declaration, Brekka plunged her sword into the bowels of Gloomullah, then twisted and stabbed upward with a powerful thrust to her heart. Gloomullah's face showed absolute shock and disbelief. She let out a scream such as a panther makes when struck by a spear, followed by a gurgling groan. Her fat body melted over the bed. The sheets soaked up the blackest of blood. Then her morbidly obese body sank into the bed just like an enormous rotten tick.

The paramours glommed together, simpering, and cringing. They were terrified at Brekka's presentation of violence.

Brekka cleaned the tarry blood off her wave blade on the bed sheets and moved nearer the cringing boys. "Stop your whimpering. It's not manly. You boys need fear nothing from me. We'll see to it you are cared for. Now pick yourselves up and follow me before the Grodor come and slay you." Then turning to Yiska said, "Do you know the quickest way out of here?"

"We have to get back to the small room, but the Grodor will attack if they see these paramours with us and no Grodor or Hags attending."

"I guess we'll just have to fight our way out of it then. And all this for some pretty, pretty, perfumed boys. Here," she pulled a blanket from a nearby shelf, "you all walk behind this blanket and keep yourselves covered. Yiska, you watch them, and I'll keep the hall clear by going ahead of you and slaying as I go."

"First, let me grab the noogs." Yiska said.

"Just leave them," Brekka said. "I don't want to play their evil game."

"You don't want that. These boys will turn into some sick dogs if you do. It takes at least a moon to get them off the noogs. You have to keep reducing the drugs or these men will become unbearable to be near. Worse than a sow in heat."

"Very well then, bring them." Brekka saw how the boys gravitated towards Yiska, probably seeking the familiar. But anytime they looked at Brekka, they trembled with fear, sowered their eyes, and tweaked their faces.

Yiska grabbed the noogs in one arm and held the corner of the blanket with the other. She said, "You, the dark haired one with the purple shirt, hold the other corner of this blanket, and the rest of you follow if you want any more noogs."

Opening the door a crack, Brekka peeked out and saw two Grodor putting some sort of bedding in one of the rooms. As soon as they disappeared behind a door she signed for Yiska to hold up the blanket and follow.

Yiska said, "You purple shirt. Hold the blanket up higher, if you don't want to be killed."

"My name is Simalah." The purple-shirted paramour with the raven black hair ventured.

Brekka said, "So, you all do have a tongue."

"A learned tongue, I might add." The golden blond with the white blousy shirt declared. Brekka admired the boldness he was suddenly projecting. It pleased her they were starting to display some courage. "And my name is Jimaloh." He proudly patted his chest.

"You need not think we are dumb just because we are silent," The red-haired boy in the tight fitting blue shirt said. "My name is Rimalum. But why did you kill the Queen All-Giver? We will lose everything, now."

Brekka said, "Rimalum, do you understand the difference between good and evil?"

"Yes," Rimalum said. "To serve the queen's needs is good. Those who serve deserve favor. To do evil is to not listen to the queen and to refuse meds."

"Boy, I am going to have to separate the night from the day for you all." Brekka said shaking her head. "She has told you this to keep you ignorant; in a state of innocence to serve her own selfish needs. If you want to know what evil is, then I tell you it is Gloomullah-Elli-Termis."

"How can she be," Simalah said, "she is the All-Giver."

"She is the All-Taker. You poor fools have been utterly deceived, trapped in this tomb by that fat old spider. She has kept you blind in her web to the fact that there are whole other worlds outside these walls. Worlds of beauty and glory such as you have never seen. And worlds of terror and ecstasy to be experienced." She motioned with her drawn lady sword for them to keep moving.

"But there is nothing but death outside of the citadel, and killers. Gloomullah told us so." Jimaloh said, as he scratched his head, struggling to dispel his disbelief.

Brekka said, "Ssh! Here come some Grodor."

Six Grodor came out of one door in the hall, walked down three doors and they all entered another room.

"That was a close call. I wasn't expecting them to come out of there." Yiska said.

"What's in these rooms?" Brekka inquired.

Rimalum said, "The blue doors are where the paramours live and the doors that are green are the computer rooms. The yellow doors are the cafeteria, and the white door is the library."

"You lost me." Brekka said, "What is a computer and cafeteria?"

"So you don't know everything?" Rimalum said.

"I never said I did." Brekka shot him a fierce glance and thought, *Smart ass,* but found herself admiring his spunk.

"Well, computers are pretty basic, it's a machine that teaches us everything, and on which we study and learn. And a cafeteria is where we eat our meals."

"Well, in my world we learn from Skalds and Lore Masters, and we eat food at a table with our families. Maybe I don't know what a computer is, but have you ever seen a tree?"

"On the computer."

"No, if you have never been outside the citadel, then you've never seen a real tree. It's more beautiful than anything you can possibly imagine. And you were raised by Grodor. There is no way you could ever know the tenderness of a mother or the calming protection a strong-hearted father can give."

Two more Grodor came out of a yellow door and went into a green door.

"Alright, they're gone."

Rimalum said, "I guess I have not ever seen a real tree. And I don't know what a mother would be like, though I watched a lamb being nursed by a ewe in a film once, and it looked so tender."

"Well, you will soon enough learn these things first hand. A rich world of experience will open up to you such as you have no basis to comprehend at this point."

Brekka held her sword ready for any Grodor that might surprise them. "Now, Mister Wise Guy answer me this. What were those mirrors Gloomullah was looking at?"

"It wasn't a mirror. That was a computer screen and she was watching old movies."

"You've lost me. What's a movie?"

"It's dramas of what the world looked like when Gloomullah was young. She watches them all the time and cries over her youth. Though she cries, she says it's because she likes them."

"Strange..." Brekka said, finding it difficult to believe Gloomullah might have had a heart. Suddenly she was interrupted by three Grodor coming out of the door in front of her. Her mind kicked into battle mode, and she slew them before she thought. "Hurry, help me drag them in a room."

"No time," Yiska said, "Here come six up the hall behind us. Run!"

As they dashed off, they slipped and fell on the glossy floor several times. The strange honking of a goose could be heard, but Yiska said it was no goose. It was an alarm. Finally, they made it into the small room and Yiska pressed the up button. The doors closed just when the Grodor were within arm's reach. As the numbers on the room decreased and Brekka's stomach felt like it was flying down to her feet, Yiska said, "That was too close for me."

Brekka said, "Here's the part, where I ask you. How do we get out of the citadel, since you said they seal the doors closed?"

"There is a button that unseals the doors."

The small room stopped at the fortieth level, which was ground level of the control center. They got out of the elevator and walked to a door. Yiska unsealed the door and they walked out into a large lobby. There was not a growling in sight. Yiska pressed another button and they walked out into the sunlight, to streets filled with dead growlings and Pitters. Going Snake had put them all to the sword and apparently pursued them to the compound to the south, as masses of troops were gathered there.

Rimalum said, "It's just as Gloomullah said, there are killers out here. Look there is death all around us."

"That's because this is a war zone, and a battle has just been fought. Look, I know you've lived sheltered lives, but from now on things are going to get much better for you and a hell of a lot more real than that sub-surface world you were living in."

Far to the south where the troops were gathered, Brekka saw that the battle with the Pitter legions and Kanarus was still raging on. She could see Kanarus had managed to blow another hole in the Pitter compound, but no one was entering. She knew she would have to secure her captives before joining them, so she looked to the north where she had told Xarela to await her return. She took off her shield and reflected the sunlight off of it, signaling Xarela to come for her. Looking back to the south she saw the detachment of Dog Soldiers riding back. It was the Going Snake.

He rode up swiftly to her, signaled for a young brave to bring her Cycnus, and said, "My lady Brekka, I was worried that I'd never see you again."

She overheard the three paramours say, "The Lady Brekka. She's a lady, like in the books on the Middle Ages."

Brekka and Going Snake both looked briefly at them, then Brekka said, "It is accomplished, Going Snake. The Dark Queen is dead. I've been to hell this day. I've freed three of her captives, but they are not yet convinced that they were captives. It will take a while to convince them. I'll wait until Xarela comes, then send these captives with an escort to safety, and I'll join you in the battle."

"That is why I am here, my lady. Kanarus sent me back. He wanted us to take the citadel, but we couldn't find a way in. Once the Far Seers spotted you coming out of the Citadel, he sent us here and said you'd be our way in. He doesn't care whether you kill the Grodor and the Growlings or not, but he wants the captives to be freed and to be secured in our camp before nightfall, my lady."

"So mote it be! We shall await Xarela and then we'll free the captives." Brekka said as she sheathed her sword.

Yiska turned from the three paramours and said, "My lady, Brekka. If we return to free the virgins and paramours, the Grodor will release the chapinapes."

"My Gods!" Brekka said, "Is there no end to the monstrosities of this land? Tell me what in the hell the chapinapes are."

"They are similar to the creeps only taller. Chapinapes stand five feet tall. They were made from the seed codes of a creature called Chimpanzee and some other ape with souped up aggression from melanin grafts out of rats. Powerful, vicious, manlike creatures with fangs like wolves and a bite stronger than a panther's. They can grab with a force greater than any man. I once saw one tear a Pitter limb from limb like you and I could do to a straw doll."

Brekka and Going Snake stared at each other. Then Going Snake said, "No worse than that grizzly you faced off as a child."

"I only survived that because my father came to my rescue."

"Yes, but it was the tools of man and courage that slew it." Going Snake said, "We've got the tools. We nurtured the courage. And Kanarus gave the command."

"Speaking of Kanarus, how goes the battle with the Skull Worm?"

"We have made a great slaughter, lost a lot of men, more than he wanted to, but it's all we can do to cut our ways through them slowly because of all their numbers. They are currently pinned down behind another wall the growlings had built. We blasted through, but it would be too costly to enter. They are the Skull Worm's elite troops. We're trying to determine what the best way to roust them out is, but Kanarus said he will no longer risk his men in another direct siege."

"That is good. He is not trained in direct siege tactics. Besides, we are going to need living warriors to one day carry this battle to the heart of the empire. Have you seen Ruhm anywhere?"

"Yes, he's trying to circle their fortification, riding the walls to study their weakest points. He saved Kanarus' ass from a frontal assault. That's one hell of a shrewd cavalry officer you have there, my lady. Perhaps if we hit the Pitters from several directions at once we can succeed in drawing them out of their cover."

Rimalum boldly came right up to Brekka's shoulder and said, "Is that a horse?"

She smiled at him, "Yes, a real one."

"May I touch it, my lady Brekka?" He said, copying Going Snakes courtesies.

Going Snake said, "This one picks up fast, doesn't he?"

"Apparently," Brekka said smiling, "Go ahead, you may touch it."

She watched curiously as Rimalum walked over to Going Snake's Horse and touched it. "So big, so warm, so strong. Sima, you've got to feel this, it breathes like a furnace."

Sima said, looking to the sky. "I'll be there in a minute. I think that great light there is the sun. It's as warm as the heat lamps, yet unreachable." He stretched his hand towards the sky and jumped.

Jima was crouched to the ground, studying the dirt. "I've found tiny, little creatures here running in a line on the floor and the floor is made of powder."

Going Snake opened his eyes wide and smiled. "These people are going to take some time to teach, aren't they, my lady?"

"That goes without saying. They're intelligent, but have evidently never been exposed to anything but the caverns they lived in."

To the north, a cloud of dust signaled the arrival of Xarela and the Spanix fyrds. He rode up to Brekka, saluted her and said, "My lady Brekka, Os-Frith! I presume jou got the orders for us and the Dog Soldiers to free the captives and take them back to the camp. Kanarus wants any Moxo people if jou find them in there. He said he will give back jour cavalry once they run reconnaissance for him."

"Going Snake just gave me the orders. I suppose I have no need of my Hickoryan cavalry, so Joself and Rodriegelf, I want you to watch these two gentlemen, and answer any questions they may have. They have never seen the real world, so be patient with them." Then turning to Rimalum she said, "I want you to be my guide through the citadel, can you do that?"

Rima said, "I can tell you everything I know and where everything is, but I do not know where the virgins are kept. We were told we would die if we touched them."

"Well, Yiska knows where they are. And you shall surely never die from touching a virgin. In fact you may discover what natural life is truly all about once you do. I promise you it will be far more rewarding than that brood sow you serviced."

Brekka turned to her troops and said, "Draw your short swords and follow me." They went up the stone stairs, entered the door and marched cautiously down the corridor.

After going down the corridor for seven man-lengths, Yiska said, "Here, this is the door to the maiden's dorm."

"Going Snake," Brekka said, "We part company here. Take your Dog Soldiers and follow Yiska to free the maidens. Get them to the surface immediately, and be on the lookout for those chapinapes Yiska warned of. Xarela, Rimulum, and my fyrd will assist me in freeing the paramours. But Yiska says we'll have to return tomorrow to rescue the bulk of the maidens and paramours, as the lower floors have already been sealed off." She waved, "See you above, Blood Brother."

# CHAPTER 16 :

## THE SHEPHERDING OF THE CAPTIVES

**B**REKKA RODE TOWARD CAMP WITH Yiska by her side. They had easily rescued what maidens and paramours were in the unlocked floors. They would camp in the desert again until the citadel was claimed and all the halls cleansed of the ferocious creatures patrolling the many floors.

"What about the Grodor?" Brekka inquired.

"They now know their queen is dead," Yiska said, "and they all scrambled with the hags into the shelter in the deep caverns below to avoid the release of the chapinapes. We met no resistance freeing the maidens."

"I'm wondering what shall happen to them."

"My take," Yiska said, "is that they shall reunite with the Growlings in the upper chambers of the citadel. They'll have to re-purpose themselves, and that could take several days. Now they are like a queenless hive of bees. Problem is, Gloomullah alone held the formula to make the Noogs. Once they wear off there's going to be a lot of unhappy growlings, Grodor, and Pitters. Not to mention the control of the skin walkers in the deep caverns below."

"You mean to tell me she controlled the skin walkers, as well?"

"Yes, they live even deeper in the earth. They were the messed up experiments that she allowed Yggep to make. The ones she couldn't control, she banished into the Poisoned lands. They made them from mixing the blood codes of naked mole rats with the aborted live fetuses of maidens and had women from the slave camps beget them. When Gloomullah learned she could not trust nor rely on Yggep, she created the chapinapes in retaliation, and started training me as Yggep's replacement. All she told you in her chamber was to honey coat what she has done and lay all the blame on Yggep. Gloomullah only pretended to turn her face from Yggep's experiments. She really wanted Yggep to raise an army up to take over the Pitters. But all Yggep accomplished was the torturing of endless maidens and creating the hosts of monsters that now plague the Poisoned lands. When Gloomullah learned it was Yggep's intent to be queen of the world, she immediately switched her plan by negotiating with the Pitters for Noogs and refusing Yggep entrance into the citadel so that all Noogs could only be gotten directly from the source..."

"Gloomullah, I am sure, must have been shocked when she learned you, too, had betrayed her."

"I never betrayed her. I was never one of them. My grandmother made me Navajo. It is a heritage the Diney may never forsake. We are born with a sense of what is holy and recognize instinctually that which is not."

# CHAPTER 17 :
## THE TAKING OF THE CITADEL

C EOLWULF'S LOG: IT IS THE *tenth day of the Hay Moonth, Knut the Reapers Day in the year 603 H.S.O. As I am honored to be Chief Skald in the Ndee Lands, Kanarus asked me to scribe for him here in the Poisoned Lands. Kanarus made great strides in driving the Pitters into the fortress while Going Snake had successfully driven the Growlings into the safety of the citadel. The Lady Brekka along with the Navajo Maiden, Yiska, successfully accomplished the assassination of the evil queen, Gloomullah, and they escaped the citadel unscathed, bringing with them three young paramours whose sole function had been the pleasuring of the queen.*

*For seventeen winters, these pretty boys, named Simalah, Jimaloh, and Rimalum, were conditioned to service the queen both sexually and socially. They claim that there are many more like them who service the other scientists, all elderly females. They also confirmed Yiska's description of the College of Virgins who served as assistants in the laboratories as well as serving as menses donors. According to Yiska's estimate, these virgins currently number three to four hundred, and there are more in the citadel, yet unredeemed. They lived like termites in the labyrinthine bowels of the citadel. It was a stunning pronouncement.*

*Kanarus did as much as possible during this first day of battle, and succeeded in forcing the Pitters to shelter inside the fortress. His archers rained down volleys of arrows in unrelenting deluges. But as the sun marched across its final fourth of the sky, he ordered his forces to return to the safety of the base camp in the canyon where they had defended themselves against the night creatures and where they were far enough away to prevent likely attacks from the enemy.*

Brekka and Yiska had returned to base camp with the three paramours before the main body of troops arrived. The journey had taken an inordinate amount of time. The boys were awestruck by the sunset, and even by the scrubby desert plant life. Apparently, their contact with nature had been only through the magic screens they called computers. At first, they were both fascinated and terrified by the painted ponies Brekka had procured from Going Snake. Coaxing them onto the horses' backs had been an exercise in patience. It was difficult for them to grasp the concept which any Herewardi or Apache child of four winters had easily mastered. Ruhm had just ridden in with his cavalry and the boys marveled at their uniforms.

While Yiska took charge of the boys, Brekka held a debriefing conference with her Lady Knights, who were especially interested in her description of the killing in the lair of the Queen of the Underworld. After she gave them a rundown, she ordered Freyxus to formulate a strategy dealing with the virgins and paramours.

As she walked with Cisne, she was startled by a tug on her upper arm. Ruhm wore a pleasant smile as he declared, "Why does it not surprise me that the Lady Knight was successful? Still I was very worried for her welfare. Be careful tomorrow, my love. I worry about you taking too many chances. You know my prayers will be with you, and I don't want even one scar on that pretty face of yours." He gave her a gentle kiss on the forehead.

"Don't try that patronizing flirtation with me, Ruhm Lee. And worry is simply a way of praying for that which you do not want to happen. So stop worrying. I thank you for your concern, but it would interest me all the same, what God do you pray to for help?"

"Just god, as Ceolwulf the Skald said, 'I'm a non-theist'."

Brekka frowned. "Whatever that is? Sounds Greek to me."

"It's just we Hickoryans are not as specific about who god is, as are your people. We believe in the Christ and the Bloody Rood, but we merely acknowledge that there is something greater than us all, that has the general welfare of all mankind at heart or else we should have all perished long before now."

"Oh, I see." She was delighted to know he was discussing spiritual matters with Ceolwulf.

"May I walk you back to base camp?" he asked with a flirtatious grin.

"Suit yourself," she said, as she made her way through a contingent of returning Fyrd Warriors.

"What was the Dark Queen like?" Ruhm asked, as he gently smacked his thigh with his rider's crop. "The awful Harridan everyone feared so much."

"Oh!" Brekka paused, a feeling of disgust settling in her stomach at the thought of all that black blood pouring forth from the swollen tick. "She was awful looking, Ruhm. She looked like a bloated toad with wrinkles. Just like a rotting carcass. And she had the blackest most self-serving heart I have ever felt. Honestly, several things come to mind when I think on her. First the toad, then she reminded me of some brood-sow with all her lackeys and drones sucking at her teats. Like a bunch of little Grodor piglets."

"Did she say anything to you?" Ruhm asked, as they came upon Yiska directing the paramours, Sima, Rima, and Jima in the basics of setting up camp and preparations for the long night. "Anything about the Amerikans?"

"Oh yes," Brekka said with eyebrows lifted. "She talked about how warped they had become. Then she tried tempting me with power, drugs, and control. She was like the Demon Tempter the Quailor talk about. What's his name...? Satan."

"What do you mean?"

"She told me she would elevate me to be Queen of Queens over all peoples, even the Pitters, if I would but spare her and let her live as she had been living."

"So what did you say?"

"I told her she was a selfish old lizard who was blinded by her vanity to the misery she had generated in the Ea-Urth, and then my Ur Fyr directed me to slay her, that the Ea-Urth might be rid of her and her kind forevermore. Honestly, Ruhm, it was like stabbing a rotten, bloated, old crocodile." Then turning to Yiska, Brekka asked, "Yiska are you willing to accompany me on the morrow into the citadel that we may put an end to all this evil and slay the Growlings and the Grodor?"

"I am prepared to go anywhere with you, my lady, where so ever you command, but it may not be necessary for you to slay either the Grodor or the Growlings, and thereby acquire the rest of the paramours and virgins without loss of blood."

Brekka felt puzzled. "Why ever not? My goal is to rid the land of abominations."

Yiska's eyes brightened. "Of course, you may slay them if you wish, but they may prove very useful. Once you slew Gloomullah they are as a riderless horse. If we can persuade them you are the new queen, we could likely take over the reins of government and they will follow you anywhere you direct."

"How am I to do that?" Brekka said as she glanced back at Ruhm and Cisne for support.

"We must go to the Grodor Central Chamber tomorrow. They are in a defensive mode, so we will have to face the chapinapes or dog men, but if we can make it to Bufo, the Head Eunuch and the Hag Scientists, I will explain that you are the new queen and that they are to serve you now. Bufo will, in turn, go into the citadel and command the obedience of the growlings under their commander, Grumpus."

"What about the hags? Weren't they Gloomullah's compatriots as well?"

"I cannot predict how they will respond, but at least they know Gloomullah supplied them with the drugs to keep them young. If you agree to continue their supply of Noogs, they should be content enough. At any rate, what resistance could they possibly offer?"

Ruhm said, "Well, that all sounds way too dangerous to me. Why not just throw some Beast- Stoppers in their chamber and be done with it?"

"I know it won't be easy," Yiska said, as she grasped a braid of her hair, "but I know these Grodor, and they are not inclined to do evil. It would be a shame to kill them merely because they innocently and dutifully served their queen; especially if that loyalty could be transferred to us. It would work in our favor."

Brekka thought for a moment before declaring, "Yiska is right. This is a better way than slaying everyone. Mayhap they can give us of their sciences. For that to happen we will have to speak their language."

Ruhm looked at her with his head cocked to one side, as if he couldn't believe his ears. "And that language would be?"

Yiska explained, "Gloomullah controlled the commanders with her Noogs; drugs so addictive that you'd give your own children for them, once addicted. We can offer the drugs in return for their compliance." Yiska paused. "But once we run out, there's none to replace them, because she alone possessed the formula."

Brekka smiled. "Perhaps we cannot replace them, but I'll bet we can have a substitute made."

Ruhm said, "What are you thinking?"

"My medicine man, Siwel the Chartreusean, can come up with a substitute." Brekka turned toward her waiting handmaidens. "Ynys, would you go to the tent of Siwel and tell him I need to discuss a matter with him right away?"

The banana-green handmaiden said, "As you wish my lady."

As Ynys darted off for Siwel's tent, Yiska asked, "You mean the green-skinned Witch Doctor?"

"Yes, he's unexcelled at herbs, knows the opiates, sages, and mushrooms of greatest power; he was trained under Xelph, Face-Of-Stars, and Zschamillah. I shall consult with him on this matter. If anybody knows, he will know what to do."

Yiska nodded. "About the chapinapes, that won't be an easy matter. We were lucky we didn't encounter them earlier. They're viciously aggressive. All you can do is kill them and that is at best a dangerous affair." Yiska looked over at Rima, Sima, and Jima. "Oh, I've got to show those three how it is we build a fire. I'll just be right there if you have any more questions, my lady."

"That's fine. I got all I wanted from you." Brekka shook her head as she addressed Ruhm. "Poor boys, don't even know the basics of living in the real world."

"Poor boy or not." Ruhm said, "That one there," He pointed with his head at Rima, "has an eye for you, Brekka and that's for sure."

"Custus Ruhm Lee, do I detect a tinge of jealousy in you?"

"That you do, my lady, and just to let him know you're all mine," Ruhm paused and took Brekka in his arms and planted a passionate kiss on her lips that warmed her to the soles of her feet. Then backing off, he declared in his usual cocky tone, "That kiss should brand you as mine—and mine alone!"

Brekka struck Ruhm on the shoulder playfully. "Why Ruhm Lee, you cad. What got into you? What's everybody going to think now?"

"Only that which I've always known; that we were meant for each other."

"And when did you come to that conclusion?"

"It's too private to talk about here. Suffice it to say I had a night vision of the woman I should marry."

Brekka hid her surprise. "Honestly, Ruhm, I don't know if you're serious or mocking me." She saw his eyes grow intense and knew he was sincere. "Well, you better quit dallying around here," she swatted him on the back, "and get your men set for defending us from the skin walkers and creeps tonight. By the gods, Ruhm Lee, don't you ever pull a surprise like that on me again. You hear. Now be off!" She secretly relished the experience and almost wished he'd do it again. In that briefest moment Ruhm's eyes had conveyed something to her she had never seen until that moment. He was connecting to her at a spiritual level. He was beginning to express spiritual maturity. Something she had hoped for, but had given up expecting.

He turned and looked back at her with those loving eyes. "Good night, my sweet lady knight. Sleep with the faeries!"

"You nasty devil, you! There will be fat chance of that tonight. It's likely we'll all be sleeping with Trolls and Demons on the prowl about our tents." Brekka smiled. Still reflecting on the pleasantness of the unexpected kiss, as she busied herself building a fire and setting some bread sticks over it. She gave one final look at Ruhm, who waved and smiled as his dashing figure faded off into the twilight.

Rima walked cautiously over to her and said, "Brekka, was your groom unable to please you?"

She frowned, noting how caring his face looked. "Whatever do you mean, Rima?"

"I just saw that your groom kissed you, but did not bring you to any satisfaction. If you wish, I shall be glad to bring you to satisfaction, I am skilled in making a woman purr."

"Rima, you have a lot to learn about our world. Ruhm is just a very good friend of mine. I have never known a man sexually and will not until I am married. There's a different world awaiting you. You are no longer expected to service anyone you don't want to service. You are a free man who can choose what you want your life to be from now on."

"Then I choose to service you. I am sure it would give me great pleasure to bring you to satisfaction for I have never known anyone as flawlessly beautiful as you. It is truly more stimulating than I can tell you, but I'd be very happy to show you."

Brekka was frustrated. "Yiska," she called out, "would you help Rima to understand the world he is living in now. I've got to prepare for the creeps and need to get some food in me."

"Certainly, my lady. Rima, stay with me and let Brekka tend her own business."

The fires and torches were lit bright that night. As the moon drifted behind a dark set of clouds, silence shrouded the land like a sodden blanket. Kanarus stood his first watch with his wife, Wilona, and his guards, while two-thirds of his men slept. Brekka had Xarela do likewise with her troops. The unnatural hush ended when the mules began braying, followed by the pluck of bow strings and hissing screams; then came the sounding of the hunter's horn that signaled full alert.

The attack of the creeps had begun. Just then, the stench of the Shit-Devils filled the air like the stinking breath of Hell as it quaffed over the camp in sickening waves. All who smelled it scrunched their faces in revulsion. The sound of alarm echoed throughout the camps, and the creeps spread out with clicking insect sounds bouncing from all directions. Brekka held high her iridium and gold shield in one hand and with a torch in the other she swept the light from the iridium side through the desert landscape. At the same time she reflected on the words of Govannon, "This is no normal shield. Once you learn how to be at one with it, you will have its amazing powers revealed to you." She fiddled with it while she moved it about. Placing her hands in various places over its surface to feel different vibrations and temperatures depending on where she placed the hand.

As she swept the reflected light across the desert, shrill cries arose en masse from the bush, as if the shield collected the light and concentrated it into a deadly beam that scorched the demons and set the brush briefly to fire before the cool night dew suppressed it. creeps leapt like grasshoppers, hopping by the thousands through the air for cover behind the darkness of the sage brush Shadow and creep could hardly be distinguished.

Then as the light of her iridium shield swept out even farther, ghastly large creatures, the size of a man, could be seen approaching in great numbers, like a parade of ghouls against the dark desert night. They looked naked, with folds of yellowish or grey-pink skin that made them appear like plucked chickens walking through the brush. Large dark eyes on their heads appeared to be fogged over and were not reflective of any light whatsoever. From each of their mouths sprung four long teeth, fangs, or tusks the length of a man's foot. Two pointing up and two of them pointing down. The creatures walked upright with their forearms before them like a mantis, their grunts sounding similar to a drift of hogs as they lumbered forward with awkward ponderous strides.

All were bent on attack, but it was obvious from their disorganization that they operated under instinct, with no central direction or command. Brekka thought, *Sometimes chaos can be even more deadly than strategy.* The light of Brekka's shield did not affect them as it had the creeps, for they ponderously loped toward her, like something out of one of her worst nightmares.

As she turned towards her Spanix Fyrd she said, "Xarela, take a bow shot at that large one in the front."

Xarela took careful aim, and soon an arrow found its mark right in the shoulder of the troll. It didn't even flinch or break stride. "Nothing, my lady. The Tro keeps coming."

"Hurry, fire another."

Again an arrow sank into the creatures head, but not a whimper was heard. Just those persistent, annoying grunts. Yiska came up to her and said, "My lady, these creatures feel no pain. You will have to behead them if you are to stop them at all."

"For Os sake, what are they?"

"The Grodor call them skin walkers, but they are some of the creatures Yggep made in her experiments with fetuses and naked mole rats. They are the failed experiments. They proved to be completely unmanageable."

"They are an utter abomination, that's what they are. Draw your swords and cut off their heads. Xarela, send a Beetle to tell the other commanders to do likewise."

"Si-jyes, my lady." Then turning without seeing an available Beetle said to his youthful Lieutenant, "Vasquezelf, tell the other commanders that they are to cut off the Tros' heads."

"Si-jyes, my Commandant. Cut off the Tros' heads." He drew his hand across his throat.

It wasn't but a few seconds later that one of Trolls sent his tusk through an Apache's head like a rock pick.

Kanarus had already engaged with the skin walkers. He had one skewered on his spear which hung in mid air gnashing with its teeth and slashing at Kanarus with its long claws. She saw Vasquezelf yell something at him and then Kanarus pulled his sword and severed the head off the Troll. Soon his fyrd was following suit.

A wave of skin walkers came loping into her camp, the smell of fresh prey causing them to pick up their pace. She quickly thrust a torch in one of their faces, dropped it as it backed away, then swung her sword and sliced the head of the troll from its shoulders. She turned, only to find another one coming straight for her. Xarela interceded and hacked at its neck, half severing the head as it continued to march on after her. With a swift swing of her blade Brekka quickly finished the job. Its head plopped with a thud in front of her while its body clawed at the earth, with those badger-like claws cutting grooves in the desert floor as surely as a plow share.

The fighting went on for several hours. Kanarus ordered every able-bodied warrior to fight in shifts of seven minutes, then to rest through three rotations before resuming fighting. Occasionally, creeps made it in and left severe bites and infectious scratches on the legs or any exposed part of the body. Just after a wave of creeps struck, it was followed by a wave of snucky punks that required one to kick and fight with both hands and feet simultaneously. Everywhere Brekka looked her warriors were plucking off snucky punks and slamming them to the ground, or kicking them through the air like rats, while others stomped on them or clubbed them.

Brekka's shield rotated in sweeps across the desert terrain, and the creeps ran in swarms from its beam. But more irritating than the thousand beady eyes were the little clicking and chirping sounds that seemed to come from everywhere. These creatures swam through darkness like schools of minnows in water; sweeping through camp in swarms of infestation. Siwel's beaucerons made short order of any creeps, and her faery-hounds killed more than their share of the snucky punks. A special type of chatter went up near the dogs which made the creeps move away from them like ants before a burning coal.

The chattering noises continued near Brekka and were so disorienting as to make her turn to one side while a creep gnashed at her from the other side. The clicking made the killing twice as hard, like mud makes walking twice as hard. But by the fourth hour, the remaining skin walkers had been beheaded and the creeps along with the snucky punks quickly fled for the sage brush at the approach of false dawn and the hounds.

The dead warriors were carried from the field and placed on a bonfire to prevent the desecration of their bodies. After ceremonies befitting their race, each was consigned to the flames. Kanarus called for all who had wounds, bites, or scratches to come to the Medicine Tent where the Quailor Hospitalers cleansed and doctored the wounds, and Siwel poured a powerful herbal decontaminate in their wounds, covered the wounds in honey and dressed the wounds with dried sphagnum and swaddling. Soon the camp had quieted down enough for people to catch up on what little sleep they could.

The guards of the third shift had kept the fires burning for those wanting an early breakfast. The Faery-Hounds were released and renewed their barking, which forced any of the hidden creeps to retreat farther and farther into the chaparral. A peace finally settled over the camps, with the first rays of the sun having sent the Trolls back to their lairs. As the last hound was summoned back into camp, the remaining War-Hounds were brought out and showed no more interest, the camp settled into the aftermath of the nightly horror.

Brekka was so exhausted that she managed a few hours rest sitting up against a large trunk in the pre-dawn hours. Her last conscious memory was of Ynys and Wilona tending her scratches and wounds. Occasionally, she woke to the braying of a nearby mule thinking it was the scream of a creep, then quickly drifted back to sleep. In her dreams horrible demonic faces hissed at her and chapinapes tore at her from every doorway, while she ran across the back of a gross fat crocodile twisting to snap at her as she plunged her spear down its throat. It was a fitful sleep at best.

When she finally awoke, the sun had moved up the sky with its warm rays shining brightly, casting a warm blanket of peace and soberness to her mood. But as she rose to her feet her mood quickly changed when she saw the stacks of skin walker bodies, morbid piles of their heads, and creeps bestrewn over the ground, as if somebody had scattered a bunch of slimy-skinned cats and skinned bear carcasses all about the camp.

She rubbed her eyes, then stretched.

Wilona said, "A gruesome sight to awaken to Sister, isn't it?"

"It makes me sick," Brekka said. "This whole business is so sickening."

"But then," Wilona said, as she packed her gear, "it makes you rejoice to think that by your hand in slaying Gloomullah, you have brought an end to all such creepy things. Brekka, the elves and faeries danced in the heavens last night, and sang songs of praise to your name before the throne of the All-Father."

"You say that as if you know it to be so."

Wilona smiled warmly. "As a mortal daughter of the gods, these things are made known to me, and the glow I saw on your necklace let me know they were present."

Brekka took her iridium necklace in hand and looked at it. "Strange that you should say so, because Freyxus had mentioned it to me during the battle." It gave her great comfort to know that the gods were with her.

Yiska emerged from the tent to join them. "The snucky punks managed to terrify the paramours last night. Although they have but few abrasions, they are behaving like they've been mortally wounded. And God forbid, any of them gets a scratch on their pretty faces."

"Nothing that a Herewardi gauntlet won't remedy. But we must keep in mind they are as tenderfoots similar to our four-year-olds. Show forth patience, they will be weaned in time."

After ordering Yiska to distract them by exposing them to the sunlight, Brekka turned her attention to the surrounding horizons and spied Going Snake walking towards her from his camp. He had seen her through the tent door, and was waving to catch her attention. He walked around the campfire to get to her, then saluted and smiled. "My lady, Kanarus has directed me and my Dog Soldiers to assist you in the rescuing of the captives. Once that is accomplished, I am to shepherd them north into the safety of the strength of the hills in Salmalhuer."

"What about the Moxo Maidens that Kanarus is so intent on securing for my Fa? According to my Fa's message, they most likely will be clothed in red."

"Kanarus has put them under your wing, so they are to go to Taxus with you."

"I can't understand why Fa would risk their safety by sending them with us. Surely they would be better off amongst the Presters." Brekka shook her head. "Even though Yiska has claimed they have been well cared for, they can only be a burden on us. For Freya's sake, the Presters would care for them better than I am able to."

Going Snake looked at her with a frustrated expression. "I don't ask questions of those I trust. It is the will of the Lord Kanarus, and especially Sur Sceaf, that you separate the Moxo and that they not travel through the mountains with me."

"So be it." Brekka checked herself. "I shall hate parting company with you. Of all my support commanders, you are my most valued. No one does reconnaissance better than you." She smiled warmly. "And of course, you are my dearest friend."

Going Snake turned crimson. "Perhaps, someday I shall be more than that to you."

"I shall stew upon that thought, but in the meantime, please consult with Freyxus and Verushka about the strategy we have devised to regain the captives."

"Without delay, my lady!"

As Going Snake took leave, Brekka considered how close she felt to him. So close were their families that he was like a young brother to her. They had not even made themselves blood-brothers. So she recognized she needed to shed those big sister feelings and recognize him as the skilled warrior he actually was, he being a most dependable shadow in any battle.

One of the Beetles brought Cycnus, and Brekka was about to mount when the snort of a horse caught her attention. She looked over to see Ruhm Lee approaching her tent on his grey steed, Spitzer.

As his horse strode up beside her, he said, "I see my fair lady is still as gorgeous and beautiful as always. At least the little creeps didn't scratch your pretty face." Then, he quickly diverted his attention to her maids and said, "Os-Frith and good morning, my lovely ladies." He tipped his grey hat at Brekka, Wilona, and the rest of the Lady Knights.

Brekka turned away with a smile only to catch Ynys frozen in a stare of utter admiration at Ruhm.

Brekka thought, *I have to admit, at times he is irresistible.* "Os-Frith, Ruhm." She checked the cinch on her saddle. "You sure look cheerful this morning." Brekka said flirtatiously, "You must have slept better than the rest of us."

"Why do you say that?"

She threw her hair back over her shoulder, "Because you look so full of piss and vinegar. That's why!"

"As well as could be expected amidst that swarm of demons last night. Fortunately, minimal casualties, but plenty of nasty bites and scratches. And what's this piss and vinegar stuff? I spoke nothing but honey and molasses just now."

"I just want to keep you on your guard, buster!" Brekka said with a wink at Ynys. "So what brings you to my camp so early?"

"I had to wish you well today in your campaign against the Grodor and the Growlings."

"Yiska has given me every confidence that it will go well. She says if we can get into Bufo we can probably negotiate their submission to our authority. They should yield to my command, at least now that Gloomullah is dead. Problem is we may not be able to get through those chapinapes in one day."

"In that case, you can wish me well, for I will be laying siege to the Pitter fortress. I don't like being outnumbered and trying to breach a solid stone wall, even with the shoot powder. We would never be able to get close enough to make it effective. This type of warfare is always too costly, and not the type of warfare Kanarus and the Ndee are used to, either."

"Ruhm, I wish you well. May the saints, Russell and Ev'Rhett, guide your sword to victory over the enemy host. May your arrows drink their share of Pitter blood, and may your scramasax slit its share of Pitter throats."

Ruhm appeared confused. "You mean those rascals, Russell and Ev'Rhett, your twin brothers?"

"No, no. I meant the Godhi of olden days for whom they were named, but you will find the Thunder Twins will do well enough in any pinch."

"I suppose you are right, but Kanarus is sending the Thunder Twins as escort to the refugees under Going Snake, that is, after we have freed the rest of them. So I'll be all alone in this campaign. I suspect it's going to take more than a week or two to get into the Growling Fortress where the Pitter Army is holed up."

Brekka walked over to his horse, took his scabbard in her hands, drew his sword, and kissed it. Then she took the white scarf from her neck and tied it about his left ankle. "Go in peace and with my blessing, gentle Hickoryan," Brekka said with an encouraging smile. "May the blood of your rebel forefathers cry out for vengeance through you this day and in the days ahead, for our road is a long one. I hope we end the trail as much friends as we are here today, Ruhm." She blew him a kiss.

"Thank you, my lady. I would slay the whole Pitter empire alone just to hear you say that again at the end of our trail."

She pressed his boot with a squeeze and said a silent blessing upon him. Ruhm winked, goaded his stallion with his heals, and rode off to lead his cavalry.

Seamisch rode up next to Ruhm and reported, "Commander Lee, I had to replace John Miller on the wall. His wounds have reopened and the Green Doctor has just cauterized them. He refuses to allow Miller to leave the medical tent for three days. Apparently, his blood needs to rise in him before he can move again."

"Who'd you replace him with?"

"Young Stillwell. He's like a wolf cub ready to try his teeth."

"That's acceptable, but only if you pair him with his brother, Frank. He has a calmer head."

"Knowing your propensity for keeping hot heads on leash, I'd anticipated such and have given the order."

Ruhm grinned. "You know me too well, my friend. As I, too, know you and your propensity for the ladies, particularly those who are unusual or exotic."

Seamisch laughed. "True enough. Especially that lime tart with the long brown hair. But when I saw how she panted for you like a fawn at a brook, I realized that no one could break that spell."

"I think you're imagining that. She's just respectful."

"She's respectful, all right. All you have to do is snap your fingers and she'd be at your heel. But, of course, you are oblivious to anyone but the Lady Brekka." He grinned. "I have to tell you, my old friend, I enjoyed your company much more when you liked the chase of skirts as much as I do."

"I have to warn you, Seamisch, not to ply any of your wiles on any of Brekka's ladies. The Herewardi sanction no shallow relationships. If you offend one, you offend them all. As part of the Syr Folk, we must honor their laws just as they honor ours."

"I hate to say it but Brekka's put a spell on you. She wears your heart like a ring."

Before Ruhm could answer, Seamisch swung his horse around and galloped back to his men.

Ruhm wanted to be angry, but honesty dictated that he concede to the truth. Seamisch was right. Brekka did wear his heart like a ring. Just the touch of her hand squeezing his boot thrilled him and made him eager to submit to any request she might make of him.

Suddenly, he was plunged into the dark abyss of that terrible night vision of Brekka dangling by one foot from a Dead Tree surrounded by thousands of evil black crows coming to feast on her. He did not understand visions, what they meant or how they were to be interpreted. But he knew the Herewardi put great store in them. The only person he felt comfortable revealing such deeply personal information was Thunder Horse, but he was far away on the Isle. As he had gotten to know Going Snake better on this campaign, he considered sharing it with him, but had not summoned the courage. Besides, he feared that Going Snake might confirm that this was an evil omen. Ruhm could not endure a world without Brekka. Instead, he had determined he would stay close to her and protect her at all costs. But now, as the distance between them increased, he felt powerless to watch over her.

Though it felt a bit alien, he felt the need to call upon something higher than himself. Taking a deep breath, he prayed silently, *Oh, God, whoever you are? Please don't allow any harm to come upon my beloved Brekka. I love her more than life, and though I know I am not worthy of her love by reason of all my youthful swiving and sinful desires, please do not take her love away from me. It would break me and blot out the light of my life. Amen and amen.*

# CHAPTER 18 :

## THE GRODOR OF THE CITADEL

WITH KANARUS AND THE FYRDS in the lead, and Ruhm, Going Snake, and the Thunder Twins right behind, Brekka, her Twelver of Lady Knights, and her Spanix Fyrds arrived at the Citadel at mid-morning. The wall they had obliterated the day before was cleaned up, and the foundation of a new wall was hastily being laid with the mud still sticking out of the laid brick. A net of hissing string had been placed over the area around the hole.

Kanarus led them through the gate and up to the citadel where Yiska said, "It's apparent they have seen us coming and fled into the citadel. The brick is left unfinished. The mud is still wet. Yet the Growlings have already started to rebuild the wall against the skin walkers, indicating that someone inside the citadel is still in command."

"Not the Pitters, I hope."

"Not possible," Yiska said, "More likely Bufo the head eunuch, a wise and good-hearted servant to the core."

Kanarus turned to his sub-commanders and ordered, "Ruhm, once again, you assault the right flank, and Going Snake, you take the left. I will continue the assault on the gate."

Both men nodded their agreement. Brekka noticed Ruhm looking her way as Kanarus declared, "Well, here I leave you, my lady, and here I shall come for you at the fourth point of the day mark. May the All-Father grant you a double measure of his ur fyr to accomplish the feat you have been assigned to and to which my wife says you were born. We unfavored mortals, on the other hand, hope to lay siege to the Pitter fortress and return to the encampment before dark falls with at least some small token of victory."

"Not so, my lord," Wilona retorted, "How much more favored could a mortal be than to be wed to Woon's daughter?"

Kanarus smiled, "Or to share a beloved son together."

Brekka saluted, "So mote it be."

Kanarus gave Wilona a kiss good bye and then goaded Sun Charger on. As Kanarus rode for the fortress Brekka called out, "Kanarus."

He swiftly swung his steed about and said, "Yes, my lady."

"Have you noted there are no Pitter banners flying on the fortress walls?"

He turned again and stared. "I see it is so. Can this mean what I think it does? Hold here and do not enter the citadel just yet."

Kanarus signed for his scouts to ride out and report the status of the Pitter compound. They rode off on either side of him and saluted as they departed in haste.

While the scouts sped off, the cavalry dismounted and took a drink from their flasks, cinched up their saddles, groomed their horses, and relieved themselves.

Kanarus said, "I don't even see any smoke rising from the fortress. Something is very wrong with this picture. Are you sure, Yiska, the Pitters have not pressed their advantage and entered the citadel?"

"That is very unlikely, my lord. Pitters have never been granted admittance into the citadel, and they have always feared to enter, perhaps believing they will be overcome by dark magic. They are only cooperative enemies at best, and despite their overwhelming numbers they have no way of forcing an entry."

"Then the Pitters have fled in the night."

Brekka noticed that the vaunted leader of the Kaninchen Irregulars did not appear dismayed or even surprised. "And why not? They know they have had their feet cut out from under them here. They can't afford to sustain any more losses like we gave them in the desert of the Apache Lands, and they knew we didn't want to suffer casualties from the skin walkers for their sakes. So they probably took a run out the south gate for the Taxus Zongas as soon as we headed for camp yester eve. It makes perfect sense. I take my hat off to the Skull Worm on this one. This will prove most fortuitous because it will give us the manpower to more easily seize the citadel. Then, all we have to do is follow their blood trail back to the Taxus."

Wilona observed, "You must be right, here come the scouts. They would not have made such a speedy return if the Pitter legions were still occupying the fortress."

The scouts reined in their horses, sending up a cloud of dust. "My lord," the tawny young blood said, "They are fled. There is no one there. The tracks lead en masse to the south. There are a few hundred camp whores. The place is otherwise a haunt for nothing but ghosts."

"I can see now, this Skull Worm, though his forces are as numerous as a plague of locusts, scorns a fight with us anywhere but on his own turf and terms. It appears, he is used to fighting an offensive war, and, as Arundel predicted, our offensive strategies are unsettling to him. Very well, hold here, sharpen your blades and groom your horses. I shall accompany the Lady Brekka and her Twelver with my Twelver into the citadel."

"Ruhm said, Lord Kanarus, please permit me to accompany you and the Lady Brekka."

Kanarus deliberated for a moment, before stating firmly, "Frankly, Ruhm, I need you and your cavalry up here and in command. Should anything go awry, only a seasoned cavalry officer could get us safely back to our camp. We must be in control of the field should the Growlings elect to attack."

Ruhm wanted to argue, but Kanarus' commands were not to be questioned. With one final salute, he rode off to position his men.

"If I may offer counsel, my lord," Yiska said, "it would be best for Brekka to appear to be in command here. The Grodor cannot comprehend a male as anything but an under leader."

"Certainly," Kanarus said with a smile, "if it will make things easier. Actually, I'm used to that. It's no different than home."

Wilona slugged him with the back of her hand. "My Dear, I'll have you remember, you chose your Bride-Covey."

"But only with your help, my Love."

Brekka led on with Yiska showing the way to enter the citadel. She pressed a large button on the wall before the door and it gave admittance.

Kanarus was shocked that no person had opened it. He darted glances in all directions searching for who could have opened the doors, and entered with his sword drawn.

Yiska said, "They will likely release the chapinapes or perhaps the dog men, once they detect we have entered the citadel. You must form a very tight phalanx against them. If it's the dog men, you must remember they can only be killed by a spear to the heart. No other wound will slow them down, for like an armadillo they are too armored in bone and muscle to take a blade anywhere else."

"What about the chapinapes?"

"They are vicious, horrifically strong, manlike creatures; made from creatures called Chimpanzees, Gelada Baboons, and Rat seed codes."

Kanarus nodded. "Yes, Brekka told me these abominations are pure Demons and Trolls, but what about the Grodor? What should we expect?"

"Once we get into them, they will likely yield. I'm betting they would only attack if there were a queen to guard. Bufo is acting queen, but should capitulate when we present Brekka as the new queen." Then Yiska led them all to a purple door. Fortunately, they encountered no opposition. In fact, the hallways were deserted. Yiska explained that once the laboratories had been compromised, the Grodor would fear that a disease had been released and would refuse to enter that area. She waited until she had their attention and said, "We shall have to divide. I will take Kanarus and his Twelver first. Brekka you can take your Twelvers down after us."

"But this room goes nowhere," Kanarus said. "What are you talking about?"

"You will see. It will open into another hall soon."

Brekka smiled at Kanarus' puzzlement, but realized she still couldn't grasp how it all worked either. *What was it Yiska said, oh yes, like a bucket lowered into a well.*

After both Twelvers arrived on the bottom level, Yiska said, "We must proceed down this hall until we come to the white door. That is where Bufo governs from."

Kanarus said, "You mean to tell me we have just come down through forty levels of caverns in a moving room?"

"That's exactly what we have done."

"By the gods of Neorxnawang, there is a strange magic found in this place!"

Brekka couldn't resist, "It's just like lowering a bucket into a well, Lord Kanarus." He gave a puzzled and uneasy smile, nodding confusedly as if he was not sure he understood.

Yiska warned, "If the Grodor have detected our presence, they will have released the chapinapes or the dog men." No sooner had Yiska finished speaking than a clamorous racket filled the hallway before them.

Brekka ordered, "Draw your weapons. Here they come." Kanarus stood on her left, and together they formed the phalanx just in time to propel a wave of blood-lusting apes who attempted to peel away their shields in raging screams. It was shear madness. Ahead of them sounded the smacking of hundreds of ape feet on the hall floor, letting Brekka know they were in for a long battle. The screams were too loud to shout commands, so she had to trust in their training and signing.

The chapinapes were like a pack of wolves on a hot trail. Through a crack in the shields she saw their horrible canine teeth flashing from the long manes about their heads. No amount of stabs through the shields dampened their ferocity. One had to be sure they were dead before stepping over them, as their hands were capable of as much mayhem as their teeth. Inconveniently, Brekka could not employ the Beast Stoppers in such a confined area.

Pointed teeth gnashed at Brekka through a break in the shields, and a Troll's hands grabbed at her shield as she thrust her blade through its throat, only to be followed by another mouth full of snarling teeth tearing at her shield. She thrust her blade through those hollow, sunken eyes as it howled like a rabid dog and pounded out its fury with powerful kicks that pushed her backwards, and opened the shield wall. Kanarus was forced into dealing with two ravenous heads at once. One of them grabbed his blade so tightly he couldn't free it.

Freyxus swiftly smote the hand off the ape, and Kanarus ran his blade through the other's throat. They hurriedly closed the shield wall long enough for Brekka to shout. "We need to fall into the doorways and fight them on three sides."

Soon the apes began falling at a rapid pace, but everyone was exhausted. Yet the inhuman predatory creatures would not relent. The ape faces were filled with wolfish fangs, and their hairy manes were flecked with the foam and froth of their rage. Brekka could hardly lift her sword again. A cruel hand choked her wrist even through the metal greave. Kanarus brought his blade down hard on the beast's wrist and Brekka had to break the grip loose from the severed hand.

By and by the tirade settled, as fewer and fewer apes were left. The combat lasted another half hour. Kanarus delivered the last death thrust into the chest of the final Troll, and everyone collapsed against the walls and sucked hard for breath. Exhaustion settled on Brekka like a heavy slumber, and she could only move at a greatly diminished pace.

After they paused for what felt like an eternity, Kanarus said, "Demons of the infernal pits, was that ever exhausting. Thank the Gods they did not have swords." Kanarus looked to Brekka, and she saw he was waiting for her to make the next move.

She rose up and said, "Yiska, show us this Bufo." She paused, bent over to catch another breath. "And I pray to the gods he's amenable to our plans."

Yiska led them to the large white door at the end of the hall. Upon entering the white chamber Brekka saw a large pudgy man dressed in a white diaper sitting at a table with eight other pudgy bald men, likewise attired, and all so similar that only the age of the leader singled him out at all.

The Grodor were startled, but when Yiska stepped forward, smiles wreathed their faces. Yiska announced, "Greetings, Bufo. I am sure you know Gloomullah Elli Termis is dead."

Bufo stood up and said, "Hail Yiska, we shall adore you as our New Queen."

"No, no! You must not, I am to be the Under Queen. I worship only the New Queen, Brekka Copper Locks, who slew Gloomullah for not ruling properly. You would do well to worship her in my stead, as I do, for she is a fierce and mighty queen capable of swift retribution."

The eunuchs stood up in unison and came forward from around the table to prostrate themselves before Brekka. Bufo then rose up straight, while remaining in a kneeling position and said, "We are honored to greet you, Great Queen."

Brekka noticed they appeared to be happy to have a queen to direct their lives and relieve them of the responsibility of such a weighty stewardship. All rose to their feet and stood around like big smiling babies. She suppressed the urge to laugh at the comedy of it all. It felt like a primary school play. But she didn't laugh, and she showed a friendly bow at the neck. After all, this is what they were conditioned to. She would operate in their system for now.

Bufo rushed into speech. "We have continued in our services until you appeared before us, and I acted as Queen that order might continue to prevail. We have charged the Growlings to rebuild the wall, and we shall run the electricity along its rim once it is complete, so as to keep the rogue skin walkers away and restore the security of the citadel and the compound. The dog men fled into the desert last night when the doors became jammed. All that remains is for us to be sure the control center is free from disease. We will return there when we rescue the rest of the paramours."

Yiska hastened to assure them, "Queen Brekka and I have taken the necessary steps to cleanse the area. It is safe."

Brekka looked at Kanarus. He signed continue. She said, "It is well, Bufo. Have your Grodor continue with their labors, while I communicate with you through my spokesman, Yiska."

"Yes, my queen. We prefer Yiska. She is always kind to us. Not like Natasha, or Yggep, Under Queens of former days.

Brekka thought of all she had ever heard of Yggep. Yggep the Bitch of Brimestone had always only ever been spoken of as the ultimate evil. She saw that even here, in the realm of darkness and the dark sciences, she was also a much detested figure. She was sure Yggep's eyes were turning up in Hell to see her works being brought to naught, and that gave Brekka a sense of utter satisfaction. She took a deep breath and asked Yiska, "How may I take control of the citadel?"

"It is already yours, my queen. Shall I take you to General Grumpus and have him and the Hags submit before you?"

"I would very much like that," Brekka said, as she contemplated how she would show them what good a benevolent leader could work for them.

Bufo led off with the Grodor following like a file of ducks waddling along, and escorted them down the hallway to a large black door. When it opened, she noted that this moving room was large enough to hold both Twelvers and the Grodor. Bufo waited until everyone gathered in. Brekka then felt the jerk of the room and the feeling that her stomach was sinking as she saw the numbers above the door getting smaller and smaller. Then, the numbers reversed and got higher and higher. Kanarus's eyes took in every detail as they rose. Utterly intrigued, he backed himself securely against the wall and held it with both hands spread.

Bufo said, "I see, you travel with your favored paramour, queen Brekka." He was looking directly at Kanarus. "Yet, I perceive you are still virgin. Most curious for Bufo to ponder."

Yiska said, "I think you will find many things will change for the better Bufo. The new queen is a very good person. More kind than I am."

Brekka saw Bufo was unable to control his childlike grin, and joy seemed to bubble out of his face. The doors opened and two grotesque-faced growling guards stood before them in shock. Their faces resembled the seared face of a pig roasted over an open fire.

Bufo said in his comical voice, high for a man of his size, "Take us at once to General Grumpus."

The guards were puzzled, but complied immediately with the demand.

They followed Bufo and the two guards through another black door where sat a large blister-faced man in a khaki green uniform with a large carbuncle on his head above his left eye. Around him stood five Lieutenants. He rose and saluted Bufo, as if Bufo was the biggest man in the world. Brekka felt the comedy of it all, to see this towering monster yield before the little Bufo, and seriously considered this was the stuff of silly dreams.

Bufo pointed to Brekka. "General Grumpus, this is our New Queen, Brekka."

Then to the north of the general she saw the drift of Hags, whom Yiska called Scientists, like a knot of toads with their mouths agape. Brekka couldn't tell if it was fear or amazement that swept over the faces of the Hags, but their eyes were wide with wonder of some sort.

Grumpus fell on his face and stretched out his arms. Then he rose to his knees and said, "Queen Brekka, all that I possess is at your service."

Yiska commanded, "You Scientists, show submission."

They immediately bowed at the neck and placed their hands out in front of them with palms down. Likely, they were too old to kneel or bow.

"Please, rise and render me a report," Brekka commanded.

Grumpus reported, "We have broken communication with the Pitters as was the order by Bufo. We have begun rebuilding the wall, and we are trying to work the gardens the slaves have left untended."

"It is well. As your new queen, I wish you to continue to receive all my orders through Bufo, and he through Yiska as my Under Queen. I want you to know there will be some big changes around here. First off, there will be no more experimentation on any living creatures, except what I sanction. Secondly, your noogs shall gradually be changed for better noogs. Thirdly, I am having skalds and godhi brought here, and bufo and the hags shall teach them all the functions and technologies you know. Now, I shall be gone for a spell, but you shall follow Yiska in all things as if she was me. Is all this clear?"

"It is clear, my Queen." Bufo said.

"It is clear, my Queen." General Grumpus said as he rose slowly to his feet.

Then one of the hags came forth. She was, like the rest, wrinkled all over, clothed in some sort of white canvas-like coat with short grey hair. "I am Griselda Limburger, the head of this team of scientists. In the future would you please refer to us as scientists and not as hags." Her face had a quirky nervous twitch on one side. "And now, may I ask, are we going to be given noogs equivalent to the ones we were receiving."

"I would hope so," Brekka said. "But you must know that you are in the rotting age of life and therefore are a hag."

"Hag is just too painful for our ears, my dear. And what about the secretions we are used to getting to keep us alive?"

Brekka looked at how anxious the looks of the hags had become. "Those are to be discontinued. There is little point in extending human life beyond the natural seasons of the span of years. It is an offense to the gods."

"Perhaps you will revisit your decision on this," Griselda said, her twitch now even more pronounced. "We need to be kept alive long enough to impart all the knowledge we have of the Amerikans."

"Perhaps, you are right." Brekka remembered Yiska's counsel to yield on this point. "Tell me, did you live in the time of the Amerikans?"

"Yes, as did three of my colleagues."

"Do you know what went wrong? Why did the Amerikan Civilization crash?"

"I suppose there were many snowballing factors, but as near as we have figured out, it was a combination of world-wide corporate greed and natural catastrophes. The corporations became more powerful than people or governments and seized control of the sciences. The corporations even owned the governments of the earth. Together they became a world-wide powerful secret government operating on black budgets outside the will and oversight of the people. They suppressed the alternatives available in energy, medicine, and psychology to a world that was starving for them."

"What do you mean?"

Griselda continued, "Well, for instance, there had long been a cure for a disease called cancer, but it was suppressed for profit's sake. Early on, it was discovered that magnetic energies could replace the destructive effects of petroleum based energy, but the inventors were either murdered or sent to prison for subversive activities of terrorism. The government designed laws that could be employed to designate anyone who opposed them as a terrorist. No one had any rights at all. The Amerikan Constitution became a sham. They even discovered viable cures for mental illness with vitamins, minerals, nutrients and beneficial bacteria, but these were banned by the pharmaceutical corporations and reviled as dangerous. There were deflector screens that could block bombs and shelter whole cities from tornadoes and hurricanes, but they were never employed because there were bigger financial gains to be had from rebuilding or even eliminating certain segments of rebellious societies. They had secret ways of seeing to it that targeted populations mysteriously died off. Finally, the Universe itself was disrupted by an array of meteor showers. The foundations of society were by then too eroded to rebuild much of a world to be proud of. Ethnic wars arose as did class and religious wars. As for us, we could not have asked to be placed in any safer place. It's what Gloomullah called the water hole, and she said we were the crocodiles that controlled it. We were safe here in the citadel surrounded by the Poisoned lands and being the only ones, to our knowledge, with any operative and sustainable technology left. Unfortunately, Gloomullah, like the corporate world she came from, used it all to her own selfish end. The rest of us were mere scientists wanting to advance science for mankind."

"Scientific trespass if you ask me. You were children playing with matches and sharp instruments you should have never been allowed to have. But then it seems your government had no adults in charge to begin with."

"I was just trying to recap history for you," Griselda said, strongly affected by Brekka's swift layout of ethics.

"Thank you for recapping the history for us. The Skalds shall be very interested in what you have to share, but I am a warrioress and swift to judge."

Yiska walked over to Brekka and whispered a message in her ear. Brekka then looked over at the Growling commander, "General Grumpus, are you aware you have a general dealing clandestinely with the Pitters for your overthrow."

"No, I am not," the grizzled general said looking about the room, "Who?"

Brekka said, "Is there a General Tibereon in your midst?"

"Why yes," Grumpus looked at a particularly hunched back general across the room and pointed, "That is him. I have considered him one of my trusted advisors."

"I have ample proof should you require it. I will have it sent to you."

Grumpus glared at the hunched back general. "That shall not be necessary. Your word and your will are adequate."

"Then I shall leave him for you to dispose of as you will, but know that he was plotting your overthrow and the overthrow of the citadel. He has taken bribes and gifts from the Skull Worm."

Grumpus pointed with his head, and the guards swiftly took Tibereon away without a struggle. Then Grumpus said, "He shall face trial and if found guilty, be hanged to death."

"Tis well. For now I shall be looking for a place to camp and set up government here at the Citadel."

Kanarus spoke up, "If it's alright by you, my lady, I think we should move our troops into the fortress until the other troops of Arundel arrive at our rendezvous point in the Taxus."

Brekka smiled. "Anything beats spending another night in the Creep Zone, but considering the time it would take to move camp tonight, it would be better just to stay put until tomorrow. The creeps are one thing, but the dogmen are loose somewhere near the fortress. We will bring the camp here first thing in the morning." Then turning to Griselda said, "I shall want you to give a full accounting of your sciences and magic to our skalds and godhi when they arrive."

Kanarus said, "I shall send out pigeons to let Arundel know the recent developments, and to tell him we will be able to meet him in two moonths at the village of Kerr by the river, as was written in the master plan. That should give us ample time to rebuild the wall, secure this place, and get the skalds and godhi in here working."

After the meeting with General Grumpus, Bufo introduced Brekka to Toador, the Master of Paramours, and explained that Brekka was the New Queen, and that he was to follow her orders. Although Toador resembled the other Grodors, he was several inches taller, coming to her shoulders instead of just beneath her breasts, and his bald head was slightly more conical than the others she had seen. Again, unlike the others who Yiska said were sexless, he made up his face in a flamboyant style, with eyeliner and cheek rouge, reminding her of the peacocking He-Shes of Eugene.

"I am at your service, my queen." He stretched his arms forward and bowed deeply. "What would you have me do?"

"I would have you to take me to the dormitory of the paramours and release them to my care."

He gasped. To her surprise he appeared heartbroken. It occurred then that he had acted in loco parentis and thought she was robbing him of his only source of identity. Quickly she added, "Rest assured, I shall rely on you to continue their tutelage and education." She smiled. "Please permit me to compliment you on your excellent tutelage in educating these young men."

He smiled just like a happy baby, and even let slip a charming giggle.

After bidding a farewell, he led them down to the queen's underworld domain. One of Brekka's first orders was the disposal of Gloomullah's body and the purging of the chamber. Upon Yiska's advice, she had the body fed to the few dog men left as a symbol of total rejection.

Toador led them along a wide corridor to a bright blue door at the end.

As he opened the door, the paramours recoiled, frightened looks on their faces. All eyes fixed on Brekka and her weaponry. Several of the boys huddled close to one another in mutual comfort.

But when Kanarus and Red Knife entered, many of the boys actually cringed. Yiska explained in a low voice, "They fear the war paint, and the weapons, and men of such commanding size."

According to Rima, the boys ranged in age from fourteen to Rima's age of twenty-two. The boys who were younger were housed with the captives until the age of thirteen when Toador and his two assistants selected the finest among them.

At the far end of the room, two Grodor stared with startled eyes before bowing. "Master Toador," they said in unison.

At a nod from Brekka, he began addressing a terrified audience of young men. "Brothers, in the shadow of Gloomullah's death, a New Queen has emerged."

A collective gasp raced through the room. One of the more precocious young men spoke up. "Master Toador, how did our beloved queen die?"

Yiska stepped forward and declared, "I will answer that. She has been slain by a more perfect queen." She turned to Brekka and bowed slightly. "She is to be called Queen Brekka.

"A Queen am I." Brekka said as she looked into their terrified faces. "And my Under Queen is Yiska, whom you already know. All of you are to follow and obey me in all things."

Rima took it upon himself to speak up. "Brothers, you will find Queen Brekka to be most pleasing in all things."

She was relieved to see them relax and prostrate themselves before her. Shaking her head she said, "Get up. Gather all the towels and blankets you can carry and follow us through the halls of the citadel. We shall be leaving the citadel, and you will be travelling under the sun and the stars of the heavens."

An astonished buzz arose among the paramours. One of the younger paramours asked, "You mean we are actually leaving the citadel?"

"Yes. We will teach you to be agents of your own life and shapers of your own destiny. And by Frey, the God of Captives, I will make it so."

Brekka calculated that there were in all, one hundred and thirty of them. Even the older ones behaved more like short-haired lackbeards, pushing and shoving and giggling. Occasionally she caught looks that ranged from lust to adoring admiration of the lady knights, and sometimes looks that bordered on utter terror.

As they marched down the hall, a horrific scream echoed off the walls. It sounded like a mix between panther and human. This was soon followed by others, and Brekka hurried her fyrd between those she protected and what she imagined was the arriving hordes of Hell. She remembered her youth as a sheepherder, and how she and her dogs would stand off a coyote attack. She got one dog moving the sheep to the safety of the cote while she and the rest fended for the flock.

"Unfortunately, Bufo released the chapinapes yesterday because he feared the intruders were part of the Pitters legions newly arrived above. Once released, the only way to cleanse the halls of them is to release the dog men. Like the chapinapes, they are impossible to control and many fled into the surrounding deserts. So what I'm saying is, there is still cleanup to do."

Kanarus exclaimed, "Dog men, another fashioned monstrosity of the Poisoned lands."

Toador corrected, "No, the dog men existed before the Poisoned lands. They were brought here by the Amerikans when they built the citadel, and were used to police the perimeter. Even Gloomullah and the scientists weren't capable of exercising the same control, but they were able to contain them and used them to control overpopulation of the other creatures."

The racket of hoots, screams, and grunts grew louder before the first chapinapes made it around the corner, thick maned and frothing at the mouth. In a rage they pounded their chests before hurling themselves on all fours down the hallway. Brekka shouted the command, "Shields to the fore, swords drawn. Prepare to thrust."

As the first chapinape hit the shields, Freyxus thrust, and the creature screamed a horrific scream as its hairy severed limb fell under foot. Once again she felt the impact of one of the beasts pulling at her shield and she thrust up her lady sword into the groin of the troll. Then all the shields were struck at once, and the cries of the chapinapes were deafening. They came with such fierce force that there was no time to rotate. Freyxus was grabbed by the ankle, and Brekka swiftly sliced the hand from the chapinape's body. Yet the hand continued to grip Freyxa's leg, and she was forced to pry its tight fingers loose.

One pulled her shield away, and she was forced to drop back while Pata stabbed the beast through its sternum. But nothing they did stopped the flow of chapinapes, so Brekka shouted, "Divide your wolf-packs into thirds and take the next door you come to. We'll hit these bastards from front, back, and sides."

As they backed their way down the hall Brekka opened the next door and she, Freyxus, Verushka, and Pata all entered. Now, as the apes charged down the hall, the Fyrd could strike them from the front, the sides, and the back, and the killing was greatly accelerated with the Wolf Packs of Kanarus and Red Knife giving cover to the Lady Knights.

After over an hour and a half of the furious combat, Pata severed the head of the last chapinape and gasped in exhaustion. Cisne had safely led the paramours out ahead of them, but Brekka could tell they were traumatized by the battle. The screaming of the apes still echoed in her head.

Upon exiting the citadel, Kanarus took his leave in order to consult with Ruhm on the progress of securing the assets of the citadel, fortress and underground.

Brekka then had Rimalum explain what had happened for the paramours. He did so with as much as he already understood. But once outdoors, the paramours appeared far more curious about nature and sunlight than afraid of what had just happened. The horses and the sun were the major objects of their curiosity. Some stood with arms wide open taking in the sun, and others actually stared direct into the sun and had to be told to avert their eyes.

After a period of active experimentation of exploring the dirt and a couple weeds, Brekka noticed Rimalum was whispering to the larger part of the paramours and they were unitedly eying her like a new girl in a classroom. Rima pointed at her and then at himself, and it brought her back to memories of her first days in the training of weaponry at the academy, and how Hrylwulf boasted that he would be the one to win her heart. She dismissed Rima's boasting as the usual wishful thinking of sex-crazed young males, knowing full well none were a match for her.

She felt like a school teacher over a bunch of primary age boys. "Don't stare into the Sun! Stop the pushing! Don't touch the horse around its tail!" Observing that Xarela was having similar problems with the virgins Brekka screamed, "Arggh!" Threw up her arms and said, "Xarela, I could just strangle them."

They all went silent and stared at Brekka with a renewed terror. "No, I am not going to strangle you. It's just an expression. I'm just impatient with how you all behave. Try to quiet yourselves and sit until we can get things moving here. There will be time enough to explore the outer world later."

Xarela wore his shit eating grin. "Gotten the best of you, have they, my lady?"

"Well, I'm sure as hell not going to be their baby sitter. What are you laughing at?"

"Jou, my lady. I see jou fight in the tournament, wrestle down calves in the rodeo, out fight any man in staves, yet jou can't handle this small group of boys. It is just so funny."

Brekka growled at him. "Grrrrh!"

Toador stepped forward. "Allow me to relieve you of this burden, my Queen."

"Gladly."

With one raise of his index finger, the boys came to order.

Soon Going Snake emerged from the citadel along with the Dog Soldiers, shepherding a mighty host of captive maidens. The girls were from many far-flung nations.

Going Snake walked to Brekka's side. "Looks like your mission is accomplished, my lady."

"How many do you estimate you've freed?"

"It was impossible to get an accurate count, but I would guess at least twelve thousand. Their Grodor were very helpful in calming their fears. Speaking of which, my lady, I think it would be wise to keep these virgins from commingling with the paramours, or instincts will soon be kicking in, if you get my drift. It's not hard to see they are sharing flirtatious glances. As soon as the last of them leaves the citadel, we'll march to the base camp."

"It is well. I'll shepherd the paramours, and your dog soldiers can take the virgins. Now shape it so."

"I shall shape it so, my lady." Going Snake saluted and commanded his dog soldiers to mount, and formed a shield about the captives, and a detachment between the two sexes.

By the time they made it back to the base camp in the canyon, there were only three hours of daylight left, and Brekka was exhausted. White Crow and the Cheyenne Warriors greeted Brekka with a nod of their heads as she entered the camp. They had kept camp and amassed piles of firewood for the long night when the creeps, skin walkers, snucky punks, and muckle-mark-steppers would likely come out to plague them. She had no idea whether the dog men would come or not, but Yiska indicated the dog men would in all likelihood feed on the skin walkers.

"White Crow, may I count on your warriors keeping these captives safe tonight?"

White Crow surveyed the maidens and then looked over the young paramours before nodding. "It shall be done, Buffalo Woman, but I did not think there would be so many."

"It appears the Pitters have been very energetic in the slave trade. These maidens come from the four directions of heaven. Some were even born at the citadel. Over there, those are Mexus, and this first group here, you can tell by their accents are obviously Hickoryan, and those there are definably Citriodoran by the colorful strings in their hair. There's even a group dressed in red cloth. They're Moxo. The gods only know where they came from, more than likely the far ends of the Ea-Urth, but definitely from beyond the borders of the Southern Woods. It will be a long process sorting these refugees out as to where they all go. And most are probably orphans, so that is going to complicate their placement even more."

"What would you have me do, my lady?" Yiska said.

"Since you already know many of these maidens and have shared in their plight, I would ask you to address them and tell them what has happened, what horrors to expect tonight, and assure them that hopefully, after tonight, they will have a life of freedom from fear and captivity. I'll talk to the paramours."

Going Snake rode close and dismounted. "What is your will, my lady?"

"We'll just hunker down here, get some rest, and await Kanarus' orders. He'll likely call on us for protection from the creeps."

About an hour before sunset, a great cloud of dust arose in the south. Soon the thunder of thousands of horse's hooves beating the ground filled the air with a rumbling that echoed off the canyon walls. Brekka was amused at how the paramours watched in utter amazement.

Going Snake's Far Seers, Mole Finger and Shark-Moon-Boy, were summoned. Mole Finger looked into the approaching cloud of dust and said, "It is Kanarus and his armies returning. And there follow many hundreds of refugees. *Many* hundreds."

"More refugees?" Brekka said. "Where from?"

Going Snake shrugged his shoulders. "More than likely from the Growling Labor Camps."

Brekka waited for Kanarus' return, eager to discover the identity of the new-found refugees. As he approached on Sun Chaser she looked up and said, "Hail Kanarus, Was Hael, and Os-Frith."

Kanarus dismounted from Sun Charger and walked up to Brekka. "We've freed the slaves the Growlings made to serve Gloomulah in bitter toil. Would you believe we found over thirty thousand of them in camps outside the southern gate. Some two hundred are Herewardi."

"Why didn't you just leave them in the Growling compound?"

"They said when we knocked down the wall that it had a barrier atop it that was all that kept the crazed and wild skin walkers, dogmen, and creeps out. We took away their only protection so now it befalls us to protect them. We didn't wish to expose them to that danger, and because General Grumpus said the Growlings had no room for them inside the Citadel, we had no choice but to bring them here."

"With so many people to protect, the slaves will have to arm themselves and help repel the creeps and snucky punks."

"Fire and water as well as your shield will protect us from the creeps. Unfortunately we already used all the gvorkel juice on the horses and mules to protect them. Let's hope it has a long persistence. I'll put the seasoned warriors on the front line to protect against skin walkers and nihtgangers. Take into consideration that most of these captives are used to hardship and toil and are probably pretty effective with a stave or club, especially, the younger ones."

"Between the Pitters and our forces, we may have killed the vast majority of the skin walkers last night."

"I wouldn't count on it. The creeps and snucky punks seem to have endless numbers. We don't know much about how they were made or what witchery went into the mix."

"One thing I know, my sister knights and I are already exhausted from fighting chapinapes," Brekka said, half hoping they wouldn't engage in any more fighting tonight, but realized it was her exhaustion speaking and that these things were out of everyone's control anyway.

"At any rate take heart, we'll be out of this os-forsaken place by tomorrow. Red Knife has discovered a water hole on the plateau to the north. We will water the horses there before nightfall and also fill our skins and barrels for tomorrow's journey."

As they began arming the captives and herding the horses and mules and asses up to the water hole, Brekka went in search of the Herewardi captives, hoping to see someone she recognized, when a young man hailed her. "Brekka, Brekka the Lady Knight, hear me."

She rode up to the youth of about fourteen winters. Like so many Herewardi of Zamora, the boy was a golden blond with tanned skin, and though very thin, had the tall build of most Zamorans. "Do I know you, young man?"

"No, but I know you. I am Otr." He pointed to another lanky blond youth of nine winters, "This is my brother, Orendel. We are kin of Freyxus and still mourn her loss in the colloseum."

"By the gods, lads, it gives me great pleasure to tell you that Freyxus yet lives and rides with me. In fact, she will be along here directly. She thought all her kith and kin dead. She will be so delighted her brothers are yet alive."

# CHAPTER 19 :
## ARUNDEL'S MARCH TO SALMALHUER

ARUNDEL MARCHED HIS ARMIES ALONG the edge of the Great Salten Sea high in the Rocky Mountains of the Prester Lands. It was a clear windy day causing their banners with the mark of Hrus to flap in the breeze like the clap of pigeon wings. Along the edge of the Salten Sea were various crystalline salt formations resembling faery castles, created by centuries of winds and water lapping at the shore. Ahead were miles and miles of white salt flats leading to the distant snow-capped mountains through which they were to pass.

Ary called a halt, dismounted and picked up a column of salt, two breadths of a man's hand in thickness. It was surprisingly heavy and warm to the touch. Carefully, he examined its sharp crystalline angles and crevices before lifting it to his nose. It smelled strongly of the sea. Cautiously, he placed his tongue to it, and gave it a lick. "Pure salt," he said and handed it to Yellow Horse.

Yellow Horse took it into his hand, examined it and licked for himself. "Incredible. No wonder the Prester merchants are so rich. This stuff is worth more than gold, and here it forms itself right along the lake's edge whereas we have to use pots to extract it from the sea." He passed it over to Redelfis, who first sniffed the shimmering chunk before him. "Not bad," he declared, grinning. "Puts me in mind of salted pork or fish."

Yellow Horse shot him an amused look. "Is eating all you ever think of?"

"When I have an empty belly, yes." Redelfis dropped the chunk, which shattered at his feet.

Ary remounted, and the others did the same. "This reminds me of a large white and silver plate."

Yellow Horse shaded his eyes and stared toward the mountains. "And here come the ants to eat us now."

Ary, too, shaded his eyes. He recognized the banner at the head of the column of riders, a black angel on a field of white blowing a golden trumpet. "Rest easy, men. They're presters, no doubt come to greet us."

Approaching at a full gait, their leader was a tall, broad-shouldered wild-looking man, completely the opposite of his clean-shaven men in tow. He reminded Ary of Wose with his long, grey, unruly hair and wild beard whipping in the salt air.

The wild-looking man signaled to halt and yelled above the wind, "A hail and a welcome to our allies, the Syr Folk! I am General Aaron P. Rockwell, Grand Commander of the Prester Forces."

"Os-Frith! I am Lord Arundel, Supreme Heretoga of the Syr Folk Forces and Paladin and Commander-in- Chief of the Confederated Nations under the High King Sur Sceaf. Hail and well met."

"A great honor, my lord. I have heard much good of you, Lord Arundel, Son of Sur Sceaf. You are also the one they call King of the Ness, are you not?"

"That would be me."

A.P. Rockwell acknowledged him with a nod and a brief smile. "We have received report of the battles you were engaged in, Lord Arundel. Reports are that you wrenched back the lands westward from the Pitter fiends. We also have news of the campaigns of Lord Kanarus, south of us. He has successfully, at last report, entered the Poisoned Lands in pursuit of the Pitter legions controlled by the Skull Worm."

"That is most curious. It is even as I thought," Arundel said, "the Skull Worm is fleeing, and the rats are abandoning a sinking ship. Skull Worm is gathering his armies to the east, because he can no longer stay the onslaught of our hosts. Hryre Seath fears rebellion in the east and wants his core protected. But Os be with Kanarus, for he marches into Hell itself in the Poison Lands."

"I do not envy him. I shiver to think what horrors await their eyes."

"Have you any word of the Lady Brekka?"

"Only that she rides with Kanarus."

Arundel felt his stomach tighten. For days he had been second-guessing the decision he'd made to send her into the Poisoned Lands. And yet, the ur fyr had not urged otherwise. Either she was the Lady Knight of prophecy or she was not. Nevertheless, he was at least comforted by the fact that he had placed Ruhm as a protector to be near her.

General Rockwell's craggy face suddenly split into a huge grin. "By god, is that not my old friend Rip?"

Rip had been riding very silently for the last two miles behind Sur Sceaf, and his voice now came almost as a surprise. "A.P., you old buzzard. You haven't changed a bit."

Rockwell rode up beside Rip and gave him a powerful side hug from his horse, "You damned old apostate, you. I should roast you alive for leaving us. Do you realize how many boring meetings I've had to sleep through since you left to 'find yourself'," he said in an altered voice. "I'm so tired of sitting in councils with those dry balls. There's nothing more I'd like to see than you coming back, dusting off the holy books, blowing the cobwebs out of the other apostles' heads, and assuming the mantel of your apostleship once again."

Rip shook his head ruefully. "You know that's not going to happen, my old friend. I've managed to find my true self among the Wood Lords. Freedom from all the powers under the heavens is something I long sought."

Rockwell sighed. "I feared such was the case." He turned to address Ary. "We have prepared a place for you and your troops to camp while we await the arrival of the Hutters and Chief Sun Cryer of the Buffalo Nations along with his allied war chiefs. My troops will be camped on the East Bench along with you so that we can become familiar with your chain of command and mode of operation in the field. Once we leave this land, I will surrender my command to you, Sir Arundel."

Arundel nodded. "It is well. When do you expect the arrival of the Sun Cryer?"

General Rockwell squinted into the sun, ran a hand through his unruly hair, and said, "He arrives in two days. Sent word that he brings the hutter volunteers along with the hospitalers and the dog sled teams you sent to teach them. I am pleased the hutters will assist us in keeping our food and supply lines operating. Probably a good idea that your hospitalers will be providing medical treatment as you have directed, too. I've done lost more than my share of good men in the field. Just couldn't get them the doctoring they needed."

The glint of Rockwell's eyes reflected a sober taciturn sort of man. Arundel found him most curious, almost a Wose, and yet not the same fire for vengeance, more a creature of devout duty. What stories must lay concealed behind that wild hair and beard. And just as Ary thought on the matter, he noticed a little red dog hiding in the long hair under Rockwell's ear. Perched there on his shoulder all the time.

Arundel said, "I see you have your pet with you."

Rockwell reached up to his shoulder and scratched the dog's head, "That's Gryphon. He's my eyes when I'm scouting. He will let me know if I'm being followed. Never barks. Just licks my face when there is a Vardropi near. That way the enemy doesn't even know I'm aware of them."

"That is simply brilliant," Arundel said. "We have a lot to learn from you. Please, lead us on to our camp and we will just follow you in, General Rockwell."

"That I shall do, and President Silas Rampton has requested to dine with you this evening at the Dutzendteich, where you may meet with our leadership and discuss coordination and correlation of our resources. I will come by your tent around five on the sundial and escort you there."

"Tis well. I'll bring Rip the Prester to help us overcome any cultural barriers we are not aware of, he being a master of both our worlds."

Arundel set up the red leather pfalz command tent and pitched camp on the high bench to the east, overlooking the Prester City of Salmalhuer in the valley below them. He also set up his wives' tent next to it, then gazed out over the city; blowing his warm breath on his hands and rubbing them vigorously together to stop the biting cold and keep them warm while the women started a fire in the tent and began the unpacking.

As Ary watched an eagle sail over the vast vistas, he noticed the city looked like it was arranged in block after block of square streets and square homes with one central building that resembled a giant silver turtle shell, which Rip told him was their tabernacle, a place of worship. Like the Herewardi, the Presters believed in open communion with their god, and revealed knowledge. Like the Quailor, they were an orderly society and not given to the usual vices of the surrounding rogue nations; that of drinking, gambling, whoredoms, pharmaceuticals, or the other vices. Indeed, they resembled the quailor in many respects, but had additional scriptures, which they held to be as sacred. What the Sharaka called the White Man's Paper Gods.

After Ary reviewed his troops, and all of his armies were secured in their camps, Rockwell arrived to escort him to the Dutzendteich, a large two story yellow wooden building in the center of the city. "The builders named it for the twelve ponds that surround us to which we have likened our apostles, as we consider them repositories of heavenly knowledge. In your language, the Dutzendteich translates to the Hall of the Dozen."

"It reminds me of the sacred pools near Holihs Pond just outside the Ness. The Ele-Anoreans consider it a place of revelation and spiritual renewal."

After surrendering their mounts to waiting grooms, Ary and his men followed Rockwell up tightly constructed stairs into the mansion. The door was opened for them by servants dressed in black coats and white shirts with strange narrow cravats. The hall ran into a large foyer through which he could see a group of men sitting around a long table. Some appeared to be Presters, dressed in black suits and white shirts and others appeared to be Jywdic, dressed in all black with peyos dangling at the corners of their heads and the usual black skull cap of a Haredic Jywd.

With the motion of his hand, Rockwell led them to four empty chairs near the head of the table with the motion of his hand. "Please, be seated," he told them, before turning to a sober silver-haired gentleman at the end. "President, this is the Lord Arundel, King of Ele-Anor-Ness and Commander of the Confederated forces, with whom you requested to dine. The Red Men are his First Lieutenant, Redelfis, and the Second Lieutenant, Yellow Horse. Additionally, Lord Arundel brings Rip the Prester, well known among us, to communicate as seamlessly as possible with us." He then turned to Ary. "Lord Arundel, this is President Rampton, Prophet, Priest, and leader of the Presters."

Arundel nodded his head at each member of the Dozen, as General Rockwell went down the table introducing the twelve members of Rampton's council. One by one the introductions came, and then Rockwell introduced the three members of the Jywdic City-State of Esdraelon, hailing from just south of Salmalhuer. They were attired in the traditional long black gabardine coats.

"Lord Arundel," the oldest Jywdic gentleman said, "I am, Rabbi Derschowitz, delighted to see you here in the appointed year, and I greet your lieutenants as well as one of the former members of the Dozen, Brother Rip, always a fair mediator between our two peoples." He turned to Rip and smiled. "Brother Rip, your presence has been sorely missed."

"Rabbi, I have missed your counsel, and am most pleased to rejoin you in this most portentous council."

"Portentous indeed. For twenty years I have awaited the arrival of this day; when all the free tribes would come together as one mighty army to throw off the Pitter yoke, and break the back of their power over the earth forever more."

"It is a day long sought after and long prophesied, Rabbi," Arundel said. "Let me commend President Rampton on the fine city you have erected here."

President Rampton acknowledged the compliment with an austere nod. "I trust you find the accommodations of your camp sufficient for your needs. It gives you a commanding view of our city, patterned after the old one we came from. It is but a shadow of what we once were before the mountains slid over us and the earth changes altered us permanently. Then it was quite a long time before we could rebuild our faith. Seeing as all the factions vied for leadership with some saying, 'lo, here is the anointed one,' and others saying 'lo, there is the anointed one'. Finally, the mantle of leadership distilled upon us and we have come to restore all things as afore."

Arundel smiled and said matter–of-factly, "We are comfortable indeed. My wives always see to that."

Rabbi Derschowitz's jaw dropped and President Rampton's eyebrows shot up. "You travel to war with your wives?"

"Well, not all of them. I have only brought three of the ten."

"What a curious practice." President Rampton gave the other dozen a guarded glance. "It is told in our old histories that our people once practiced multiple marriages, but gave up the practice long ago; even before the natural destructions and the Great Quake."

"Did you find it advantageous to give up such a practice?" Arundel inquired.

"There is no way to know, but judging by the number of Herewardi tribes, I would say it has served you very well. What would you say Rip?"

Rip smiled. "I believe we Presters let the flame of our culture burn out long ago in our efforts to please the other nations. I have told Lord Arundel, I believe we are a mere shadow of the Presters of former days. They wouldn't even recognize us as one of them. Though I must in all honesty say, I found my marriage to Presterdom was sweet in the beginning. I was not long among the Herewardi when their light shone bright and warm upon me. For the first time I felt truly at home and their doctrines were delicious to the taste. My eyes were ever after opened to the awareness that all anybody needs is within the silent chambers of their own breast."

"And I thought I was the only one given to stating the painfully obvious but unspoken," Yellow Horse said with his hands in the air and eyes held wide open.

Ary said, "Please, Yellow Horse, don't get started. This is an internal matter."

Yellow Horse gave a mischievous grin and went silent.

President Rampton displayed no open offense as he answered "Yes, Rip the Wandering Apostle, who went in search of the lost flame. I am happy for you that you found what you were searching for. Perhaps, if we can defeat the Pitter Empire, we'll find a world similar to the one we left. Pity is that the Pitters have cost us all so many losses all these years. And you Rip, once sat at our table and ate of the bread of our faith. Though you have found a new path, we hold no ill feelings towards you. You were a good man then, and I am sure you are a good man now. We only seek to hold together the fragments of the kingdom our predecessors left us, in the hopes of one day obtaining the restoration of all the lost keys and words of the kingdom we once possessed. Perhaps you shall yet help us find our way back."

Redelfis chimed in, "And now the day has arrived in which we shall avenge the blood of our fallen fathers together."

"Well, we at least do not have war blood to atone for as do you. We have been relatively secure in the arms of these mountains, but our losses were great from the Pitter cattle raids and the interruption of our trade lines. Not to mention their total disregard for our sovereignty. But if I may not now give you a total picture of our history, it is as Rip said; we lost the flame."

His recounting was interrupted when servants began delivering plates of mutton, corn, potatoes, and beets. After three months of subsisting on dried meat and acorn bread, Ary found himself salivating at the mere thought of eating hot, fresh meat and potatoes.

"Yours is a story I have been made familiar with as told by our skalds and ambassadors. In looking around, I marvel that you are able to make such a waste howling wilderness into something that produces such abundant food. As Rip often said, 'Just add water and stand back.'"

They laughed.

One of the apostles remarked, "Yes, we have made the desert to bloom. By the way, I am Dilworth Johnson. I wasn't sure you caught my name in the introduction of so many at once. I gathered the troops we will be placing under your able command."

"I thank you for your efforts," Ary replied before taking a bite of the juicy mutton and chewing slowly, savoring its flavor. It had a more sage-like flavor than his grass-fed flocks. He made a mental note to see that his wives received a portion. "The joining of our forces has had a terrifying effect on the pitters. In times past they have always assessed us individually as enemies. Never dreaming we would bind together as one force. Now, they do not know how to calibrate our united strength. I think it has put them on the run and struck a chord of fear in their hearts they are not used to. We thank you for your efforts in this grand alliance."

"Oh," Silas Rampton said, bright eyed, "It was no effort at all, and it will prove a good thing to put our differences aside until all this is over. So many of our young men are chomping at the bit to take the war to the Pitters instead of having to constantly post vigilant guard and never knowing from whence the next attack will come. What I'm saying is that it'll just be good to go on the offensive for a change."

Yellow Horse talked with a piece of mutton still in his mouth, "You realize of course, Dilworth, that once we get into Pitter and Vardropi lands, our forces will still be greatly outnumbered."

Dilworth said, "But don't we have them on the run? Have I not heard, they have already been driven out of most of the west?"

Arundel swallowed his beet. "We still have to root them out of the Poisoned Lands and the Taxus Lands. I'm thinking it may go one way or the other."

"What do you mean?" Dilworth asked.

Arundel studied the faces of the Rabbis and the Dozen who all ceased eating to hear. "Either they will put up a stiff fight to keep those lands or they will forfeit them so as to maintain their legions for their home turf. It depends on how strong they estimate us to be. They'll not want the science of the Poisoned Lands to fall to us and yet they have no control over Gloomulah and the Growlings. Also, they will do all they can to keep the war from going to the east. The Taxus Lands have been the base of all their operations in our lands, and they will be tough to uproot with all those strong bastions in Taxus."

Yellow Horse said, "Even if we take those lands..."

"We will take them!" Redelfis interrupted. "There can be no 'if'."

"When we take them, we have only ridded them out of our lands. They are like a school boy running from a bunch of neighborhood kids. Once they get in view of their older siblings, they will suddenly grow far more brave; which means we'll have to take on their older siblings by marching up the Missip to Quirenopolis and take the Banner of the She-Wolf from the Vardropi. It is a maneuver they will never anticipate."

Rabbi Derschowitz said, "It makes me to shudder. We came from those lands and damned few of us survived that trek. Dire Wolves, Waheela, fierce winters, with Quant and White Rogue Tribes who have forsaken all codes of decency robbing and harassing us in our blood soaked march. I pray to god, you do not succumb to the trials we had to face."

Rabbi Bubber added, "But we Jywds were city-dwellers and did not have the weapons or fierce training you Herewardi and Sharaka possess."

Rockwell inquired, "But why go so far north after we've secured the Taxus Lands? Why not just secure the Taxus and be glad the Pitters are no longer in the west."

Arundel answered, "Because, striking the She-Wolf at Quirenopolis will leave the empire out of balance. But, even more importantly, if the Bamboo Plantations bloom, they will produce the fruit that stimulates exponential growth in the Pitter population and if that happens, we'll be hopelessly overrun in less than ten years. It's all got to happen now on the war plan we established. Besides, the south lands are now filled with

Hickoryan rebels. By us attacking the north, it will draw the Pitters in many directions to aid the Vardropi and give the Hickoryan rebels the chance to break the yoke of Pitter rule once and for all. The more the Hicks invest in this war, the better the transition to a free and sovereign government shall be for them."

"I fear greatly for you, Lord Arundel. Quirenopolis will be hard to get to and is very well fortified," President Rampton declared. "The city itself is mostly underground. And then--then there are the beasts of the north that Rabbi Derschowitz mentioned. Few there be that brave passage in those wild parts. And supply lines are hard to maintain in melting snow. It's too hard. Nigh impossible, in fact."

"Hard, yes, but impossible, no;" Arundel stated with conviction, "It is more likely that we can break the Vardropi at Quirenopolis than it is that we could ever penetrate through Pitter dominated lands into Nu-Yalk and Hormah. If we knock down Quirenopolis first, it will be like striking the kingpin, and they will never suspect that to be our plan. The trick is to get their legions running back and forth until we wear them down with confusion. Besides, we want to cut the outer roots of the empire first so that the core will have no support or reinforcement when we hit it like a large wind. It is better we hit them from many directions to spread them as thin as possible and then strike with the concentrated force of a cyclone at their core."

Servants began laying plates full of nut breads before them. Arundel took one and buttered it, then savored the sweet tastes. One of the Jywdic members waved his hand for Ary's attention.

"Pardon me, Lord Arundel, I am Rabbi Horowitz of B'nai Scholomo. I have heard much of your victories, and we do also pledge the support of the Jywdic City-State of B'nai Scholomo in Esdraelon. It is well known that you have vibrant Jywdic communities in your midst and that Jywdic Fyrds will be marching with you. Indeed, we have heard that they begin to rival us in numbers, and we have heard in dispatches of their heroic deeds at sea under the Jywdic Commander, Zeru-Herewardi. Do you have any conflicts with them per se, or are there any precautions we should take in the mingling of our troops with yours?"

"I think not. At least I can recall no problems with our Jywdic fyrds, but you must know, they are an intricate part of Herewardi Society. The Jywdic troops you will be sending will be led by Sol-Om-On Sunchild, himself a Jywd of great renown and a devout follower of the Torah. My wife, Macbah is Jywdic, the Daughter of Rabbi Amschel ben Levi. Perhaps you should ask such a question of her when you visit us."

"I would be most curious. We have heard that the Rabbi Amschel has greatly altered the Jywdic teachings, and have even heard he denies the existence of the holy city of Jerusalem."

"I am not so much sure that he denies it, as that he said it has passed away into a history that no longer has any significant relevance, beyond being a mythical aspiration. He believes that his Jywdic communities can best express themselves as a new City-State in the Confederation of the Syr Folk, and that his Jywdic seed code will naturally unfold like a Tree of Life without any archaic strictures to suppress its growth."

"Well, Jerusalem is at the core of being Jywdic."

Yellow Horse responded, "Evidently not, because there are Jywdic communities that thrive without it and consider themselves every bit as much a Jywd as you do."

"We have managed to form our Jywdic community here without having to alter or change. I just can't believe to do otherwise that they can be considered to be true Jywdic."

"And that should always be your prerogative," Arundel interjected. "I have found it is always better to let families settle their own quarrels." He smiled at the Rabbi.

President Rampton laughed and said, "Yes, it will be the strength of all free peoples if we learn to live in tolerance of our differences. Isn't that right, Rip?"

"That is right President Rampton," Rip answered, "and I appreciate I had the freedom to explore our differences without suffering your censorship or jading our friendship."

Rockwell said, "Lord Arundel, your skill as a general and a warrior are unexcelled, we know. But I have a question which has run around my head for months now."

"Sure, what is it?"

"I notice you keep the council of your court jester, who is a red man, and that your other lieutenant is also a red man. What is that all about? Are you Herewardi or are you Red?"

"It is our belief that anciently the red man owned all these lands and that we shall be the instrument in restoring them back to much of their former inheritance under what we call, manifest destiny. Yellow Horse is born a red man, but he has been made a Blood Elf, which means he is accepted as Herewardi. Believe me, he tends to float freely between both worlds. Indeed, you will find that the history of the Herewardi is closely intertwined with that of the Red Man. For the Herewardi and Sharaka have done a lot of crosspollination in the last five hundred years. I, myself, have some red blood.

"Now, in Herewardi culture the jester is a valued member of the royal court. Yellow Horse was adopted by Muryh the Master Builder. But because Muryh was always so busy building, Yellow Horse grew up in my house under Sur Sceaf's fatherhood. As a Jester, under Herewardi law, he can say anything he wishes. When I get too haughty or full of my own vanity, it is Yellow Horse that grounds me and shows me I am not seeing all there is to see. Besides, his counsel is mostly good. And as for Redelfis, he is my most trusted friend since youth, our fathers being blood-brothers and we being in the same wolf-pack since youth."

Yellow Horse explained, "Jester is a role I have much enjoyed, because you won't find anyone with more vanity or faults than Lord Arundel."

***Jesse ben David's Log:*** *The Blood Moonth, the Half-Moonth of Ullr, 603 H.S.O. Although I was assigned to be Lady Brekka's scribe, Lord Arundel has commandeered me. From sun up until sundown Arundel watched as the armies of Sun Cryer poured into the Great Salten Basin through the eastern canyon of the Great Rockies. It was called Crack Canyon, because it was the place where the mountains split apart in the day of the earth cracking, great quake. Lord Arundel had me catalog the numbers of soldiers, wagons, and mule trains as they came through. The numbers of the Buffalo Nations were most impressive.*

*I was also charged with arranging for a meeting with Sun Cryer, A.P. Rockwell, Heinrich Gutmensch of the Hutters, the Quailor hospitalers, and Betsy and Karl Throckmorton with their dogsled teams, and the leaders of those groups in preparation for their march to the Taxus lands. This took place in Lord Arundel's Pfalz command tent.*

*Lord Arundel pointed out the horrors we may encounter in the Poison Lands. He emphasized just how important it is to destroy the Pitter legions here in the west and secure a firm base in Taxus before launching a campaign against them in the north, south, and east. And he explained how a navy would have to be built and launched from Taxus within three moonths. It has been an exhausting day. I was grateful for the assistance Lord Arundel's wife, the Lady Macbah, gave me, in organizing the records.*

*The next step in our journey will carry us into the Taxus. Lord Arundel's primary mission is to secure the Omala and build a seaport on Elves' island. We leave as soon as we complete the refugee shelters for the rescued captives of the Poison Lands. Lord Arundel is most anxious for the arrival of the next Silver Harrier who should bear news of the battle of the Poisoned Lands.*

# CHAPTER 20 :
## GOING SNAKE AND THE GOAT'S LEAP

W HEN BREKKA AND YISKA ENTERED the laboratory of the
citadel, Siwel was demonstrating to the hags his method of
grinding reishi with a mortar and pestle. Brekka was amazed
at the way the hags hung on his every word like a bunch of curious
students.

The Chartreusean healer responded to Brekka's greeting with
obvious pleasure. He had been working steadily since coming to the
citadel shortly after Brekka's forces had secured it. His first priority,
after tending to the recovering Hickoryan patients, was a cure for the
blains and boils of the Growlings. Brekka had been so busy she had had
little time to consult with him, but she knew he had been working on
conconctions for the past two months.

"So glad you stopped by," he said with eager enthusiasm. "The
woman and I have seen great progress in just fourteen days time. I
believe they can be healed of their awful condition."

Astonished and pleased, she glanced at Griselda seated opposite
Siwell at the metal table. "I thought it was a permanent condition."

"That is what Gloomullah always led us to believe," Griselda said.
"But this magic man shows us otherwise." She pointed to her face. "See,
even takes away my crepe wrinkles."

Brekka narrowed her gaze for a better look. Perhaps some of the
wrinkles *had* smoothed, but not enough to make a significant change.

"That looks like mashed mushrooms. Surely the cure can't be so simple?" She leaned closer for a better look.

"A major ingredient, yes, but added to others."

"My people use mushrooms for many ailments," Yiska offered. "Some are very magical."

The healer with the pale green skin nodded vigorously. "Years ago I treated a girl with horrible pustules on her face with green slime from the giant worm and with tea from the reishi mushrooms to which I also added a little elf wort. Within one moonth she was healed, and the pustules never returned. Since then, it has become a standard treatment among our healers. Three days ago, I exposed three of the Growling women to the same regimen and believe it or not their blemishes are crusting over and fading." He got a mischievous look on his face. "I believe they may become quite delightsome in appearance."

"How did you come by the giant worms?" Yiska asked.

"I keep them in a box of humus in my wagon. They come from the Isle of Ilkchild. I packed them here for just such a purpose. It's important I add some of their native soil every so often."

"And the reishi mushrooms?" Brekka inquired.

"I always carry them in dried form."

"Siwel, you Chartreuseans never cease to astound me. The gods of nature speak to you with more clarity than anyone else."

Blushing a darker green, he said, "For most of what I've learned, I have Xelph and Queen Zschamillah to thank. But healing the Growlings' skin problems is only one of the things we've accomplished. Hear this! I have managed to reverse the drugs Gloomullah used on the eunuchs. Bufo, Tudo, and Krodo have all allowed me to administer the remedy on them. And what results! With a mix of an herb called Macca and several potent mushrooms I have doubled the size of their ballocks. Bufo is already saying he wants to become a paramour, and possibly, I'm hearing a deeper voice."

Several of the hags laughed and Griselda said, "If they continue to grow bigger balls, it'll be a good thing we got all those virgins out of here. Now maybe some of us ladies will have a chance after all."

"I'm sure the Grodor won't be as pliable as they have been once they become intact males," Brekka said with a sigh. "But these Growling women you have treated must be quite pleased that their complexions are improving. Gloomullah had them thinking they had been eternally damned to look like the walking dead. I'm sure it was to control them, but now there is hope. By Almighty Woon, there is hope. And where there is hope, shackles and yokes shall be broken."

Griselda said, "That reminds me, Queen Brekka, shall we scientists be given the pills to maintain our libido?"

"Griselda, you astound me. Does it not seem unnatural to you to want men a fraction of your age? Look at the moon, for Freya's sake, even it has its waning phase. But, upon second thought, you have been very cooperative and if there is medicine to make you feel fire in your thighs and it harms no one nor robs anyone of their will, then I suppose I could consider such."

The hags exchanged excited looks, and Brekka bit off a sigh. Who was she to judge?

Quickly, Siwel changed the subject, holding up a green finger, "The Growling women are still far from our perception of pretty, but, that could change in another month or two of treatment."

"Beauty is one of the greatest gifts a god can bestow," Brekka said, as she contemplated the ramifications. "But Siwel, you say you have only treated three women. How will you ever supply all the other Growlings?"

"Ah hah!" Siwel said holding up his green finger once again. "I've got a host of them working in the gardens piling up manure and mulch to get a large worm crop going. Soon, I will be able to treat all of them. In times past the Growlings wouldn't even think of getting their hands dirty in the gardens. That was the work of slaves they captured. Now they are becoming like the Chartreuseans and view the garden as the healing chest of all their woes. That which they formerly esteemed the least they have now come to love and value the most." He laughed his musical laugh. "You should see them, hoes swinging, shovels digging, hods full of mulch and all the while, singing tree songs I taught them. It's a beautiful sight to behold, Lady Brekka. Reminds me of my former days in the gardens of Arym Gael."

"As much as I hate leaving you here at the citadel, I can see that your work here is very valuable. Train your replacement though, for we shall eventually need you in the war effort more than here." Brekka smiled. "How pleased the Growling will be, if they can be brought to normal lives, free of the disease and all that makes humans look displeasing. The gods have planted the desire for beauty in us all because it is a spiritual food. Siwel, you are truly a wizard."

"And Lady Brekka," Siwel said with a flirtatious look, "you are a delight to work with."

"Thank you, Siwel, but please forgive me. I must see Going Snake off. He's taking the host of refugees to Salmalhuer, an arduous trek at best."

Although Siwel was a good looking man whom she found very endearing, he lacked the armoring of muscle she preferred in males. He would be a good friend. Nothing more.

Leaving the citadel, she and Yiska wound their way around tents and campfires until they came to the camp of the three paramours she had "adopted."

Sima, Rima, and Jima lit up like lamps when they spotted her. After calling out a greeting, she turned her attention to the throng of refugees massing near the gate. Her brothers, the Thunder Twins, Ev'Rhett and Russell, sat mounted on their white steeds. Nearby, a groom held the reins of Going Snake's white stallion White Lightning, the get of White Fire, while Going Snake stood looking over a list of supplies provided by the Hutter Quarter Master.

She approached him in deep thought. "Greetings Going Snake. Is all well?"

He turned his bronze face towards her, his long black hair hanging loose. "Just making a final tally and it appears we are short of axes."

"Go ahead and mount. I'll have a Beetle get some from the Quailor Quarter Master and have them brought to you."

"Thank you, my lady." He handed her the list before taking the reins from his groom and swinging easily into the saddle. "The sooner we get started the sooner we can return."

Brekka looked over the vast throng of refugees, raised her arms up into the square of the swan blessing and said, "The gods be with you until we meet again. May they smite your enemies before you, mark your trails into safety before you, and bring these captives to freedom and a safe haven." She lowered her arms. "Going Snake, take good care of these refugees and guide them like tender lambs through the mountains. They are not seasoned to hardship as are we. Be a gentle shepherd."

"You know, I will my lady." He saluted and held up the red feathered spear. "Yeoh Wah!" he shouted before nudging his horse forward. Soon the caravans of refugees were off on the trail to Salmalhuer. She watched as they snaked their way into the northern horizon. She prayed, *There goes one of my most valuable warriors. Please watch over and protect him, Father Woon, and keep him from harm's way. Temper the winter weather for them.*

The Lady Brekka raised her arms up in a swan-swear and pronounced one more final blessing: "May the gods and Thunder Beings watch over and protect you. May your enemies be devoured by the flames of Woon's judgment and may the Manitous give you the cunning of a fox, Going Snake."

As he smiled at her, he saw her wet eyes and felt the warmth of the blessing sink into his heart. *It is always an honor to serve you, my lady.* He swung his stallion around and was soon accompanied by the jointly commanded fyrd of Russell and Ev'Rhett.

How he wished Brekka were riding alongside him! His brother Redelfis had always thought of her as a mere sister, but Going Snake had long suffered the fires of attraction. Try as he might, he had never detected any of the slightest signs of reciprocity. *Perhaps she thinks of me as just a little brother? But by the gods, she is the most beautiful woman I have ever known.*

He looked over the long train of refugees, mostly young females dressed in white smocks and shod in moccasins, which would almost certainly wear out before the trek's end. Perhaps, by then he could persuade them to toughen their feet by going bare footed. They each carried a bed roll and a ruck sack and would in all likelihood need that one blanket while passing through the mountains. He had seen Sharaka infants that were more seasoned than these girls, and as for the troop of paramours, they were little better. Their age and masculinity gave them potential for enduring the trek better, but even a five-year-old Sharaka boy would have more stamina than they demonstrated.

At his signal, the companies of dog soldiers and fyrds took their protective positions alongside the refugees. The trek would take them from the citadel of the Poisoned Lands up the trails through the mountains to Salmalhuer.

Rip the Prester acted as their guide. Rip had been sent down from Salmalhuer by Arundel to pilot the refugees back, being the much experienced mountain man from those parts who knew the safest and shortest passageways.

Going Snake was compelled to drop down on a southerly course to avoid the creeps and skin walkers, then swing far to the east and turn northwest for Salmalhuer in the top of the Rockies. He was looking forward to getting this mission over as fast as possible that he might join Brekka in her Taxus campaign.

Against twilight on the third day of the march they were setting up camp in a large mountain meadow when Going Snake made his rounds. He stopped by the sloppily hung tent of Rima, who looked up at him with a smile. "What do you think Going Snake? Did I do a good job?"

It was a pitiful sight, but he understood that in many ways these paramours were still very much like children. He walked over to Rima and said, "You're getting the knack of it, but I think you just need to tighten these stakes a little more."

Going Snake took it upon himself to pull the stakes out one by one, stretch them taunt and pound them back in with his tomahawk.

Sima frowned. "Ah, I wondered why the walls were all sagging." Once again Going Snake helped pull up stakes and re-position them for the paramours.

Jima had made several attempts to get a campfire going, but failed. Going Snake managed to rein in his impatience as he began patiently teaching the boys the basics of fire-building.

Jima had a gleam in his face and looked dreamy. "This is the most beautiful place I've ever been, Going Snake, so many new colors and interesting things to examine. So alive! Nothing like the citadel." Suddenly, his lip quivered, and he began to weep.

Going Snake was puzzled. Was he crying because he could not get the fire started or was it because the forced march was too draining on him? He placed a hand on Jima's shoulder. "What's wrong Jima?"

"Why? Nothing is wrong." Jima looked up with a smile as tears streamed down his cheeks in rivulets.

"Then why do you cry so?"

"Because, my heart is filled with joy at all the beauties that surround us here. All above and all around, everything is beautiful. Look at these meadows with their flowers and listen to those birds. Hear the hum of bees and look how that bird soars through the clouds."

Going Snake smiled at him and thought they truly are just children. But as he looked out across the meadow, he thought, *Why did I not see how beautiful this place is too? I need to thank the Thunder Beings for the beauty of this moment. By the gods am I so blind that I do not look anymore?*

He took the bow out of Jima's hand and told him, "You have to keep on this bow if you want to start a fire. If you let it rest, it just cools back down and you won't get enough heat to start your tinder."

Going Snake ran the bow vigorously back and forth in his hand. Out the corner of his eye, Rima drew near him and said, "Going Snake, is the Lady Brekka not pleased with us that she should have us sent away?"

Going Snake started blowing the tinder and soon the spark caught it on fire. He began stacking small pieces of kindling on the fire while Sima watched intently. "So that's how it's done."

"Yes, that's the way it's done," Going Snake said and then answered Rima. "Brekka was not in any way displeased with you."

"Then why has she not kept us for her lovers? Are we not very pleasing to look upon?"

"I am sure you are pleasing to look upon. She is trying to teach you that you are so much more than just breeding bunnies. It will take you many moons to understand that you are beings with many dimensions and she wants you to learn to be warriors, workers, free-thinkers, husbands, and fathers. That's why you are under my care and tutelage, but you must develop your own moral code that you can live by."

"Does not being a father require one to be a breeding bunny?"

"Not exactly. Trust me, there are many aspects of yourself that you do not yet understand or know, and much also for you to unlearn. Once you have the reins of your own heart, you may ride to great heights. Then there's still much you must learn about the spiritual aspects of love."

Rima said, "But we have never seen such beauty as Brekka radiates. I don't know what to call it. Is it grace or attraction that Brekka possesses? We don't have words to describe how much she stimulates us. All of us have had dreams of lying with her. Is this not spiritual connection enough?"

Going Snake stifled a chuckle, shook his head, and said, "No, it is not a spiritual connection enough. It is the dream of boys. You will know when it is enough because the person you love will be dreaming as much about you as you are of her. I do not wish to demean you, but I know Brekka like a sister, and it will take a very special type of man to finally win her heart."

Rima fired off, "A man like you. I could see how fondly she looked upon you."

"No, no, you don't understand. Our love for each other is like brother and sister." Internally he didn't want to believe that, but his heart told him it was so. "I'm probably not her type of man either, though I find her very attractive as well."

Jima said, "What type of man is it that she wants? So we can woo her properly."

Going Snake could see by their facial expressions that they were deeply sincere. He thought for a moment. "First off, I am sure he would have to be Herewardi. He would have to be a kingly sort. A warrior. A spiritual man. And a lover. All the things my Herewardi wives have told me they looked for in a man."

Sima looked thoughtful. "So we must find out how to become Herewardi and learn your ways of being kingly, spiritual, how to be warriors, and I think we have the lover part down very well already. Then we can all go to Brekka and bring her our love."

"I am sorry this is so hard for you to grasp, but if she was to accept your love in marriage it could only be from one of you. You see, the Herewardi women do not marry more than one man."

"Well, why not?" Rima said, "You have many wives?"

"I only have three, two that are Herewardi and one that is Sharaka. But I will tell you, the Herewardi have found, through hundreds of years that marriage of more than one man to a woman does not work."

"Why not?" Rima asked.

"Because male energy is opposed to male energy, whereas female energy compliments female energy when in balance. With some awful exceptions I personally know of. You need to give your education in our ways at least twelve moons to ripen so that each of you can learn to be your own man and find your true selves before you take on the ways of our world. Be patient my friends and I will help you as much as I can before the Skalds arrive to teach you the path of truth and light."

"Skalds," Rima repeated. "What are Skalds?"

"They are learned men and women, sent to teach us the way, the truth, and the light. I studied under them as a youth." He saw their puzzled looks, and then clarified. "You know; the meaning of life and why we are here, where we came from, and where we are going."

Going Snake placed some larger logs on the fire. "There, you've got yourself a fire now. See how we worked the bow to get a spark, then added tinder, then kindling, and finally the larger logs? That is how it will be with your educations in our way of life. You are at the stage where you have to work hard to get a spark going, then add the smaller basics, then a little more, until finally you can use the big things and have a warm spiritual fire burning in your hearts; What the Herewardi call the Ur Fyr and what we Sharaka call the Great Spirit." He looked up and saw the grooms gathering the horses and taking them to the ropes for tying. Behind them followed the dog soldier guards.

Rima appeared annoyed. "Work! Everything in this world requires so much preparation and work. If you want to eat, you have to prepare your food. If you want warmth, you have to prepare your fire. You have to prepare your tent if you want shelter. And you have to prepare your woman, if you want to be joined to her. So much work."

Going Snake laughed before scanning the camp. His right hand man, Talking Stick, was addressing the order of the camps and completing his duties. Campfires burned in circle after circle of white tents. Each camp containing approximately one hundred people, and there were thirty camps of refugees alone. Hoots and cries went up as the horses and cattle were rounded up for the night. Mooing and whinnying carried through the air, and the camp took on a calm feeling with the approaching twilight.

He returned to his conversations with the three paramours. "I think you men are starting to get it. You need to start teaching the other paramours. It's a type of work you will come to enjoy. In fact labor improves most anything. Not only in the art of love, but in every act which we set our hand to do. The next time we meet I'll tell you about the joy of having children and a family, but for now I need to finish my rounds and meet with Russell, Ev' Rhett, and Rip. Tomorrow, Rip tells me, we shall pass through some exciting terrain, and you shall see some lofty mountains that will rob your breath with their beauty."

A soft warm breeze blew in from the south, lifting Going Snake's hair like a wispy brush over his back. He walked on until he came to the refugee camp of the virgins and noticed a white woman of particular beauty tending to the blisters on another woman's foot by carefully wrapping it in swaddling. It was apparent that most of the virgins at least knew how to cast a tent, and several already had soups and bread cooking over their campfires which were delivering their delicious odors across camps. The gentle sound of wooden spoons clunked out a rhythmic beat as he walked over to the virgin bent over and tending the other girl. Surprised that she was so adeptly bandaging the foot as if she had much experience, Going Snake declared, "It would appear you have some skill at this."

She looked up and he was instantly struck by the depth of beauty in her grey eyes. "Yes, I am trained in the healing arts. I was an assistant to Griselda for five years." She smiled and his heart pounded in answer. There was a connection that unseated him momentarily.

*Oh, Chief-Maker, what is this I am feeling?* Her steel grey eyes were embedded in fair rosy cheeks framed by long curly tresses of tawny hair that sent out a glistening sheen in the fire-light. He guessed she was around twenty winters. Her lips were a subdued vermillion that smiled invitingly at him. He was lost in her face for a long silence. "Well, we could certainly use your skill. We are in need of a good doctor. What is your name?"

"My name is Bithia," she said as she stood up and wiped the hair from her face, "and who might you be?"

"I'm Going Snake, the commander of this expedition."

She smiled, "I'm glad you are a going snake and not a rattle snake." They laughed. "I saw you prancing about on that white horse of yours. Thought you might be the leader. You must be proud to sit such a stallion. You look every inch the warrior on him."

"My father taught me to be proud, but never to brag about my possessions or abilities. Still, this horse is a colt of the great White Fire, the High King Sur Sceaf's famous stallion."

"I do not know Sur Sceaf, but that horse is the brightest I've ever seen. I haven't ridden a horse since I was captured at age twelve, but I've never forgotten the feeling of traveling over the land like I was gliding between heaven and earth. Nor can I forget the sensation of racing down out of the grass covered hills of home."

"Where would your home be?"

"We were Hutters in the Montan. My family was killed by the Vardropi, and my sister and I were sold to Gloomullah. My sister went into the camp of Brimestone and never returned. I became a favorite of Gloomullah. It is one thing to know there is evil in the world. It is another to live through it and to have its claws embedded in your heart. It's brought a hatred in my heart that won't be quenched."

"The baleful Vardropi are godlessly cruel, and Brekka has told me that Gloomullah was possessed of an evil ghost spirit."

Going Snake felt a strange mix of emotion. There was compassion, but a keen sexual attraction, and spiritual link he could not understand. *I shall want to know you far better, Bithia though I am sure your wounds run deep.* The pungent smell of juniper and sage filled his nostrils, and the sweet feelings of love filled his soul.

A horse trotted up and snorted behind him. He turned and his first lieutenant, Talking Stick, was mounted on his paint. He wore nothing more than a loin cloth and moccasins. He saluted, "Chief Going Snake, the horses are secured, the Dog Soldiers and Fyrds are camped on the perimeters, and the guards are all set. I shall now take leave of my duties."

"Tis well, Talking Stick. We will take a long needed rest and rise late on the morrow."

Talking Stick smiled and rode off. Going Snake turned his attention back to Bithia. "If it is alright with you, I shall come in the morning. I should like to know you better."

Bithia smiled, "I would like that very much, Going Snake."

As he walked on, he thought, *The Supernatural One Upon Who It Thunders has awakened my heart to this woman. Something great is trying to happen to me. Oh Grand Father, is this your way of telling me to let go of Brekka?*

It was midday and very hot, up high in what the Presters called the Rockies or Uintas, but the Herewardi had named the Jotund Spine. As Arundel took a swig from his water flask, he was pleased to look out over the roofs and see how many cabins they had completed for the expected refugees. While Arundel supervised the building of the cabins, Redelfis trained the Warriors of the Buffalo Nations in the fighting arts of the Herewardi, called Raumaulkin. He could see from the roof he was standing on that Sun Cryer's braves were enjoying the exercises. Then he returned to hammering down the shingles as he thought about how much he missed his other wives, all of his children, and his enchanted home in the Hyf at the Crater.

His reverie was broken when Yellow Horse came up the ladder with a fresh bundle of shingles, unceremoniously dropped them, and said, "I hope we complete these cabins soon. My ass and knuckles can't take much more of this kind of work, Ary."

Arundel continued hammering. "I just tell myself, that whatever has a beginning, will have an end, and set my mind to doing whatever is at hand."

"We've built twice the long cabins the Presters have and will finish up before them," Yellow Horse said with pride in his voice. "When do you think the refugees will arrive?"

"Oh, I give them another ten days at most; though I suspect Rip knows some short cuts. Once they arrive and we give them an orientation, we'll turn them over to the Skalds and the Presters for sorting. It won't be an easy matter to place all of them. It could take a couple of years to determine where they should all be finally situated. Brekka sent me a pigeon requesting I send three of the paramours to Moon Door. Says she thinks they have potential and that Ilkchild will delight in their stories."

"She probably has a crush on one of them by now. I hear they are all a bunch of very pretty boys. She probably wants to make them Herewardi because I don't think that relationship with that Ruhm guy is going to work. You know, he's one of those stubborn ass Hickoryan type. Kind of like that Merriman Wallanwood the Strict, who married his daughter off to your brother, Il-Alim. All of 'em, unyielding as mules." Yellow Horse chuckled, cut the bundle of shingles open and took up his hammer. He hammered for a few shingles then said, "I've been thinking, my lord, are you looking forward to the Taxus Campaign?"

"Like nothing I've ever done before. It is the land of my Longfather, Arundel the Great. If we take the Taxus Lands, I think we have won this war against the evil spirit in the west. True, it will become far more costly, but once we have a foot firmly established in Taxus, it may be all over for the Pitters, for that will be the pivotal point of the Great War. The only thing that could tip that equation in the other direction is if the Bamboo Bloom is not thwarted in time. Word of our victories will spread, and it shall kindle the resistance in the South Lands as far as Flar-Dah and Jaw Jaw; thus softening the soil for our entry into the eastern lands. We have heard there are solid secret militias throughout the south lands, a strong resistance force in the mountains of the firginias, and quilombos; black guerilla bands, that dwell in the swamp lands. Amanuel was taught that martial art there. You know, he calls it capoiera. He lived in a quilombos for two years before moving on to the west. It is of course, only my hope they will all rally to our cause."

"And if they don't."

"Then the war will be protracted for another generation, and by then the Pitters will have a population explosion, and our war will become too awful to even contemplate."

Yellow Horse had a sad look on his face. "You don't seem altogether confident the guerilla forces will aid us."

"You're absolutely right. The Hickoryans have been taught we are immoral, and Amanuel tells me the quilombos teach that they never want to shadow whites again. Even call us White Devils. Perhaps Ruhm can persuade the Hickoryans, and Amanuel the Blacks. It seems the blacks were evilly dealt with in the Amerikan Empire, had their culture totally diluted and were forced to be the shadow of White Culture. We may have many cultural obstacles to overcome before we can convince them that our cause is their cause. If everyone thinks only of their own tribal needs, we could all find ourselves on the wrong end of the stick and the Pitters on top."

"Or worse, extinct."

# CHAPTER 21 :

## TROUBLE IN THE MOUNTAINS

"THE QUICKEST TRAIL INTO SALMALHUER is just beyond that pass."
Rip the Prester pointed toward a break in the line of mountain peaks.
Going Snake figured it was an hour before high noon on the
thirteenth day of the Hot Moonth. They'd been on the trail for eight days.
Two days earlier the desert landscape had given way to the mountainous
terrain of Juniper, Pinyon, and Yellow Pine. "Even at our usual snail's
pace, we should make it to the pass before nightfall."

As Going Snake turned back to announce the need to pick up pace,
the scouts he had sent out at the crack of dawn to survey the way ahead
came storming back. Here-Yggr, Sur Sceaf's Son of Taneshewa's hearth,
and the other scout, his Herewardi lieutenant, Uffa, were clearly excited.
"We spotted four Vardropi legions heading directly toward us from the
north, Commander," Here-Yggr reported. He brought his white stallion
to a full stop next to Going Snake's.

"They have a large group of female slaves in tow," Uffa added. "We
had better figure out some sort of swift retreat or they will run over us
like a herd of buffalo."

Going Snake glanced toward the mountains. "Retreating swiftly is
out of the question. Look around, Uffa. We, too, have a large contingent
of females and they are almost all afoot."

As soon as the scouts had returned, Ev'Rhett and Russell rode up.
"Russell and I could take our fyrd and hold them while you get the

trekkers back to the safety of that large canyon we saw two days back," Ev'Rhett suggested.

"And then what? Hold up for two weeks while Rip the Prester procures more troops from Arundel? Methinks not. Starvation is worse than death by battle."

"I think I have the solution," Rip said with a twinkle in his eye.

"Well, let's hear it then," Going Snake ordered.

Rip leaned over his saddle horn. "When Pyrsyrus and I were pirating far down in the south seas where the stars begin to re-configure, we came upon a race of Wild Men along the coast. They were given to peace and hospitality and so we shared a lot of our cargo of goods with them. They spoke a type of espagnol and thought us to be gods come from the heavens when we pointed to the north as our homeland. Well, we parted on good terms with them. And then, five years later when we returned on a voyage of exploration, we came into their cove once again and spotted a fleet of dragoons parked there."

"A fleet of dragoons, you say," Russell said as he shifted his Hugin raven hair claw. "Must have been El Yid's men."

"Probably Mexus pirates," Ev'Rhett said, mirroring Russell by readjusting his Munin raven hair claw. "They are fast learners. Probably copied our designs."

"No, it wasn't either! That's precisely my point. We, too, thought it was probably El Yid or some Mexus Pirates, but as we drew nearer, the ships appeared to be very queer looking. Once we were close enough to discern, we saw that these were bamboo and palm frond replicas of our ships. It had us completely fooled into thinking they were real ships. These wild men had made them as a tribute to us, believing that it would cause us, the gods, to return to them and give them more treasures."

Russell scratched his head, once again readjusted his raven claw. "What's your point, Rip?"

"My point is that Going Snake and you all could remain behind with the dog soldiers and fyrds to create a fake fort and camp. You could make it out of all the Yellow Pine we just passed. It shouldn't take more than a day. It would be enough to halt the Vardropi in their tracks while I escort the refugees into and over the mountain trek into the crack at Salmalhuer before we get hit by an early snow storm."

"Ingenious plan," Going Snake conceded. "But will it be safe for these unseasoned refugees? Some are sturdy serfs, but many are no more than perfumed parlor boys, and tender virgins, unaccustomed to the rigors of the wilds. Most have sore feet already, others are burned by the sun despite the hats fashioned from palm leaves."

Rip nodded. "I have considered that, and I agree it will be harder than hell for them, with steep climbs, long periods without water, and very steep descents, but I believe it will be safer than staying here or getting trapped in a blind canyon."

"But if we cannot hold the enemy, they will surely be able to overtake you and our efforts would have then all been in vain."

"Not so. There is a place high in the mountains called Goat's Leap. It is a great chasm over which we can lay long timbers and earth. We'll be able to bring the horses over blindfolded safely to the other side. Then none may pursue or make afraid, for we will pull the timbers away and by the time they could figure out how we did it, or where we went, we shall be under the Angelic Aegis of the Presters."

Going Snake considered Rip's explanation, looking for dangerous flaws. And, as his Grandfather had often counseled, "The simplest solution is usually the best solution."

"Then that is it. Get on it! Russell and Ev'Rhett, get your men to cutting timbers for a fake fort right away."

The twins exchanged excited looks, snapped off crisp salutes and rode away. Going Snake then turned to Here-Yggr, "How long before the Vardropi get here?"

"When we spotted them, they were in camp feasting on freshly killed buffalo, and showed no signs of moving on any time soon. I'd say three days at the least and likely a week at the most. They appeared to be coming from a slaving run through the Rogue Nations and Quants, and seemed none too anxious to get anywhere."

Going Snake nodded. "Rip, how long will your trek across the Goat's Leap take?"

"A week and a half, give or take a day or two. It shouldn't take more than a half day to cut and lay the timbers."

"Then you'd better get started."

Rip nodded. "I'll need at least a fyrd to help me manage so many travelers and I'll have to draw supplies from the quarter master."

"Whatever you need."

"And the two of us?" Ulla asked, watching as Rip trotted toward the quarter master's wagon. "What would you have us do?"

Going Snake bit off a sigh. "Help me figure out how we're going to defeat four legions of rabid Vardropi with only a fraction of their numbers."

The sun beat down mercilessly on the mountain bench above Salmalhuer where rows of newly built cabins stood waiting for their new occupants. Arundel paused to wipe the sweat from the handle of his hammer. Twice, it had slipped from his hand while he'd been attaching the shiplap siding, once barely missing his mocassined foot. Thanks be to the gods, this was the last cabin. He didn't mind the manual labor. After all, the strenuous work kept his muscles strong and eye-hand coordination sharp. But he doubted he could manage one more day listening to Yellow Horse's endless grumbling.

"What say you, my mumbling Jester friend? Shall we celebrate the completion of our labors with some High Desert Ale?"

Yellow Horse lifted his head with a look of exhaustion in his face. "I would say my ass is as grateful as it gets. My thumbs thank you that they only have a few more misguided hammer strokes to endure before they are free to pursue their favorite employ."

"What would that be, Joker?"

"To sit in the quiet of my candlelit tent and read the Idylls of Leofric with my dear wife, Elisheba when she arrives."

Arundel had other plans for his wives, but thought to each his own. "If all goes according to plan, our wives will be arriving in the Apache lands by the time we arrive in Kerr by the river. Once we take the Bastion at Omala in the Taxus Lands, we'll send for them. That should give us all incentive for taking the Omala. In the meantime, they can enjoy the hospitality the Apaches and Kaninchens offer."

As Arundel and Yellow Horse raised the framed wall, the last of the four, a Prester messenger came riding hard into the compound. As soon as he spotted them, the messenger dismounted and trotted over to them. "Lord Arundel, I bear you news that Rip the Apostle is three days' journey from the crack and sends you this urgent message." He handed a letter to Arundel.

Arundel opened the roll and read, *'Lord Arundel, I approach the crack near Goat's Leap with the refugees of the Poison Lands and bid you send your fyrds out before we arrive. Going Snake is likely holding off a host of four Vardropi legions while we make our escape towards you in the Prester Land.'*

"By the nine glory twigs, these are strange times. Who would have thought the Vardropi would be this far west? Yellow Horse, find Redelfis and have him sound the horn for the assembly of the fyrds. We ride through the crack to the wyhome today."

The soughing pines waved their branches in the mountain winds, and magpies sang in the tall, thick sagebrush where Going Snake and his Dog Soldiers hid in ambush astride their painted ponies. Up in a Pinyon Pine, Crying Dog signaled with the sound of a hoot owl that the Vardropi were approaching.

Going Snake spotted the cloud of dust first, then the wind-whipped banners of nursing she-wolves, and finally the massive army moving toward them like a machine. At the head of the column rode a huge man dressed in the distinctive black uniform of a Vardropi Commander. The Vardropi were not ashen colored like the Pitters, nor did they have large incisors, for they were more wolf seed code and less rat, and twice as fierce.

Yesterday afternoon, one of Ulla's advance guard had spotted two Vardropi scouts surveying the "fort" from behind a clutch of boulders. The guard had succeeded in approaching close enough to hear them discussing what they saw, but could not make out the words out as the two Vardropi were speaking Frank-Kay, a language that was prevalent in sections of the far North. However, the guard did pick up on the repeated use of a word that sounded like "Ishkummen." Going Snake had immediately recognized it as the name of a Vardropi Commander reputed to be particularly ruthless and cunning. No doubt he was the rider in black.

"Ugly bastard, isn't he?" Russell whispered.

"Arrogant, too," Ev'Rhett replied. "Making himself a target riding out in front like that. Must not be too worried."

"No reason he should be. It's not like we had time to build more than a small fort."

Going Snake had chosen the location of the hastily erected walls so that he could attack the enemy's left flank from the grove of Pinyon Pines. He considered it a gift of the Thunder Beings that the enemy had arrived just as the sun was low on the horizon. As soon as the attack commenced, the Vardropi would be looking directly into the glaring sun.

Going Snake waited until Ishkummen's features were clearly visible. "Ugly" did not adequately describe the man's grotesque, wolf-like features. In place of hair, this Vardropi had a thatch of stiff bristles running down the middle of his shaven head resembling the ridge on a boar's back.

"Get ready," he whispered before signaling to Crying Dog to sound the order to attack. Crying Dog gave out a distinctive trilling wild cry followed by Talking Stick's blood-curdling yell. Going Snake led the charge and his men followed with the fury of a nest of angry hornets into the kill zone.

As his horse charged into the Vardropi leader, the impact hurled the bristle-head off his horse. The Vardropi was stunned as he fell to the earth with a thud which knocked him both speechless and out of breath. Going Snake reined his horse in and turned around to see Ishkummen struggling to get up and catch his breath with terror stricken eyes. Before he could rise to his faculties, Going Snake thrust his lance directly into the enemy's chest, felt the armor catch, then give, as the lance head pierced Ishkummen's heart.

Ishkummen heaved a groan then fell back to the earth lifeless with his mouth wide open and his features locked in a frozen snarl. Going Snake pulled out his long tomahawk from his belt and began smashing the heads of the Vardropi cavalry who were so taken by surprise that few knew how to react to the rising tide of frenzied Dog Soldiers. The shock tactic and the blinding sun scrambled and broke the Vardropi legions usual battle formation.

With each swing of his tomahawk, a Vardropi skull was crushed or a sword arm broken. Before the Vardropi unit commanders could gather what was happening, Russell hit from one side like a clap of thunder, and Ev'Rhett struck in a lightening-attack from the rear. This broke the formation of the legions into greater chaos and sent them scampering in all directions.

Going Snake remembered what White Crow told him and yelled it to Russell and Ev'Rhett. "If you smite the Vardropi leader, the whelps will all scatter."

Going Snake continued to plunge deeper and deeper into their ranks. He felt so empowered by his success that all reason had departed, but he had so decimated the Vardropi ranks with his Dog Soldiers that those Vardropi who could, gathered into a mass, and fled back into the north.

The axiom of smiting the head was true. Mile after mile Going Snake and his Dog Soldiers hounded the fleeing Vardropi, who obviously could not calculate the force that pursued them. Occasionally, a group of Vardropi would break off and flee in another direction altogether, but the mass hung tight and headed for the high chaparral.

Fully exhausted in slaying and pursuing over some ten miles of rugged terrain, Going Snake gave the signal to halt and re-group. As he raised his arm to rally his troops a searing pain tore at his chest. He looked down and was shocked to discover an enemy arrow piercing his shoulder. He broke the shaft and tossed it away. As soon as Ev'Rhett and Russell arrived, he signaled his men to follow and resumed the pursuit across the broad plain. Despite the fire of the embedded arrowhead, he was determined to pursue the enemy in order to buy time for Rip to ensure the refugees safely got across Goat's Leap.

The sun began to set, and still they rode. Sharp pains ran through his chest, but he knew he must keep up the pursuit or lose all advantage. His strength began to fade and he remembered how Brekka had once told him that Woon can give strength in battle by sending the Valkyries to administer relief to those afflicted with pain, if they but call upon him. The pain was well-nigh unbearable, so he prayed, *All Father Woon, have mercy on your red son. Send your Valkyries to minister their relief to me. I pray thee, and I shall consecrate my next son unto thee.*

The land rose abruptly into rocky outcroppings, forcing him to call a halt. The Vardropi had embedded themselves inside a high dry rock formation, not only giving them the advantage of the high ground, but also the natural protection afforded by the rock formations of the box canyon behind them.

Going Snake signaled for Russell and Ev-Rhett to join him in counsel. To his surprise, the fire in his shoulder began to fade. Within minutes a welcome numbness settled over him.

"It seems the wolves have found a lair," he said. "If they have time to choose a new leader their strength will come back to them and I doubt with our few numbers we could take them.

"And how do you propose we get a wolf out of its liar?" Here-Yggr asked.

Russell got a mischievous grin on his face. "With fire."

"Exactly." He waited until Crying Dog and Talking Stick rode up to join the makeshift Council Fire. "We will burn them out," he explained. "Here-Yggr, position a double row of bowmen across that canyon and have them fire into the Vardropi to force them deeper and tighter inside. Russell and Ev'Rhett, set your men to cutting brush while the archers are distracting them."

Minutes later, Russell and Ev'Rhett had their men hacking brush and stacking it before the canyon, while Here-Yggr's archers filled the air with raining wolf-arrows from their long bows. Several cohorts of Vardropi sensed a trap and broke for the holes in the enclosing brush wall. Cavalry were dispensed to run them down, and Russell's men hastened to fill the holes.

After two hours a ten foot wall of dry brush rose and extended from one side of the canyon to the other. Going Snake assumed the Vardropi would think he was forming a barrier and being from the far north would not comprehend how inflammatory this dry brush truly was.

He drew on all the descriptions he had heard about the Vardropi. His father had fought them and told him the Vardropi were ravening wolves, vicious to the man, and far more durable than the Pitters. They were cruel and brutal and strictly bent on their warlike pursuits. His father had told him that unless you kill their leader, in most cases they are unrelenting in any conflict. Once the leader is killed they spend lots of time fighting, squabbling, and juggling for a new leader. He had to act while they were yet in their juggling and contending phase, for they were a savage lot, delighting in torture and reveling in collecting trophies from the dead, particularly ears, scalps, fingers, and genitalia which they wore around their necks. Ears stood for helpless victims, scalps for warriors, fingers for arms severed and genitalia from those they raped, all attesting to their subhuman natures.

Going Snake felt a sharp jabbing pain in his wounded shoulder and blood began running down his arm in a rivulet. He ordered Crying Dog to gather tinder and light a fire from which others could light their torches.

His braves dismounted and began making rough sticks into torches with torn shirts or tinder which they fashioned to the end with strips of fringe from their bags or garments. A volley of Vardropi arrows struck through their ranks and killed Coyote Foot and Frowning Bear. Going Snake called for shields up, for the wounded and dead to be gathered, and waited as his men laid larger pieces of wood on the fire.

Going Snake struggled to remount and keep his shield up, as it was shortly thereafter struck by three Vardropi arrows. He declared to his troops, "The Vardropi have re-grouped and we can only pray this wall of fire will hold them."

Each brave hurriedly lit their torches from the fire and then at his signal they cast the flaming faggots into the brush pile that caught instantly. Soon it whipped into a towering flame of rip-roaring fire tongues spreading from the westerly winds as it swept into the brush of the dry canyon like dragon's breath. Like demons fleeing from Hell, flames leapt from brush to brush to singe the howling, gnashing Vardropi legionnaires, who could not pass the wall of fire and whose horses were wild with panic and terror. Any who fled by seeking to leap through the low points in the fire wall were summarily cut down by archers or the tomahawks of Dog Soldiers.

Soon masses of Vardropi began collapsing, either from the heat or smoke that now engulfed them until all that was left was a field full of blackened corpses, charred horses, and black rocks.

The feeling of satisfaction, from having disabled four evil legions filled Going Snake with pride, and he gave thanks to the Thunder Beings and Woon. By all standards the day should not have ended in anything short of death. But, instead, the gods awarded him a miraculous delivery.

"Leave the bodies for the carrion."

"I'm sure I saw some of the enemy flee into the crevices in the rock," Crying Dog said. "Shouldn't we pursue them?"

Going Snake shook his head. "Let them go. I doubt there are enough of them to do us much harm. We must free the captives back at their compound while we still have some twitter light left."

The elation of having survived a battle with the Vardropi soon gave way to the increasing pain of his wound, which now screamed louder than a crying baby in the middle of a weary night. He said a prayer, *Thank you, All Father, for preserving us.*

Going Snake gritted his teeth and held himself awkwardly up in the saddle by his right arm. Then he signed for all to follow him back to the slave compound. He tried distracting himself from the pain in his shoulder that was throbbing like a big drum and burning like a hot tong. He turned his mind to more pleasant thoughts. He remembered his meeting with Bithia and wished she were there to tend his wound. A smile creeped across his face and then his mind bounced back and forth between pain and Bithia.

By the darkening hour they came upon the Vardropi temporary compound. Going Snake signed for his troops to surround it, then signaled for Quick Stinger to lead his Dog Soldiers in. By torchlight, they slew the remaining Vardropi, dispatching them with ease.

Inside the walls were untold numbers of young girls and a few men. One was a pedlar who looked about fifty winters in age, with silver hair and a leather hat, coat, and pants who stood by a canvas covered wagon.

"Hail Sharaka Chief, the name's Timothy Lighthorse. I'm a traveling merchant and was pressed into serving these bastard Vardropi. You need not think I am in any way affiliated with these rabid dogs."

Somehow, Going Snake managed to dismount without crying out from the pain. The man handed him the papers allowing him passage from a number of tribes, signifying that he was indeed a bona fide merchant and pedlar who came highly recommended. "As I watched you approach and saw your broad shoulders, your deep chest, and your narrow hawk-like face, it put me in mind of a great Sharaka Chief I once knew called Onamingo. You would not be his son,would you?"

"You sir, are a flatterer and I am not wont to trust flattery. Though I know it is the way of merchants. I am not his son. I be his grandnephew. I am Going Snake of the Syr Folk, Son of Mendaka. And the tall redhead over there, Here-Yggr, is Onamingo's grandson also of the Syr Folk."

"Yes, the Great Island Confederation of Nations. Out of small things proceed the great. I have heard much of them. And I did know your Father, Mendaka. Chief of the Di-Ahman, I believe."

"Man, the only thing that concerns me now is, can you tell us what the Vardropi were doing this far west and south of their homeland?"

"The Vardropi were on a slave run heading for the Poisoned Lands. They hoped to trade these young female slaves from the rogue nations to the Growlings, like the Pitter do, in hopes of gaining some of the new weapons and noogs the Growlings purportedly offer." The merchant glanced around. "Tell me, did you manage to kill that bastard, Ishkummen?"

"We did. As well as the majority of his legionaires."

"Then you were lucky indeed, because I have heard of greater armies than you being defeated by them. But I see you are yourself not without wounds. And I'm thinking I had better dress that wound before I give you the bad news."

"What bad news?"

"No, no, not before I dress your wound, Chief."

Crying Dog rode up beside them, saluted, and said, "Camp is secure."

Going Snake shot him a pained smile. "Good! and Crying Dog, would you please tend to White Lightning for me?"

Crying Dog glanced at the pedlar. "Of course."

Going Snake handed him the reins and Crying Dog led the stallion away.

The Pedlar used a small billows to blow into a small kiln he had on his wagon and stuck in an iron poker.

"How fast can you remove this arrowhead?"

"Faster than you can say Timothy Lighthorse," The merchant said. He went to his wagon, got a sharp knife and pliers, and handed Going Snake an onyx cup with a concoction in it. "Here, down this first."

Going Snake could tell by the smell it was best to chug it all down in one slurp. He drank quickly, choked, almost retched. "Oh, Thunder Gods. What devil's concoction is that?"

"Pulverized acorns with a heavy crop of blue mold on them mixed in some birch beer." Lighthorse cut open the sleeve of the shoulder, then latched onto the broken shaft with his pliers and at the same time cut into the muscle tissue to allow for the arrowhead to be slowly tugged out.

Going Snake felt his eyes roll back in his head and as though from a great distance he heard the merchant's voice. "Now stay with me. Stay with me." Lighthorse gave one mighty tug, before presenting the bloody arrowhead for Going Snake's inspection. As soon as Going Snake took the arrowhead, the pedlar grabbed him by the arm and plunged the white-hot poker into his wound.

Going Snake yelled and at the same time, drew up a fist to smash the pedlar in the face before he stopped himself. The man clearly knew much of the healing arts. "Thank you, Pale Horse."

The jovial merchant gave a comical laugh and said, "T'weren't anything. Glad I could be of service. Though the name is Lighthorse."

Going Snake was about to reply when Talking Stick rode up with Here-Yggr.

Here-Yggr pulled his horse in close beside him and said, "It grows late Going Snake. Shall we strike camp here for the night?"

"Yes." He glanced at the merchant. "It grows late, my friend, and we must set up camp among you. Take me to see the slaves and let me speak with them, and then be so kind as to tend the wounds of my men. Do you have any other medical supplies?"

"I have plenty of alcohol and bandages," Lighthorse said, scratching his head as if he was wondering if he'd ever be paid for it, then continued, "perhaps a little opium, and some few other medicines. And as you see all about camp, there is plenty of buffalo to eat." Then the merchant walked over to Here-Yggr who sat astride his horse, tugged on his pant leg, and asked, "Is there any Cygnus among you?"

Going Snake said, "There is no sickness among us just the wounded and injured as I said."

Here-Yggr smiled. "I perceive you are a fellow traveler, Timothy. We shall talk later about the Cygnus."

Going Snake furrowed his brow at Here-Yggr and thought, *What a curious interaction,* then followed Timothy to the slave compound.

Timothy opened the compound gate, which was made out of crude Pine branches. The captives were still tied to poles in rows and looked both gaunt and bedraggled, unlike the healthy slaves he had seen in the Growling compound.

"Yeoh Wah!" he shouted.

Several of his dog soldiers came running through the gate. Talking Stick and Crying Dog accompanied Russell, Ev'Rhett, and Here-Yggr into the usual council fire that customarily takes place after every battle to determine what could have been done better.

Going Snake said, "Gentlemen, permit me to address these slaves first. Use your knives and free these poor unfortunate souls. I shall not enter council until I am assured they will all be fed and properly cared for."

The men immediately set to freeing the young women, who proceeded to rubbing their wrists for relief from their tight bindings. Going Snake saw a barrel, turned it upon end with the help of Ev'Rhett and despite his shoulder wound, climbed atop it. "Dearest children, we are come to deliver you out of the hands of your slave masters and to bring you under the wing of freedom and protection. I am Going Snake of the Syr Folk Nation and we shall take you to the place called Salmalhuer for sanctuary, where we will make an attempt to locate your friends and relatives for you. I see there is plenty of buffalo and we shall see to it that it gets divided up with you soon enough. My men shall not eat or drink until every one of your bellies is full and satisfied first."

Talking Stick signed for his braves to see to the freed captives needs.

"There is one more thing I must ask you, Chief Going Snake," the Pedlar said lifting off his hat and scratching his head. "It's the thing I said I would not tell you until I dressed your wound."

"Yes, what is it, Horse White?" He knew he had gotten the name wrong once again. "I'm sorry, Lighthorse."

Lighthorse smiled, "I can see you've lost a lot of blood. I'll cook you up a mess of buffalo liver. But what I wanted to ask first is when you burned those Vardropi, did any escape?"

"I reckon no more than a fourth to a third may have escaped over the mountain. The rest burned. Why?"

"Then you don't know that there are four more legions east of here and that they will likely return here on the morrow or the next day."

"By the Thunder Beings! Dammit, I wish I had known that right off. Why didn't you tell me?"

"Because I knew you wouldn't have taken the time for me to address that wound and it would have killed you if I hadn't cauterized it."

"Here-Yggr, would you please record our emergency council and meeting. Lord Arundel will want to know what happened here."

Here-Yggr reached into his haversack and pulled out pen, ink well, and tablet. "It shall be done."

"That means," Ev'Rhett said, "we've got to get these women out of here and over the Goat's Leap before they come."

"That's exactly what it means," Russell said. "Ev'Rhett and I shall hold those bastards off while you do it."

"No, I must do it," Going Snake said.

Talking Stick cried, "Chief, you speak in the name of duty and not wisdom. As your first in command, I am asking that you let Crying Dog and I fight the Vardropi legions while Ev'Rhett and Russell lead the captives to freedom."

"Why don't we all go north and avoid the confrontation with the Vardropi altogether?" Timothy put in anxiously.

"For two reasons: one, that it is a sacred obligation to avenge the death of a blood brother. And, two, we must clear the route to the Taxus for the Syr Folk troops and hospitalers. Better to use the element of surprise once again."

Going Snake knew he was no good for any further combat, knew Brekka greatly valued Russell and Ev'Rhett as two of the strongest pillars in her army, and he knew he greatly loved both Crying Dog and Talking Stick, like brothers. He said, "I cannot make this call. The gods must choose who will stay and fight, Ev'Rhett and Russell or Talking Stick and Crying Dog." He paused looked up at the sky and prayed a silent prayer. *Oh, Grandfather, please choose who will stay and fight. Let it be done according to thy will.*

As he looked down he saw the scramasax in Russell's pant leg, reached down and pulled it out, then walked over to a nearby upended whiskey barrel and said, "Russell, you stand to the north and Talking Stick, you stand to the south. Lighthorse, you will spin this knife and whomever the blade points to, will be who stays and fights. It is the gods' will."

The four repeated, "It is the gods' will."

Lighthorse said, "Dammit, I hate to have anyone's fate resting in my hands." He closed his eyes, stretched out his hand, and spun the balanced blade, which made several revolutions then slowed down to point clearly at Talking Stick.

"It is settled," Talking Stick said. "It is a good day to die."

Going Snake felt his guts tighten and fell upon the shoulders of Talking Stick and wept.

"Do not weep for me, my blood brother. I shall join my fathers in the Other World. But there is one request I have of a good friend."

Going Snake pulled his heart together and said, "You need but name it."

"I wish that none under the age of eighteen winters to accompany me."

"But that's half the Dog Soldiers."

"Suffer it to be so, my brother. These Young Bloods will sing my praise beside every campfire."

"It will be so."

Talking Stick struck arms with Crying Dog as they looked into each other's eyes and said, "We shall tell all of our men to prepare to enter the Other World and we shall every man take more than double our share of Vardropi out of this world today."

"Then hear my vow, Talking Stick and Crying Dog, your families shall be well cared for and your sons will know what great warriors their fathers are."

Going Snake reached with his one good hand to his belt and unfastened a small white deerskin bag. "Here-Ygrr, will you do me the honor of emptying the contents of this bag on to the barrel."

Here-Yggr took the bag and poured a pile of soft downy feathers on the top of the barrel. Going Snake then reached down with his right hand and began sprinkling the eagle down over the heads of Talking Stick and Crying Dog. "Thus, I call upon the gods to give you the strength of eagles and the powers of heaven."

Three days after Rip's Prester Messenger had arrived in Salmalhuer informing Arundel of their predicament, Arundel entered the camp of Going Snake which was an hour's march from the Goat's Leap. Ary, his fyrds, and an exceedingly large force of dog soldiers from the Buffalo Nations under the Grand Chieftain, Sun Cryer had crossed the Goat's Leap using Rip's brilliant engineering feat. A host of young women stood back huddling together, as he and his Fyrd of Heorls approached. "Hail Going Snake."

"Hail, my lord."

"This is not the sight I expected to see. I rejoice much in the living gods that they have preserved you alive and that your enemies do not wear your scalps. It is a testament of the gods' love for you."

"My lord, such love is too hard to bear. I can never replace what this trek has cost me. We took the Vardropi totally by surprise and that gave us the advantage. I immediately killed their leader in the chaparral. Whereon, we laid the blade unceasingly to them in a chase, penned them in a high and dry canyon, and set them to the flames with a brush fire from hell. But a quarter to a third fled over the rugged mountains and mustered four additional legions we knew nothing of. I had to divide our forces to get the refugees to safety and since I was wounded, we let the gods select who would stay and fight while the rest of us fled for Goat's Leap. The Pedlar spun the Norn's Knife and the Wyrd Sisters chose Talking Stick. It was they stuck their hand in the wolf's mouth that we might have time for safe passage."

"Son of Mendaka," Arundel roared, "my hatred for the Vardropi is tenfold greater than it was. I mourn for the loss of your men. You are every bit the Great Warrior your father is and I could have never made such a wise decision." Arundel said as he grasped Going Snake on the shoulders.

Going Snake could only scrunch his face in pain, feeling his heart burst with compassion for Talking Stick, Crying Dog and their braves. "And you, my lord, are known to be every bit as great a warrior as your father, the All-King, Sur Sceaf. Your praise humbles me."

Russell and Ev'Rhett rushed to greet their eldest brother. "How much further to the Goat's Leap?" Russell asked.

"No more than three miles. Once you cross Goat's Leap it is a gradual slope down into the valley of Salmalhuer."

Going Snake exchanged looks with the Pedlar. "Ary, I can but ask a favor. Once we cross the Goat's Leap, we will be safe. So I plead with you to join the battle and deal them double the wrath they deserve."

"You have my swan swear on that."

General Rockwell had become a doting father figure to the three paramours. Going Snake was a bit apprehensive until Rip had explained that the general and his wife, Prunella, had recently lost two boys about the same age to drowning in the Provo River. The Rockwells had even opened their home to the boys, who were enthralled with their new surroundings. They were fascinated by the bicycle and antique artifacts, which they were able to identify from their lessons taught on the magic screens.

It had been a week since Rip had lead them down from the mountain and through the crack into Salmalhuer. Going Snake was immensely impressed with the way the Presters had prepared for the refugees. The dormitory cabins with their simple pinewood furniture were airy, bright and welcoming. Each was able to accommodate four hundred beds, and although it was tight quarters, no one complained.

Upon inquiring, he had learned that the Presters had provided one dining hall for every twelve cabins. Though simple fare, the food was hot, tasty and nutritious. Prester women, and Hutter and Quailor hospitalers had collected clothing, blankets and shoes. The hospitalers had worked overtime seeing to their medical needs, while rotational volunteers attended to their personal needs, serving as cooks, laundresses, teachers and entertainers.

Any who wished were invited to work on the many Prester welfare farms on the outskirts of the city where they learned agricultural skills. Going Snake discovered that the Prester culture was similar to the Quailor with their seventh day being a day of worship and rest.

After the midday meal General Rockwell invited Timothy, Going Snake, Here-Yggr and the paramours to take a tour of the city's magnificent Tabernakle where a new musical implement called an Organ had just been installed.

Going Snake found himself even more fascinated than the paramours by the immense pipes reaching nearly to the ceiling and the polished wooden box with three rows of white and black pickets. General

Rockwell spoke with a man who had just seated himself in front of the pickets, and then beckoned the paramours to join him there.

Going Snake, Here-Yggr and Timothy took seats beneath the apex of the dome. Although he was accustomed to the amazing buildings in Godeselle, Going Snake decided they could not compare to this building. On the way to the Tabernakle, Rockwell had explained that not one nail had been used in its construction.

Suddenly, the music began, swelling and soaring into a sweet melody that stirred his blood and yet soothed his soul at the same time. It was as though he had entered the Summerlands, romping in a field of flowers and riding on the wind that carried him back to his beloved boyhood home. For a moment, he even imagined running behind Fur Puller in hot pursuit of a coon.

He was even more amazed when he realized this magical music was being played by Rima. Stunned, he stared at the boy's fingers racing over the black and white pickets.

Suddenly, the organ crescendoed, then stopped. Rima rose from the bench, turned to face them, and executed an elaborate bow. Going Snake didn't know the proper response so he held his hands together in a sign that it was good. At the same time, Timothy rose to his feet, clapped his hands and shouted, "Bravo! Rima, bravo."

Rima beamed like an excited child. "That is my favorite piece. It is called the magic flute. Gloomullah forbade me to play it in her presence because she did not like the message that the queen was evil."

Rockwell called up to them and said he was taking the boys on a tour of the pipes.

"You know, for pansies those boys are pretty talented," Timothy drawled.

"It's not their fault they are pansies. They're just stall-raised bullocks. Once they fall under Ilkchild's tutelage, they will be as tough and manly as the best of our Young Bloods."

Going Snake took a deep breath. "While the three of us are here alone, I have a question. You and Timothy seemed to be communicating in a way I did not understand." He turned to Timothy. "It seemed to mean something special when you asked Here-Yggr, is there any sickness among you?"

Timothy exchanged a surprised look with Here-Yggr, who nodded. "I'm surprised you had to ask. I was actually using the word Cycnus--

C-Y-C-N-U-S—the word for Swan and the name of Brekka's horse. I'm surprised your father has not enlightened you."

Going Snake frowned. "Enlightened me how?"

"Have you never heard of the Sire Sheaf?" Here-Yggr asked.

Going Snake searched his memory, then shook his head.

Here-Yggr hesitated before saying, "I see no reason you should not know about it. After all, you are a red king, and married to a white queen and, worthy of such secret knowledge. The Sire Sheaf is a secret kind of seed bank, designed and created by the Roufytrof to ensure the perpetuation of the Herewardi Tribe. Its members are chosen by the Roufytrof to live amongst other nations while keeping their identity as Herewardi secret. Asking if there is Cycnus among you identifies the speaker as Herewardi. If the listener is not Herewardi, he will hear you asking about illness, but if he is, Herewardi he will hear Cycnus and answer with the correct sign and token."

"I admit to still being confused. Timothy, you don't act like any Herewardi I know. You have no wives or children, the most sacred duty of the Herewardi."

Timothy laughed. "On the contrary, I have a wife in Citriodora, a wife in Samathracia down in the Taxus and a wife in Balmor on the east coast. And at last count, I had eighteen children."

"That's part of the genius of the Sire Sheaf. They are like chameleons, able to blend in to any society. Some may appear to be Hickoryan, some may appear to be Sharaka, and some may even be Prester. And I have even known a few Quailor."

Going Snake was still digesting this and wondering if his father might be a member of the Sire Sheaf when Rockwell and the boys reappeared.

Jima offered them a huge grin. "Father Rockwell is going to treat us to something called bread pud-ding. He says it is the most delicious food on earth, and only his wife can make it so good."

"And you three are also invited."

As they exited the Tabernakle, a deep-throated bell tolled from a tall bell tower in Tabernakle Square. "Methinks Lord Arundel has been spotted approaching."

Going Snake hurried back to the refugee camp on the bench above Salmalhuer. By the time he arrived, Arundel had just dismounted, and Going Snake hurried to his side. A quick survey of the horsemen told him that Talking Stick and Crying Dog were not among them, and his heart sank.

As soon as Arundel spotted him, Going Snake hurried forward. "We encountered the legions ten miles from Goat's Leap and slew them in the mountain meadows. The mere fact that we encountered them so quickly testified that they were hot on your trail. Since there was no sign of your Dog Soldiers, we backtracked to the Vardropi encampment where we found thirteen of your warriors still alive on the pillories."

"Was Talking Stick and Crying Dog among them?"

"No, the only brave I recognized was Talking Stick's son, Swan Tear. I am sorry to say we found Talking Stick disemboweled with his hands drawn tight into fists. When we pried his fingers open they were full of eagle down."

"Where are the thirteen warriors that survived? I see none among your host."

"They have remained with a fyrd to assist them in proper burial and to erect a monument to the brave men who held their ground rather than yield. Those who survived said that Talking Stick kept the torture extended by challenging the Vardropi to cause more pain than they were. He mocked them from the pillory so that he could buy you more time to get over Goat's Leap. The remaining warriors will rejoin us before we embark for the Taxus in two days time."

Going Snake swallowed his tears of grief. "His name will be sung at our campfires."

"The skalds shall record their names and deeds in the Book of Heroes."

# CHAPTER 22 :

## IN THE HIGH DESERT AT SYR-RUS-SALEM

T HE EARLY MORNING STORM HAD washed the dust from the air, and left the High Desert around Fort Rock sweet with the mingled scents of Juniper and Artemisia. Yeoman farmers were tilling the freshly irrigated fields, and merchants were opening their shops along the streets of the city of Syr-Rus-Salem. During the past sixteen years refugees from Citriodora, Frisco and the Mexus as well as Hickoryans fleeing west had sought the safety of the fort, indeed, so many that a new city had been formed.

Together the King and Queen of the High Desert, Starkwulf and Va-Eyra, had made the High Desert an altogether prosperous land, insomuch that there were no poor to be found among its citizens, as every man and woman had their craft and labor.

The brilliant sun of the After-Light moonth was climbing over the towering rock walls of Fort Rock when Starkwulf sweet-talked Va-Eyra into a stroll in the private garden she so loved.

It was here among her beloved roses and wisteria that he had confessed his love for her. And here where they had married sixteen winters ago. Though her hair was now more silver than auburn, and laugh wrinkles edged the corners of her green eyes, she was still as beautiful as the day he had first met her twenty-seven winters past.

He had thanked the gods every day since that she returned his love.

"Shall we sit, my love?" he asked when they approached her favorite arbor.

She glanced up at him with a twinkle in her eye and smiled. "Need you ask?"

"My dear, I would never presume to take anything for granted when it comes to m'lady's wishes."

"Dear heart, you are as full of hot air as one of those cerulean balloons we saw when we visited the Ness." She settled onto the wooden seat and adjusted her skirts. He sat next to her, leaned close and kissed her.

"By the gods, Va-Eyra, even though I enjoyed spending time with Hartmut and Meny and their family in Salem, it feels damned good to be home again."

Va-Eyra nodded. "I agree. Although it was fun helping Meny set up her new home. "I'm glad Hartmut tore down the old place where he and his first wife lived and built her a new house of her own. I don't think she stopped smiling the entire time we were there."

Starkwulf understood Hartmut's actions all too well. He, too, had suffered the loss of not one, but three wives and his children, slaughtered by the Pitter attack on Zamora. His happy years with Va-Eyra had helped him heal, but he would never forget the family of his youth. "In another year the quailor will be able to supply our armies with most of their provisions, and the citizens of Fort Rock will soon be enjoying their agricultural genius."

Va-Eyra chuckled. "Can you believe how much Shug Knight has changed? I remember Surrey describing him as half con-man, half disreputable pirate. Now he's a prosperous country squire and well-respected leader. Thanks to him, the Columba Rogues are keeping order so that all other rogue tribes now obey Syr Folk law.

"Eyra-Elf all but worships the man. Allowing Shug to foster him was a good decision. Under his tutelage, our son has shown his proficiency as a warrior in mopping up the remaining Pitter Hell-Rats. I couldn't be prouder."

"Nor I," Starkwulf replied, putting his arm around her slender shoulders and giving her a gentle hug. "But I give you the lion's share of the credit. He has much of your spirit and dedication."

"And your grit and stamina." She snuggled closer, and he kissed the top of her head. "I'm certain he will equal Syr Elf's prowess in battle."

"But I can honestly say, for a man of his tender years, I did not expect this much. He's made the high desert so safe that the Klamath and the Sharaka have taken back their inheritances, and I honestly believe we are in for a long stretch of peace here."

Va-Eyra raised her fingers in the sign of the dove, "Sssh! You mustn't tempt the Dark Elves!" She looked in his eyes, "I'm just happy I have my man with me, the days of the Wose but a memory, and the fear of your dying in impossible missions behind us forever. Frankly, I will be ready to retire to a contemplative life when Syr Elf returns from the war and finally assumes the mantle of king."

He drew her near and kissed her, reveled in the warmth of her clinging body, and the sweet smell of her luxuriant silver and auburn hair. Their lips met once again when he heard someone clearing their throat very loudly. Opening his eyes, Starkwulf saw Eyra-Elf, standing a few feet away, a leather dispatch tube in his hand.

He was proud of the dashing figure his son cut. The Young Blood of nearly sixteen winters had inherited his mother's thick auburn hair as well as her flamboyant nature. However, he had inherited his powerful physique from his father. "The spitting image," Surrey had claimed, pleasing him to no end.

"Don't you two ever tire of dallying and kissing?" Ey teased. "Shouldn't the honeymoon be over by now?"

Starkwulf pretended to glower. "All I know is that a rude young man is intruding upon our alone time. Someday, you will understand."

"Oh, I understand, alright, though I hate to admit it before my parents, for I shall be taking Swan Bee, the daughter of Sur Sceaf and Taneshewa's hearth to wife soon. Her mother has given her blessing and now Bee and I only await the approval of her brother, Alfheah, since her father and Arundel are off to war."

Va-Eyra clutched his arm. "That is marvelous news, Ey!" she exclaimed excitedly. "Your cousin is a real jewel, the very best of blood." She shifted her gaze in his direction. "Don't you think so, Starkwulf?'

"Without question, the best of stock. It won't be the first time our blood has overlapped with that bloodline. And, of course, I'm doubly pleased, since Sur Sceaf is a dear friend and brother of arms to me, a man of the gods, without question, royal of the seed to the core."

"We're shooting for getting married on the Ghost Moon here at Fort Rock," their son said with a smile that immediately disappeared. "Forgive me, I almost forgot why I'm here. A silver harrier just arrived with this dispatch from the high king himself. It's addressed to both of you." He stepped forward to hand the dispatch case to his father.

"Mind if I stay to hear its contents? Might be he's sending his personal approval of my proposal to Swan Bee."

"Go ahead. Stick around," Starkwulf sighed, pleased that his young son showed so much promise and proud of his good looks and intelligence. "But I can see it's a war dispatch by the seal. Not likely to have anything personal in it."

Starkwulf removed his arm from his wife's shoulder and opened the cap to retrieve the rolled vellum. He quickly scanned Sur Sceaf's neat penmanship, then seeing nothing that would not be for Ey's ears before commencing to read it aloud.

My dear friend Starkwulf and my beloved Sister Va-Eyra.

May the gods ever bless and watch over you. I write to tell you of our many victories which I have listed on the second skin of this vellum. While in the Mexus Lands, we encountered a vast army of inhabitants from the far south who are called the Moxo. The gods smiled on us when their leader, Ehira, agreed to ally his army to the Syr Folk cause. It was with his help that we defeated the Pitter legions of Commissar Grindlseath.

Even so, Starkwulf, I am in urgent need of your services. The victories we have obtained have not been that costly, in part because of the assistance of the Moxo. But these are but minor skirmishes compared to what lies ahead. The major forces of Pitterdom still lie eastward of the Mys-Isis River, with many Zongas, Bamboo Plantations and Dominiker allies. The battle for the Omala is the beginning of the real war, and it is imperative that we meet the target dates established by the Roufytrof if we are to defeat the Pitters before the Bamboo Bloom arrives.

Now our spies tell us the Emperor Hryre Seath has decreed the west is forfeit, and that all legions are to return to the core of their empire at Hormah at once and to avoid any costly engagement with the Syr Folk while carrying out this order.

I have been prompted by the ur fyr to ask you to join with me to secure the Omala and, thence, march with me into the core of Pitterdom. I realize this request is beyond any reasonable call to duty, and you need not fear any obligation unless the ur fyr prompts you likewise. If the ur fyr prompts you to continue your duties to your people, please ignore this plea, for I understand loyalty to those you rule.

But should the ur fyr prompt you to once again take up the sword of righteousness against the dark elves, you can join the caravan of wives at Denio at the end of the Steens. In anticipation of your reply, I have requested Paloma to wait there for a silver harrier, who will report your time of arrival or your decision to remain at Fort Rock.

With all respect and love, Surrey

"Absolutely not!" Va exclaimed heatedly. She snatched the vellum from his hands and hurled it through the air. "I won't hear of it. You have rendered service to the folk well in advance of your vows, and I forbid my man from leaving me ever again. I would die for love within a week."

Her eyes were determined as flint and her fists were drawn tight, ready for a fight. Ey was thunderstruck, his mouth open in shock.

"So, dear wife, I am to believe your objection is a wish to avoid further separation. Is that correct?"

Her nostrils flared and her face grew as red as her favorite rose. "You're damned right. I will never stay awake another night worrying about my husband's whereabouts, nor will I ever tend an empty bed again. My life already had its share of loneliness, and I've already laid one very good man in the grave. I could not bear to do that again. Can't and won't."

Starkwulf smiled at her. "You are as feisty as your beloved Jaguarundi Cats, you are. It's a damned pretty sight if I must say. Don't you think, Eyra-Elf?"

"Fa, I think you're digging your grave deeper. I wouldn't provoke her, if I was you."

"Va-Eyra," Starkwulf said. "What say you we both go together? We were an unbeatable fighting force here in the high desert. In the name of our ancestors, let us finish the capstone of this generation and be part of the history of our people forever that our children may glory in our name."

"I'll have to give that some thought," she said cautiously with a pensive frown on her face, "but who would rule the high desert kingdom? Syr Elf is off to war."

Starkwulf turned his head toward the Young Blood and Va-Eyra turned to him as well then said, "Why Eyra-Elf, of course!"

Their son appeared horrified. "But, Fa, I'm only fifteen and am about to marry."

"Let me sight your mind that when I was fifteen, I already had two wives and ran the largest sheep ranch and horse stud in Zamora. You have shown great leadership and have already been selected as the commander of your Young Blood Twelver. You will have the counsel of the High Mayor of Salem, Hartmut, and the support of Shug should you require consultation or aid."

Ey looked a bit overwhelmed, but also deservedly proud. "I am humbled by your confidence, and I swan swear I shall pattern my reign after Elrus of Olden Times."

Va-Eyra cracked a smile. "So mote it be."

# CHAPTER 23 :

## 'REMEMBER THE OMALA'

**J**ESSE BEN DAVID'S LOG: I *Write this entry as the sun breaks over the eastern Taxus skyline like a fiery disk in a grey-cast sky. Arundel and Sun Cryer waited for the fyrds, Dog Soldiers, and armies to assemble before marching to Kerr by the river where they were to rendezvous with Brekka and Kanarus. They had a joyous reunion, recounting their triumph over the poisoned lands and their having secured it as a Syr Folk asset.*

*Kanarus delivered a letter from the High King, Sur Sceaf, stating that he was engaged in a campaign to rid the Mexus of the Pitters, and that he had encountered a mighty army of fiercesome warriors from the far South wood, a people known as the Moxo. Sur Sceaf also ordered Kanarus to separate the captured Moxo Maidens, eight hundred in number, from the others and bring them to the Taxus. He reported that they are a hardy group of maidens and are eager to be reunited with their people.*

*Kanarus also sang the praises of Brekka and her forces in the execution of her mission to destroy the evil queen of the Underground. Ceolwulf has given over to me his record of the taking of the poisoned lands and would now be my full time assistant, but he will accompany the Lady Brekka into the Taxus Hilly Country to record her deeds at Banderas and Leakey.*

*Once Lord Arundel was satisfied that both Kanarus and Brekka were fully prepared for their assigned tasks of taking the fortress at Banderas* and the fortress at Leakey, he shouted out, "Yeoh! Wah! Remember the Omala!" and ordered them to rejoin him at San Arundel, otherwise known as the ancestral City of Omala from which the Lord Arundel II had ruled over his peaceable kingdom for three generations in the days when the Herewardi walked wholly in the path of the elves and were of one heart and one mind. Now, we march from Kerr onward to recover the Omala, which is a shadow of its former splendor.

A partial list of those under the command of Lord Arundel include one hundred forty four Syr Folk fyrds, seven thousand braves from the buffalo nations, twelve thousand dog soldiers, four thousand Hickoryan cavalry, two thousand Chartreusean cavalry, five thousand Cerulean cavalry, and ten thousand Prester cavalry as well as smaller forces from various allied groups.

Following a safe distance to the rear are three thousand Quailor and Hutter hospitalers and countless wagonloads of medical supplies pulled by teams of sorrel mules bred for stamina and steadiness on the battlefield.

Since the Taxus is known for an abundance of cattle, sheep, goats, and a variety of wild herds, Arundel has formed a special fyrd composed of skilled hunters who will provide fresh meat to supplement the battlefield rations.

*Jesse ben David's Log:* On the third day of the trek we came upon the Omala. The Lady Brekka is to begin the campaign to regain the Taxus by leading the attack on the Pitter Zonga at Banderas in preparation for the siege of Fort Leakey, the Pitter's most powerful stronghold in this region, containing upwards of ten thousand trained Pitter and Dominiker troops. Once the Arundelean monastery of the Godhi, Leakey is considered a jewel of the Herewardi cultural history, and if re-captured will represent a great spiritual triumph for the Herewardi.

In addition to her famous Twelver of Lady Knights, Brekka is to have under her command her Brother Il-Alim's Bush Master Fyrd,

*Custus Ruhm Lee's Cavalry of Grey Ghosts, Sun Cryer of the Cheyenne, his son, White Crow and their dog soldiers, Going Snake and his dog soldiers, the Spanix fyrds, the Thunder Twins with their fyrds, and her White Buffalo, Ma-Za-Ma.*

*Arundel's plans to retake the Omala are contingent upon Brekka's speedy success. Arundel confided to me that he has assigned her this vital mission after conferring with her and consulting the seer stones given to her by their father, Sur Sceaf.*

The stone and adobe Fortress of Banderas had been erected on a huge mesa of granite that towered over the flat plains surrounding it; once a vivid red in color, the adobe walls had been scoured by eons of wind and sun to a pale pink hue that contrasted starkly with the thick abundance of grey-green chaparral and sagebrush.

Brekka sat atop Cycnus on a knoll just beyond an arrow's flight, studying the fortifications with Ruhm, Il-Alim, Sun Cryer, and White Crow. Many thoughts and strategies went through her mind as she considered the best plan of attack.

Alim was the first to speak. "Our Herewardi ancestors knew how to build the perfect fortress. According to my tutors at the academy, the walls are three feet thick, and the two gates are nearly that thick with timbers of hickory brought all the way from the Forest of Arwood."

Ruhm stared at the khaki-clad legionnaires on the parapet. "They hold all the fortified high ground and they're locked down secure. I, for one, would prefer to wait for some siege machines before proceeding any further. Maybe we could employ a toulucan or two, and at least a couple of Arundel's Magonels. Otherwise, I don't know how it can be done."

"To be honest Ruhm, I don't know how I'm going to do it either, but we're going to do it. By the gods and all my elven ancestors, I am commanded to take Banderas and that is what I'll do."

Ruhm's lips slanted into a wry smile. "I would expect nothing less, my single-minded Lady Knight."

Brekka found herself laughing. The man really was a charmer. "Besides asking Ary for Toulacans and Magonels, which he doesn't have, what would you suggest I do?"

His pleased grin warmed her all over. "Thought you would never ask. First, I'd call for the fortress to surrender," he said. "If the commandant refuses, we should reconnoiter to find the points of easiest breach in those walls and use the exploding powder like we did at the citadel. Or, we could pile rocks and dirt up against the wall like a ramp and herd sheep into the fortress."

Alim laughed. "Imagine the Pitters' reaction to being attacked by a flock of devil sheep."

"Maybe we can find some dogs to send them, too," Ruhm added. "They can't dig their way out through tunnels, because the Herewardi built on granite foundation, and we've only spotted one gate. But, if the Pitters can resist our assaults and have adequate supplies of food and water, then we'll just have to wait them out."

Brekka nodded her approval of his assessment. "I like the first two steps you suggest, but I've never known a Zonga commander to surrender. It's against the Emperor's orders. So you're correct. Most likely we'll have to smash our way through, or build earth up against the walls. But what is sure, Ruhm, is that I'm going to take this zonga if it means I have to sprout wings and fly over them."

"Spoken like the fiest you are! However, I just don't want to take unnecessary losses of my men, when waiting for Arundel would be the prudent thing to do." Turning to Brekka's Brother, Il-Alim, Ruhm said, "Even when we used to hunt together, she always had to be in at the kill. It's her damned nature." Ruhm threw his hands in the air. "Arggh! Wisdom was never your sister's best foot. She's too damned reckless for me, Il. I can't tell if she's a lunatic or a heroine. You know why?"

Il-Alim shrugged.

"Because I'm not sure there is a difference!"

Il-Alim rolled his eyes but remained silent. But Sun Cryer darted a stern look at Ruhm and said with a furrowed brow, "Hey now! Bite your tongue, Ruhm! Do you not know she is the Buffalo Woman? Know you not that the Thunder Beings ride with this woman? The towers of this world will fall before her like anthills before the buffalo herds. Leave her to find the will of the Thunder Beings, and then follow. "

"Father," White Crow said, "Ruhm cannot see with the eyes of a warrior, though he be a great one. He is only blinded by his love for Brekka and his frustration at not being able to protect her from harm's way. A pointless effort in war! For loss comes to us all."

Sun Cryer nodded his head, folded his arms and looked forward in a silent frown. Then after brooding for awhile said, "If you cut off the Pitters supplies and block them from their work farms, they will soon be desperate. There are too many legionnaires in there to properly feed and water. This fat bear can't last in those walls for more than another week, Buffalo Woman. I say we give them battle."

Brekka nodded. "I am grateful for your suggestions, all of you. I will take them all into consideration, but, ultimately, I must rely on the ur fyr." She glanced at the troops stationed strategically around the fortress. "Now, for the time being, have these troops maintain their positions around the fort. Il-Alim, have your men make a mud bath for me here on this mound, and then have them build a privacy screen and bring me a tub of water and soap for bathing."

Ruhm shook his head. "I've been around you Herewardi long enough to know there must be a reason for this…unusual order, but I'm damned if I can figure this out."

Il-Alim answered for her. "It is a ritual that warriors often perform before battle. Similar to your Hickoryan baptismal ceremony. Brekka is going to draw strength from Mother Earth before the battle starts. It is a ritual to invoke the elements in our favor."

"I see. And are we all to do the same, my lady? And if so, do we strip naked?" He gave her a leering grin. "I volunteer to wash your back."

Brekka wanted to be angry with him for mocking a sacred ritual, but she knew him well enough now to realize he meant no disrespect.

"Not a chance, Buster!"

Her brother laughed. "Careful, Ruhm, or she just might wash out your mouth with some of that mud."

Ruhm raised both hands in surrender. "The offer's always open, my lady."

She ignored the frisson of excitement his words evoked and let out a sigh. "Now if you'll forgive me. I shall make ready for battle." She shot a piercing glance at Ruhm. "Know you not, Ruhm, the Goddess of Nature has shaped me. She is the one who made me the she-wolf I am. If you had your way, you would defy her, and make me into a poodle or some worthless lap dog, but I am of another race. I am of a warrior race."

While Brekka returned to her tent to pray, Il-Alim had a contingent of his men dig a pit and fill it with crumbled Taxus earth and water before stirring it into a sluice of mud. At the same time, others constructed a privacy barrier of piled chaparral and sage. Next they carried two collapsible leather tubs to the enclosure and filled them with bucketsful of sun-warmed water from the stream that ran alongside her camp.

Once all was in readiness, Brekka entered the enclosure followed by her handmaidens who helped her remove her armor and weapons before she stripped down to her one piece underwear that bore sacred runic marks sewed on by the able hands of Redith the Seeress. Gingerly, she slid belly first into the mud soup and squirmed and rubbed the mud through her hair and over her face and body. Finally, she was fully covered in the wet grey earth so that only her eyes were free of the mud, signifying she had taken on the strength and protection of Father and Mother Ea-Urth.

Careful not to slip, she got to her feet and stepped from the sluice pit. After shedding the muddy underwear, she stepped into the first foaming tub. Ynys held fresh clothes and Wyth attended her with towels. Outside the blind, the Lady Knights sang and prayed as they bore the cleansing waters. "Oh join us in this battle Ea and Urth. Cover us with thy protection. Make us one with thy purposes."

The Twelve Lady Knights carried leather bucket after leather bucket of slushing water in to Brekka as she rinsed the mud from her body and hair. Emerging from the now muddy bath, she dried herself, and then stepped into the second bath. Sinking down until only her head remained above the water, she contemplated the task that lay ahead.

For twenty years she had worked diligently to master the skills and persona of a Herewardi Warrior. The path that lay before her was fraught with dangers, some she had trained for, others unknown and unknowable. Anticipating the road ahead left her both terrified and exhilarated.

This time she bathed with soap and washed her hair, rinsed thoroughly with fresh buckets of water brought into the enclosure by her Lady Knights. Wilona then led her Sister Knights in a prayer of consecration. Raising her arms to the swan square, she said, "We consecrate, dedicate and set apart this Lady Knight as the Sword of Righteousness in the Hand of Odhin."

The others answered, "So mote it be!"

Brekka turned to Freyxus. "Please summon Xarela to my tent. I will meet with him shortly."

Wilona then raised her out of the tub with the strong grip of Howrus, and she towel dried herself and her hair in the hot Taxus Sun. After Brekka's hair was thoroughly dried, Wilona, Ynys, and Wyth assisted her in donning fresh under garments and a white Gambeson while Pata and Cisne braided her hair. Next, she donned the distinctive silver chainmail of the Lady Knights.

Wilona tightened Brekka's codpiece and Ynys put Brekka's belt on her with a buckle that bore a Magnolia with a molded large golden honeybee in its center and under her belt hung five plates with engraved beehives symbolizing the fifth sabbath, which rested against the cream-white loin cloth that hung to her knees. These plates were invested with magic under the forging hand of Govannon who designed them to protect her feminine parts. Over her shoulders were secured three-tiered shoulder guards with the mark of Hrus ornately embossed on each one. Then Wilona solemnly fastened her vambraces on her forearms, and greaves on her shins, each with embossed Herewardi Knots that so aptly concealed her scramasaxs. Brekka had Wyth hide scramasaxs on and about her body, a trick she had learned from the Apache, Chiggibbah, and one she always took pains to follow.

Next, Ynys ritualistically held up the Pertha Torc and placed the twisted gold band on her neck, and Wyth carefully put the head codpiece in her helmet, stuffing the copper ringlets of her hair and braids up under the cod piece for cushioning from blows to the head. Wilona smiled warmly and placed Brekka's iridium helm on her head. Once firmly seated, it served to enhance her powers of thought, for it, too, had been fashioned by the Alchemist, Govannon, especially for her.

Intricate in design between her eyes the helm bore the Golden Eye of Howrus, from which sprang silver swan wings upon a golden band of Hawthorn blossoms that curved over each of her eyebrows. Atop the helm rode a spherical diamond with shimmering facets on an iridium bee cell called the Shem. Finally, Ynys fastened a pure white cape over her shoulders, securing it with a double raven's broach.

"You are ready for battle, my lady," Ynys declared. "May the gods protect you?"

Ruhm was the first person she saw when she exited the blind. His mouth dropped open, and those steely eyes glowed like the Taxus sky. The woman in Brekka delighted in his admiration.

In his honeyed Firginia accent, he drawled, "My lady, you shine as brilliant as the rising sun."

Sun Cryer shot a look of impatience in Ruhm's direction. "I told you, Proud One, she is the Buffalo Woman, the brightest star of the Thunder Beings."

Xerala listened to Brekka's plan without interrupting, then made a few valuable suggestions. Once the plan was fully understood by both, the two of them exited the Pfalz Tent to find Going Snake waiting. He was accompanied by Walks-As-He-Talks, and as if by cue, the two brought Ma-Za-Ma the White Buffalo, with its plated-silver armor up to her. Ma-Za-Ma was compliant to their lead, but it was apparent that he had but one master, and that was Brekka. The bull expressed his pleasure at being near Brekka with a loud snort that sent Going Snake and Walks-As-He-Talks into a laugh.

Going Snake threw back his long black hair and declared, "He sure knows his master."

She scratched behind his wooly ear and mounted. "Yeoh! Xarela, it is time to set our plan in motion."

The dashing Spanix officer bowed his neck and signaled for his fyrd to mount. Brekka had carefully chosen Xarela for the initial pretext for a battle, knowing that he would fully follow her instructions without question.

A dust devil danced through the chaparral below them and gradually twisted a path through the stretch of land between them and the enemy. Going Snake looked up at Brekka, his hand still on the halter of the great white bull, "I'll take that dust devil as a sign from the Thunder Beings that they are stirring up trouble."

"Well read," Brekka said, and then turning to her Spanix commander she said, "Xarela, while I parade Ma-Za-Ma before the enemy host, prepare the sacks of whale oil for the gates of the fort. We will create a distraction here while White Crow is positioning his troops to the south. Once the gate is burned down, I'll lead the charge in."

"My lady," Ruhm protested, "We don't know what awaits us inside those gates. Shouldn't we do a test run first, before you venture in?"

She got that smothering feeling in her chest once again. "Ruhm, your counsel is wise and logical, but I am led by the Ur Fyr. Even the plan I have devised does not seem the course I should take, but it is the direction the Ur Fyr leads me in, and that is not always down a clear path. I will follow the Ur Fyr over any plan devised by mortals. And the Ur Fyr bids me to press my attack. The plan to draw them out is only the best I can come up with at the moment. In this way we can test their strength and see what we're really up against in there."

"Ur Fyr? We're gonna gamble our lives and the lives of those who fight for us on your feelings? If a plan sounds bad, and your advisors all agree that it is bad, you should listen. Not only do we *feel* this is a bad idea, we all know it is a bad idea. Maybe your ur fyr is really hubris, and you are walking yourself into a fool's death. Have you thought of that? What if the ur fyr has given me knowledge and tells me that you are endangering yourself?"

Brekka glared at Ruhm. "You best watch your tongue Ruhm, or you will find yourself released from your position."

Ruhm  glared back at her, silent in thought, then warned, "At least be aware of that crow they have at the gate."

Brekka looked across the wide valley for a plow's length at the Crow, a machine with a heavy arm like a crane with a hook on a rope that is used to grab the armor of unsuspecting assailants and lift them off their horse. To her surprise, the crow did not appear to be in a position to hook anyone, so she proceeded with her plan to mount Ma-Za-Ma and parade him beyond arrow's reach before the gate; a distraction while Xarela's men fixed the leather sacks of oil to the gates.

Ruhm, being the strategist he was, was forced to bite off his words. He shook his head and walked away. Brekka gave Xarela a nod.

He turned to his lieutenants, "Joself, Rodriegelf, as soon as your men have all the oil sacks in position, rupture them, but beware the parapets, they could throw down hot oil, hot lime, or boulders, and for gods sake watch out for the crow. We'll shower them with arrows, but they could still get a shot or two in on you. So instruct your men to shield themselves at all times."

Two bands of Spanix warriors rode up to the gates of the Zonga while the remainder of the Spanix fyrd offered cover with their unrelenting shower of arrows. Brekka goaded Ma-Za-Ma on, feeling the might of his motion beneath her. She felt empowered by the strength of the beast and its powerful shoulders. She leaned down and tapped its wooly shoulder and it bellowed loud enough to turn every Pitter head on the wall. The distraction was but a moment, but it allowed six Spanix soldiers to puncture the bags of oil with their spears just in time to miss a load of rocks and lime dumped from the parapets. Brekka gave a silent prayer of gratitude, for the rocks struck where the six had moments before stood. She assumed the Pitters did not use hot oil for fear of its incendiary qualities, which meant they had already guessed her game.

Soon the Spanix wolf pack returned swiftly to their ranks. It was of small consequence that the Pitters guessed her intent to burn down their gate for now the oil was soaking the timbers. Visibly more Pitter bowman ran out along the walls like rats scurrying along a rail, this time waiting for the next attack. Meanwhile, Brekka continued to ride her white buffalo back and forth like a tiger in a cage while White Crow led his dog soldiers out wide to come back around to the south gate from which he was to launch a similar attack on their rear.

She signed from her mount for the war horns to be blown with two blasts, signifying all troops to prepare for the false siege. Anything to get the enemy disoriented, somehow draw them out, and make them vulnerable for attacks. Overhead an eagle screeched, and a large silver cloud came over the hosts of Brekka, making it considerably cooler. Sun Cryer smiled at her and marched out to join her, his dog soldiers and the lady knights following as they rode through the dusty chaparral towards the imposing fortress. Fox-On-Fire, Hoarse Flute, Lone Dog, and Chiggibbah waited with their warriors atop the hill facing the fort.

A warning trumpet blasted from Russell's fyrd and Brekka saw the gates opening. Cohorts of legions poured out the gates like some khaki ooze, led by mounted black clad priests. She swiftly signed to Russell's fyrd on her left to hold back. Then she signed to Ev-Rhett's fyrd on her right to do likewise, while her lady knights, the buffalo dog soldiers, and the Spanix fyrds marched head on to grapple with the legions. Going Snake rode up with Brimhilde bringing Brekka's white horse, Cycnus, in tow, and in full battle armor. Brekka swiftly dismounted from Ma-Za-Ma, who gave a blast of disappointment from his nostrils and she remounted Cycnus who wore a golden swan-winged helmet.

She signed for her archers to release a volley of arrows, forcing the Pitters to close ranks. Then she led a mounted charge, careful to fend off the Pitter pikemen. Her cavalry on well-armored horses plowed down the enemy like a scythe. Cycnus reared and brought his hooves smashing down on a line of Pitters as Brekka smashed skulls with the broad side of her axe and cut off their swinging sword arms in the fray. Occasionally, she employed her sword on Pitter soldiers brave enough to open their shields.

Although the initial attack hammered the Pitter cohorts into temporary defeat, the surge of fresh Pitter troops proved impossible to hold. The risk of being surrounded by them grew too great. She sounded for a trumpeted retreat, and at the same time signaled to Russell and Ev-Rhett's fyrds to engage so that she and her troops could safely dislodge from combat and take the high ground behind them for greater safety.

As she swung Cycnus back around atop the hill of their encampment she saw that the Pitters had sent out couriers in several directions. Presumably this was a plea for reinforcements, that at least let her know they felt threatened enough to call for aid from other Pitter zongas and forts. Now the Pitter cohorts were backing up into the safety of their fortress. She looked over at Ruhm who was straining at the bit to get into the battle and signed for him to attack the fleeing Pitters with his cavalry.

The yells and the screams now sounded even louder from a distance than they did in the close up alarm of conflict. It was like watching a battle between a wasp nest and a bee hive, so much did the rolling and fighting resemble the conflict of insects. Ruhm's fresh cavalry hit like a sharp blade at the scattered pursuing legionnaires, forcing their bugler to summon them back into an even tighter formation. Then another surge of Pitter Rat Packs emerged from the gate and once again began a forward advance. This time they came dangerously close up the hill towards Brekka's encampment, but the chaparral broke their tight cohorts, and soon Chiggibbah's archers decimated the Pitter ranks.

Brekka signed for her Spanix fyrds and Lady Knights to ride with her. She went forth slaying and to slay the Pitter legions as they came up the hill. Every seven minutes her forces rotated. With Russell and Ev-Rhett applying constant pressure from the sides, and Chiggibbah's bowmen from above, they were able to affect a great slaughter there on the breast of her hill after two hours of furious combat they reached a stalemate.

Brekka could not move the Pitters beyond the bottom of the hill because of their great numbers, and they could not advance their cause up the hill to her encampment due to her fierce fighters repeatedly rotating.

By day's end the Pitters bugled a retreat back into their Zonga to lick their wounds, and Ruhm's cavalry cleaned up the field of wounded Pitters by putting them to the sword and rescuing the Syr Folk wounded. Brekka had the wounded taken to the quailor hospitaler wagons where they were treated for wounds and Chiggibbah's men gathered the dead for proper burial.

Brekka had a flaming arrow shot up in the air as a call to the war council. All the leaders and her scribe assembled at her Red Command Tent and gave Ceowulf the counts of their dead and wounded. Sharp Rooster, a runner from White Crow's braves, showed up at the door. "Buffalo Woman, White Crow sends me to report we were sorely beaten back into a retreat and could not soak the south gate with the oil. We had to ride far off before we could find high ground and the Pitters stopped pursuing. White Crow asks, is it still your will that we put fire to the south gate?"

Brekka paused and walked back and forth for a moment, then turned to Sharp Rooster, while her commanders sat in anxious expectation around the council fire. "Sharp Rooster, sit in council with us. We are discussing our tactics for the morrow. Then I shall have an answer for you. Do you have a tally of your dead?"

"Yes, my lady, we have lost a tenth or fifty two dog soldiers. Our superiority as horsemen is the only thing that kept our losses low. White Crow did everything he could to carry out your command."

"White Crow has done very well. Did you get that number, Ceo?"

"Yes, my lady. I've received a full tally from all the commanders. Most have lost twice that number."

Brekka masked her expression to hide the sorrow she felt. "This has been too costly a battle. We must find a way to penetrate those gates or they'll cut us down like one cuts up a big log; Piece by piece."

"What do you propose, Buffalo Woman?" Chiggibbah asked.

"We have to get under their skin somehow? Have you any proposals?"

Sun Cryer said, "I thought Ruhm's idea of tearing a hole in the wall, particularly while a distraction is going on, was a good idea."

Russell said, "What sort of distraction?"

Ev-Rhett said, "I say we give those gates another dowsing with whale oil, and this time, make sure they burn."

Brekka said, "My thoughts precisely. We have to convince them we can beat them. Today they learned we can hold them, but they have not yet learned we can take them. Tomorrow we shall show them our steel by penetrating through that front gate."

"Hear! Hear!" the commanders all said.

"Sharp Rooster, return to White Crow and tell him to mount guard at the south gate at three hours before noon. If the Pitters attempt to escape, make it too costly. We want to pin them down inside the walls for the killing."

"It shall be done, my lady."

An alarm blast came from the trumpeter. "Ceowulf, attend the alarm and report the cause."

Ceowulf was gone while various commanders discussed different distractions and tactics. When he returned he said, "It was one of Chiggibbah's scouts, Rolling Horse. He said a Pitter legion is marching by torchlight from the west."

Brekka took a deep breath. "It is as I expected. They fear they are pinned down and have sent for reinforcements. Chiggibbah, take your Ndee guerillas, ride out, and nip the flanks of that legion. Perhaps you can defeat this legion before it even reaches here. They'll never suspect an attack in the night, and they certainly won't know your numbers or cunning."

"It shall be done, my lady. And I'll have the head of their legion on a pike before this gate by tomorrow." The tall Apache chief stood up and bowed his neck as he exited the command tent.

"Your advice is always wise, my commanders, yet there will be times when I appear to act contrary to wisdom and counsel. I ask you to be patient during such times and bear with me. Take comfort that I must plot my course according to the promptings of the Gods and Thunder Beings whose sight supersedes all else. With that in mind, I wish for Sun Cryer to be the Chief Commander if anything should happen to me. He is wise of years and has counted many successful battles in his day. Wilona shall lead my lady Knights."

The Commanders answered, "So mote it be."

Brekka noted that Ruhm never spoke a word. His silence was most uncustomary. She could see that if he stayed in her ranks there would be too great of a toll on their relationship. She knew the time had come to re-assign him to Arundel's ranks. She would sleep on it, and on the morrow make her final decision. She went over the plan with her commanders and they worked out how the siege would be executed on the morrow. She then excused everyone for a much needed sleep. Ruhm left in silence without so much as a good night.

As Ruhm entered his tent for rest, Loosestrife said, "Captain, I noticed you lost it out there today. I've never seen you treat Brekka like that before."

Seamisch turned in his sleeping bag and said, "That wasn't you Ruhm. I know you have too much respect for that lady. You acted insubordinate to her."

Ruhm's face flushed with shame. "And I feel damned terrible that I was insubordinate. I hope you two don't think I'm going Herewardi on you, but a while back I had a night vision. It was of Brekka burning and hanging from a tree as a mummy. It was the most powerful experience of my life. It felt so real, and today when I saw the oil being placed on that gate, I just feared her immanent destruction was at hand. In my mind insubordination was better than her death."

"Yep," Seamisch said, "you're becoming Herewardi. Don't tell me our captain is a dream interpreter now. Next thing we know, you'll be peeping into stones and foretelling future events."

"I'm serious, Seamisch."

"So am I. You've got to return to your Hickoryan roots and rely on your cunning, logic, and reasoning. The sleeping mind can make us dream most anything. Half the times it's just the workings of our emotions, and frankly, I've learned you can't trust emotions. You've seen what stupid things your men are capable of when they become love-sick puppies. Now your love for Brekka is clouding your good judgment."

Loosestrife added, "Yeah Captain, you need to stop obsessing about the welfare of this Herewardi woman. She's making you crazy. Perhaps if you got a little strange you wouldn't be so imbalanced."

"I don't think I could do that. Not that I don't want to. It's just that I want to be as pure as I am capable of for Brekka."

"Alright," Seamisch said, "we've heard this one before. You just keep chasing your ghost lover. I'm sure you'll be married next month. Or was it next year? Keep this up and you are going to be an old man bachelor. And by the time you choose a woman that will actually marry, you'll be gummer."

After a restful sleep, Brekka awoke to a bright morning and steamy heat. After waking her Twelver, Brekka and the knights donned their battle regalia and ate a hasty breakfast, after which she had Freyxus sound muster.

The guards who had the pre-dawn watch reported that all seemed quiet beyond the fortress walls. "The torches were refreshed as ordered, and burned bright during our watch, my lady. Pitters were spotted atop the walls, but initiated no hostile activity. We assume they were merely the night guard."

Eyes narrowed against the blazing sun, Brekka stared at the formidable walls. Splotches of dried black blood marred the serene pink adobe and the hard-packed ground below, testifying to the battle that had raged there less than twenty-four hours ago.

Once the troops were assembled, she held counsel with her commanders in the Pfalz Tent. The Taxus heat had already layered sweat beneath her armor, several of her commanders were equally uncomfortable.

"We continue today where we left off yestereve," she commenced briskly. "Sun Cryer and Ruhm, hold back on the hill along with Ev-Rhett and Russell. Fox-On-Fire, take your dog soldiers on a run down the east road to cut off any Pitters that might be coming to the fray from that direction. Going Snake, you and your dog soldiers surround the fortress, and at my signal, send forth the Herewardi Rain. Xarela, you and your Spanix Warriors will aid the Lady Knights and me in laying siege to the north gate."

Once she judged the others were in their battle positions, she signed to Going Snake to commence the arrow barrage, which was also the signal for Xarela to proceed as planned. He sent a mounted Spanix warrior forth with a torch and a sack of oil to light the oil-soaked gates, but the unlucky youth was shot down by a Pitter arrow before he was halfway to the gate. A second one tried running with a torch and met the same fate.

The crow swung its large wooden arm into position in front of the gate, ready to hook the next assailant. A clear distinct prompting of the ur-fyr came to Brekka as if it was the whispering of Woon, the All Father, *'Ride out. Be my offering this day, Daughter of King's Blood. Let them take the rattlesnake in their hand from whose venom they shall never recover.'*

Just as Xarela raised his hand for a third runner, Brekka signed halt, and rode out on Ma-Za-Ma. She took the torch from the next runner and rode directly up to the gate while at the same time keeping a careful eye on the lethal hook tracking her movements.

A heretofore hidden door in the middle of one of the gates sprung open. Too late did she sense any danger. A black clad Pitter with a whip appeared in the opening and with a snap of his braided lash, tore the torch from her hand. Another crack and the rawhide lash wrapped around her neck. Never had she known anyone to command a whip so skillfully. But this tall dark form was cunningly adept at it. She was set off balance by the jerk of the whip as her assailant tugged it tight about her neck and pulled her completely off her mount. Gasping for air, she struggled to free herself, only to be flung against the iron-hard timbers before being jerked unceremoniously upward. Desperate for air, she clawed at her neck to get free and to breathe once again while she kicked and struggled even as she was hauled through the small door. Her vision began to dim, and her chest burned.

Half-choking she struggled to free the coils from her neck, but it had tightened even more and too quickly. Her vision now went blurry. Then darkness poured over her.

When she returned to consciousness, she was being dragged along a platform, down some wooden stairs to a large courtyard by khaki-clad, bald, ashen colored Pitter troopers with callous brutal hands, and no regards for her comfort.

Once conscious inside the Pitter Zonga, she could see the legions were armed to the hilt with pikes, spears, armor, shields, and broad swords. There were so many that they reminded her of a barrel of salted smelt. Most of the walls had buildings up against them to increase their thickness and utility. She quickly made a mental note of where the walls were thinnest. From the smells that accosted her nostrils, the latrines were overflowing and the air was filled with swarming flies.

Empty bottles of the Mexus drink called Tequi-lah were piled against several of the pillories. The hemp-weed smokes of the Pitters, what the Herewardi called rat turds, littered the ground. Among the Hickoryans these rolls were called ignorant weed, and were considered a bane to good health.

It was then she spotted three toulucans aimed directly at the north gate. Pitters were busily stuffing the metal mouths with cloth bags of shoot powder. She faulted herself for not anticipating their presence.

With twists and turns of her hands, she struggled to free herself from her bindings, but the Pitters were escorting her rapidly to a large pillory whipping post where the sinister tall black clad Pitter shouted, "Bind this serpent to the whipping post and we'll milk the venom out of her pretty white breasts."

She waited till they backed her against the post, then using the post as one point of a brace and thrusting out vigorously with both legs, kicked two of the bald, tattooed soldiers who were attempting to tie her. They tumbled into the dirt causing the other Pitters to laugh in derision. She felt momentary pride, only to see the tall, ugly bald Pitter in his black cowl approaching her like the crow of death. There was a tattoo of a broken cross between the most brutal and cruel eyes she had ever looked into. Briefly, she caught sight of his face as he stormed towards her with his yellow gritting teeth and prominent incisors. With little decorum he brought the butt of his broad sword smashing down on her forehead.

She awoke to blood running from her nose and foggy vision. An effort to move her hands to her face made her realize she had been firmly tied and bound to the post. The acrid stench of black smoke assaulted her, raising her consciousness. Somehow, her men had managed to set the gates aflame. For smoke was now coming through every available crack in the timbers.

No doubt Sun Cryer had taken command, bent on rescuing her, as well as carrying out her plan. She had to warn him not to come through those gates.

Once again the smell and stench of the courtyard made her want to retch. Taking deep breaths, she struggled at her bonds until the tall black figure moved closer to her once again.

"So the snake-witch awakens, does it?" His voice was harsh and tinged with mockery. Black-clad priests below the pillory guffawed.

"What say you, men of Angrar, shall we have this witch raped by our soldiers or scalp her muff for a trophy to hang on my pike?" The Pitter thrust up a large black pike from which hung his gruesome trophies of scalps and muffs. The response from his fellow-priests was mixed, with some shouting "rape" while others yelled "pike."

Ruhm's words of caution washed over her. If she had requested reinforcements from Ary and Kanarus, they could have starved these hellions out. The putrid latrines were evidence that disease would soon run through this place like a bloody grass fire.

But she'd sworn to the Roufytrof that she would lead by the ur fyr rather than the counsel of men and, in return, they had promised her that if she did hearken only unto the ur fyr, she would always have the favor of the gods. For some things cannot be discovered by any means other than the spirit of inspiration.

Still she found herself confronting a flood of regrets. Regrets that she had not married in that first flush of her youth when she and Ruhm were so young. And oh, the unbearable thought of not having had any children. Remembering the promptings of Woon, she cried out loud in prayer, "All Father Woon, save thy daughter from the tangle I've gotten myself into. Permit me, thy daughter, to fulfill the full measure of my creation."

The dark figure mocked her in his scratchy voice, "All Father Woon, save your little witch. Is she seeing faeries and elves?" Suddenly, she heard the bellow of Ma-Za-Ma from outside the wall and took satisfaction in the sudden fear that crossed the face of her hecklers.

*It is enough. They fear my witchy powers. Oh Father Woon, thou art mindful of me. The sign is well taken.*

In a thunderous crash the gates crumbled and collapsed in a pile of flames. Sparks swept through the gates like some mighty spirit had just entered and flame burst through the gate's timbers with a vengeance. A skinhead Pitter soldier ran up and said, "Commissar Skull Worm, the gate door has collapsed and the confederate forces are re-positioning."

The dark figure in his conical hat and robes, the Skull Worm himself, shouted, "Prepare the toulucans and hang this snake over the flames of the gates by a flaxen cord! That Sheep-Lord, Arundel, must be too

squeamish for a fight and had to send one of his wives to do his dirty
work. We'll hang the bitch and when she dies, I'll choose what parts I'll
eat first. Now, snap to it! It'll buy us more time for my surprise attack
from the rear." He turned with a sinister smile on his face.

Brekka swallowed hard at the thought of hanging and realized, *He
thinks I'm Ary's wife, Zscha. That may play in my favor.*

Two Pitter Priests cut her loose from the pole, then retied her hands and
cinched them so tightly with a flaxen cord that blood dripped from her wrists
as they forced her up the stairs. The cord was thin and smooth, but exceedingly
strong. The Citriodorans alone knew how to fashion such a fine rope. After
they double secured it around her hands with several knots, they hung her
over the wall by it, lowering her slowly until she hung just above the flames.
Heat waves rose as high as her face and her feet felt torturously aflame.

The Skull Worm shot her another sinister grin, then shouted out,
"Prepare the cavalry, and at my signal charge out the back gate. Keep
that witch hanging until I leave. Then drop her ass in the fire. When they
attempt to rush the gate, let fly the toulucan fire."

A legionnaire came running, leading a scruffy black horse. As the
Skull Worm mounted, he shouted, "Anybody hungry for roasted witch?"

The host of demonic soldiers roared, "Eat her! Eat her! Eat her!"

Brekka was able to swing and wiggle, twisting to look from the
gates at her people gathering in battle array. She caught a brief glimpse
of Sun Cryer struggling to restrain Ruhm from coming to her aid. Her
hands tied, she could not sign that toulucans were about to blast her
armies to Niflheim and back the moment they entered the Bastion's
gate. Nor could she sign that the Pitters were going to launch a surprise
cavalry charge from the rear of the Bastion. She only knew White Crow
would be there in the back. She trusted he would be able to outmaneuver
the Pitter horsemen.

Her thoughts were interrupted by the Skull Worm, who shouted,
"Tease them! Lower her slowly into the fire, but do not suffer her to
burn yet."

The flaxen cord she hung from began to screech as they lowered
her. She choked on the smoke as the flames seared her feet and lapped
at her face. The metal on her armor made her to feel like she was a piece
of bacon on a hot skillet. She struggled to wriggle free and to lift her
burning feet, but they continued to lower her into the tongues of flame.

Skull Worm shouted, "Pull her back up. They're taking the bait. You see how it's done. Just keep them distracted a little longer."

Over the crackle of the flames, she heard Sun Cryer call all the troops back to the hill. For a moment she was puzzled. It was as if Sun Cryer could read every move of the Skull Worm in advance.

Then she thought about how the Priests of Angrar actually did cannibalize their victims, and she struggled once again to get her bindings off, not wanting to be buried in their foul stomachs, but to little avail. She was angry that she did not suspect the whip that took her captive. Ruhm must have thought her foolish, charging in like she did.

Looking back over her shoulder, she saw the Skull Worm signal to his Pitter horsemen that it was time to ride out the back gate, and she tried to shout a warning to Sun Cryer, but the distance was simply too great.

"The sheep-eating bastards are withdrawing," the Skull Worm shouted triumphantly. "Roast that witch again. See if that'll bring 'em back."

Once more, she felt the flames reaching up for her. The very soles of her feet began burning inside her boots. The pain grew so intense that she could do naught but kick, squirm, and cry out, as if that might relieve the burning in her feet. She kicked her legs, then noticed a scramasax on her ankle. She felt it with the calf of her other leg. They had not bothered to search her, and probably mistook it for decoration with all her other armor. She managed a glance down to see if her feet were actually on fire. The gates were almost completely consumed when a sudden wind whipped up and caused the heat to move away from her burning feet. The Skull Worm yelled, "Raise the witch."

As she was being raised up to the level of the keystone in the gate, the pain was so intense in her wrists that her fingers went numb. She twisted to see where the Pitter Horsemen were and saw them riding off towards the back gates of the Zonga. Her mouth was dry and she thirsted like she had crossed a desert. As she twisted back around she could tell Sun Cryer was not yet aware of the surprise attack. She groaned over the losses this would inflict, possibly even the death of his own son, White Crow.

Two ravens flew to the beam from which she hung and grokked loudly. Her arms ached and felt dislocated as she hung there, unable to do much of anything but witness the losses. Breathing now was laborious. Looking up, she saw the ravens circling overhead, and she cried out, "Oh, All Father, hear the words of my mouth. Oh, All Father hear the words of my mouth. Please suffer me to take vengeance upon the killers of my people. Please free my hands to wield my scramasax."

The ravens descended like black knives out of the blue sky and alighted on her hands which caused the Pitters to roar with laughter, certain the ravens had come to feast on her, starting at her bloody wrists. In the distance, Chiggibbah returned from battle and held up his arms in a swan victory salute, giving her anguish of heart some relief that he had defeated another legion.

"Now is the great day of my power, when I shall wreak havoc on these confederates by burning this mistress of strife and battle like the rattlesnake she is!" Skull Worm shouted. "Let's end this plague on our empire once and for all." Turning on his black horse he shouted the command, "Let burn the witch!"

For the third time she was lowered into the fire, which no longer burned high, but was now mere simmering coals. Instead of taking flight, the ravens continued pecking away at her knots. Suddenly out of the brush emerged her twelver led by Wilona Saga-Jah-El-Ea and they were given cover by Chiggibah's excellent Apache bowmen. She now understood that Sun Cryer created his own diversion by withdrawing the troops so that the Twelver could get properly positioned for an attack.

As the priests lowered her further she began swinging in an effort to avoid the coals below. Wilona took careful aim with her bow and shot an arrow at the rope, but the rope refused to be sliced, attesting to its Citriodoran origins. The ravens continued to pick at the bindings on Brekka's hands until they loosened with a swift release, sending Brekka plunging into the edge of the hot coals. She sprung out of them faster than a rattlesnake could strike, suffering the scorching heat of the coals momentarily, but exhilarated at the freedom from her bonds.

She collected her senses and fled, limping to the arms of her Twelver who had rushed to her side. By the time the Pitter soldiers dashed out for her, she was running with Wilona for the safety of her Shield Maidens. Brekka held her scramasax in her numb hand, where upon, she turned, and together with her twelvers, hewed down the Pitter attackers like panthers disembowel pursuing dogs. They raced on toward Sun Cryer.

The Pitter Rats that followed were quickly dispatched by Chiggibah's bowmen, who left a black stack of Pitter dominos all the way back to the fortress.

As Brekka hobbled up the knoll on nerve-raw, burnt feet that pained her more than she could stand, she strove, in her mind, to shut out the pain. She approached Sun Cryer on his painted mount and he declared, "Brekka thrice burnt, I knew the Thunder Beings would not allow the Buffalo Woman to die before her time. You are a blessed war goddess."

Breathlessly, Brekka said, "I was not... so... convinced... a few moments ago." Her burnt feet now felt singed to the bone and burned even more intensely than when she was in the fire, making walking or standing unbearably difficult.

Sun Cryer said, "Chiggibah has returned with some curiously uniformed dominiker prisoners. He destroyed the Pitter legion that was coming up the south road, and if you were not in such pain, you'd see him planting the piked head of the Pitter commissar, Lincsterbe, even now before the eyes of the enemy host within."

"It's great news, Sun Cryer. My faith was sorely tried this day."

Ma-Za-Ma became too much for his handler, broke loose, and came directly to her. As she stroked his wooly head, dancing on first one foot and then the other, she said, "Ruhm, take your men to the rear. They're launching a charge on White Crow there."

Il-Alim said, "Shall I launch my fyrd through the front gates, now, my lady?"

"No. By the gods Tyr and Thor, everyone hold here. I have a new strategy. Death awaits anyone who enters the Pitter's front gate and that's what they are hoping we will do."

She signaled to pull all the troops away from the front gate and although it was a very hot day, a large silver cloud rested over their camp which provided cooling shade that was not afforded the Pitter Zonga. Brekka noted the two ravens that had picked her bindings free earlier. They circled over her, then flew into the silver cloud and disappeared.

***

Even though Ruhm was pleased that the lady knights had come to Brekka's rescue, he thought it should have been him. Though Seamisch had tried to reason with him, he had stalked off into the chaparral, needing to compose himself before facing Brekka again.

Breaking off a branch of sagebrush, he twisted it in his hand and struggled to calm himself. His emotions were like a beehive that had been upended. His fury at Sun Cryer for preventing him from going to Brekka's aid was equal to his terror at nearly losing the woman he worshipped and adored. *Damn that woman! Why does she continually reject the wing of my protection? Why does she stubbornly insist on risking her life repeatedly, placing me in the position of having to stand by helplessly with my hands tied?*

The vision he had kept coming to mind. It terrified him. The Herewardi considered it a gift, but he considered it a curse. He had never been schooled in revelatory powers, and didn't know whether visions were written in stone, or if they could be altered. Not knowing was a source of constant torment, and awakened him from his sleep in horror on several occasions.

*No*, he thought, *I can not allow her to martyr herself out of single-minded zeal for the cause of her people. Whether she approves or not, I am going to save her from her delusions of winning this battle single-handed.* Suddenly, he tossed the mangled twig to the ground and stalked off up the hill.

Brekka turned at his approach. Without pausing, he swept her off her feet and into his arms. She opened her mouth to speak, but he stopped her with a kiss. Shocked into silence, she glared at him.

"Save your rebuke, my lady. The torments of Hell cannot equal the torture you put my soul through this day. I would allow myself to be drawn and quartered before I would allow that again. I would defy the king himself if he tried to restrain me. I cannot and I will not lose you."

# CHAPTER 24 :

## THE TAKING OF THE OMALA

**D**URING THE REIGN OF ARUNDEL the Great, the City of Omala was a land of splendor that ran with milk and honey, dates and figs, and herds of cattle and sheep without number. It was written that Arundel the Great had maintained a stable of sixteen thousand of the finest horses to be found anywhere. It was in this stable that the famous Sire Horse, Woon Shadow, had been birthed. Many were the champion steeds that had carried his seed, including Sur Sceaf's own beloved White Fire, now enjoying the verdant pastures of Valhalla. Sur Sceaf now rode his get, White Thunder.

A man of great vision, Arundel the Great had sought out the finest builders and architects to create the most splendid city in all of Herewardom. From far and wide he recruited the most learned of Skalds, and it was said, the women of Omala equaled the elven race in beauty, grace, and intelligence. It had come down through the folk mouth that Arundel the Great had received what they termed The Opening; a state of total awareness. During his stewardship, the Herewardi citizens of the city spread the canopy of Herewardi peace, wisdom, philosophy, and law as far south as the Mexus Lands and as far north as the Buffalo Nations, so that no Pitter dared come to hurt or make afraid.

After this city enjoyed several generations of peace and prosperity, a Bamboo Bloom produced the fruit that stimulated the Pitters into a frenzied breeding cycle that caused their population to explode.

In normal years a Pitter female could birth no more than one or two children per year, but every forty to fifty years, when the bamboo bloomed, and they partook of the bamboo fruit, it was not uncommon for them to have seven or eight offspring a year. Since the average Pitter child reached sexual maturity at eight winters, every Bamboo Bloom resulted in an enormous population spurt.

The City of Omala that once entertained elves had now become the haunt of the Dark Priests and their Pitter minions. Long had the blood of the Herewardi saints cried out from the Omala's soil against the murderous Pitters. Now, after five generations, Arundel the Great's direct descendant and namesake sat mounted on a white steed and contemplated the righteous rule and reign of his Longfather.

It was a momentous moment in his life—and for the Herewardi-- and as was his custom on such occasions, he asked the blessing of the gods. *Oh Elf Father and Faery Mother, in prayer I come to you for victory over the alien Pitters who have inhabited and usurped the land of my longfathers for far too long. Restore us, I pray you, unto our former inheritance and let holy beings once again attend our councils and join with us in lifting the spirit of mankind to loftier heights.*

The City of Omala sat on the banks of the San Arundelf River in the Taxus Hilly Country. The original wall built by the most skilled Herewardi masons five generations earlier had been erected of solid limestone three feet thick. Within the walls stood a large rock bastion resembling a castle of olden times, with its finished ashlers shining bright in the morning sun. Set in a parkland setting of trees, shrubs, and palms, the Bastion towered over the large white limestone homes of the early Herewardi.

After taking the city, the Pitters added a second wall, consisting of a stone foundation on top of which sat an upper wall of brown mud bricks. Gates of thick timbers provided entrance from all four directions.

From the hill he had chosen as his vantage point, Arundel and Kanarus scanned the flat terrain surrounding the fortress and discussed the most advantageous positioning of the troops in the forests, so as to keep the Pitter scouts from ascertaining any accurate count.

The Pitters dwelt within the inner wall. The space between the inner and outer walls contained only a few thatched huts and served as a place to train their troops, process slaves, sort cattle and hogs, and for the local nations to come pay their taxes and tithes. Beyond the outer wall lived poor Mexus and Hickoryan laborers in small weather scoured wooden huts surrounding finer built yellow wooden homes that housed the Dominiker Overseers who managed the extensive gardens used to supply the city.

As soon as Arundel ordered the fyrds to take up the positions he had selected, Dominikers fled into the safety of the fortress, while the Mexus and Hickoryans took their goods and began moving away from the city and the pending conflict. As they moved past the fyrds, they saluted and shouted blessings on the fyrds. Several stopped to give the fyrds intelligence and descriptions of gates, dormitories, and positions of weaponry.

Ravens alighted on a nearby Pecan Tree while Arundel awaited the return of his two Hickoryan spies, Huwe Kroket and Wil Krosser. His was a formidable force, consisting of twenty six fyrds, the Hickoryan cavalry, the immense armies of General A.P. Rockwell, and the masses of Apache Nations that rode with him.

Always fiercely aggressive and impatient, Chief Chise rode up the hill, accompanied by his Twin Brother, Zoot. Both saluted Ary and Kanarus with their spears. "When do you think Krocket and Krosser will return, Lord Arundel?"

"They should have been back by now," Kanarus said. "Ary sent them over the wall early last night."

"Perhaps they were killed, Sikyatavo." Chise said to Kanarus as he paced back and forth in front of Lord Arundel. "I grow antsy in this dull idleness."

Ary said, "I don't think the Pitters would know Kroket and Krosser are ours. They blend too well with the local Hickoryans here. They're just being more thorough than usual. If they are scouting out the inner wall and the half-acre fortress, it will take them a while. I've just underestimated the timing."

Chise frowned. "I am surprised the enemy allowed us to take this high ground. It makes for a perfect command post, gives us a view of the activities within the wall and without, and now it will be harder than hell to roust us off this hill."

"I knew this hill from the history books. It will serve as our command post for some time. Our commanders will be able to strike undetected from the several wooded areas before the enemy knows it."

Zoot interjected, "My scouts report there are massive herds of longhorn cattle to the south. Are you thinking what I am thinking, Chise?"

"Alright, you two are worse than Ev'Rhett and Russell," Arundel said. "What are you conjuring up?"

Chise said, "If we can breach that outer gate, we could stampede the cattle through it and penetrate the first wall a lot easier."

Arundel stroked his forked beard. "That's brilliant. That would save lots of lives, disorient the enemy, and make for a smoother penetration for our troops. At least we wouldn't have to wait for the Magonels to get here."

He raised the signal for his young Green Beetle messengers, who rode quickly to his side. "Yes, my lord?" one asked.

"Hrolf, ride back to the base camp and tell Roger Gornall to bring half of his best drovers and report to me."

"I will shape it so, my lord."

"Heorot, you accompany Hrolf and fetch Siwel to me. Tell him to bring all the ergot he has and to report right away."

"I will shape it so, my lord."

As the two messenger boys dressed in green to distinguish them from the Silver Harriers, rode off toward the west, Kanarus, Zoot, and Chise continued to pace back and forth like caged wolves.

Suddenly Chise cried, "I see Kroket and Krosser heading up the hill! There, just on the edge of that forest of Madrona."

Turning to look, Arundel said, "Marvelous! Our army operates on good intelligence and nobody is better than those two wild men at getting it."

The two scouts ran up to Lord Arundel and saluted. The tallest of the two buckskin clad Hickoryans, Kroket, spoke first. "My lord, it is even as you thought. The outer wall is too long for them to properly defend, but the inner wall shall not easily be taken. We also searched out the fresh water well in the center of the interior bastion. It is precisely where you said it would be. From this large adobe pool alone they draw all of their water for their troops."

Krosser took off his felt hat and wiped his brow with a red bandana, "There are ten legions or about forty thousand Pitter soldiers and approximately four hundred priests camped in or about the fort. Some of the merchants said there have been many queer happenings of late, and one said he overheard a commissar say they must pack everything up for Elves Island and be out of here before next spring. Said that's why they've spent months gathering all the crops, herds, and tripling the taxing and tithing on the citizenry."

"I command three thousand seven hundred and forty four fyrd troops. Chise and Zoot each have five thousand, and Rockwell has his twelve thousand. That makes twenty-five thousand seven hundred and forty four if counting all the Buffalo Nations, Spanix Fyrds and those under Brekka's command, should we need them." Arundel then asked Krosser, "And the commissar in command, did you discover his name?"

"Yes, it is verily the devil himself, Sanangrar the Sinister."

On the hills before the fortress at Banderas, as the sun climbed in the east to its zenith overhead, Brekka called Going Snake over to her and drew lines in the dust showing three stations where he said the walls were likely the weakest. "How are your men doing with the battering rams on the mud bricks of these three places?

"They've been hammering away since before you were hung, according to your directives, my lady. I'll have it finished before you can say Robin Good Fellow. At least we'll have a breach big enough for three horses to pass through within two more day-marks on the sun wheel."

"Then shape it so," Brekka approved.

She reckoned now was the time for Going Snake to strike because, while the Skull Worm had attempted to create a distraction for them, he had also created a distraction for his own troops. So focused was he on the surprise charge of his Death Head Horsemen. But by the time Ruhm Lee routed the Death Heads and returned to Brekka's command, she had marshaled her Spanix fyrds for a total assault on three walls at once. She directed troops from her litter atop the hill while a quailor hospitaler dressed her feet in aloe vera and honey, and wrapped them in swaddling. She could no longer be part of the muscle in this battle, but she sure as hell wasn't about to withdraw her teeth from a prize like the Skull Worm. Besides, she now had a personal vendetta to fulfill.

Once the battering rams struck their final holes through the weak points of the walls big enough for three horses to go abreast, Xarela led his troops through the breach in the southern wall, drawing the Pitter forces to respond, while Russell led his troops through the breach in the west wall and Ev-Rhett charged headlong through the breach in the north wall. Brekka knew the Pitters were too tightly packed to maneuver well and her men were proving her right, for all the cohorts were too focused on Xarela's fyrd to re-gear for a fight from the east and the north at the same time.

Brekka sat impatiently on her litter and was stirred from her anxiety when she saw Itza-Chu of the Buffalo Nations riding hard towards her. She almost leaped to her feet to receive him. He reined in his horse and said, "My lady, the Skull Worm, upon seeing his predicament has fled through the south gate with his Death Heads and Priests, going in the direction of the Omala. Going Snake wants to know if you would have him pursue them?"

"How many did we slay before they fled?"

Itza-Chu said, "I would say, upwards of two thousand, though no count has been taken as yet."

"Tell him to stay his course and concentrate on purging the fortress." Those words fell hard from her lips. She wanted so badly to pursue the Skull Worm and roast his feet over an open fire, but knew she was not up to a battle with her burns tormenting her as they did. "All of our energies must be focused on laying siege to this zonga at Banderas. Nothing else matters. Let Lord Arundel deal with the Skull Worm as he sees fit."

White Crow rode up, his expression foretelling bad news and spoke almost trance like, "My best men, Fast Rattler and Rock Bear were killed. Horse-On-Fire is badly wounded as is White Man's Ghost."

Itzu-Chu said, "And we have many wounded and at least ten dead, my lady."

"It grieves me. We shall mourn their losses. You men stay with your wounded," Brekka commanded, "Verushka, get the Hospitalers on the wounded right away." Then turning to Freyxus , "Take count of our dead and wounded and report back immediately."

By the fourth Sun Mark Freyxus returned with the report of thirty dead and one hundred and thirteen wounded. As Freyxus read off the list of the dead she winced. Uddo, a fourteen year old runner, a Green

Beetle, had been killed, she shook her head and beat back tears. Uddo was the only son of a woman who had never married. He was a son of the Fifth Sabbath, an 'Ev-Rhettson,' as the Herewardi call them. Brekka raised her arms and ordered, "Give our dead the full honors of a burial. Bring the wounded to me and let the infirm remain here. Everyone else, clean up and prepare for a swift march by the seventh sun mark."

The hospitaler who was dressing her feet pleaded, "Please, my lady, you are in no condition to walk or even ride. You need to heal or you'll be in a fever by the seventh sun mark."

"That gives us three sun marks to work then," Brekka said, ignoring the kind hospitaler. She painfully walked over to her Ma-Za-Ma, mounted and led another attempted siege. She bested the now demoralized troops of the Pitters whose leaders, priests, and death heads had all fled, presumably to Omala.

By the sixth mark on the sun wheel the last Pitter was put to the sword, and Brekka rode on Ma-Za-Ma through the gates from which she had only that morning hung. Now victorious, she rode with her Lady Knights to the cheering of the Hickoryan, Spanix, Herewardi, and Buffalo Warriors. They shouted, "Hail Brekka! The Thrice Burnt Buffalo Woman." She brought her White Buffalo up a winding stairway to a halt in the center of the court of the Zonga where she had earlier been bound and suffered her brutal assault by the hands of the Skull Worm near the pillory. She summoned her stewards. "Bring me three large chests from the base camp, as quickly as possible."

Sam Wagoner, the hospitaler, came up to check on her again and she waved him away. The intoxication of victory overrode any pain she may have born and besides, her heart was already set on the next victory at Leakey. Sam walked away shaking his head.

"Three large chests, yes my lady, we will shape it so!" The young beetles rode off in the direction of the base camp.

Ruhm rode up to her on his sleek grey mount, Spitzer, dismounted, looked up at her, took Brekka's hand and kissed it. "Very well done, my lady, I cannot tell you how I fretted over your welfare. When I saw you hanging and those damned crows starting to eat you, it brought back a night vision I had of you. I would never be able to survive your death."

She felt both love and indignation pulling her heart in two directions at once. "Ruhm, those were ravens, not crows, and they were helping me, not eating me. They freed me from my bonds."

Ruhm looked surprised. "All the same, had Chief Chise not restrained me, I would have come to your aid." He paused, and then exclaimed, "How in god's name are you riding? You better get to bed, right now."

Brekka pulled her buffalo alongside Ruhm's horse and led him off to privacy in some chaparral. She realized she had done Ruhm a great disservice by not dismissing him the first time he showed any signs of insubordination, but love had blinded her, and it had fogged her reasoning the same as when one blows hot breath on a cold mirror. She couldn't allow for it any longer. He was definitely fogging her judgments. She took a deep breath and spoke in a strained whisper, "Can't you see Chief Chise should not have had to hold you back. And that is the problem here, Ruhm. You assume too much familiarity with me, as witnessed by your insubordination lately, and your inability to accept me as your superior in matters of warfare. I hold you guilty of contradicting my intentions this morning. I see I have no choice, but to have you removed from under my command and placed with Lord Arundel."

Ruhm's nostrils flared and his face went red with fury. She held up her finger to his face so as to indicate she would tolerate no protest. "Believe me, I know your worth, Ruhm, and I value you greatly as a commander. As a cavalry officer you are unexcelled, but our special relationship has no place in the roads that lie ahead of us. It would only be an impediment to the both of us. Go to Lord Arundel with my blessing and praise for a job well done. And as for us, we shall let the gods sort our relationship out later."

Ruhm gritted his teeth just to keep from speaking. His jaw muscles pulsated at his temple, and his nostrils were distended like an enraged stallion's. Even in his rage, he was a hell of a handsome man, and cut the finest features she had ever seen. But she could not ever before remember seeing his face have so much anger written all over it. Her heart grew soft for him out of pity, but she continued resolute in her decision, nevertheless.

She felt she had to give him some flag of hope. "Ruhm, soon, I sense we will be plunged deep into this conflict; not to drown us, but to purge us and make our mystical union stronger. But for now our paths must part. And I pray we may meet as friends when next our trails cross."

Ruhm stared in silence for a moment in what she took for disbelief, then without speaking, pivoted on Spitzer, and swiftly rode off.

White Crow and Sun Cryer exchanged looks as Brekka returned. They were unable to tell what Brekka had said, but Ruhm's swift ride let them know something unpleasant had gone down. Brekka dismounted from Ma-Za-Ma and handed his reins to Walks-As-He-Talks who had brought her Cycnus for a smoother ride. She limped over and mounted Cycnus. "Men and brethren, noble sons and daughters of the confederation, lady knights, lend me your attention. We are going to secure this Zonga as our fortress from here on, and I have a mind to take the Zonga of Leakey a very special gift. And it shall all be won fresh from this oven of our affliction."

Chise looked alarmed. With a furrowed brow he asked, "A gift, Buffalo Woman, why ever a gift?"

"Because, my lords and Ladies, I studied the ways of the Pitters under the Rune Singer and Lore Master, Wheelursun, and he has taught me those things that will most affect the sinister fiends we are now facing." Then turning about on her steed so as to make eye contact with as many of her troops as she could, said, "Who, who, who, I ask you, is the strongest man in all of our midst?"

Going Snake said, "Why none other than Sigurd of Zamora, the Horse Master."

She scanned the troops for the giant blond. "Bring Sigurd of Zamora before me."

There was a rumbling murmur in the crowd before Sigurd appeared before Brekka. She dismounted on sore feet, and faced off with Sigurd. He stood fully a head and shoulder length above any of her other men, with muscles piled on muscles. "Sigurd, divest yourself of all your weapons and armor."

"As you wish, my lady." He proceeded to unbuckle and unlatch his armor with the help of two compeers and walked up to Brekka, smiling in his loincloth and shirt only. He was the making of a god in physique and form, but also like some school boy expecting a joke was being played on him by his teacher.

"Stand before me."

The tall blond pulled out his hair claws, shook his head to release his mane of straw colored hair and then stood like a chiseled golden bull in human form, his sky blue eyes flashing both wonder and puzzlement.

"Sigurd, I want you to fight me."

Everyone murmured in confusion. Sigurd said, "I cannot fight you, my lady. You go on burnt feet. If I win, then all will mock me for fighting an injured woman. If I lose, then they will mock me for being beaten by an injured woman."

"Sigurd, I do not wish to play with your emotions, but only to show my people that the greatest of enemies may be brought down by the simplest of means. I need you to demonstrate this to my people and I will apologize in advance if I cause you any embarrassment. Will you suffer this embarrassment for your lady?"

"You know I will, for you, my lady."

"So then, I command you as your Heretoga to fight me with all the strength and cunning you possess. It is my command."

"Only as you so command, my lady."

Sigurd took a deep breath, smiled at the crowd. His muscles running down his chest and belly looked like sculpted marble and ever much as rock hard. His broad shoulders and deep back left little doubt of the power of a mule he possessed inside that mighty frame. Brekka had to chuckle as he proudly, and confidently posed for the audience like a strutting cock. Then he charged Brekka like a bull buffalo. She quickly side-stepped him like a matador. A laugh went up through the throng of warriors. Sigurd turned and this time held both arms wide to hook Brekka in either direction she would choose to sidestep him. He secured her in his powerful bear grip and said, "Now, my lady, do you concede I am the strongest?"

She smiled and said, "Sigurd, no one can doubt you are the strongest." Sigurd released her, she twisted and brought her hand swiftly up into his groin, up under his loin cloth, and into his man bulge. He fell to the earth in sheer nauseating agony as she clutched tightly his man sack. There was total silence for several seconds and then uproarious laughter rang out.

Brekka let him go, remounted her steed as Sigurd rolled on the ground recuperating. Brekka smiled and ordered loudly, "Someone get some fresh Govannon's Ale for our beloved friend and brother, Sigurd of Zamora, the strongest of men. He's hung bigger than most bulls I've tied. He's a good sport man. Give him a round of applause." A roar of appreciation went up.

Brekka said, "Forgive me Sigurd, I have not done this to trifle with your emotions, or to make you play the role of a fool, but you proved that you were the strongest man and I merely proved that all enemies have their vulnerable spots."

The Beetles came riding back in their acid green clothing from the base camp with the three chests and unfastened them from the mules. Then carried them before Brekka, saluted, and said, "It has been done as you ordered, my lady."

After Sigurd had regained composure, he came up to Brekka and said, "I had always heard you were cunningly deceitful in fighting, but I did not expect that one from a maiden."

"We maidens are full of surprises. Nor will the enemy expect what I am about to do to them. Ahead of us lies the legendary Pitter Zonga of Leakey, our once and future monastery, which like you, Sigurd, is at least ten times our strength. If we march right away, we can make it to them by midnight with a special gift that just may lay them in the dust before us. For as my brother, Lord Arundel has oft said, 'You can take the legions, like a rabbit, by their ears. You just have to find their ears'."

Sigurd who had finally regained composure enough to move about easily, held up the much prized ale one of the beetles poured for him, and declared with a big smile, "You want us to grab the Pitters by the balls. Is that it?"

White Crow said, "My, what big ears you have, Sigurd."

The crowd roared.

"In a manner of speaking, Sigurd, that's exactly what we will do. The Pitters do not think as we think, and it is a mistake to ever assume they do. They think we are freaks because we possess many wives. But we think they are freaks of nature because many of their priests practice celibacy, not to mention their rat and wolf seed codes. It is a known fact that the Pitter religion teaches that if a man loses his balls in this life, he will be born queer in the next life. Unlike the Vardropi who enjoy their same sex partners, it is something the Pitters greatly disdain. Now, to you and I, this is all utter foolishness. But to them it is as an unshakable truth. Therefore, I command you to strip down these Pitter Rats and cut off their man parts until these three large chests are full of balls and yards and by Hollar and Herman, we'll give them as a present to the Pitter Zonga at Leakey. And in the chests we'll present them with a note to tell them what to expect from us, and that the Skull Worm has fled from a mere woman. A Herewardi witch!"

Cheers went up from the throng. She finally yielded to the hospitaler to tend her burned feet that had begun to ooze a clear fluid. Her troops quickly set themselves to the task of emasculating the Pitter corpses with their scramasaxs. When all were finished and washed up, Brekka ordered the host of young Beetles to remain behind, haul the twelve hundred and some bodies of the Pitters outside of the walls and to burn them in bonfires.

After summoning Thunor-Tyrson, the commander of the Shasta fyrd, she ordered him to secure Banderas as a Syr Folk asset, and then to remain on site until redirected by Lord Arundel. After he departed, she summoned a Silver Harrier and delivered a verbal message which he was to take with all haste to Arundel, proclaiming their victory and reporting her coming march to Leakey. "My lady, with your permission, may I also relate to Lord Arundel and his camp the details of your combat with Sigurd of Zamora?"

She laughed. "If you wish."

The hospitaler said, "My lady, I do wish you would stay and heal. Even I, but a peaceful quailor, know a fresh army fights better than an exhausted one."

"I thank you for your care, Sam Wagoner, but we shall not likely fight tonight. The gift I bring the Pitters at Leakey will be better than a slow knife in killing them inside those walls, and we shan't have to lift a finger to do it. By the morrow, we'll have our strength back and I shall rage with Berserker ferocity should even one of them step outside those walls."

She signaled the trumpeters and sounded for the forced march to Leakey.

Ruhm rode away from Brekka in a rage. He had chosen not to say anything to her because he knew it wouldn't be pleasant.

*I loved her with all my heart. Laid my most private feelings on the table for her and everyone to see and what did she do? She ripped out my heart, tossed it on the ground and trampled it into the dust. All those years I patiently courted her, biding my time, respecting her dedication to some mystical calling, she'd been merely toying with me, and making a mockery of me in front of my friends and family. I was made a fool for love and she strung this ignorant Hick out like a fish on a line and then used me for bait.*

*And now she's deliberately humiliated me publically, calling me out in front of my men for insubordination; all because I was willing to give my life to protect her.*

Rage boiled inside his head and churned in his gut.

*No more!* he vowed silently. *Never again am I going to allow a woman that much power over me. From now on I will swive whomsoever I will and show loyalty to none. Apparently, the vision I had was nothing more than the play of my love-intoxicated brain just like Seamisch said. My friends tried to warn me that she was simply toying with me. Men are nothing more than mice under her claws. Fool that I was, even when I saw the affect of her powers on Going Snake and the paramours, I had failed to recognize that this was her usual manner of controlling men.*

*But no more. The scales have finally fallen from my eyes. I will no longer chase after a mirage. From now on, I am Ruhm the Swiver.*

That night in camp as Ruhm was stirring the hot coals of his fire, he realized that both Seamisch and Loosestrife had given him a wide berth all evening. It was as if they smelled his wounds, and no wonder; he was bleeding to death deep inside.

Sitting alone with only a flagon of ale for company, he once again reflected on the night vision that had caused him to become so alarmed whenever Brekka was exposed to danger. Now he wondered if the heathen gods had deliberately planted this in his mind to trip him up, perhaps to drive a wedge between the two of them in order to prevent the bloodline of their precious jewel from being polluted by the blood of a mere Virginia Hick.

Once, while riding alongside Wilona, he had broached his concerns about the Herewardi obsession with the purity of their bloodline. She had assured him that there would be no impediment to his being 'grafted in', and such was her sincerity that he believed her.

*But perhaps the Herewardi gods have a different opinion, and have deliberately hurled this stumbling block in my path.* Humiliation sparked inside his head as he realized he had come dangerously close to stepping across the abyss and becoming Herewardi, but no more. *From now on, I will take pride in my Hickoryan heritage and beliefs. From now on, I will entertain no romantic thoughts of Brekka. I shall see her as simply a co-commander of the Syr Folk forces. I will put her forever behind me, but I shall never heal of this wound.*

# CHAPTER 25 :
## POMER IDO-ANUM

**B**REKKA LISTENED AND LOOKED OUT her tent door. She stepped out in the open and stood gingerly upon her feet atop the knoll. In the breaking dawn light of the Taxus Foothills she looked directly across at the Leakey Zonga. She had awoken with an eerie feeling that something was very wrong, and as she looked the picture didn't look right. An irritating mocking bird hammered out its perseverated tweets and twits. The sheer pain of standing on her burnt feet made her more irritable than she was accustomed to and she would have strangled the bird if the opportunity had only presented itself.

She looked up at the fortress. The walls of Leakey were void of any guards or bowmen. She called for her runner and told the beetle-green clad youth, "Fetch Going Snake and Chiggibbah." Then she yelled over to the white tent with the red cyclone painted on it. "Xarela, line out your troops and report for duty. My tent."

She took one last look at the fortress, shook her head, then hobbled painfully back into her tent where she lowered herself down gently onto a stool to the wincing faces of Wyth and Ynys. "Sisters, would you help me dress for battle this morning?"

Shortly thereafter, Going Snake and Chiggibbah arrived together on foot. Brekka said, "Gentlemen, have the guards reported anything unusual?"

Chiggibbah looked at Going Snake and said, "Nothing!"

"Nothing, my lady," Going Snake repeated. "But upon awakening I noticed the noise within the fortress was far quieter than yesterday. No bugling, no shouting. Nothing." The tent walls began shaking as Xarela lined up his horsemen outside."

Brekka hobbled over to her armor, carrying her stool to sit upon and relieve the pain in her feet. She summoned Wyth and Ynys with a sign to help her dress. "Comrades, have you eaten?"

"Yes," Chiggibbah said, "we breakfasted together."

"Then I charge you to gather a group of cryptic stalkers and scout out what's happening at the Zonga while we dress. See what you can discern and report back. I'll join you with Xarela as soon as I am geared up and have had a good breakfast."

"We will make it so, my lady," Going Snake said. They both bowed at the neck and left the tent."

Brekka walked out the tent to review the troops. She winced as she stepped on a sharp pebble. She forced composure and saw that the troops were ready to ride. She returned back inside to eat breakfast with her Lady Knights and her hand maids. As she parted the tent door she could see a somber expression on Ynys' face. The other Lady Knights busied themselves cooking breads and eggs. But she could tell by their looks they had all been discussing something that they squelched the moment she walked back in. The air just had that feeling of hush after a conversation which she was not meant to be privy to. She saw that Ynys' face was twitching and said, "What is it Ynys? What have you got in your craw?"

Ynys flushed, twisted the rag she was holding and said, "Do you really think it wise to remove Custus Ruhm Lee from under your command, my lady?"

Brekka took a swig of kefir, swallowed, looked into the brown eyes of her green hand maid and said, "Ynys, I know how much you girls all fawn upon Ruhm, so I understand how you feel, but his type of insubordination can grow and become contagious when the odds go against us. And by Thor's Hammer, my disapproval then would be a lot more painful than what I did. It's better for now that Ruhm and I take different paths so that we do not grow to hate one another."

Ynys set her jaw and Brekka could tell by the way she walked off that the decision did not suit Ynys. Brekka wished she could have had Ruhm near, if for no other reason than to hear his gentle voice or witness his caring hands always attentive to her every need. But no more. That is the problem. I have to do this alone. She looked back at Ynys. Ynys busied herself by straightening the tent in a painful silence, which Brekka interpreted as her method of coping with the disagreement they had just had.

Wilona however was determined to see to it that the matter was laid to rest. "Ynys, once you are married you will understand that a man like Ruhm may value you above everything else in the world. But they cannot resist the urge to protect you, even when you're perfectly safe. That's one of the reasons I'm here fighting along side Brekka instead of being stuck in Kanarus' tent. Love him, I do, but I have come to fight and give godly advice as I was born to do."

Wyth folded clothes and said across the tent, "Ynys, the battle field is no place for a romance. It only stirs up your feelings to confusion. I can see Brekka is right in removing Ruhm from under her command. The lines were getting fuzzy and neither Brekka nor Ruhm knew how to draw them. As the lady knights all say, 'We fight now. We love later'."

The sounds of troops moving and Xarela shouting orders in espagnol filled the air. Freyxus flipped the bacon in the skillet, and the other lady knights sat at the table shooting glances at one another and drinking kefir or munching on biscuits. Brekka realized she and Ynys were the morning's entertainment. She could also see several of the other ladies were disappointed at her decision to release Rhum. Only Wilona had flashed any true encouragement in her expressions. Wilona got up, walked down the table and secured a fresh crock of kefir, then returned to her seat beside Brekka.

Ynys said, "I just hated to see him go. I love his presence. Just to hear his voice makes my heart flutter. I can't help it he's like sunshine to wet seed. He makes me sprout."

Brekka could see the matter was not going to go away. Wilona took a sip from her kefir, looked at Brekka, and said, "What's the plan for today, my lady?"

"I would prefer to initiate the siege, but the Lord Arundel has commanded I wait his arrival, and now it appears that may be as much as a week away. He's sending us a supply line, which means he wants me to hold here until he comes. If Ruhm talks to him, he'll probably send me back to the Omala with the Moxo girls, and I so want a piece of this action. This is the jewel of all the Pitter fortresses in the west.

Elven Lords once taught here. Many of the hymns of the Godhi were composed here, and heavenly elves are said to have been common visitors. It was the heart of Herewardom at one time, a monastery of elven learning, and I want it."

Wilona stared at her for a moment then said, "Well, then don't let anything stop you. Seek a pretext and together we'll root these bastard, rat turds out of Leakey. If Arundel has sent no direct orders then you are open to use your discretionary powers as any commander would be."

Brekka was seized by the thought of a victory. "Pretext, you say. No, I know I could justify a pretext, but in all honesty, Ary has always given me free rein and he is in charge of the War Road. It would feel too much like insubordination. All the same, we'll parade around the Zonga as we did yesterday. It keeps the Zonga on alert and plays havoc with their nerves inside. It makes them think we have some secret agenda or something. I have read, in the Bok of Leofric, of many battles won simply from properly applying suspense against the enemy. Besides the gift we gave them, the chests of genitalia, has made them very nervous. And these damned feet. I'd be scaling these walls if it weren't for them." She stood up, walked awkwardly over to Freyxus, put a hand on her shoulder and snatched up a piece of bacon, whiffed the smell and said, "Wilona, Freyxus, Verushka, and Brekka; we four could scale those walls and wreak utter havoc." Then she chomped down on the crispy bacon and smiled. "I'll wait til my feet heal and Ary either comes or sends the necessary reinforcements. But I'll be praying for a miracle all the time we wait."

Wilona looked at her with her amber eyes before saying, "The key word is wait, the hardest part of any war."

Wyth said, "My lady, Commander Xarela is at your door. Shall I grant him admittance?"

"Yes! Show him in."

As Xarela came through the tent door in full fyrd uniform with red surcoat, black pants newly pressed, and polished boots, he said, "Senora, what is the order of the day?"

"Why don't you sit here at breakfast with us, Bro-Son? We have to wait for Arundel's arrival before any attack, so eat, and talk until we can rouse ourselves for another parade about the fortress."

Darting his eyes towards the breakfast table, he said, "Oh, this is so much better than what we were eating in our tent. It would be a pleasure."

Brekka said, "Pass the Xar some of that omelet and one of those raisin muffins."

Ynys said, "Anything for our tall dark gentleman."

Xarela smiled then took the plate of omelet and commenced to devour it in delight. "Much better than refried beans with kefir."

After the hardy breakfast and a quick reading of the mail, the rider had just delivered, Brekka turned to Xarela and said, "It would seem Pyrsyrus is due to arrive in the Taxus Lands in three days. He's being directed to the Omala where Arundel is rebuilding and setting up our Command Base for the winter."

"But," Xarela said, "That means we're staying in Taxus when we could be marching east, freeing compounds, and laying the Pitters to the edge of our knives."

"Xar, your father is too wise for me to ever question his orders. He is after all, my Prophet, Priest, and King. Not to mention, my favorite brother. Just as we use suspense to arouse this Zonga to foolish ventures, so also, I believe, Ary wants the news of our victories to spread through the south lands before we enter them and in that way, stir the blood of those southern rebels. It will soften up the soil for our planting the ideas of confederation among them. Besides, just because Arundel is spending the autumn and part of the winter in Omala, doesn't mean the rest of us will."

Wilona admonished, "Ary is the anointed of Woon. We would all do well to always remember that."

"Well, with that in mind," Brekka said, "let us go out and call the men to order for the parade." She looked at Xarela just getting his first muffin. "Xar, you finish eating first. My soul is not content with this quiet idleness anymore than yours is. I'm going to stir up some trouble inside this hornet's nest."

As Brekka exited the tent she waved at Walks-As-He-Talks, who brought her Ma-Za-Ma. She mounted the white buffalo in her full regalia, and Wyth placed her diamond topped Shem upon her head. As she looked over the horns of the buffalo, Going Snake and Chiggibbah ran up with their cryptic scouts following, somewhat out of breath.

He held his hand up to Brekka and sucked for air, "My lady...the Pitter legions...are fled!"

"What? How could they have fled without us hearing them or seeing their torches?"

"We suspect it was through a tunnel we found that runs for four plow lengths out the south. After all, we arrived here in the dark and could not assess where to place our scouts that night. Now the only people left inside are the camp whores and slaves."

"Could you detect where they went?"

"Their tracks all lead southeast. They're presumably heading for Elves Island in the Taxus Bay. It seems you really hit them in their balls."

"Now I am at a quandary. I don't know whether to pursue or secure this Zonga. Did I grab the rabbit by his ears or did he run out the other side of his hole?"

Wilona said, "My lady, I believe you should do as you know Arundel would do. The Pitter are amassing their forces in the east. They do not want to fight us here and drain off their much needed and valuable fighting forces. Once word of their losses here hit the peoples of the east, it will arouse the resistance in their occupied lands to a frenzy, and they are going to need far more troops than ever before to continue to hold the non-pitters in subjugation. They will have the Rdokians and Hickoryan rebels to deal with, and untold Freedom Fighters will seize the opportunity to sabotage and rebel from one end of Panygyrus to the other. The Pitters will also want to protect their core. The Emperor Hryre Seath is no dummy. He knows this war has turned on him and he doesn't want to fight on two fronts. He'll dig in and wait for us to come to him."

Freyxus agreed, "That is as I see it."

"Very well then," Brekka said, "we shall stay and purge this Zonga. Send a messenger to Arundel immediately informing him of this strange turn about. But damit my blood is up for the hunt. I was so hoping to go in for the kill. Chiggibbah, take your dog soldiers and at least nip the heels of those fleeing Hell-Rats all the way to Elves Island."

Chiggibbah gave a big smile. "It shall be done, my lady."

Freyxus said, "That is the wise thing to do, my lady. Hold back your huntress blood for another day, secure this jewel as the asset it is, and let Chiggibbah herd the bastards into the corral at Elves Island. There, Arundel can slaughter them like cattle in a pen.

"Then let us leave a small force to secure this monastary. Let the Godhi run it and we shall depart for the Omala to meet with Ary and father as soon as my feet our healed."

"We shall make it so," Verushka said as the Lady Knights all sported a smile and saluted.

"That way we'll get to see Ruhm at the Omala," Wyth said with a big toothed smile.

It was a sunny autumnal day in the Omala and most of the Syr Folk seemed in a festive mood as Arundel passed them mounted on Sun Charger, a Silver Harrier had alerted him that his wives and children were less than two hours away. His heart skipped a beat with excitement. He dismounted and tied Sun Charger to a Chaste Tree. The warm gentle wind coming off the river teased the pampas grass plumes that glistened in the late morning sun light. As he walked down the cobble stone street of the inner bastion, he took a path along the river where the yellow Ginkgo leaves overlapped the Red Oak leaves, giving off the sweet smell of fermentation that he so relished in Ele-Anor-Ness. The scent stirred memories of autumnal dallying in the parks with Zschamillah. Looking up at the beams of sunlight which danced through the Magnolia branches above, he paused in a moment of serenity to listen to the Boat-Tailed Grackles fill the air with their rich deep songs.

Fyrd warriors and dog soldiers were dressed in their finest and most colorful clothing, barely even recognizing him in time for a salute. Not only were the people in a festive mood for the elven fair, but today, his first wife, the bee-mother was due to arrive. The Queen Zschamillah would be arriving with his other wives, their retinue, and a host of Herewardi, Ele-Anorean, Chartreusean, and Cerulean settlers. Additionally, the Pyringean Pirates under El Yid and Juan Carlos were traveling with them.

Regretfully, the High King Sur Sceaf and the Moxo Hosts had not yet arrived on schedule for this momentous occasion, the re-dedication and re-settlement of the Omala.

Ary examined the outdoor stage on the San Antonio River, renamed the San Arundelf River for his great ancestor who had fled from the

Firginias to set up a Herewardi realm here several generations before. He had often thought how, maybe, he should call himself, legitimately, Arundel III, but then thought it just sounded too pretentious. How glorious it was that in his lifetime they had regained almost all their ancestral lands in the Taxus and how now, only the Isle of Elves wanted reclaiming from the Pitters. But the conquest of the Isle of Elves was in his war plans. Shortly after the worshipful high holy days of the elven fair were over, he was purposed to launch an all out attack on Elves Island, provided the Pyringean Pirates arrived on schedule.

Tonight the drama of the death and slaying of the Grand Elf Howrus on Mount Heredom would be reenacted, as it was every year for the last five hundred plus years in any and all Herewardi realms. Only now, instead of the Herewardi fleeing ever further and further to the west, the tide had turned on the Pitter empire, and the enemy was now the one doing the fleeing further and further to the east. It was what Long Swan referred to as, 'reversing the blows of death.'

The table where honored guests would sit was positioned at the front, facing the stage. Clumps of bananas growing to each side of the stage framed it. Arundel sat alone under a large old Oak, the Tree of Kings, and wrote down his thoughts for rebuilding the city into the thriving center it once was. He pulled out a pad and began sketching gardens and henges, a temple, and a globe theatre; for Shakespeare was holy to the Herewardi.

It was mid day when a triple blast from a trumpet signaled the arrival of queen Zschamillah and her retinue. Arundel hurried over to Sun Charger and mounted. As he rode to the front gate to greet his family the very air seemed filled with autumnal magic. It was warm, but crisp. Colored leaves fell from the tree bowers, but the trees still looked full. Great flocks of robins, grackles, and cardinals filled the greenery with bird song, and the grass hoppers sang their swan song. The gold cup of summer was pouring out its last drops as the red cup of autumn was splashing on the tree leaves. Autumn was closing in.

Much had happened since the caravan from Godeselle left the isle three moonths before and traveled to Fort Rock to be joined by the High Desert fyrd. He knew Sur Sceaf had sent a dispatch requesting Starkwulf join in the war which was not originally in the plan, and yet now he saw what looked like the noble warrior approaching on horseback with his silver queen riding by his side, leading the procession of wagons with the fyrds from Fort Rock under Syr Elf's command. They had linked up with the larger caravan coming from the Isle of Ilkchild, and were welcomed by the wagon masters as an additional protective force in ushering the families safely to the Omala. Starkwulf and his desert queen were attired in the silver garments of the High Desert Kingdom. They shone like the moon in the red back ground of their fyrds, marked by the Jaguarundi banners they carried.

Arundel thought, *How ever did father persuade them to come?* He felt pride in having the greatest hero of Herewardom fighting with them, and knew the counsel his Aunt Va-Eyra would offer would be of immense strategic advantage.

Then his heart skipped a beat as he laid eyes on his own queen, who sat in her open buggy with her long red hair shining like molten copper and draping over her shoulders in loose ringlets. She wore a shimmering chartreuse dress with periwinkle colored collar and cuffs. On either side of her sat their four year old son, Leofric, and their six year old daughter, Cygbee. The rest of her children rode in the fore of the carriage, and one of his older son's donned the uniform of a Young Blood fyrd. Yjr Young Blood rode mounted on a Fjord horse to the side of his mother's wagon. Ary saluted him, and said, "You've done well, Yjr."

"Fa, it is so good to see you. I have mastered the Flame Elfhabet and won three consecutive archery tournaments."

"You must tell me tonight at the feast, Yjr. I am anxious to see your mother."

Ary goaded Sun Charger on and rode up next to them, kissed Zschamillah warmly, then reached over the carriage and grabbed first Cygbee, placing her on the horse at his back, and then grabbed Leofric with one hand under the arm, heaving him over to sit on the saddle in front of him. Ary kissed him on top of the head and said, "How's my little tiger?"

The child looked up and said, "Have you come home, Fa?"

Arundel glanced over at Zschamillah and had to laugh, "I suppose I have, Son."

Cygbee leaned around and handed him a note.

"What is this my dear?" He said as he smiled at the curly-haired, red-head, eyes as sparkling green as emeralds in a cool mountain pool.

"It's a poem I made for you, Fa." She darted a glance back at her mother, who indicated with a nod that he should open it.

He opened it by shaking it out. "It reads, 'Bee happy. I am Bee. Therefore, I am happy.'"

"What a wonderful little poem, my little honey bee!"

She scrunched her nose and said, "I knew you'd like it. And Fa, we saw a twister near Tahlequah. Lady Taneshewa said she grew up with them, and Lady Grandmother Paloma said Twisters are the Norn Sisters spinning space and time together on their distaff. But to me, it looked like a giant funnel of wind pulling up trees."

Arundel smiled, heaved the children back over into their wagon, and then clucked for Sun Charger to walk on and rode up beside his two spanix wives. As he looked into first one face and then the other of these dark-eyed beauties, he reflected how Gabrielle and Isabelle had been concubines to Gorge the Guatemalan, but Gorge had scorned to lay with them because Gorge preferred his male lover. So they went to a behanding and announced before the Law Stone that they were divorced. Whereupon they traveled to the city of Ele-Anor as gardeners, and Arundel came upon them laboring in the queen's orangery where he often retired to read ancient lore. He took a special liking to them. They were playful, hard workers, and above all else lively. They were approved by Zschamillah and he married them, raising them first to the status of cifes or near wives and then to be his eleventh and twelfth wife.

"How are you, my lovely ladies?"

They grabbed his hand that he put forth to touch them with, and Gabrielle said, "We have so missed ju, husband. It is so good to see ju are still alive. All the way here, all I do is worry, worry, worry over ju fighting those awful Peetters."

Isabelle patiently waited, while Gabrielle repeatedly kissed his Arundel's hand. Then she held her nursing baby in one arm, took his hand and kissed it. "Tomorrow, I make ju jour favorite fried red peppers dipped in chocolate. I bring the peppers and chocolate with me."

"Ladies, you treat me too well." He reached out, "May I see my daughter?"

"Ju may see her. She is so cute."

Arundel took the warm little bundle in his arms and it smiled. "What did you name her?"

"Juanita, I name her. Ju remember the letter I send ju."

"You called her Guajote in the letter."

"Oh, that is 'cause she is like a little turkey. See how fat she is." Arundel smiled, kissed the baby on the head and said, "Here's our little turkey back." The two wives laughed.

Following directly behind was Ilkhava with her five children. Then came Lyr the Chartreusean wife with her green skin contrasting dramatically with the white sarong she wore. Her three children rode with her, waving and shouting "Daddy, Daddy, Daddy." She called out, "I have been praying to Cernunnos for your welfare, my husband."

"And Tyranus has heard your prayers, my love."

Ilr, another Chartreusean wife with her three children signed her love then said, "I was explaining to Xipe how our gods are similar to yours, husband. You say Tyranus and Thor, we say Cernunnos."

"They do appear to be the same."

Then Xipe, his Cerulean wife smiled as she passed by, her blue skin and plum colored lips setting her apart from even her own two children's flesh color and blond hair. She signed, "You are all mine."

Finally in a wagon together, traveled Aethelthryth and Aelfgyva with their children. His heart leapt in him for the love he had to all his wives, and he sent up a silent prayer of thanksgiving to the Faery All Mother that his wives had been spared any harm or accident in such an arduous trek as they had undertaken. He looked forward to showing them all the glories of the City of Arundel the Great.

He yelled from his mount, "Hail and Os-Frith, ye daughters of the sacred Isle of Ilkchild." Then riding to the head of their train he said, "Follow me, and I shall take you to your quarters at my mansion where you may bathe, find fresh clothing, and prepare for the day's festivities with all your bride-sisters."

Arundel then rode alongside the buggies, wagons, and carriages, saw that Zscha had brought a company of beo-ceorls (bee keepers) with her, and cracked a smile. He continued welcoming and kissing each wife as he passed. Then he led them by horse, to the Castle Arundel, the Bastion's original name.

After arriving at the Lord's Mansion, his wives were greeted by their bride-sisters that had gone with Ary as well as their servants. They greeted one another with much weeping and hugging. Arundel dismounted and lifted two of his sons who were punching at each other into each of his arms. "Lads, I want you both to be warriors, but we must always refrain from fighting a brother."

"He punched me first," Thorgood said, turning his head away from his brother.

"Did not. He said I wet the bed last night and I didn't," Freyred said.

"Words can be as bad as a punch. No more hurtful words or punches boys. It's time we become a family again. The rule is: always helpful behavior, never hurtful behavior. Alright?"

Both of them shook their heads and darted off to explore the long porch on the castle. The bride-sisters turned to the grooms to take their horses and buggies to the livery, while several took advantage of the stop to change the diapers of crying babies. Eight of his little daughters were chasing each other through the lawn, and the servants looked fit to be tied. Other servants gathered everyone's baggage up and followed them into the mansion house.

Aelfgyva said, "What a splendid palace, my lord." She greatly admired the large columns, the pointed arches, and the beautiful bay windows, the red tiled roof and the tiled porch. "Not to mention this lovely garden. Zschamillah was so worried there would be no garden."

"Wait til you see the parlor and the ballroom. Its walls are made of walnut wood and the tables of pecan. There is even period furniture from the times of our Longfathers. And the kitchen is so big you'll have to send beetles as runners if you want to talk to your sister wives."

Queen Zschamillah punched him in the side, "Husband, I never know whether to believe you or not. But I had no idea the Main Land of Panygyrus never ends. A moonth ago I thought we must surely arrive any day, but I was assured by the Fyrd-Heretoga, Ilrundel, that we had yet another moonth to go. Then, when we arrived in Apache Lands, I thought we were surely there. Yet still there was another leg to go, and in the driest lands I have ever seen. When I said I'd go to the ends of the earth for you, I did not know the earth was this big."

Arundel took Zschamillah in an embrace and kissed her. "Would you believe you have only come half way across the Panygyrean Main Land?"

"By Queen Ele-Anor and all the Iluloika, must you yet travel that far to the Pitter nest?"

"We must. The war is only half over, dear. But forget that for now. These are the good times. Let me show you to your room, since you will be staying with me tonight. Ilklilith will show the other bride-sisters their rooms, and the nannies will take the children to theirs."

Arundel's chartreusean wife, Lyr, said with an excited tone to her voice. "Did you have this place built, my lord?"

"No, dear, it was builded by Herewardi stone masons for my Longfather, Arundel."

Aethelthryth said, "Well, I hope you had the place cleansed of all the demons and spirits of the Dark Elves before moving in."

"We did, my dear. We purged the place with Ash, Hyssop, Sage, Magnolia, and Hawthorn, even burned oak leaves and then burned all their paintings and images of Angrar. And if that wasn't enough, we placed Elfwort and Magnolia, in each room and I personally dedicated it to be filled with and shielded with ur fyr."

Aelfgyva said, "I hate to think of the demonic practices and tortures that must have gone on in this castle."

"You all needn't worry. It has all been pronounced clean. Remember, the Omala is one of our ancestral homelands. I would not doubt, but that our ancestors have come back from the Other World to dance upon our roofs this very moment."

Aelfgyva said, "I cannot wait until we take back the Firginias and the Merry Lands. The rune singers sing such lovely tales of those sacred homelands. How they are filled with the greenery and the bounties of nature."

Gabrielle interjected, "Where is my darling son? Where is Xarela?"

"He'll be along directly. He's with Brekka right now."

"Well, ladies, I am going to show Zschamillah to her room. All of you may clean up for the elven fair while I do."

As Arundel started up the stairs, Aelfgyva said, "No double dipping now Zschamillah, it'll be six days before I get him."

Zschamillah turned on the stair and said, "I've never known that to slow him down any. There's always plenty for us all. And let her who has never double dipped step forward and she can have my place tonight."

The bride-sisters all laughed, but none stepped forward.

The elven fair was a great success. Ary took delight in every aspect of the festivities. Surrounded by his wives and children, old friends and brothers and sisters in arms, he felt exactly like a nomad returning to a familiar hunting ground and water hole. While he sat with his inner circle at the head table, reminiscing and discussing the war road, his wives took the opportunity to visit with old friends at other tables, their familiar laughter and happy smiles wonderfully soothing to his war weary soul.

Watching the passion plays in company with his wives and older children, competing in the tournaments with his young blood sons, presiding over the festive board in company with his friends who'd trekked past the dragon's back with him—these activities had always played a large part in his growing up years. Now that his wives and children had joined him, he was as much at home as he had been in Namen Jewel or Ele-Anor-Ness. He intended to embrace every day that the gods allowed him respite from the war road, which from this point on would only grow more and more intense and costly in lives and losses.

As he observed three of his wives enjoying the company of El Yid's bride covey at their table nearest the stage platform, he noticed, for the first time in his recollection, Brekka and Ruhm sat at opposite tables. Brekka sat with her lady knights and handmaidens playing a knife and card game, while Ruhm left his company and sat with some Hickoryan friends and some very cozy Mexus girls playing cards.

He had not questioned Ruhm closely after the hickoryan and his cavalry had arrived in Omala, but during the following weeks, he had noticed a change in Ruhm's demeanor. Not only did he seem more reckless, but he also had an edge to him. Zscha had remarked on that as well.

"A young man who has been disappointed in love oft times turns surly," she had told him with a sigh. "Remember how short-tempered you became when I rejected you?"

Ary did not like to dwell on the angry young man he'd been then, and he found himself mildly sympathetic to Ruhm. Still, he had to trust his sister's judgment in matters of command.

Tankard in hand, Ary sat back in his chair and let the various conversations flow over him. Large piping hot beefs were winched over to the table on chains. Porters laid out spitted ducks and geese on the festive board, while milk maidens passed out leather pitchers of mead and ale from large wooden barrels. Braised guinea fowl with lovage, braised chicken with chervil, served with nettle, leek, and lentil soup or celeriac soup along with eggs on hops in a nettle puree. Side tables with golden breads and butter were brought within easy reach.

Directly across the table, Starkwulf had just returned with a plate of sweetmeats, which he presented to Va-Eyra with a courtly bow before planting a deep kiss on her lips. "Sweets for my sweet lady wife," he teased as he resumed his seat.

Ary's aunt actually blushed. He had never seen her so happy.

He selected a finger tart from the plate she offered, thanked her and savored the lemony taste. "Starkwulf, how in Middle Ea-Urth did Fa ever get you to come out of the High Desert?"

Starkwulf grinned. "Couldn't resist. The peace became so great after we had cleansed the High Desert of Pitters I couldn't resist the chance for action again. And when my darling Va agreed to ride at my side, I knew the gods had spoken my fate."

Va-Eyra gave her burly husband a fond look. "The thought of making a pilgrimage to Mount Heredom was utterly irresistible, especially in company of this big old bear."

Starkwulf laughed. "I have to admit my motives were far less spiritual, the chance to participate in cutting off the head of Hryre Seath, now *that* was impossible to resist."

"I'll drink to that, my friend." Ary saluted him with his tankard before taking a sip. "And I, for one, am very grateful to have you and the Desert Queen, as well as your children and their fyrds as compatriots in the battles that lie ahead."

Starkwulf smiled at Va-Eyra and said, "Anything for my people. We figured, Herewardom's welfare is our portion. And to show how committed I am, I have brought several barrels of High Desert Ale with me, which I shall tap only when the High King arrives."

Tall, powerful, blond-haired Ilrundel approached the head table with his very pregnant redheaded wife, Lily, clinging to his arm. "What's the next step in your battle plans, Lord Arundel?" he asked.

Ilrundel resembled a more powerful version of Ary's good friend, Ilkchild, the Wizard of Moon Door, and it felt as if he were conversing with his old friend again. "We've been discussing a plan to attack Elves Island in the Bay of Taxus."

Ilrundel smiled, turned his head to Lily, and said, "Oh, yes, the Isle of Elves in the days of Arundel the Great. The Lore Master, Wheelursun, taught that so elevated was Arundel II's court that Forty-Four of them achieved Lore Master status. It is written the Forty-Four Wizards met on the Sacred Isle of Elves in great moots in megaliths of stone circles with the very gods of Osgard and Valhollar in attendance."

"I would that we could achieve that level of civilization again." Lilly declared, "In Ilkchild's letters from Moon Door, he has repeatedly declared that it was his goal to make moon door like unto the City of Elves, in splendor, wisdom, and the arts."

Ary nodded. "And I believe he is well on his way to making it so. You should visit the Marbled City someday; a city of philosophers and wizards. It is truly the jewel of the jungle." Ary drained his tankard just as Ruhm arrived with the young quailor, Alf Hegele at his side.

"My lord, forgive the interruption," the eldest son of Hartmut and Mendaho said as he snatched off his black hat. "I have waited for the appropriate moment to tell you. On our way here from our encampment, we encountered a strange sort of fellow. Called himself an Appalachian, name of Pomer, said he had very important business with the Lord Arundel and asked if I could get him an audience with you. Declared he was an Ambassador of the Rdokians. I told him I would talk with you, took him to my wagon, and asked him to wait there for an answer."

Arundel exchanged looks with Ruhm, who nodded. "An ambassador from Appalachia," Ary mused aloud. "How appropriate is it to have arrived on the Elven Fair. Tis a sign from the gods, for I have never had any word from them before. Nor have our merchants or spies ever reported anything, but marginal contact."

"The Rdokians are fiercely independent, have an inherent mistrust of strangers, and have heretofore relied only on their own strength to hold off the Pitters, my lord," Ruhm explained.

"Then please, let him enter, and make room for him at the festive board." Arundel flagged down a Green Beetle messenger boy. "Sydda, go to Alf Hagele's wagons and fetch a man named Pomer here as swiftly as your feet can carry you."

"I will go fetch him, my lord," the Beetle said, and he rushed off.

"With your permission, my lord, I will return to the cards." Ruhm grinned. "I'm winning!"

Ary laughed. "I noticed. But winning at what, I wonder."

Ruhm grinned, turned and left without answering.

The Beetle soon returned with what looked like a wild man. Indeed, he probably was. Soon a murmur spread through the tables as the celebrants watched the stranger following the Beetle between the tables.

Tall and thin, the appalachian was dressed in buckskin and a wide brimmed leather hat. His stride was long and confident, his movements fluid and measured, the walk of a warrior.

When he reached the table, Arundel stood to offer a formal welcome.

Pomer took off his hat to reveal a head of long brown hair and piercing blue eyes, a mustache and a tiny strip of beard running from the middle of his lower lip to his chin similar to the Herewardi Royale. "Damned glad to meet ja, Lord Arundel of the Syr Folk Confederation." He turned his hat over and bowed. "I'm Pomer Ido-Anum, Son of Hoor Yew-Anum, from the hilly country of Roaring Springs in the Virginias."

"Os-Frith, Pomer Ido-Anum," Arundel said, letting the name role off his tongue. "Please sit to festive board with us." Alf Haegele pulled up a wooden chair for Pomer and one for himself. "And you join us too, Sydda."

"The pleasure would be mine, for I have ridden many days ride through treacherous woods and swamps filled with robber bands and rat packs with little sustenance, save only what I was able to kill under way, and nothing cooked, and certainly not the bounty which you here display. Last meal was a coyote and that didn't set well. In all my days, I ain't ever seen such fixins as y'all have."

Pomer Ido-Anum took the chair next to Ary, nodded at Starkwulf and smiled at Va-Eyra. "Beg pardon, ma'am. I hope I'm not dressed too coarse for your company."

"Not at all, sir," she replied with a twinkle in her eyes. "I have always been partial to buckskin on a man."

Looking pleased, and a bit more relaxed, Pomer pulled out his large hickory handled knife and stuck it in the table before glancing at Sydda, who had stationed himself nearby. "Boy, I'd be real grateful if'n you would fetch me a plate of them vittles."

Sydda glanced at Ary, who nodded. "Better bring two plates."

As Sydda hurried off, Pomer declared, "Word has come to our ears of the great victories you have had against the western half of the Pitter Empire. I've been sent to confirm that report."

"You heard correctly, although I'm surprised, that word has traveled so fast in Pitter Territories."

"There be many who hunger for just such news and have feelers in many lands. Some of the swamp foxes sent us runners telling us of your victories. That news was like a fly touching a spider web. It wasn't long till we and all other freedom seeking peoples got the word and spread it to all of our allied encampments." Pomer Ido-Anum stared at Ary, his eyes displaying the cunning of a guerrilla fighter, a look seen only in the eyes of a fox, as he declared, "It is said that you have broken the flood of the Pitters and that they are draining out of your lands back into the empire of the east faster than rats leaving a sinking ship. We have seen legion after legion passing through our mountains. Long have my fathers waited for such a day. When we heard of your father, noblest of kings, the Great Sur Sceaf, and his victory of Moon Door, that tale has been sung around our campfires by the singers for nigh two score of years now."

Sydda returned with a large tray bearing two plates and bowls, which he deposited with great care on the table before serving first Ary and then Pomer.

"Thanky kindly, boy," Pomer said, ruffling Sydda's fair curls.

The boy looked both startled and pleased as he took up his station again.

Ary sipped his leek soup and noticed Pomer waited for the cue to drink his own so he looked at the soup and nodded. "You must have thought we went dark."

Pomer's face lit up at the taste of the leek soup and he drew his lips into his mouth with utter relish as if to suck in the last drop of it. "We did. There were many years of silence before our web was agin shaken by the victory of the shield-maiden, which we heard through the Quilombos, and we knew the time was at hand for the final battle. Since the days of our Forefather, Rdoke, we have done battle with the

Pitters and have been driven and afflicted from hollow after hollow by their armies even to this day. There is not a stretch of the Appalachian Mountains that we do not know like the backs of our hands. The Pitters have searched for us in every cess-pit, lion's den, and fox hole the mountains have, but have never stopped our resistance or tapped our whereabouts without us detecting their presence or moving before they could get into us. It is our belief that you will soon be coming east, and though your victories in the west have been great, you must know that you are now coming into the pit of vipers themselves. They will be far more formidable in their eastern zongas because they have been in possession of those lands for so long, and now they have summoned the very demons of hell to aid them."

"You mean the Vardropi?"

"Not just the blood thirsty Vardropi, no siree, I am saying they have the eaters from the stars. You will not be successful without us. The eaters will know your every move and guide the Pitters straight to you. We can show you all of the emperor's weak flanks; show you where to retreat to, and where to hide in places they may not enter. I am saying we will fight with you against the pitters, but needed to warn you they will easily repel you, unless you outfox them with the cunning we possess."

Arundel frowned, "You are saying they have spies among us and that is how they know our every move?"

Pomer shook his head as he downed a swig of ale. "Wow! That's good stuff. No, there are dark demons that serve Hryre Seath; moth men; the eaters with leather wings that suck the life out of man and beast, and watch us in the night. The Mountain Witches tell us when they are coming so we can hide from them."

Arundel felt sick at this news. "I can see you shall prove to be a most valuable ally. But we have not heard of the likes of such things yet."

A Milk-Maid passed with hot bread. The mountain man stabbed a loaf with his knife and commenced tearing off chunks. He offered Arundel a piece, and broke a piece for Alf and Sydda before tearing into it with his teeth.

The way Pomer mantled his bread and ate it like a watchful cougar darting his eyes in all directions told Arundel he was a man of constant battle-readiness, and that all his survival instincts were so finely honed that it must have required great courage to walk into such a gathering full of strangers. He suspected that beneath this mountain man's cool exterior raged the fires of centuries of enduring the oppression under the pitters. He knew he was looking at fired and beaten steel that had no dross left in it, and that such a race as this could prove decisive in any battle.

For some unknown reason, perhaps because Arundel was thinking about Ruhm's homeland, he shot a glance over at the Hickoryan, who was tightly embracing a Mexus girl. Instinctively, Ary shifted his gaze in Brekka's direction. His sister was pointedly ignoring Ruhm's actions, confirming his suspicion that a serious rift had indeed come between the two lovers. This charade with the Mexus girl was Ruhm's way of saying to Brekka, 'it's over.'

He recalled the Lady Redith's wise counsel which she had written him in the days he was troubled over his tempestuous and trying love for Zschamillah. 'Love takes strange and winding paths.' Still it made him sad to see such a long relationship severed in twain by the war.

Pomer ripped off a piece of duck, shoved it into his mouth, chewed twice and swallowed. "Well, what say ye? Are you with us or not?"

Ary grinned. "I would be a fool to say no, but I would ask you to agree that I am to lead the forces under my command. Also, when my father, Sur Sceaf arrives he will assume full command. For, you see, we are come to utterly rid the land of Pitters and to establish a Confederation of Nations from the eastern sea to the western sea. This is our manifest destiny; to bring the rule of law, liberty, equality, self-determination, and constitutional government to all men, and to restore the inheritances of all tribes to their rightful tribal lands."

Starkwulf leaned forward to ask. "I'm still curious, where do these flying demons come from?"

Pomer looked around, and then pointed up, "From the stars. They have furious eyes that are red as hot coals, teeth like a boar hog, and a long, piercing pink tongue." A look of monstrous fear filled Pomer's eyes and then all color left his face, washed away like ash. "They are the haunters of the dark, and I've lost a couple good men to them."

Arundel wondered what manner of thing could affect Pomer so. He looked around and his table had grown completely silent. Everyone at the table was suddenly attending their conversation. He took a drink of mead to still his own heart and said, "Then we shall meet them with our flying ballooners and send those demons back to Hell together with Hryre Seath."

# CHAPTER 26 :

## THE BATTLE FOR ELVES ISLAND

**I**T WAS A FORTNIGHT AFTER THE Elven Fair, and in three days it would be the new moon, perfect for launching the guerilla attack on Elves Island. El Yid had spent much of those two weeks sweating in the hot Taxus sun, building kayaks. Following the instructions of Raven's Tongue the Tlingit, he and his Pyringean Pirates had constructed more than a hundred of the odd-looking crafts. After carefully testing them on the San Arundelf River that flowed past the Omala Citadel, and finding them sound of hull and easy to maneuver, he had them painted black, as he planned to use them in the dark of night.

Once all were loaded on wagons, he went to say goodbye to his family. It was only a short jaunt to his assigned tidy stone house overlooking the river, the haunt of a former Dominiker officer. With a heavy heart he saw that his entire family had gathered on the porch to bid him farewell. Their time together had been much too short. Still, he treasured every moment.

One by one he kissed his wives, Judith, Rebekah, and Ystersaex. As though sensing the dangerous nature of this assignment, each of his ladies clung to him tightly before releasing him.

"My lord, I shall pray to Woon for your safety in this battle," Ystersaex said in an emotion-choked voice. "I have an uneasiness that I can't shake. Lord Arundel is asking too much of you to spearhead this attack. There are too many Pitters gathered to Elves Island. It just doesn't sit well with me."

"And this from the wife that just a fortnight ago said, 'Herewardom's welfare is our portion.' Did you not mean that?"

"I just mean to wish you *waes hael*, and yes, I meant it, but I did not mean for you to lay your life so cheaply on the line."

"But if not me, who? We are fighting to retain the freedoms granted to us by god. Shall I not take my turn on the stage of war?"

Pyrsyrus had put El Yid in charge of the attack on Elves Island, while Pyrsyrus would be busy gathering the materials and directing his Quailor craftsmen in the construction of the newest palace of the seas. The great ship was not only to be a floating palace, but also a warship. It was being designed as the mother ship for servicing the dragoons and directing the naval campaign against the Pitters on the eastern seaboard. Both the taking of Elves Island and the building of the sea palace were time bound and of equal importance, requiring that Yid and Pyr take different courses before they rejoined their forces.

After El Yid hugged and kissed his wives goodbye, he addressed the children who ranged in age from seventeen winters to Ystersaex's new born son, Anglechild. "I want you all to do your chores, study Torah, and keep one another safe while I'm gone."

Young Joseph, the ten year old son of Judith's hearth, pulled on Yid's arm, "But, father, I want to be at sea and fight the Pitters."

Yid smiled and tousled Joseph's dark brown hair. "The best way for you to fight the Pitters is to study Torah. Keep the Torah, and the Torah will keep you."

Joseph looked puzzled "But Ystersaex's children don't study Torah."

"Now, you know she is not Jywdic, and we respect her beliefs the same as she respects ours. That's what life is all about."

Etti-Dorpha, Ystersaex's eldest daughter of only twelve winters spoke up, "Besides, Joseph, we Herewardi have to study the Forty-Four Laws *and* memorize every word by rote. And I'm also reading the journals of Myra-El."

Yid blew everyone a kiss, walked off the porch, and took his black horse from his oldest Son, Thorjudah, who wished him *"Waes hael."* He muscled his horse, swung it around and rode off.

By the time he and his black-clad Pyringean pirates rendezvoused with Arundel and his armies, the wagons containing the kayaks had been covered with canvas just like the rest of the supply wagons which contained materials and tools necessary for constructing ships. Ary's plan was to rid Hewes Town of Pitter occupiers before using the harbor to launch the kayaks.

Three days later the enormous wagon train arrived on the outskirts of Hewes Town. Arundel set up base camp on the Bay of Taxus, from which they could see Elves Island, the last Pitter Zonga left west of the Mys-Isis River.

Spies had earlier confirmed that the Pitters had been using this harbor to load their belly ships with legions and supplies before transporting them to the critical plantations of Flar-Dah and Wymouth where the Pitters mounted a rigorous guard over their Bamboo Fields.

El Yid spent the day studying the Pitters' movements on their anchorage at Elves Island, in an effort to determine which ships he would capture for future use by the pirates and which he would simply burn.

As he watched, several belly ships departed, riding low in the water indicating that they were fully loaded. He counted ten others that were being loaded. Later that evening he went to Ary's Pfalz Tent to detail his overall strategy for taking the island and securing the commodities stored there. Ary was particularly interested in his description of the large warehouse-like structures near the shore, and the endless line of handcarts and wagons transporting goods from them to the ships. If successful, Yid and Arundel's attack would ensure all those vast supplies would soon be in Syr Folk warehouses.

"You do realize, Ary, that this will be as difficult as an ant pushing a boulder uphill, but do it we must."

"The plan is true, the plan is square, and you will make it so. I will destroy the Pitters at Hewes Town and then join you in taking the Isle. No doubt their spies have reported no sign of our ships approaching, so most likely they will not expect an attack on the Isle until we have the means of transporting our armies there. This mistaken belief, of course, will work in our favor."

Brekka had already begun her far-reaching attacks when Ary rode off to begin his siege of Hewes Town.

After returning to his camp, Yid ordered his men to take the remainder of the day to get rest and refreshment for the arduous battle to come.

Just before sunset a messenger rode up to El Yid to report, "Lord Arundel's fyrd has destroyed the Pitters on this side of the Bay in Hewes

Town and wished me to tell you that you need not fear a surprise attack. Also, the Lady Brekka's Spanix fyrd is now sweeping through the countryside, freeing the captive slaves by the droves from the agricultural compounds. Both anticipate joining you here by deep nightfall."

"Please tell Lord Arundel that I will make the island ours, and to be prepared to begin boarding the Pitter vessels at my signal. Until then, he is to stay out of sight, so as to convince the enemy that our main goal is the taking of Hewes Town and the securing of the compounds, supplies, and work camps."

Once the twilight had passed and the sky darkened to a colly black, Yid gathered his Pirate Guerillas around him. Quickly, he went over the plan one more time. He had divided his men into three groups—one to board the ships on the south end of the anchorage, one to board those to the north and the third which was under his command would capture the ships in the center.

"Unless the Pitters have altered their routines, there should only be skeleton crews aboard, but I must emphasize one more time that we must be as quiet as a synagogue mouse. Then, as soon as you secure a ship, put only enough men aboard as is necessary to safely pilot them back to the harbor at Hewes Town where Arundel shall load his fyrds. Then return and repeat the process over and over, until we possess all their ships. We'll deal with the supplies later. Go with stealth and take no unnecessary chances. This labor must be complete before dawn's light, so let us make all due haste."

He and his pirates donned the distinctive black bandana of the Young Lions of Judah with the letter Shayn on the forehead. Yid had selected this symbol to mark his men as holy, and to remind them that they were always under the watchful eye and protecting hand of God. Seth Moss, leader of the Columba Rogues had chosen a dove as his sigil, while the leader of the Herewardi, Ullr-Ruh, selected the Elwas Rune sigil.

"By the God of Abraham, Isaac, and Israel lets launch."

The Jywdic pirates replied with the traditional "Amen", the Herewardi with, "So mote it be," and the Columba Rogues with "Get down, boys." As stealthily as possible, they carried the kayaks from the wagons to the bay and launched them under cover of the New Moon.

Upon reaching the middle of the bay, the three groups split apart and headed for their assigned targets. As soon as Yid's kayak reached the first ship in his sector, he tied the pointed bow of the small black craft to the anchor chain, then slipped into the water, holding fast to the rusted chain while his men did likewise.

Then, like an army of black frogs, they climbed up the chain and over the railing. Swiftly, they fanned out, moving from deck to deck, silently dispatching the sailors they encountered before moving to the sleeping quarters below deck where, with great efficiency, they slew the sleeping crew.

Once the ship was secured, Yid left a skeleton crew aboard before he and his men climbed down the anchor chain and into their kayaks. Once all the ships had been likewise secured, he would give the order to sail the commandeered vessels to the port of Hewes Town where the fyrds would board in order to launch the attack on the Isle.

This process was repeated until all ten ships had been captured and dispatched to the harbor on the other side of the bay. Yid and his men then searched nearby dormitories and officers' dwellings where they found mostly longshoremen and Pitter quartermasters in charge of loading the thousands of crates stacked in rows inside the warehouses and on the quayside.

Once this initial phase of their attack had been successfully completed, Yid declared to his men, "Good work men. If you can picture a single ant rolling a boulder up a steep hill, that's what we did. Now we will push that boulder down the hill to crush this nest of vermin."

By dawn's early light the belly ships were returning and unloading Syr Folk fyrds, Hickoryan cavalry, and Buffalo Nations' dog soldiers onto Elves Island. The combined forces swept across the island, systematically surprising enemy soldiers in their homes and camps. Slowly, slaying as they went, they fought their way to the far end of the island. Casualties had been surprisingly light, the result of an unexpected knifing or clubbing.

But when Yid and his men came to a Pitter compound built on a bluff overlooking the Taxus Bay, all that changed. This compound contained elite troops, experienced in battle and skilled at repelling an attack. Even worse, this compound was unlike any Yid had ever seen, with narrow slanting windows, thick bricked walls, and iron gates. Yid suspected this fortress dated from the time of the first invasions in the day of Arundel the Great, for he knew of no such Pitter construction.

As the casualties mounted among his men, Yid signed for his commanders to pull back their men and wait until Arundel arrived with reinforcements.

When his men appeared dismayed at the order to stand down, he explained, "If there was not a danger of burning the rest of the island down, we could burn them out, but Ary has charged me with preserving as many structures as possible. Besides, this one is clearly of ancient design, and therefore, doubly valuable."

Yid was exhausted, and most of his men gave every indication that, despite their protest, they were grateful for the rest. "We will make camp here and wait for Ary to arrive. Let him decide how he wants to handle this."

At two points on the sun dial past high noon, Arundel arrived at the South compound to confer with El Yid on a viable strategy. Yid had done an excellent job of securing the island, and this was like a fly in the otherwise perfect soup. Arundel wanted as few casualties as possible, for he would need every man for the march eastward when the Mud Moonth arrived. He was frustrated with waiting, but seeing the hospitalers dressing the wounds and caring for the injured convinced Ary they must proceed more cautiously. Herewardi military decorum dictated that a commander must put the life of his men above all other considerations. His father repeatedly counseled his commanders that any strategic maneuver that placed the lives of the men in great danger needed to include their voice before it could be made.

As soon as Yid and his men had eaten, Arundel asked him and his two senior commanders to confer with him in his Pfalz Tent. "We could starve the rats out of their nest," the commander of the Rogue contingent, Seth Moss, son of Shug, offered. "They have the high ground, but we control access."

White Crow pulled out a strip of jerky from his saddlebag and took a bite. "That's one way of getting rats out of their hole," he said. "The other is to smoke them out."

"I considered that," Yid told him. "But I decided against it for two reasons. One, I feared to cause a conflagration that might destroy this end of the island. And two, I believe this compound has great historical value to the Herewardi and deserves to be preserved if possible." He glanced Ary's way and raised his eyebrows. "Have I reasoned correctly, Ary?"

"You have, my friend." Ary smiled his gratitude for Yid's respectful understanding of both Herewardi values and culture.

Ruhm thought for a moment before suggesting, "Why not build a wet fire instead? There's plenty of greenery around here to use as fuel. The fire will be more smoke than flame, and won't spread more than a few feet."

White Crow glanced at Ruhm with a new look of respect in his dark eyes. "I agree," he said.

Ary caught the eager look on White Crow's face. Several times the Chief had reminded him that his braves needed frequent blood spilling or they became restless. Soon the idleness would generate fighting.

"Well done, Ruhm." He gave him a pat on the back before ordering him to set his men to gathering fuel for the fire. "Hack down those green cattails and gather any green herbage. Stack it near that compound. Throw water on it. Keep the ground moist and cut a firewall so no fire spreads into the dry grass. We'll smoke these damned rats out."

He turned to White Crow. "Your braves will be the spearhead in this battle."

"That's fine," White Crow said. "But how do you propose to get that green stuff to start once it's soaking wet?"

"Whale oil. The hospitalers carry barrels of whale oil for their lamps."

Once the materials were piled several feet high around the building by shielded men, the whale oil of the hospitalers was poured on the thick green thatch. White Crow then shot a flaming arrow into the herbage, and flames ran slowly along the surface of the piles followed by a choking, thick, billowing smoke that blotted the building completely out of sight. A freshening breeze from the bay drew the smoke through the compound where it lingered suffocatingly thick.

Ary ordered, "Archers, commence with the Herewardi rain!"

The Pitters inside hacked and coughed, and cried out in pain as the arrows found their victims. After the third barrage, the iron gates opened, and Pitters spilled out in a ragged turtle phalanx over the porch and down the stairs.

White Crow signaled for his archers to flood the porch and doorway with arrows, and then charged over the dead and writhing bodies of the Pitters, hacking everything in front of them with their long tomahawks. Some Pitters ran wildly from the building and scampered for the water, but were summarily shot by Arundel's crack archers. Inside the compound, it sounded like a panther had been released into a saloon brawl, with crashing furniture, screams, and wild raging red men bent on obliterating the last of the Pitter Hell-Rats.

There was a long silence. Then White Crow strode out of the compound with the head of the Pitter commissar in hand. He hacked and choked a few times, then rolled the head over the fire wall like a bowling ball. "Hail, Lord Arundel." He choked from having inhaled too much smoke. "Care for some bowling?" Choked again, and said, "It is a good day to die, my lord."

Arundel nodded. "And, it is a good day to slay Pitters." Then Arundel walked over to the severed head, rolled it face up with his boot, and said, "Damn it. I do not know this commissar, but I do know it's not the Skull Worm or Sanangrar. Cowards that they are, no doubt they were among the first to flee the Isle by ship; and I had so hoped this was going to be their end."

Brekka walked over and examined the head. "Ary, this is the Commissar Xombro."

"And you know this how?" Arundel asked.

"He bears the crescent tattoo of a Dominiker on his temple and no one else has funny looking ears like this. Xombro was the only other Dominiker besides Balaban and the Cha'Kal operating here in the west. I fought him in Zamora."

"Leave it to you sis, to reveal the hidden."

A roar of hails exploded from White Crow's dog soldiers as word spread that they had just killed Xombro. They shouted choking war cries of victory, for Xombro was known amongst them as 'The Evil Spirit,' by reason of all his foul deeds against man, woman, child, and beast in their home lands. Brekka's Spanix fyrd joined in the jubilant victory cries followed by Ruhm and his cavalry. The Pyringean Pirates saluted the heavens silently with their swords raised, as was their custom, like a congress of ravens.

After a prolonged parading around the Pitter compound, Arundel cried out from his mount. "Today marks the end of Pitter rule in the west and over their subjugate peoples! And to cap it all off we take this head of Sherman Xombro, the Evil Spirit, and cast it into the sea for crab bait!"

With that proclamation, he hefted the head, walked to the edge of the bluff and hurled it into the sea where it hit the water like a shot put with a loud splash. Then, turning back to all of his men said, "This sacred isle shall be for Pyrsyrus to launch his navies from. This city of Elveston was originally where the monastery of Elves was established at the place of the Great Megaliths. It shall be returned to that purpose again. Sur Sceaf has decreed in the war road that Juan Carlos de Sajones is to govern this isle, and assist us in speedily building a navy by which we may plague the Pitters with clipper ships and dragoons up and down the eastern seaboard of the Aegirean Sea. And for this purpose, the Lord Pyrsyrus is also come to supervise it. Once he has built his sea palace, it will act as the mother ship that will be a floating command post far from shore as well as a supply ship for the Pyringean Navy."

Dubbed the Ringhorn Sea Palace, it was designed specifically to service Pyrsyrus' dragoons and the clipper ships of Juan Carlos' Mexus Navy. It would provide food, critical medical treatment, and issue battle directions. Upon this ship the wives and younger children of the seamen might abide in comfort and safety in the long days of the Great War ahead.

"When I return to the Omala, I will arrange for the quailor timber men to supply you with all the timber and labor you Pyringian Pirates will need for the ship building. I will also draft local men to assist you in this labor, and Juan Carlos will set to building his clipper ships.

"May the names of El Yid, Seth Moss, Ullr-Ruh and White Crow be written in the books of the rune singers as great men of valor, and may the glory of the Pyringean Pirates be sung in all our taverns and folk moots. I charge you men to write a new chapter in the exploits of the Pyringean Pirates. Meanwhile, the Godhi of the Roufytrof shall come to cleanse this isle and re-establish their Odhinic monastery by the megaliths our longfathers planted here. So mote it be!"

Three days later, back at the Omala, Ary stood at the open window of the stone tower in the Bastion, watching as an endless line of warriors, both mounted and on foot, made their way up the winding road that ran from Hewes Town to San Arundel, the Mexus name for the Omala. Behind them came countless wagons, cattle, sheep and horses; enough, to fill a small city.

The young quailor, Alf Haegele, had awakened him earlier than he wanted to arise, since he had stayed up so late planning the construction of war ships with Pyrsyrus, Yid, and Juan Carlos and determining which eastern seaboard cities to strike and when.

Alf had been on watch, and summoned Arundel from his bedchamber to see the magnitude of armies approaching the Omala from the south. "My lord, that's got to be the largest army in Middle-Ea-Urth," the lad exclaimed in awe.

Arundel regarded the serpentine movements of the approaching hosts, the numerous flashes of red, the clouds of dust and flapping banners. He, too, had experienced a moment of awe when first he set eyes on the multitude. "Alf, you may very well be right. If I hadn't seen the fyrd banners, it would have been a most terrifying and unwelcome sight. At least now I understand why, in part, the Skull Worm didn't offer much resistance. He had to have known these armies were coming directly for him."

"But who are they and where did they all come from?"

Arundel stared transfixed for several minutes. "Moxo! They're called Moxo. Least that's what the messenger pigeons say. Said they are from the deep woods of the south, beyond even Guatemala, from a place called Bolivaria. Places no Syr Folk have knowingly ever been." He grinned as he caught sight of his father's banner leading the procession. "Come, lad, ride out with me to meet them."

Sur Sceaf rode to the fore of the fyrds with his necessary contingents and officers, and Gorge, a translator. Though bred to the saddle, he found himself eager for a respite from the long days on horseback. Though he hated to admit it, he was feeling his age.

He knew not the age of Ehira, only that the Moxo chief had long passed the bloom of youth. Still, he had endured the forced march nobly and was even talking about what he would do to the Pitters when he caught their emperor. Had Ehira not said, that "Once the Moxo make a vow, they will never break it," and he had vowed to track those who stole his daughters "to the ends of the earth, until the soil drinks their blood, and the sun witnesses it."

A few minutes later Surrey spotted two riders coming toward him through the rising dust. One of them was Arundel astride Sun Charger. He knew not the other, though from his somber black attire, he had to be Quailor.

Turning to Heimdal, he ordered the trumpeter to sound the traditional greeting on the hunter's horn. The large cattle horn with golden ornation blasted long and hard.

When the riders drew nearer, he recognized the youth at Arundel's side as Alf, the son of his dear friends Hartmut and Mendaho Hegele.

Sur Sceaf said, "Gorge, translate for the Moxo as we make introductions."

Gorge saluted, "It shall be done, my lord."

"Waes Hael and Os Frith Arundel," Sur Sceaf said, "thou harbinger of a new day, and always as welcome a sight as the Morning Star."

"Hail, Sur Sceaf, King of Kings. I should have expected you two weeks ago and never expected your arrival to be at dawn's early light."

"It took two weeks to even reunite these mighty armies." Then turning, Sur Sceaf said, "Permit me to introduce to you our new ally, Chief Ehira of the Moxo, and his generals, Yuku and Nubube. They have come to obtain their captive daughters and to join us in our fight against the Pitter Empire."

"The Lord Arundel welcomes you Chief Ehira," Gorge translated, "Your daughters have indeed been located, and anxiously await rejoining their father at the Omala where they shall join you in a feast of celebration."

"And their father looks forward to meeting them," Ehira smiled as Gorge translated, his face showing deep satisfaction.

Sur Sceaf was suspicious of his own thoughts as he looked at the brave beside Arundel and said, "Forgive me my man, I know I must know you, but your name fails me."

The brave sat tall on his painted mount. "I am Lone Dog of former days, my lord. I am the one who roughed you up many moons ago, unfortunately at a time when I counted Standing Bull a friend and brother."

"Lone Dog, how is it you come to ride in Syr Folk company? For the last I saw you were as a traitor in the company of the Standing Bull."

Arundel held his arm up, "Father, please, I brought Lone Dog that he might answer his redemption to you. Both Kanarus and Chiggibbah now vouch for him. He has given us the best of service in the Poisoned Lands. He has earned his way among us for that alone. He comes before you under the law of Herewardi redemption."

Lone Dog had a mournful look about his face, "I understand it would be hard for you to forgive a traitor, but in truth I am not a traitor. When I heard you and Mendaka speak at the Elk Spirit Crater of the future, I knew your words were true, for they burned inside of me. But my eyes were sewn shut by the life long friendship I had with the Standing Bull. I chose a crooked path. After I realized that Standing Bull made a covenant with the Devil Cha'kal, I broke all bonds with him and fled to Apache lands to make my path straight again in Chiggibbah's service. The Lord Kanarus will vouch for my honorable career as a warrior all these years."

Sur Sceaf said, "It pleases my heart, to see you have redeemed your name. I welcome you back, son of Red Dog. Please ride with us and tell me your journey. But first," he turned to Arundel, "Lead on son, we are weary of much travel and have run low on supplies and you can't know the longing I have for the faces of my beloved wives."

"I should probably mention Going Snake will be marrying Bithia tonight, and Lone Dog here will be marrying Yiska. With the reuniting of the Moxo and you with your wives, there will be a great and joyous feast. I hope you are up to roast beef, corn, sweet potatoes, and saddle of hare in dill sauce. And, oh yes, your sister, Queen Va-Eyra and Starkwulf have brought you a few kegs of High Desert Ale which they had to fiercely defend."

Sur Sceaf felt his mouth salivate, licked his dry lips, and said, "Right now I'm hungry enough to eat a horny-toad. Did you say saddle of hare in dill sauce?" He smacked his lips once again and wiped them with the back of his hand as Arundel nodded his head. "And High Desert Ale, you say. Well, I'll be damned if my old friend didn't think of everything to cheer a weary heart. It's what he promised me we'd eat together the last time we parted. And to think he even brought my favorite sister with him, the she-cat of the High Desert herself. I'm sure that's a tale to tell. As Ol' Crooked Jack used to say, 'All is well, when the trail comes to a good end'."

***Jesse ben David's Log:*** *On the fourth day of the dark moonth, also called Spear Shaker's Day, 603 H.S.O. the High King Sur Sceaf arrived in Taxus with his fyrds, Mendaka with his dog soldiers, Khem and his fyrds, and three massive armies of Moxo, a people formerly unknown to us from the unexplored Southern Nether Lands of Bolivaria, but who have the appearance of being red men. Red is also the color of choice in their clothing.*

*Just past dawn Lord Arundel rode out from the Citadel at Omala to greet his father. In the moonth since he has taken possession of the citadel, fyrd members have enthusiastically worked to restore the Holy City of Omala and purge it of all unclean objects, idols and abominations. The Lord Arundel has studied extensively the history of this Ancient Ancestral See and has resolved to restore it to its former glory. The Syr Folk forces gathered here have been more than eager to assist the masons and carpenters in returning the citadel and the city to their original splendor.*

*Under the advisement of several lore masters from Moon Door who have accompanied him for just this purpose, he first placed a carved jade Eye of Howrus atop the tallest minaret as an invitation to the gods to watch over this city. Next he restored the swan fountains throughout the city, but was indignant to discover that the sacred font in the courtyard in front of the capitol had been profaned by the addition of a statue of Angrar. After ordering the statue pulverized to gravel, he spread the pebbles before the stables.*

*During the restoration of the font, a bejeweled golden casket was found in a small stone box cleverly hidden beneath the hooves of the eastern facing Wissent, the traditional hiding place of the Herewardi kings. The lore masters were overjoyed to find a treasure trove of cryptic plates inscribed in the flame elfabet. Included were many parchment scrolls containing written records from the beginning of the citadel, written in the hands of Lord Arundel the First and the Second, detailing secret communications with the ascendant elven masters on the hermetic mysteries.*

*In the ancient days, visiting elven lords and ladies from other realms had instructed them in the ceremonial ways of the light elves, which include the value of pageantry to instruct the populace in the elven pattern of worship, gentility, and grace. Other parchments were filled with seed code maps and patterns of man, beast and plants, which they had observed and chronicled. They found Herewardi culture depicted in drawings and on ceramic plates, many portraying women in colorful flowing dresses and men in well-fitting cordovan leather and shiny knee-high boots. The homes appeared well furnished, with ornate chest and chairs, fine plate and glass wear, offering a vivid portrayal of the daily life of the longfathers. Lord Arundel was particularly fascinated by the portrayals of the horses with their tasseled bridles and feathered headdresses. Lord Arundel the First appeared to favor tassels and saddle blankets of light blue, while his son, Arundel the Second, also known as 'The Great,' seemed to prefer gold adornments. When questioned, the lore masters explained that it was Arundel III personal duty to bedeck his horses in red in order to follow the pattern of the sun, whereupon rising, it appears pale blue, in its glory it is gold, and its setting is red. This all betokens father, son and ur fyr.*

*Ehira, Chief of the Moxo, upon observing the white horses of the fyrds with their ceremonial red tassels and feathered headdresses, immediately ordered his sub-chiefs, Yuku and Nubube, to adorn the horses of his cavalry in like manner, to which King Sur Sceaf replied that he would make it so.*

*Expecting a large force, Arundel has prepared a suitable campsite on the vast plain outside the wall where shade from the pecan grove is plentiful and the San Arundelf River is within easy walking distance.*

*Upon arriving, Sur Sceaf received an abbreviated report from Arundel concerning the various battles and successes. After that he was pleased to hear that a double wedding had been planned for that evening between Going Snake and Bithia, one of the rescued captives; and Long Dog of the Klamath Tribe with Yiska of the Navajo. Sur Sceaf had been taken aback and demanded to know if this was the same Lone Dog who had ridden with the traitorous Bandidos led by Standing Bull. Arundel revealed that he was the same man and that he repudiated Standing Bull in an effort to save his own soul and never partook of any of Standing Bull's pollutants. He has sworn that he has never harmed any innocent, nor betrayed the Syr Folk, and now comes under the tongue of good report of Kanaras, Chiggibbah and Red Knife, who declared that his deeds after joining their forces would more than atone for any crime he had committed. Sur Sceaf was skeptical, but since he believed in the path of redemption, he was willing to accept their good report.*

*Sur Sceaf expressed delight at spotting Alf Hegele, Hartmut and Mendaho's eldest son, among the Silver Harriers. He had been present at the baptism of the boy at age twelve, and was both humbled and honored at being asked by Meny and Hartmutt to serve as Spirit Father to the lad.*

*Alf has grown into a strapping young version of Hartmut, and has inherited his sharp wit and quick tongue from Meny. Seeing the pleasure his father took in speaking with the lad, Arundel asked Alf to escort Sur Sceaf to the citadel where his wives awaited him.*

*Meanwhile, in the camp of the Moxo, Chief Ehira and the other fathers were reunited with their daughters. Later that day, Sur Sceaf's personal twelver delivered twelve snow white stallions bedecked with red tassels and head ornaments, gifts from Sur Sceaf and Lord Arundel to Ehira.*

*Overcome, the chief expressed his gratitude by pledging eternal allegiance to Sur Sceaf, whom he professed to love as dearly as his own father.*

As Sur Sceaf rode toward the citadel with Alf Hegele, he reached into the rune pouch attached to his belt and retrieved the first rune his fingers encountered. It was the Ivory Os Rune, known as the God Rune and the Rune of the Seer, which when blindly chosen would give him the power to see through illusions. He realized that he needed to invoke this power to its fullness. He held the rune in left hand and reached for his scramasax with his right. Using the needle-sharp point, he pierced his left index finger, and then expelled a few drops of his blood onto the rune.

*Ye Princes of Osgard and Odhin, Mighty Lord of Valhalla, hear the words of my heart. This rune tells me that I must rid myself of all dross and illusion.*

As he looked up from the rune, he beheld a larger than normal raven, the color of jet, sweeping down from a tree to viciously spear a mouse, which he read to mean that he must become deliberately vicious when dealing with the enemy.

*Oh Odhin, give me the fire of our elder ancestors and allow me to deliver the death blow to the Pitters they deserve.*

As he returned the bloodied rune to the pouch, Alf appeared both puzzled and intrigued. "Forgive me, my lord, what ritual have you chust performed?"

Sur Sceaf smiled at the lad. "Do you have knowledge of runes?"

"My father told me that your god and father, Odhin, who mother said was the greatest of elves, gave the Herewardi the runes as markers in life."

"Exactly right. They have come down through the well of time to mark the path and show the way to those who wish to see. My father taught me to consult the rune before making any important decision."

"But where did Odhin get them?"

"They are not of this world, they came from the stars. All Father Odhin gave them to us after receiving all wisdom and knowledge while hanging for nine days from the world tree. During this time he was given a wise and understanding heart that allowed him to interpret the magic of each rune. The Skalds say that the runes will return magic to Middle Ea Urth. Magic is the knowledge and power of the Upper Worlds."

Alf blinked. "My mother believes in magic, but father says that what he cannot reason with his mind or find in the holy scriptures, he leaves alone."

Sur Sceaf laughed. "Your father is a good and wise man, but he has already exceeded the reaches of his forebears. He was never one to reject truth he discovers through his own experience, but remember he must remain within the bounds of the fold he governs."

Alf laughed. "But mama has no boundaries, and she has told me there is not an inch of space that does not contain mysteries and creatures to be discovered. Many times she has said the paper gods are not for her."

Sur Sceaf smiled. "Meny has always been a seeker of truth. But what do you believe?"

"I am approaching Rumspringe, and I plan to explore every avenue available. Yellow Horse has promised to be my guide." He grinned. "I can hardly wait."

Sur Sceaf was about to answer when he caught sight of the Omala spread over the Taxus countryside like a city of splendor, huge walls, large mansions with slate and tile roofs, the See of Arundel the Great. A lump formed in his throat. He never thought to see such a day. Although the War Road had dictated that the Syr Folk arrive here by this target date, in the core of his being he truly did not see how that would even be possible. On the day the Roufytrouf had approved Arundel's plan, he nearly expressed his belief that the unfolding was too fast, but his son's extreme confidence, persuaded him to swallow his doubts and lend his full support to the plan. And now, here, he was, about to enter the fabled city of his ancient ancestors where elves once walked with men.

"My lord, Lord Arundel has allotted you the Bragi Hall, a most illustrious mansion." He pointed to a three story red brick structure with a black slate roof. "Can you see, your banner already flies, as your wives have taken up occupancy there."

Sur Sceaf gazed in awe at the black flag containing a bee hive within a solar disk enclosed in a red footprint of a ewe, symbolizing that the Herewardi are to pursue the ewe and the honey bee to fertile lands. His heart began to thud, and his body hummed in anticipation of seeing his wives and youngest children.

Not able to wait any longer, he spurred White Thunder into a gallop and headed for Bragi Hall.

Eight Winters old Yr-Raven of Swan Hilde's hearth, born when the Wissent was in the Solar House, dashed into the foyer of Bragi Hall and shouted at the top of his lungs, "Fa is coming! He's here. Everybody, he's here! White Thunder is way ahead of Alf the Harrier." The golden-haired lad spun around and raced back to the veranda.

Faechild's heart leapt. For nigh unto nine months she had been waiting for this moment, as had her sisters. Both Ahy and Moonie had just finished suckling their babies, born while passing through the land of the Kaninchens, and came rushing into the foyer directly behind Paloma.

"Remember, sisters, only Ahy and Moonie shall bring their babies to meet their father. If you have not already instructed your nannies and governesses to keep the children in the orangery until Surrey has greeted us, do so now."

Swan Hilde spoke up. "Yes, yes, you've only told us this a dozen times since Ary sent word Surrey had been spotted approaching. If any of your brats destroy any of my plants in the orangery, there will be hell to pay."

Lana, normally the peacemaker, said in an exasperated tone, "And thou hast only told us this a dozen times."

"Or more," Shining Moon muttered.

"Sisters, enough," Paloma ordered. "It's time we receive our husband. He will not be pleased to find a contentious household."

"I agree," Faechild said as she threw open the ornate red oak doors and stepped out. Her sisters followed with Paloma exiting last.

"Remember to line up in reverse order," she called. "The first shall be last, and the last shall be first, but he's my man tonight."

As her sisters rearranged themselves, Faechild peered eagerly down the paved promenade lines framed with towering Pecan trees. "See mothers, I told you he's coming," Yr-Raven exclaimed.

Swan Hilde glanced at Paloma before telling her son, "Thank you, Yr, for your excellent watching, but now it's time for you to join your brothers and sisters in the Glass House."

"But, mother--"

"No buts, you know the rules."

Reluctantly, the boy left, his running footsteps echoing through the high ceilings.

Sur Sceaf requested another round of High Desert Ale for he and his compatriots. Paloma planted a kiss on his lips as she passed it over to him, and Lana brought everyone some of her sweet breads. The festivities with old friends and family after the rigors of warfare and forced marches through the deserts of the Mexus Lands made the music and entertainment like entering the heavenly halls of the elves above. Va-Eyra competed with Sur Sceaf's wives to see to it all his needs were being met, and she and Starkwulf amused Ehira with tales of Sur Sceaf's youth. Gorge didn't know what he should translate for Ehira, but translated the account Va-Eyra told of Sur Sceaf being bound and entombed in the bottom of a pit by a Pitter Rat Pack and how the ravens had warned Mendaka to come and rescue him at the edge of death.

Ehira was so enthralled by the story that he repeated it to his three daughters. The eight year old asked if she could see Sur Sceaf's scars for proof and so Va-Eyra took the girl by the hand and led her behind Sur Sceaf. She lifted his shirt, and the little girls eyes widened as she gasped, and put her hand to her mouth. Soon the other two daughters of Ehira had to see for themselves and showed equal shock.

Taneshewa said through Gorge, "It's alright, I kiss them better every night."

Ehira laughed.

Nubube said, "What I'd do to have a woman of your beauty kiss my scars."

Gorge twisted his face like he didn't mean to translate that and then Ehira grabbed Nubube's mug and said, "Enough drink for you." Gorge translated.

Ehira turned to Taneshewa and said, "He's always weak when it comes to beautiful women. Now he drinks too much and the lid is off his big mouth. His father was a great friend, but I fear he lacks the strength of his father."

Taneshewa nodded and gave Ehira a gracious smile.

Ehira's daughters gathered around him like bear cubs and he showered them with every praise imaginable. It was all too apparent he loved his daughters without equal.

Ehira's daughter whispered something in his ear, and he belted out an enormous laugh. Then he went stone quiet. "You know, Sur Sceaf, you grow on a man. I have come to honor and love you as much as a brother. I have searched many years to find good men to rule my people wisely with. I have spoken with the shamans; I have listened to the women and children, the workers and the braves. Yet never have I found the wisdom and integrity that you have. Your ways of judging and ruling constantly astound me. I want my people to have the wisdom your people show. I want to make my world as orderly and refined as yours is. I am not only bound to fight for you by reason of my vows, but I choose to fight for you because I know it is the right way. I feel it in here." He smote his breast.

Sur Sceaf said, "It is merely the accumulated wisdom of the ancients. I will gladly share it with you, my friend. Good government under good laws makes all to prosper. The war is half over. We will swiftly set to securing all of our assets here in the Taxus and then we must branch out and embrace the other theaters of the war to the east, where the enemy is still deeply rooted.

# THE END

# AUTHOR BIOGRAPHY

Russ Howard was born in the north end of the Shenandoah Valley. He grew to manhood in rural West Virginia, where the mountaineer culture conveyed to Russ a sense of fierce independence, which is a running theme in his books. In his youth his first passion was for the animals he kept, an assortment of creatures from owls and pigeons to chipmunks and foxes. As he entered adolescence he developed an obsession for running and became an accomplished cross-country and track athlete.

His education spanned across international borders. He attended four major Universities in three states and for a number of years he lived abroad as a student in various German cities as well as Kitzbuhl, Austria. During his stint there he learned to love and appreciate the German tongue and culture.

He is greatly influenced by English literature, Germanic, Keltic, and Slavic mythology. He is an admirer of the operatic genius Richard Wagner, the political innovator and democratic theorist Thomas Jefferson, and reveres J.R.R. Tolkien as the greatest modern story-teller. Russ's spiritual philosophies have been condensed from sources of mysticism and Kabballah. He especially praises the works of Rudolph Steiner, Bruno Bettelheim, and Martin Buber.

Most of his life he worked as a Mental Health Investigator, and a Marriage, Family and Child Therapist. Now Russ lives with his wife Kathryn, a dancer, in Roseburg, Oregon. He spends his time as an avid gardener, small-scale farmer, and shepherd.

Thank you for reading *Brekka*. I hope that you fell in love with the heroes, hated the villains and laughed with the jesters.

If you liked the book, please leave a review for this book on whatever platform you purchased it. Every review gives me renewed vigor to carry on with the stories of Panygyrus, and leads other readers to enjoy the fantastic world you have come to love.
Thanks again, Russ L. Howard

*Brekka* is the eighth book in the eleven book series, ***The King of Three Bloods***, which follows the many trials and tribulations faced by the freedom-loving Syr Folk. If you enjoy this third installment, you are humbly, though excitedly, invited to continue your journey with all the many colorful characters in book nine, ***El Yid.***

Be sure to check out

**TheKingofThreeBloods.com**

for future book releases, articles by and about the author and other news concerning the series.